Phyll

CIRCUS OF WONDER

SHARN W. HUTTON

For more information visit sharnhutton.com.
Book design Sharn Hutton.
Map design © Sharn Hutton 2021.
Cover illustration Andy Catling © Sharn Hutton 2021
First edition February 2021.
10 9 8 7 6 5 4 3 2

For those who dare to believe.

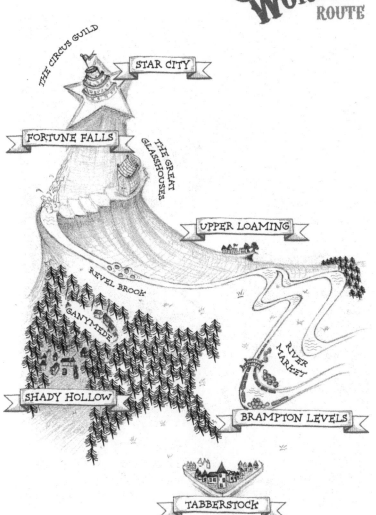

CHAPTER ONE

The Horseshoe Path

Phyllo Cane had a better place to be.

Now was the time to be free in the crowd and he wasn't going to miss it.

Released from the jostle at the gate, that night's customers strolled arm in arm onto the Horseshoe Path, and Phyllo wanted to be amongst them.

He pushed past the ticket booth and into the throng.

The smell of buttered popcorn filled his nose and stalls of sweets sparkled with sugar in the evening's golden light.

Above the crowd jewel-bright balloons bobbed in a jolly huddle, just one drifting on, its ribbon now grasped in the firm grip of a fist. Its owner, Phyllo knew, irretrievably enchanted.

The magic swelled in his chest.

The path led on eventually to the big top's grand entrance, but for those still with time on their hands, other doorways promised alternative delights. Phyllo wanted to witness their awe. He wanted the hairs on his arms to lift with vicarious wonder.

This was the last fully non-magical town on the route and the amazement of *ordinaries*, experiencing the delights of his circus, was still his favourite thrill.

He found Roly waiting just inside the gate. Together, they

1

were the sons of the Circus Confectioner and Roly had been busy making toffees. He passed one to Phyllo and unwrapped another for himself. They joined the flow of the crowd.

"These are the best you've made," Phyllo mumbled, through the caramel sweetness.

"Pretty good, if I say so myself."

Phyllo punched him lightly on the arm. "You're a genius," he said.

Roly grinned.

The steam organ parped to life and injected energy into the crowd. The automaton orchestra thumped out the opening bars of the circus theme. Tiny cymbals chinked over the big bass drum and a tinkling xylophone chipped out the refrain.

Ahead, colourful circus folk guided the ambling crowd through a gallery of toys for every child to pick a favourite. Phyllo pulled a pirate cutlass from the rack and whirled it around his head.

"To the show, me hearty, or I'll have your gizzard!" he crowed.

Roly snatched one up too. "Not if I take yours first!"

Parrying and lunging, whooping and laughing, they bumped against each other and people nearby to sweep through the throng on the rising heartbeat of the organ.

Drapes of striped silk announced the quarters of Frú Hafiz, who would reveal your destiny in return for a coin. Signs promised sights 'this way' that would 'astound, nay leave you gasping'. Visitors from the *ordinary* humdrum embraced the enchantments to lose themselves a while in the fantastic. Lazarus Barker's Circus of Wonder had come to town and Phyllo loved that it was his home.

He and his brother slipped from the pack to squeeze through a gap in the canvas. A travelling theatre in the round, this big top was the grandest Phyllo had ever seen. A hundred feet high at the centre, a canvas of midnight blue dusted with stars was its ceiling. It swept over intricate iron work and copper to hide the network of platforms and rigging – the heart of the magic. Spotlights played upon the surface of the ring, but the action was out in the stands.

With the big top already a quarter full, circus folk in sparkling costumes led ticket-clutching families to their seats: benches by the ringside or plush cushioned chairs on rising tiers. Clowns and magicians wandered through the stands, raising smiles. Toy pedlars wore sandwich-board-style racks of goods about their person, covered from shoulder to knee in rubber swords, spinning lights and star-spangled wands.

Phyllo and Roly wore costumes of a sort too: jackets made in the traditional candy-stripe of the Circus Confectioner. Phyllo's was violet and lemon and Roly's: sapphire and ginger. Both had shining buttons and sharp pointed collars.

As twelve-year-olds, the boys were required to look the part, but the pressure wasn't on to be good at the family talent just yet. When they were thirteen, then things would get serious. Phyllo knew that the Circus of Wonder had no space for freeloaders, and teenagers were expected to at least demonstrate skill to keep their place in the troupe.

Roly had managed to master a couple of recipes, but Phyllo himself was lagging badly behind. Not one of his creations had yet come to more than a sticky mess. He was trying not to worry about it. He still had time and right now all he was interested in was squeezing every last drop of joy from his freedom.

They swashbuckled their way along an aisle and into a clown who'd paused to amuse the mob of children following him around. They spun to face each other.

"Hey, Emmett." Phyllo grinned and his old pal looked back at him, more glassy-eyed than usual. He was looking a bit podgy too, Phyllo thought, considerably thicker around the middle lately and he'd cut back on the greasepaint as well. Phyllo guessed that after so many years in the business Emmett had hit upon the key strokes of the brush that created the effect he was after.

Either that or he was getting lazy. Today it was just over-large white eyelids and a red spot on the end of his bulbous nose. The effect was still good. Combined with a pom-pom tipped night cap and spotted nightshirt, he looked as affably daft as ever.

Emmett paused to consider him, straight-faced, then, quick as a flash, relieved Phyllo of his sword. "Bingo!" he called out and nodded around to the children he'd been entertaining with a wide-eyed face of delight. He turned the sword horizontally and bonked Phyllo on the top of his head. "Bongo!" The gaggle of children screamed with laughter.

A year or two ago Phyllo would have feigned dizziness and played along, but now, with all these little kids watching, it was embarrassing to be disarmed by a clown. He shuffled awkwardly and Emmett, recognising his discomfort, passed the sword back and pushed Phyllo away with a mock worried drum of fingers on his lip. Phyllo tutted, but gave him a small smile then scarpered with Roly into the tiers.

They found their father, Marvel Cane, on the next level up. He'd attracted a small crowd too, but these were eager customers, watching hungrily as he plucked jellybean batons and marshmallow wands from his cart to whirl them into eager hands. His Confectioner's coat of red and green swirled and flapped as he dipped and spun.

Somewhere in the pit, musicians started to play. A viola

and a tambourine. Their tune: a jaunty polka that was drowned out mostly by the growing crowd. Phyllo swiped two bottles of fudge-cream soda from the cart and passed one back to Roly.

"Having fun, boys?" Their father rolled his eyes.

"Delicious." Phyllo took a long pull from the soda and burped richly. Roly collapsed into giggles.

"Well don't drink all our profits, eh?"

The children in the next row along goggled at them. 'Can I have a fudge-cream soda, Daddy?' 'I'd like one.' 'Me too.'

Marvel swept three bottles from the cool box and passed them over. "I hope you're not as naughty as these two!" he said with a smile.

Phyllo eased another bag of toffees from the cart's edge and winked at a small girl in pigtails who was watching him, open-mouthed. He offered her one.

Other musicians took up the refrain, the rising waves of music gaining in strength. A minstrel in black and white harlequin robes stood on the edge of the ring, playing a piccolo. A tune that danced up and down the scales, hypnotic and alluring. The big top filled, but the sound was of circus folk one by one joining in, humming a low tune that under-pinned the melody from the minstrel. A hum that grew in strength until the air vibrated with the sound. Somewhere up high in the tiers a female voice rang out in song:

> *"Come hear our song,*
> *See the Circus of Wonder!*
> *Come join the throng,*
> *The Circus draws near.*
> *Run! Come along,*
> *It's a Circus of Wonders!*

Take your seat, plant your feet.
You're in for a treat.
The Circus of Wonder is here."

More carnies unnoticed in the crowd took up the tune with their humming, and a thousand tiny lightbulbs rippled to life about the ring. The hairs on the back of Phyllo's neck stood on end as every voice in the cast took up the song to sing it through once again, his own included. Spotlights whirled and searched the now darkened audience. At the final line they swept back to the centre of the ring to find the Ringmaster, resplendent in scarlet tails and high-shine boots, standing upon a golden platform. No-one had seen its arrival nor the Ringmaster's for that matter.

The show was about to begin.

CHAPTER TWO

The Art of the Confectioner

Phyllo came down from the step stool and slid it along to one side with his foot. For twelve years old he still had some growing to do. Just exactly the right height to be in between needing the stool to work at the kitchen counter and not. With it, the bowl was harder to control as he stirred, skidding around on the smooth marble surface, but without it his sleeves dragged through the litter of sugar and almond dust he inevitably produced. He shook his sleeves experimentally and it rained sweet grit to the floor.

Phyllo's family made all the sweet confections for circus visitors. In fact, 'Cane's Exotic Sweets & Treats' had been part of the Circus of Wonder and run by his ancestors for as long as anyone could remember. He and Roly were next in line, but they'd have to develop their talents first.

Phyllo imagined they'd make a great team. Where Roly charged in, Phyllo was considered and methodical. Where Roly liked the old favourites, penny toffees and liquorice, Phyllo enjoyed experimentation and wasn't averse to the odd hint of spice. Roly with his plump cheeks and mousy wavy hair, Phyllo: leaner, sharper, straighter. Twin brothers who were as different as they were complementary and there was still so much to learn.

Phyllo readied himself for the next part of the process. Making sweets in a big top kitchen was unlike making them in any other. Along with the sugar and butter and cream, a circus confectioner added something mysteriously *more*. Something that tingled the senses and brought back the joy of a long-forgotten holiday, for instance. Or perhaps, gave you the comfort of a favourite blanket. Remembered pleasure could come from the most unexpected of places. The talent of the circus confectioner was to add that sprinkling of *feeling* that subtly struck a chord and actually tasted good too.

Roly had already managed to produce an excellent toffee, imbued with the aroma of feeding peanuts to elephants, but Phyllo, thus far, had had difficulty making his mark.

Today was the day. He was sure of it.

His ingredients, as always, were arranged in strict order in his own personal box. He sat it straight on the counter and then pulled on his mother's old apron: a rose and lime candy-striped affair with loose threads where buttons once had been. He wrapped it tightly around himself, secured it with a knot and firmly rolled up the sleeves.

He felt sure that using this apron, rather than his own as his father would have insisted, was more likely to garner success. His aim, as always, was almond and honey marshmallows that would summon up the glorious days gone by, when his mother had still been alive.

Every inch of the small kitchen was employed to its fullest. Shelves were crammed to capacity, ingredients in neatly tied bags dangled from the arched ceiling and copper pans crowded on hooks behind the gas burners.

Travelling small definitely did not have to mean travelling light. A theory Phyllo's father had also applied to their shopfront. The tiny space beyond the counter, with doors that

8

opened onto the horseshoe, was equally stuffed with an astounding array of delicious sweets, not to mention the great copper and glass corn popper which stood six feet tall and took up an entire corner. The riveted metal bucket suspended within belched popcorn day and night to keep up with demand on show days. Today was such a day.

Kernels popped and fell softly into the gathering pile at the base of the box and buttery warmth filled the air. Phyllo took it in in a steadying breath and ploughed on. He rubbed no-stick edible wax into the edges of a large flat tin, then chopped three tablespoons of toasted almonds, which he sprinkled to cover the surface.

The kitchen was highly organised now, but casting his mind back to time spent in it with his mother, he realised it did lack *something*. On cloudy days, time spent in the kitchen with his mother had been filled with sunshine. Looking up at her, from the step-stool by the counter, he'd felt a glow like sunbathing by a natural pool, like warm porridge on a frosty morning, like beef stew on a hungry night.

He was mixing his images. He had to be clearer.

He put sugar and water into a saucepan and added two drops of honey from his precious reserved pot. The honey she'd gathered all those years ago. The last jar. He closed his eyes and stirred. Slowly. Clockwise.

Phyllo remembered the beehives and the farmer's field. His father had found them. Led the family to them laden with jars through a gap in the hedgerow, giggling and whispering. "We'll just have a jar or two. The bees won't mind," he'd said.

"And what about the farmer?" his mother had asked, raising an admonishing eyebrow. He'd waved her away with a grin.

His mother had kept Roly and Phyllo a safe distance away,

9

as his father had approached the hive. His only protection, a wet muslin cloth over his head and a pair of cotton gloves pulled over the cuffs of his apron. They'd watched with bated breath.

Removing the lid had been easy enough and it all seemed to be going terribly well, until they'd realised that the bees weren't happy to have their peace disturbed. They'd swarmed around his father in a persistent cloud as he'd prised out a tray of honeycomb, and it became clear pretty fast that the gentle drip of honey into jars that he'd enthusiastically described to them was not going to happen.

"Run, Persipan!" Marvel had yelled from the hive, "Take the children! Save yourselves!" The entire family had run away screaming, Marvel clutching the precious honeycomb to his chest and his mother swatting bees from him and Roly and running in circles to 'confuse and befuddle' the bees. Marvel had been stung, several times, but had remained good-humoured about the whole thing. In fact, they'd all laughed as he'd rubbed his fat belly and winced at every welt.

Coaxing honey from its comb had been the next challenge. They'd had no equipment so Phyllo's mother, Persipan, had fashioned a wire contraption which she'd strung inside a bucket and whirled around her head to uproarious applause. It drew the honey like a charm. His clever funny mother.

Phyllo added shining leaves of gelatine to the mix and stirred them in, then set it to simmer. The grate that sat over the burner wobbled on uneven feet and Phyllo wedged a spoon under one side to keep it steady. He'd have to watch that.

Egg whites next. It turned out that whipping was easier standing on the stool, but the extra height put him further away from his memories as a five-year-old. From here he could see every chip in the marble worktop, see out over the counter to the mud of the path. From here it was easy to see the cracks and the cobwebs. From here the magic was fainter.

He combined the syrup and egg white foam and spread it thickly in his tin, sprinkling the last of the almonds on top. It looked the part, but you never could tell. Some time in the cooler and he'd see.

When Marvel, Roly and Phyllo's little sister, Dodo, returned to the Confectionary an hour later, Phyllo was itching to see what they'd make of it. Marvel, however, was distracted.

He fiddled with the boxes of jelly beans on the shopfront shelving, condensing the contents of two shelves into one. Somewhere unseen, gears clicked into life and the shelves moved around, consuming the space he'd created. Phyllo loved it when the Machine did things like that. Only the Ringmaster understood properly how it worked, but its valves and circuits were at the heart of the Circus of Wonder. For every talent and in every cabin, the Machine played a part.

"Emmett's not himself," his father sighed at last, raking away the loose brown curls from his forehead, "He's wringing his hands and staring out at nothing. I'm worried about him. Spends too much time on his own."

"I could visit, I could take him some marshmallow," said Phyllo, leaping at the chance to bring it out of the cool box.

His family gathered dutifully around, but they'd encountered Phyllo's marshmallow before and eyed it with suspicion. Dodo got up onto the step and poked it. It stuck to her finger.

"Just needs cutting," Phyllo said, shooing her off. He flopped it out onto a board and set about chopping. The marshmallow pulled in long sticky strings that stuck to the knife, but he persisted, creating a gummy web and some vague separation. Phyllo looked hopefully to Roly, but he wrinkled his nose and their father caught the look that passed between them.

"Perhaps we should just have a try before we give any to Emmett, eh?"

He gamely pulled a chunk from the oozy mess and bit it off his fingers, keeping the stickiness away from his clothes. He sucked. He chewed. He drew air in through his teeth and paused, Phyllo thought, to savour the flavour. Then, tipping his head to one side, deliberately swallowed. The family waited for him to speak. Eventually he said, "Almonds. They're good, nice and nutty."

Phyllo nodded, eyes wide and expectant.

"Mallow texture," he said as he poked at a back tooth with his finger, "rather challenging."

Phyllo deflated, but his father reached out to put a hand on his shoulder. "It's got promise, really it has. Better than the last one."

"We couldn't get that one out of the tin," muttered Roly, and Phyllo gave him a poisonous look.

"But how does it *feel*?" Phyllo asked. He'd tried so hard to project the sunshine warmth of that day in the field. He'd seen his father's rotund figure at the hive so clearly; heard all their laughter as his mother had swung that bucket madly around her head.

His father's eyes shone. "Feeling. Yes, it does have that. Perhaps not quite what you were after. Sweet melancholy, I'd say. Not really the ticket for a circus confectionary, eh? I'm sorry, Phyllo, it just feels too sad."

Phyllo's face fell. He'd failed again. His father pulled him in for a hug. "Perhaps this isn't the right thing for Emmett today."

Phyllo tried a piece himself. It *was* sad. With the marsh-

12

mallow in his mouth the difference in his father from that day in the past was clearer than ever. The jolly Marvel of then, against today's wiry and jumpy version, wearing that ever-present expression of loving disappointment. Phyllo swallowed it bitterly.

"I'll get it," he muttered.

His father held him out at arm's length and spoke directly, "Perhaps you should move on from this one, son. Not every recipe can be a success, eh? Barnum's britches, if I listed all the recipes I've tried and failed, we'd be here 'til next week."

"I can't give it up. It's important. I'll get it. I know I can."

His father shrugged and then gave his shoulder a squeeze. "Tell you what, why don't you see if you can help me with something, eh? Take the old grey matter off this for a while. What do you say?"

Phyllo poked at the marshmallow slop and pouted, but Roly took up the bait. "Orange sherbet? Coconut ice? Ooh I know, Black Forest fudge!"

"All excellent suggestions, Roly, but I was thinking of a twist on peppermint truffles. If you would, Dodo."

Dodo bounced excitedly up and down and then dashed away through the arch which led to their living quarters. She returned a moment later clutching a snow globe. Marvel whistled and up on a high shelf yellow eyes popped open in a foot-ball-sized ball of grey feathers.

"Glumberry," Marvel said, "Peppermint truffles. The ones we made last Christmas. Call out the recipe, eh?"

He took the snow globe from Dodo and held it out for the others to see. Inside, a polar bear sniffed noses with its cub as they stood on an iceberg of glittering white. He wound the key and inside the heart of a music box tinkled to life. It started in

13

the middle of the tune, a song they all knew, about the wonderland of winter.

"Doesn't matter where it starts, we all know it right away." Marvel bobbed both hands in the air, conducting the song, and nodded along for the children to join in. Roly was first, punching up and down with so much enthusiasm that Dodo took a step back. Phyllo snorted.

"Listen to the notes. They aren't all there, but we know the tune so we fill in the gaps." It was true, Phyllo had never noticed before. There weren't enough notes for all the words in the song. "Stay on the notes and spread out. Phyllo, you're on equipment. Dodo and Roly: ingredients, please." Marvel continued to tap to the beat, fingers dipping as if playing piano mid-air.

There was no sense in resisting. Disappointed as he was, Phyllo hoped that with a bit of luck he might learn something – perhaps the very thing that would make his own recipe work.

"Ready, Glumberry?"

Glumberry pulled himself up to full height, which was about ten inches, snapped his beak and then squawked, "Yes. An excellent choice."

"Quite so. If you would, then."

"Peppermint cream chocolate truffles. Originally made three years ago at Fortune Point for the Grand Vizier to demonstrate the—"

"Yes, that's the one," Marvel interrupted, "Ingredients list, please. Experimental batch quantities, I think."

"Very well. Ready?"

"Ready."

"To begin, Madam Miniver's full fat cream cheese, one cup. Powdered sugar, sieved, three cups. Peppermint essence

14

to taste, suggested one saltspoonful. Mixed to a creamy paste."

He paused and then tapped his furry claw to the beat of the musical globe while the children scurried about and bobbed along to the beat.

Phyllo found the bowl and spoon whilst Roly pulled forward the ladder that usually hid snugly within the shelves, ushering Dodo up to the top to fetch a small green bottle.

Marvel tipped the snow globe over and back on itself, releasing from its resting place a multitude of sparkling snowflakes that swirled around the bears, sweeping over their heads to gather at their feet. The bears in the globe turned on their iceberg. Music tinkled. He took a scoop of powdered sugar from the sack beneath the counter and shot it into the air. It swept over their heads and around them, travelling the same path as the snowflakes, turning in tighter circles as it neared the countertop, finally settling in a pile in the bowl.

Roly scooped in the cream cheese with the best flourish he could muster and Dodo tapped out drops of peppermint essence from the top step of the ladder, just hitting the edge of the bowl.

Phyllo stirred, slowly at first then faster and faster, until Marvel took the bowl to work the mixture they'd made into small and even balls.

"Next," squawked Glumberry, talking to the beat, "Peruvian chocolate, one and a half cups, gently melted over steaming water."

Phyllo prepared the bain-marie and Roly thunked fat chunks of chocolate in, to melt.

"Hubert's Humbugs, one quarter pound, crushed to a powder and spread on a plate. Smother the truffles and roll through the dust."

Roly hammered humbugs in a pestle and mortar and then, when their father had given him an approving nod, tipped them out to spread over the counter.

Marvel sprinkled over a fine purple powder with an extravagant flourish and Phyllo passed him a long fork-ended pin to spear one truffle after another. He swirled them through chocolate and the sparkling dust then laid them out on a tray to set.

The spinning snow globe wound to a halt. The music box pinged a final clear chime as Marvel settled the last truffle onto the tray. He cast his eyes around his children. Sparkling sugar dusted the tops of their heads. He smiled.

"I'd say that went quite well."

Clearing away the mess that they'd made was a necessary chore, but even that had its highlights. Smears left in the chocolate bowl and humbug dust that could be gathered with damp fingertips were the cleaner's perks. Phyllo dived for the chocolate bowl just as the same thought occurred to Dodo. Their equal determination fast descended into a scrap which only ended because Phyllo wrenched it from Dodo's grip. She wailed. Marvel rounded on them, plucked it from Phyllo and gave it to his sister. "Let her have it, you know she likes to lick the bowl."

"*I* like to lick the bowl!" Phyllo protested and snatched it back. Dodo started to wail again, but he didn't see why she should get it. Because she was the youngest? He was the one who was trying the hardest. He deserved it, didn't he? He ran a finger around the bowl's inside and scooped the chocolatey goo into his mouth.

Dodo cried out, "Daddy! He's eating it!"

Phyllo clutched the bowl to his chest and scowled. "Mum would have let me have it," he said, and she would have too. Another reason why life had been better then. He and Roly had shared the spoils. Now he was lucky to get a look in.

Marvel put out his hand. "Phyllo."

He clonked it down onto the counter, pulled his face into a nasty grimace and said, "Boo hoo, I'm the youngest, I get everything." Dodo burst into tears, real ones this time, but Phyllo didn't care. He stalked off to throw himself onto the lumpy sofa in the back room and sulk. A minute or two later she came to stand over him, chocolate smears around her mouth.

"Come to gloat?" he huffed.

She held out the bowl. It was mostly licked clean, but a small section remained, the edges carefully cleared. Her eyes were glassy and pink. Phyllo's chest felt suddenly hollow and he looked away. Dodo sat down beside him and put the bowl in his lap. "You can have it, if you like," she said in a faint voice.

She was so much smaller than him, a wild mop of strawberry blonde curls on her head somehow making her seem even smaller. Strawberry blonde, just like his mum. She wore her old lime and rose waistcoat too, cut down to fit by his dad. Phyllo had wanted that chocolate so badly a few minutes before, but now the back of his throat cloyed at the thought of it. Dodo twisted one leg on the ball of her foot and watched Phyllo with round blue eyes. He sighed and put the bowl into her lap instead. She grinned a wide gap-toothed grin, "You mean it?" He looked pointedly around her chocolatey face. "You clearly need it more than me."

17

CHAPTER THREE

Aldo Volante

Phyllo picked a lolly stick from the sole of his shoe and tossed it into a barrel by the doorway. Gathering litter didn't take much effort when you worked as a confectioner. The soles of his shoes had a permanent stickiness, and over the years he'd found all sorts of things stuck there. Trailing ribbons and streamers were common. Flattened popcorn cones and discarded tickets, equally frequent. Even the odd fortuitous coin.

They'd come to the big top to find testers for their creations. It was always a nerve-jangling activity, and he smoothed his clothes as they approached the ring and attempted to tidy his hair, which was hopeless. Phyllo's hair seemed to absorb sugar from the air in their humid kitchen. It coated every strand and, no matter how many times he washed or brushed it, it always stuck out in straight random spikes, like a porcupine recently dragged through a bush.

As expected, the big top was still busy. The show might have been over, but there was always plenty to do. The cast's love for the Circus of Wonder surpassed everything else. It was their pride and joy. It was their magnificent theatre and their home. At the end of every show they'd hang up their remarkable costumes and walk the aisles of the big top or follow the horseshoe path, looking for litter or mud on the canvas. They'd seek out wobbly seats or a tear in the colourful banners. They'd clean and repair.

Flyers were scrambling around in the rigging over the ring, retying knots and topping up chalk. Signor Volante stood on the ground in the centre, shouting up streams of instructions and gesticulating his displeasure. "No, Ezio, not that one, the line on the hook. San Giuseppe save us. No!"

Ezio, up in the rigging, rushed to obey. Phyllo could see he was trying not to keep Signor Volante waiting.

Signor Volante was patriarch and head of the Fabulous Volante: the flyers who performed aerial feats high over the crowd. The star act in the show. These days he didn't get up onto the bars very often. Thick set and short, he had the sure hands of a catcher, but he'd relinquished that role to his eldest son, Salvo. Once he'd proved himself to Signor Volante's satisfaction. Now he ran the flyers from the ground.

Show time or not, the Fabulous Volante all dressed alike. Time out of the spotlight was spent in casual loose suits of baby blue. Phyllo imagined Nonna Volante up all night at her sewing machine, knocking up endless pairs of wide-legged trousers and spacious tunics. They seemed to have a never-ending supply of them, the only individual touch being in the sashes tied around their middle – the symbol of their talent. Signor Volante's was wide and intricately embroidered with an eagle.

Phyllo's father made a beeline for him, his confectioner's coat flapping out behind. Phyllo, Roly and Dodo trailed in his wake, carrying trays of truffles and marshmallow. It seemed to Phyllo that Signor Volante was considering stalking away, but he hadn't noticed them in time to get very far. They were on him before he could move.

"Aldo! Aldo! Fabulous show!" Marvel waved enthusiastic hands in front of him, "Columba looked just beautiful up on the silks. So graceful, eh?"

"Beautiful, *si*." Signor Volante's eyes were narrow. He squinted at Phyllo's dad.

"We've been creating something beautiful too, haven't we, children." Phyllo and the others all nodded dutifully. "I hate this bit," Roly whispered to Phyllo, "Wish we could just do the making and leave this to Dad." Phyllo silently agreed. His dad seemed to have earned a bit of a reputation.

Signor Volante looked over to the trays. "What is it?"

Marvel was delighted that he was showing even the faintest interest. "Come closer, Roly. Bring the tray. There's a good lad. These, Aldo, are my very latest recipe. Peppermint truffles." Roly approached, stiff-armed, close enough for Signor Volante to sniff the air above the tray. "They are the very essence of winter. Prepare to be transported to the coolest glacier, a promise of Christmas glistening in the snow." Marvel presented the truffles with a flourish.

A girl about Phyllo's age, also in flyer's blues, wandered over to see what they were looking at. A small white dog in a tutu twirled at her feet. She looked at the contents of Roly's tray and then over to Phyllo to see if he had the same. He showed her his tray of squelchy marshmallow. A dusting of icing sugar had helped them stay separate. She stepped lightly towards him, as if practising walking on a tightrope, the little dog spinning by her side. "What's that one?" she said.

"Almond and honey marshmallow. It's a new—"

She snatched up a piece and popped it straight into her mouth.

"—recipe. It's, er, still a bit of a work in progress." Phyllo inwardly cringed as the girl's chewing became laboured and her eyebrows rose. "I was going to ask mostly what people thought of the flavour, you know, what they feel about it." He waited while she fought to swallow and then rub at her cheek. "I feel like my teeth might fall out, that's what I feel! Why didn't you warn me?"

"Sorry. You were so quick."

"Well I won't be again. It's horrible, I feel horrible." She stared bitterly at Phyllo and then stalked away to sit down on a bench at the ringside. Signor Volante meanwhile was reaching out to take a truffle. No sooner was it in his mouth than he spat it out. Even Roly looked shocked, and he was used to their efforts not always being met with great enthusiasm.

"San Giuseppe di Cupertino! No! Marvin, what is that?"

"Urm. Er. Really? Goodness. That *is* a surprise."

Signor Volante ran his finger around the inside of his mouth, as if scraping the flavour away.

"Why would you do that? Peppermint is peppermint. I no want to eat perfume, Marvin."

"Too much lavender in the dust, eh?"

"Lavender? Dad – that wasn't in the recipe?" said Roly and Marvel gave him a placatory smile. "Sometimes I like to add just a soupçon of the unusual. Just a smidgeon of something from another place. To make it memorable, you see?" He continued to smile, turning his gaze on Signor Volante. "Oh, and it's Marv*el*, Aldo, not Marv*in*," said Marvel, trying his best to be polite.

"I know your name is really Marvin. You are just trying to sound more circus."

"No, no, really, it's an old family name."

Signor Volante spat into the sawdust and noticed the little girl sitting on the bench. She was quietly crying.

21

"*Tesoro!* My little birdie! What is this?" He reached out a hand and she glumly came over, settling under his arm.

"I just feel so desperately sad. I don't know why, but I do." She snuffled into Signor Volante's shirt.

Phyllo shuffled back and forth. The sadness in his marshmallow didn't just affect the immediate family then. He didn't say anything, but Signor Volante's eye's fell upon his sudden movements with suspicion. "You. What do you know about this?"

Phyllo shrugged guiltily. "It'll wear off in a minute."

Signor Volante gnashed his teeth together and glared ferociously at Marvel. "I don't know how you sell anything," he said and swept the little girl away.

"Quite," said Marvel, rubbing his hands together and looking around at the children. Phyllo was rolling his eyes. "Dad? Lavender? Really?"

Of all the flavours to add to a peppermint, Phyllo thought that one was truly disgusting. Marvel flapped his arms a little and laughed. "It was just a little bit. If you don't give it some personality no-one will remember it and what's the point of that?"

"Er, to make a sweet that someone actually wants to eat?"

Marvel waved Phyllo's comment away. "Aldo just doesn't have a refined enough palate. Not everything goes with spaghetti, eh?" He nudged Roly with his elbow, and truffles rolled dangerously about on the tray. "We just need a taster who's a bit more sophisticated. I know just the person. Come on, kiddos." Marvel strode away so Phyllo and the others had to run to keep up.

"You know who this'll be, don't you," said Roly. Phyllo thought that he probably did. Frú Hafiz, their resident Fortune Teller. She was held in very high esteem by the troupe in general and especially so by their father. Exotic and learned, she was open to the unusual – a quality essential in appreciating Marvel's creativity.

"Maybe she can tell us if anyone will buy it," said Phyllo to Roly.

"You'd think."

As expected, Marvel swept out into the horseshoe path and turned right – the direction of Frú Hafiz's cabin. But behind them, at the main gate, voices were being raised and one by one they turned to see what was happening. They could see Skinner and Bain, burly men in black and tan from the engineers, tossing a couple of cases out of the gate. Standing behind them in a broad-shouldered jacket and a stovepipe hat was the Ringmaster, Lazarus Barker himself. He leant on his cane with one hand and flicked out the other in a roll. "I'm sorry. You've brought it upon yourselves," he stated, "This serves as no more than exacerbation."

There was another voice, but it was too faint to make out. Phyllo found himself drawn towards them, to understand what was happening. The gate was wide and tall. When closed, it completely filled the only opening onto the horseshoe path from the outside world. Above it spanned an arch, lit at the edges with golden bulbs. To visitors it proclaimed: 'Welcome to Lazarus Barker's Circus of Wonder', but it said no such thing to the two people who found themselves on the other side of it now. The light from the bulbs threw an incongruous glow over the scene.

"Lazarus, please. I'm begging you," said a man's voice. Phyllo moved further around the curve until he could see out of the gate. It was Arif and Shadi, a double act called the *The Incredible Parisa*.

"This shouldn't be a shock. We've spoken about the quality

23

of the act more than once. It isn't fair on the others, Arif."
Lazarus Barker's voice was authoritative and calm.

"We'll practise, night and day. You'll see, we'll be the best
act in the show." Arif's voice had a desperate edge.

"Pfft." Signor Volante had come out to see what was going
on too and had been standing behind Phyllo without him real-
ising. "Best act, ha." A handful of others straggled out onto the
path, all interested to see what the fuss was about.

"Everybody practises day and night, Arif. That's what we
do. The fact that you are only offering to do so now does rather
point out the problem."

"I'm getting better all the time," Arif's partner, Shadi,
chipped in, "I think it was the shoes. I have better shoes now."

"A balancing act that can't stay up is no act at all." The
Ringmaster's voice was louder now, although his temper still
seemed to be even. "I have a responsibility to the reputation of
the Circus, to the troupe."

"That's us!"

"No. Not anymore."

"But where will we go? Have mercy, Ringmaster. Don't
leave us to the In-between, please!" Shadi's voice cracked,
tears not far away.

"Three times I have warned you." Lazarus turned away
from them, to face the growing crowd behind him. "Three
times I have asked them to improve," he said to his audience
at large, "A disappointing act drags the rest of us down. A bad
act ruins our reputation and then who will come to see us?"

"Ringmaster—"

"Who will come and bring their Coin, the Coin we need to
feed our family?"

Phyllo looked about the growing crowd. People continued

to be drawn to the unnatural commotion. They watched with wide eyes and folded arms.

"Close the gate."

Skinner shoved the last remaining trunk over the borderline with his foot and sneered at *The Incredible Parisa* one last time. "Be off with you," he said and clanged the gate closed, swinging great bolts into place. The Ringmaster strode away, through the gaps in the crowd. He walked tall, chin aloft. He didn't look back.

Signor Volante stepped out from behind Phyllo to greet him. "Best act in the show? Who are they kidding? They'll never come close to winning a Gilded Pennant," he said as Lazarus Barker came close. Much more than six feet tall, the Ringmaster paused to tower over them both, leaving Phyllo feeling as small as his little sister.

Dressed in a pea coat of black brocade and a black rabbit-skin stovepipe hat, he cut an imposing figure even out of his Ringmaster tails. He had a marvellous beard that curled extravagantly at the ends and he clutched his cane in one hand, by the shaft. "I must act in the best interests of the troupe. I hope everyone will understand that."

Phyllo could hear Shadi wailing from outside. It had a much worse effect than his marshmallow ever could. His father came over and took him by the hand. "Come on, son. Good evening, Ringmaster." He gave a respectful nod and tugged Phyllo away.

"Is no skin off my nose," said Signor Volante gruffly.

The Ringmaster tucked the fingers of one hand into the hip pocket of his jacket. "I'm glad to hear it, Aldo, truly I am. Everyone must play their part to support the circus so that they may be supported in return. After all, we clothe and feed, give employment and protection. There is a bargain to respect."

Signor Volante nodded, but didn't speak. Others on the path had turned to follow their Ringmaster's progress and his voice was loud enough for anyone to hear who cared to listen. "I'm a fair-minded man, but won't put my circus in jeopardy. Hard work and results built our proud company. Compromise would be our ruination. Not today. Not any day." He turned slowly, scanning the faces of his audience. Somewhere at the back, someone started clapping: fast and nervous. Then over to the other side a voice piped up: 'Hear, hear.' Unsure applause rippled out, over a sea of whispers.

Phyllo shuddered. Arif and Shadi were out. It didn't seem fair.

"Come along, children." Marvel stretched a guiding arm behind Roly and Dodo, turning them around and hustling them forward. "Let's see if Frú Hafiz is at home."

CHAPTER FOUR

Getting In Between

Frú Hafiz stood beneath her silk awning. From this angle it would have been impossible to see the scene that had just unfolded at the gate, but Phyllo felt sure that, somehow, she'd witnessed it just the same. In the shadow that the awning threw, her long black dress melted into the darkness. She could have been invisible if not for the silver chain that laced her jacket and the fine silver belt that dropped through a central loop at her waist and ended in an ornate blade at her knee.

She stood statue still, hands tucked into opposite cuffs. Her skin was the colour of moonlight, and her eyes, ice blue pools with lashes of purest white. She wore a black tail-cap with a long vermillion tassel, and a serious expression. As the Cane family approached, she nodded slowly.

"Frú Hafiz." Marvel reached out a hand and she laid hers gently over his for a moment then withdrew. "How are you this fine evening?"

"Better than some, I'll wager." Her voice was soft and clipped and betrayed her Icelandic roots.

Marvel cast his eyes down to the ground. "Yes, same for us all."

"Isn't anyone going to *do* anything?" Phyllo blurted out.

"It's not fair. He can't just throw them out. Shadi's still learning."

Marvel got behind Phyllo and encouraged him under cover. "Yes, I know, Phyllo, but I'm afraid those rules don't apply when your family isn't already established. *The Incredible Parisa* had to be great straight out of the oven, that's the thing when you've no history."

Phyllo scrunched up his face.

"That is the way the circus has become, Phyllo," Frú Hafiz agreed. "Their cards have been marked for some time. Imagine if they never improved and word got out that the acts at the Circus of Wonder weren't wondrous at all. What would become of us? The Circus families stay part of the troupe because their tradition lives on. Their talents are passed from one generation to the next. *The Incredible Parisa* had to prove they were incredible and they weren't."

"But they haven't had enough of a chance. What about helping people? What about encouraging them?" Phyllo couldn't accept that they'd been given up on.

"The Ringmaster must do what he thinks is best," his father said with an air of finality, "It's not for us to question. We have our own bread to bake, eh?" He gave Phyllo a comforting squeeze on the shoulder. Dodo clung to Roly who tried to shake her off – she kept bashing his tray with her head.

"And on that note, I wonder if you might like to try something, Frú? I have great optimism that you're going to like it." Marvel clasped his hands hopefully and a small smile flickered at Frú Hafiz's lips. "The essence of winter and the promise of Christmas," he said and took the tray from Roly before Dodo could knock the whole lot onto the floor. "Peppermint truffles."

"I don't see how, if it's all so normal and expected, that Arif

28

and Shadi were so upset. Shadi was really crying, Dad. Wailing."

Marvel waved an exasperated hand at him. "Just a minute. Give it a minute, Phyllo. You'll ruin the taste." He returned his attention to Frú Hafiz who was thoughtfully raising her eyebrows. She popped a truffle into her mouth and her expression didn't change.

"What was all that about the *In-between*?" Phyllo persisted.

Marvel flapped at him, not taking his eyes from his tester. Frú Hafiz consumed the truffle slowly, seemingly rolling the flavours around her mouth, eyes now closed. "Whispers of snow and the melody of ice," she said eventually, "Our season is coming to an end, my King of Cups."

"Is that good?" Marvel looked perplexedly from her to Phyllo, to Roly and back.

"There will always be springtime," she said.

"That's good. That's good, right?"

"Oh yes."

Marvel grinned widely.

"It is always better to look to the future than dwell in the past."

"Right. But do you like it? The truffle that is, not the future."

"Fascinating. It's quite fascinating."

Phyllo and Roly exchanged glances. Roly rolled his eyes.

"Err, right then. Anything else you might like to add?"

"Dad, what about the *In-between*? What does it mean?"

Marvel sighed, resigned to getting no sense from anyone. "It's the people who live on the circus route but don't have a proper big top to call home. Out there, in between, without a respectable troupe. They are a lawless lot, Phyllo. Beggars and vagabonds, thieves and swindlers and worse." He waved his free hand, indicating the world beyond the horseshoe.

"Performers with no circus? All wandering about on their own?"

"Some band together into Shindy Fairs. Security in numbers, I suppose. What some lack in talent they make up for with cunning. Have the food off your plate and the Coin from your purse as good as look at you. They give us decent circus folk a bad name, cheating our customers out of their money and some of the shows, well I'd not want your eyes to see them. Wrong. Plain wrong and often desperate and dangerous too. You don't want to be out there, there's no doubt about that." Marvel looked dejectedly down to his platter. "Would any of you children like to try one of these?"

No-one had much of a stomach for it.

"Let's get off home then, eh? Thank you for your time, Frú."

Arif and Shadi were going to have to fend for themselves amongst villains and thieves. Phyllo didn't like it at all. "Can't they get away from them, Dad? Wouldn't they be safe if they went into the town with the ordinaries? Into Tabberstock?"

Phyllo's father wrinkled his nose. "They could probably get away with it for a while. The Ringmaster's chosen quite a good place to eject them really, given where we're going. This is the last completely *ordinary* pitch on our route, Phyllo. From here on in there'll be more and more *charmed* in our audiences. More and more chance of meeting a Shindy Fair or a rogue group. At least here they might have a bit of breathing space."

"Do you think they'll stay here then?" Phyllo asked.

His father shook his head. "No. I'm afraid we charmed circus folk don't tend to blend in terribly well with the ordinaries. Alluring as they may find us here, it's quite a different matter out there."

Phyllo had noticed how the *ordinaries* seemed so much more mesmerised by everything. It was the reason he loved pitching at purely ordinary towns. "Have *you* been out in Tabberstock, Dad?" he asked.

"It's best avoided. Years ago, I tried to mingle by popping down to their High Street in search of interesting ingredients. They got very nervous. All sorts of accusations. You know what they did to witches. Just not worth it. The charmed have to stick with their own. That's the way it has to be."

The Cane family emerged in a stream from beneath Frú Hafiz's awning and as they gathered on the path, Phyllo noticed Emmett leaving the Ringmaster's quarters, away to their right. Head down and preoccupied, he bumbled in their direction, although at the same time seemed quite unaware of their presence.

He clutched a small package wrapped in crumpled turquoise paper under one arm and, as he came closer, Phyllo could see he was still wearing his show costume and make-up. The jolly red mouth had been smeared across his cheek and his spotty nightshirt had black grime at the knee. He was dishevelled and watery eyed, but that didn't make Phyllo any less happy to see him.

"Emmett! Emmett!" he called out, "Emmett! Come and have a hot chocolate. We could finish off our Hearts tournament."

It wasn't possible for him not to have heard, but Emmett didn't look up.

~

31

The Confectionary was all things to the Canes. It was their shop, their kitchen and their home. It was a mobile cabin, pushed into place and expanded when the circus set up. It always occupied the same spot on the horseshoe path: the very last doorway accessible to the audience before they walked through the grand entrance into the big top.

Its frontage was essentially two doors. The one on the right took up almost all of the width. Eight feet square, it swung on an enormous hinge and, when open, effectively blocked the path. It presented on its shelves a mouth-watering and jaw-dropping selection of confections. Every sweet you could think of, and plenty you'd never concoct in your wildest dreams. Squeezed generously into the racks. The marvellous racks that shifted and changed as they emptied and Marvel refilled them.

The door on the left was just as tall, but very narrow and mainly glass. This was the door that the family used when the circus wasn't open for business. Its slender dimensions encouraged them not to get fat and meant that Phyllo and Marvel had to turn sideways to squeeze in with their trays.

"Hot chocolate, then," said Marvel depositing the tray and unhooking a pan from the wall. Phyllo leaned heavily on the counter, watching. "Do you think Arif and Shadi will be alright, Dad?"

"Oh, I'm sure they'll survive," Marvel said, turning his back. Phyllo shifted his position along the counter to better see his face and, as he'd suspected, it was furrowed and pinched.

His father understood what he'd seen. "Arif's not half-baked. It's possible they'll hook up with a reasonable Shindy Fair. If they don't wander too far, they might be able to cadge a lift with another troupe. It's not like they don't have any experience. Lazarus did pick them up from the fair at Fortune Point after all. He obviously saw some talent in them there. Perhaps they can work on it. They got picked up once, there's no reason why they couldn't manage it again."

Phyllo chewed on a fingernail. "So, where did they come from? Originally I mean."

"Persia, I think," Marvel said, "I don't know how long they'd been with the travelling fairs and, to be honest, it's probably that association that's been their undoing, eh? There was a space to fill after Rufus got thrown out for stealing. I don't think the Ringmaster ever really fully trusted them."

Rufus, yes. The magician's talent for sleight-of-hand had also been useful for picking pockets. He'd been an amiable sort of chap although obviously dishonest. "I used to like him," mused Phyllo, "I wonder what happened to him."

"I heard a rumour he was worked over by the Toshers in The Big Smoke. They had the contents of his pockets and threw him in the sewer, or so the story goes. His sins came round to bite him and no mistake. A bad business."

Phyllo was horrified.

"But we're nowhere near there," Marvel quickly interjected, "I'm sure that won't happen to Arif and Shadi." He attempted to smile reassuringly. "Come on, let's go and sit down, eh?" He poured the hot chocolate out into four generous mugs. "Lead the way."

Once through the arch from the kitchen, the Cane family living quarters amounted to a single room. Bunk beds hid behind thick curtains on either side. A small log burner, with an oven just big enough to bake in, hunkered in the centre of the outside wall. When lit, it puffed sweet cinnamon reminders of cakes gone by into the air. Thick porthole windows peeped to the outside world and beneath them, bookcases groaned with years of knickknacks and books. There was a rickety and deeply uncomfortable chair, the only decent seating being a small squishy sofa which squatted with its back to the kitchen wall.

Roly and Dodo lounged conspicuously upon it, taking up most of the space.

"Table please, boys," said Marvel, clutching the tray, and Roly was forced to grudgingly vacate the seat generally accepted to be the best in the house, to help. Dodo instantly slid into it.

The boys found the brass handles set into the floor and, releasing the catch, pulled a table up out of the floorboards. They locked it off at a suitable height for hot chocolate. Phyllo beat Roly back to the sofa and sprawled on it grinning, one arm flopped decadently over its side. It was a sofa ideally made for two, but three bottoms could fit side by side, so long as you tucked in your elbows. Nobody ever sat in the chair.

Marvel scooped Dodo up, sat down himself and then put her on his lap. He produced a large pink marshmallow from up his sleeve and gave it to her as recompense for losing her seat. She dunked it happily in the steaming froth. Roly shoe-horned himself into the centre and they supped on their drinks in brief amiable silence. It was comfortable enough, so long as nobody moved.

"I wonder who the Ringmaster will get to fill in," Roly said, "It'll be difficult to find someone if he won't allow anyone who's lived in-between."

Marvel stirred his hot chocolate contemplatively. "I suppose I can understand it. What they did to his family was terrible."

"I've never really heard him talk about it," said Phyllo.

"Well why would you?" He tapped at his top lip. "The Ringmaster doesn't like to talk about it and I for one wouldn't

34

want to remind him. And, it's not the kind of story one generally tells to a child."

"I'm old enough now though, aren't it?" Phyllo thought he was quite mature enough to hear any kind of story.

Marvel eyed him appraisingly. "I suppose. It was a long time ago, but I don't think time's healed those particular wounds. A decade ago, more. Certainly, before you were born." Marvel looked up to the ceiling, remembering.

"Verne was in charge, of course, Lazarus's father. Verne Barker, a great man. He had such marvellous skill with the Machine. Three Gilded Pennant we had back then, not like now. He made all this." Marvel waved his hand to indicate their home.

"We were here, actually, in Tabberstock, for a full week of shows. Packed up like usual to move on, but when the big top set down and we went out to rig, we weren't in Shady Hollow like we'd expected, but in Verne's garden at Winter's Deep. Now I'm not talking about a postage stamp with a vegetable patch here. It was a wide sweeping lawn, plenty big enough for us, and the house, well the house was a beauty. Been in the family for hundreds of years. We used to over-winter there back then, but not anymore. Not since the fire."

"Fire?" Dodo piped up, "Where?"

"Somewhere far away and a long time ago, sweetheart." He tweaked her nose playfully and sent her out to fill up the popcorn machine with fresh kernels. He spoke in a quieter voice while she was out of the room.

"Verne took us to the house for a surprise party. He'd set up decorations and entertainment. Hot air balloons were tethered in the grounds and tumblers and dancers were cavorting about the place. They led us into the gardens for food and drinks. Such lovely things. It made a change for us to be enter-

35

tained. A point not lost on Verne, who'd seemed determined to make us all feel like important guests."

Marvel looked down into his hot chocolate and stirred it with his finger.

"As the sun started to rise, we were led into the great hall for breakfast. Verne was going to make an announcement. He was getting on a bit and I wouldn't have been surprised if he'd announced he was going to retire."

"So, what did he say?" Phyllo asked.

"We never heard. He never made his speech." Marvel fiddled with a button on his jacket and pinched his lips together. "Some said the fire started in the kitchen. Others said the gas from the balloons was to blame. They were too far away, in my opinion. We never knew, but one thing was sure: the house was riddled with people of the In-between. Verne's best intentions to do something special for his troupe hadn't taken into account the jealousy and the spite of the outsiders he'd allowed through his doors. He'd given them a chance to show him what they could do. He hadn't bargained for how terrible that would be."

He sighed and took a slurp from his drink. "Lazarus was the only member of the family to escape alive. Verne and his wife Seren, Beau and Boddington, their other two sons, were all lost to the flames."

Phyllo's mouth hung open in shock. "What about the troupe?" Roly asked, "What happened to everyone?"

"The rest of us got out safely. The great hall had doors directly into the garden. The family, we think, were gathered in a room at the heart of the house."

"That's awful." Phyllo said.

"Lazarus was a mess. He took up the Ringmaster's cane, but his heart wasn't in it. We barely saw him. I think he lost

36

himself for a while." Marvel patted Phyllo on the knee. "But he rallied. In the end."

Dodo came back into the room and tugged on Phyllo's sleeve. "Phyllo, I can't get the hopper lid on, can you do it?"

"Can't Roly do it?" Phyllo didn't want to get up. He wanted to hear more of the story.

"Phyllo," his father said, "it wouldn't hurt you to be a little nicer to your sister."

Roly gave Phyllo a smug grin and when Phyllo prised himself out of the sofa, he immediately moved into his seat. The lid was easy enough to get on when you were a foot taller, and when they returned Dodo slid into the middle spot leaving Phyllo standing. Roly looked at him with over-wide eyes, amused, luxuriating in the corner spot.

"And where am I supposed to sit?"

Roly gestured to the rickety chair and Phyllo glared back, "Shove up, Dodo. Go back where you were."

"I like it here."

"But there's no room for me. You can't wait to suck up to Dad usually."

"Phyllo, that's enough," Marvel warned and Dodo petulantly crossed her arms.

He couldn't believe it. More Dodo favouritism.

"Fine," Phyllo huffed. He didn't want to sit on the stupid sofa anyway.

CHAPTER FIVE

Giving it Everything

G oing off to bed early in a huff had its advantages. For one thing, his bed was far more comfortable than the rickety chair and for another, he woke up early too. Being up before anyone else meant valuable time in the kitchen, alone.

Phyllo slid out of bed and went to stand by the log burner. The last of yesterday's heat lingered in its metal but it wasn't enough to subdue the chill in the air. He pulled a jumper over his pyjamas and looked out at the still sleeping world. The sun was just starting to rise over Tabberstock, but not so high yet that the scene had great definition. Even so, Phyllo noticed an unnatural mound by a thicket of trees some fifty yards away. He squinted and rubbed at the misting glass. When it moved, he realised it was a person. Two people. Both figures had been lying down, but now one sat up and leant their back against a tree. Arif. Poor Arif and Shadi. They'd spent the night outside, concealed in the trees. They must be cold, he thought, and so wanted to help them, but couldn't see a thing he could do to bring them back under the big top. Breakfast, however, was doable.

He hurried to make tea in a flask and warm some muffins in the oven, then opened the little window to wave the brightest tea towel he could find to get Arif's attention. He came running over, low and nervous, checking around.

"Arif, are you OK? I'm so sorry. This is terrible. The Ringmaster should be—" Phyllo blurted, but Arif interrupted, speaking in a hushed voice. "Shhh. It's OK, Phyllo. Don't get yourself in trouble."

Phyllo passed out the flask and the muffins. "Did anything happen? Were there any In-between? Are you OK?" whispered Phyllo.

"All was quiet. Thank you, my friend. I thought we'd be safer close by."

Phyllo nodded, helplessly.

"Don't look so worried. You are a good boy. A Shindy Fair will come. We can tag along. I'll share this with Shadi and bring back the flask, OK?"

"Keep it. You might need it."

Arif gave him a small bow. "Good fortune, Master Cane." He checked around and then dashed back to the cover of the trees. Phyllo could see Shadi get to her feet and them stashing his gift in their bags. Phyllo continued to watch from his window and a minute later they were shuffling away into the trees, pausing briefly to raise a hand in farewell. Phyllo flapped his tea towel one last time and then drew it inside, feeling heavy and sad.

He was lucky to have been born into an established family. He wasn't under scrutiny yet, but now that he and Roly were almost teenagers, the clock had definitely started to tick. Children got a free pass only for so long and then it started to reflect badly on the family. He had to develop his talent and he knew he should practise other recipes, but he craved his past so badly that he could only think about getting that one recipe right.

The rest of the family were still asleep. If he had a go now there'd be no-one to roll their eyes. He padded out to the kitchen and opened the lid of his carefully curated box. Flaked almonds, gelatine, sugar and the precious jar of honey. The ingredients were simple enough. Why was producing the marshmallow so hard? It had to be in the process, he reasoned. He just wasn't doing it right.

He considered his father and his method with the peppermint truffles. OK, so they hadn't been a massive hit with Signor Volante, but Frú Hafiz had certainly found much more to appreciate. The flavour had been wrong. Unsurprisingly, lavender hadn't been a welcome addition to peppermint, but the feel had been right. His father had made the ingredients dance. Everyone in the room had worked to the off-time beat. Glumberry had read out the recipe like calling a dance. He glanced up to the top shelf where Glumberry sat utterly still, his creamy eyelids resolutely shut.

Perhaps he wouldn't enlist his help this time. Phyllo inspected the saucepans. What could he do to alter the process? How could he describe that joy without feeling its loss? His eyes slid from pan to pan: a small copper milk pan with a short steel handle; a crepe skillet, blackened beneath. He felt he had to be utterly immersed in the moment with no thought for the present. How could he do that? His eyes slide to a long silver tin with handles at the short ends, then a cauldron-like copper, suspended from the ceiling.

Scale. Scale might just do it. If he made the mix so large that it took everything in him to keep it under control perhaps that was the answer, but the ingredients in his box weren't nearly enough.

He pulled more from the shelves.

Instead of one tin, this time he laid out ten and used a

whole bar of edible wax to make sure he'd be able to get them out. At least that part had worked last time.

The flaked almonds from the stores had to be toasted and once he'd browned them in the oven, Phyllo decided to leave the gas on and the door slightly ajar for atmosphere. The warmth of that summer's day in the kitchen would surely add something.

He put the sugar and water into the great cauldron and balanced it on the gas. His precious honey was the only item which could not be topped up from the stores and he realised, with dismay, that the quantity required would leave only the tiniest amount in the jar.

He had to plough on. The heat from the oven had already warmed the room and Phyllo felt convinced that this was the one. He alternated working with his eyes open and then closed, holding the image of the beehive affectionately in his imagination, watching his mother twirling that bucket in his mind's eye as he poured the cherished golden liquid into the mix.

Now, the egg whites. Whipping them up brought him out in a sweat at the best of times. This huge quantity would be tough. Phyllo rolled up his sleeves and got up onto the step for maximum purchase. He tapped at the step with his foot twice, for luck, and whirled his whisk like his life depended upon it.

Behind him the cauldron bubbled and spat. The door of the oven crept down. A globule of syrup escaped the pot and fell into the flames with a hiss. Then another. Phyllo's whisk worked the egg whites and sweat formed on his brow. *Such a beautiful day. He laughed out loud, seeing his mother running around and around, 'befuddling' the bees.*

Syrup hissed in the flames again and the cauldron jolted on the wobbly grate. It slid, unbalanced, down off the burner. The weight of the liquid pulled it over and the whole lot sloshed in a wave over the counter and into the oven.

Phyllo swirled in circles with his mother, beating the whites for all he was worth, almost overwhelmed by the heat and a sticky sweet burning. Wait. What?

Thick black smoke poured from the oven and then turned into flames. Barnum's britches! He'd set the place alight! He dropped the bowl and dove for the controls of the burner and oven, but they weren't controlling anything anymore. Smoke filled the kitchen. Gasping, he ran to throw open the giant door of the shop, and then searched frantically for something to dowse the flames.

The oven belched out a long tongue of fire, hitting the popcorn cabinet squarely, shattering the glass and super-heating the corn hopper. It exploded with an almighty boom. Flaming balls of corn fired past Phyllo, crossed the horseshoe path and rained down on the big top canvas. The ferocity of the explosion extinguished the fire in the oven, which was just as well as a moment later his father appeared through the smoke, still wearing his pyjamas and a flabbergasted expression. He wielded a brass hand pump extinguisher which he pumped at the oven and burners, at the popcorn machine, counter and even Phyllo, covering the kitchen in a blanket of white. When he stopped, they stared at each other dumbfounded. Then his eyes fell on the burning canvas outside.

"Get the others," Marvel said, pushing past Phyllo and out to the big top. He pumped with his extinguisher at the blaze, but it was empty. "Fire!" he yelled, snatching down a banner and beating at the flames.

Phyllo reappeared with Roly and Dodo. "Wake everyone up. Stay together."

Waking everyone up wasn't much of a challenge. The

popcorn machine exploding had been loud enough to wake Tabberstock. People were out of their beds before any of the Cane children shrieked at their door. Lazarus Barker was the first on the horseshoe.

"What the devil is going on?" he roared and then, spotting the flames, dashed into the big top. The engineers swarmed about him with fire extinguishers and ladders, obeying his commands. They climbed with dexterity and clambered about the roof, dowsing the flames and tearing away canvas to prevent it from spreading. "Sink the roof!" he yelled and the centre of the canopy fell fifty feet. The engineers scrambled around the circumference, unhitching their precious canvas, detaching it from the frame. It fell the rest of the way, ballooning over the benches and wafting a great wave of hot air and sparks over the mayhem. Engineers frantically roped the roof canvas into the centre, its great weight yielding under their adrenaline-fuelled strength. Circus folk chased the sparks, snuffing them out before new fires could take hold. They tore at the walls and threw them from harm's way. People dashed up and down the path, clutching buckets of water and at themselves. They shouted instructions to each other and embraced loved ones when they found them in the melee.

At length the roar of the flames was silenced and a hush descended. As the sun rose, light poured in through the naked frame and illuminated the devastation in all its hot horror. Cast wandered about, muttering, and picked at the ruin. The Cane family stood together outside the wrecked Confectionary, Marvel's arms stretched about his boys' shoulders, knuckles white. Dodo gripped at his waist.

Lazarus Barker stood stony-faced and blackened by soot. He gazed up at what had been the grand entrance. The engineers had worked fast, but a good quarter of the canvas had been destroyed. The top tier of seating beyond it: charcoal. It could have been worse, but it wasn't good. It wasn't good at all. Phyllo was close enough to hear him speak.

"A parting gift from *The Incredible Parisa* then is it?" he said, "We'll see about that. Skinner! Bain!"

The Ringmaster thought that Arif and Shadi were to blame! Phyllo broke away from his family. "Ringmaster, no!"

"What are you doing?" Roly hissed.

Phyllo took another step. "It wasn't them, Ringmaster. They had nothing to do with it," he said.

The Ringmaster continued speaking to Skinner and Bain, who were now jogging toward him. "Take a crew. Find Arif and the girl. I'll make them pay for this." He spat the words with venom that arched his back.

"Ringmaster! No! It wasn't them; I know it."

He turned his head then to see who was talking. His eyes fell upon Phyllo in a ferocious glower. "And what would you know about it?"

"They've gone. I saw them leave before it even started."

"I saw them too, Candyfloss Boy. I saw them scuttling away into the trees this morning, minutes before my circus was aflame." He turned back to Skinner. "Do as I say."

"It was me," Phyllo blurted and the Ringmaster's eyes flashed back to him.

"It was an accident. I didn't mean to. The oven caught light and then the popcorn machine—." He tailed off as the Ringmaster pushed past him, striding for the Confectionary. He cast his eyes around the blanket of melted foam, the blackened counter, the broken glass. There was no denying its destruction.

44

"What do you know about this?" the Ringmaster growled to Marvel.

Phyllo's father looked shell-shocked. "All I know is that I awoke to smoke and flames, Ringmaster. There hasn't been a chance for explanations yet." He threw his glare to Phyllo, the first glimmers of the telling-off to come, forming.

The Ringmaster paced about the shopfront and poked at the confections, melted on their shelves. "Your stock is ruined," he said.

"Undoubtedly."

"And the kitchen is a disaster. Will it function?"

Phyllo's father stepped back into the Confectionary for the first time then himself. "I believe I'll need a new corn popper —" it had pretty much disintegrated "—and the oven looks suspect, but you never know. As for the ingredients, well that will take some investigation." He cast his eyes around the shelves mournfully. His gaze fell upon Glumberry on the top shelf. His yellow eyes were open and as wide as tea plates.

"Glumberry! Glumberry!" Dodo spotted him too. "Get him down, get him down, Daddy." Dodo rushed into the kitchen and skidded on the foamy floor, trying to get to the stepladder.

The Ringmaster stepped backward, reversing out of the cabin. His face now blank and pale. "You have your hands full. As do I," he said, then turned and strode away.

CHAPTER SIX

The Ringmaster's Word

The final shows at Tabberstock were cancelled. The circus was in no fit state to accept paying customers. A great swathe of the canvas was missing and the middle tier of seating wobbled precariously if you so much as breathed on it. The engineers did their best with what canvas remained, but they needed new fabric of a magical variety and you couldn't get that on your average high street. They patched it up with temporary tarpaulin and worked day and night on the carpentry. It needed to stack so at least they could travel.

The troupe was jumpy. Rumours percolated through misheard conversation and paranoia that the In-between were responsible for the fire, with Phyllo an unfortunate scapegoat. Others held him fully responsible. He wasn't sure which was worse.

He coped with his newfound fame by staying out of the way. After all, he wasn't lacking in things to keep him busy. In fact, the list of outstanding jobs at the Confectionary was as long as his friends list was short. They had to clear every shelf and check the ingredients for damage.

Generally, the sealed items in bottles and jars were alright, but anything that was fresh or stored in open boxes or sacks:

ruined. Everything had to be either cleaned up or thrown out and listed in an inventory. A new supplies list was drawn up for the quartermaster, but there was only so much a general shop could provide, and periodically his father would sigh and lament the loss of a hard-to-find item and Phyllo would feel bad all over again. Between them they scrubbed the whole place, top to bottom. Even the oven had not shone so well in years. The worktop above it, however, was irreversibly scorched.

They couldn't afford to replace it, but Marvel had muttered that perhaps a visual reminder to pay better attention wouldn't hurt. His initial bright rage, tempered by Phyllo's regret had now faded into a dull sort of mourning. Phyllo preferred the anger.

"I know you didn't mean to, son, but if we could keep experimental activities supervised from now on, eh? I think that would be best."

Phyllo agreed wholeheartedly. He was a disaster waiting to happen.

The Ringmaster summoned him the next day and when Marvel said he'd go too, Roly insisted on coming along. "The Cane men, strong together, eh?" Marvel had remarked but, as they'd approached the grand engraved doors to the Ringmaster's cabin, he'd wrung his hands. Phyllo knew that if the Ringmaster asked them to cover the cost of the canvas they were done for. There was barely enough to cover ingredients.

Marvel knocked, pushed the door open and Phyllo stepped over the threshold, his heart in his throat. Directly in front was a solid wall of machinery, which cut them off from the main part of the cabin in a small antechamber. Pistons and gears connected together in a brass riveted frame. Cogs meshed and bright blue electricity arced in a cage. The Machine. Phyllo had never been summoned to the Ringmaster before. This was his first up-close encounter. Marvel pushed him along to the side and around it, into the cabin and Roly followed.

It was nothing like the Confectionary. Vast by comparison, it rose double height with a great arch of ridged iron for a ceiling. An enormous circular window looked out toward Tabberstock, metal mullions dividing the scene into three.

Lazarus Barker sat behind a large boxy desk, whose straps and handles suggested it had once been a travelling trunk, and could be again, if the right levers were engaged. One hand curved around the arm of his leather chair and the other gripped the head of his cane. He drove the tip into the floor. His knuckles were white and his eyes were cold.

The Ringmaster said nothing as they approached and, as terrifying as his demeanour was, Phyllo could not help but look around at his surroundings. It was the most incredible sight. The entire right side of the cabin was filled with workings of the Machine, continuing on from the section in front of the door. The marvellous magical contraption at the heart of the Circus of Wonder. Phyllo's eyes swept floor to ceiling, over brass pipes and valves. Great cogged wheels could be spied through gaps further inside, seemingly driven by pistons. Nixie tubes and electro-magnetic chambers squeezed between copper urns. Just the faint hum of electricity suggested life. Nothing else moved and Phyllo wondered if it was sleeping.

Marvel drew the boys up to a halt in front of the Ringmaster's desk and his gaze slid from one to the next, finally settling on Phyllo. He lifted his chin a little, magnificent beard curling at his chest. "Let's hear it then," he said.

This was it. "I'm so sorry," Phyllo blurted out, "I was practising a recipe, and I was concentrating so much on the whipping that I lost sight of the syrup and, well, the heat from the oven was helping. It was definitely helping. At one point I'm pretty sure I laughed out loud—" The words fell out in an ill-advised rush.

"You laughed out loud?" questioned the Ringmaster, the expression on his face: not at all encouraging.

"Not at the fire." Phyllo's hands shot up in defence, "At the scene, in my head, at my mother."

The Ringmaster threw back his head and shook the absurdity of that statement from him. "Your mother? Make sense, boy."

"If I may, Ringmaster," said Marvel, "One of our most ingenious ingredients can be memories, although devilishly difficult to harness, I'm afraid."

"Is that so?"

"I've been working on a recipe that includes a memory of my mother," Phyllo explained.

"Because…?"

"I, er, because it was special, I guess. It was special, to me."

"Did it taste nice, this memory?"

"Not exactly, I mean, in a manner of speaking."

"It seems to me that it had no place in confectionary."

"Sometimes you have to add the unusual to make it memorable. Isn't that right, Dad?" Phyllo tugged at his father's sleeve.

"Quite right." Marvel smiled down.

"It seems to me that this unusual ingredient almost cost me my big top. It's certainly cost me six months' takings in canvas repairs. It's cost you your stores and your stock. Was it worth it, do you think?"

Phyllo had so desperately wanted it to work. "It could have been," he mumbled to his shoes.

"Was it worth it?" the Ringmaster repeated, more forcibly this time.

Phyllo shook his head, his eyes burned.

"No." The Ringmaster said the word for him. "Marvel, how are Phyllo's other endeavours? Has he produced anything of merit?"

Marvel perked up, waving his hands animatedly. "Ah, yes, he is a splendid assistant in the ring. Makes our wares very appealing to the children. Great enthusiasm."

"I see. So, he enjoys the circus. How about actual confections?"

"Um, no, not so much, as yet. He has been rather focused —" The Ringmaster held up the palm of his hand. "And Roly?" He turned his gaze onto Phyllo's brother, "How are you finding the family talent?"

"Brilliant. I mean, I really like it," Roly blurted out, "I've made candyfloss and some good peanut toffees."

"Have you now? Excellent. Excellent. It would appear it's just you that's the problem then, wouldn't it?" The Ringmaster's cold stare returned to Phyllo. He rose from his chair, moved over to the window and onto the platform by the window. He smoothed the crimson velvet of his jacket and pulled himself erect to look out at the view. "Our world is not what it once was. Our glory fades and with it our fortune. Every customer counts. Every act counts. Every contribution and every subtraction count. You too must count. You too must be supportive to the cause. What do you say to that, Phyllo Cane? Do you wish to be a valuable asset?"

Phyllo looked nervously to his father and back to the Ringmaster. "Yes, of course," he said.

"That's good. I'm glad to hear it." The Ringmaster turned to face him. One hand clutched the cane by its polished head,

the other he tucked behind his back. "You need a little vicissi-
tude. It's time we found your way to shine, wouldn't you say?
Confectionary clearly isn't your thing." He shook his head, but
was smiling, coaxing. "I think you should run the circuit."

Phyllo stared at him blankly. He had no idea what he was
talking about. His father seemed to understand better though.

"Ringmaster, no," Marvel exclaimed, "there's no need—"
The Ringmaster raised his flat palm once again, this time
directing an edge of testiness toward Marvel. "Yes. Yes. I think
it's the perfect solution."

"No, but, Ringmaster, he's still young, only twelve."

"All the better. More time for trials. Birdie Volante is only
eleven and she's already mastered basic tricks on the trapeze
and Emilio could juggle six clubs before he was six himself. I
think you just can, or you can't." He looked pointedly at
Phyllo, "The longer we leave it the less chance he'll have of
grasping anything."

Phyllo scrunched up his face, confused. "The circuit? What
do you mean?"

"The circuit, dear boy, the circuit!" He shook his head. "It's
an honour."

"Ringmaster, please."

"You've cost me dearly, Phyllo Cane. If you weren't from
an established family you'd be out on your ear, like *The Incredible Parisa*. No, this is a rite, an old tradition of the circus folk. A
last chance at impunity really, but we won't look at it like that
for now."

"What? What does he mean, Dad?"

"Surely he could have a little more time?" Marvel pleaded.

The Ringmaster rounded on him. "I'm being more than
generous. I should have you out, the lot of you. This is going
to cost me a small fortune and we'll lose shows making repairs

so that's even more Coin to the Toshers. Who's going to explain that to the troupe? Will it be you?" Anger was creeping into the Ringmaster's voice, his careful control slipping.

"Do you take the threat of the In-between so lightly? Our fading fortunes ripple out into the dark. Children's imaginations lost to technology and adults washed away on the unrelenting wave of bad news. If they can't open their hearts to us, if they don't visit us, how do you think our poor relations of the In-between fare? It is desperate times for them. They prowl outside our walls at every stop. Jealous and vengeful."

"I don't think that there are any in Tabberstock," Phyllo added in a small voice. He'd meant to ease the Ringmaster's worries, but it seemed to make him more annoyed.

He snapped back at him, "We'll have to deviate from our route to get to the canvas merchant. Shady Hollow. A poor take that will be. It's my final word, Marvel, Phyllo has to make amends or he's out."

Phyllo's father leant back, jaw flapping. "I, I see." He looked desperately over to Phyllo who still was utterly confused.

"Miss Fitz, take a letter," barked the Ringmaster and beside the Ringmaster's desk there was a burst of sudden movement.

An armoured trunk four feet across and two deep stood on four iron legs that brought its lid to waist height. On top perched a sit-up-and-beg mechanical typewriter of polished chrome and black enamel. Rather surprisingly, an octopus with slick black tentacles and shining grey suckers appeared to have made it its home. Its curling limbs snaked around from the rear of the roller. One snatched up a sheet of paper and fed it into position with the help of a second tentacle which pumped the return lever. The tentacles stilled, presumably awaiting further instruction.

"Addendum pertaining Cane, Phyllo. Today's date, Tabberstock Fields."

The tentacles flexed and curled, their tips tapped precisely at the keys. It typed as the Ringmaster dictated.

"Meeting between the Cane family, specifically Marvel, Roly and Phyllo and myself, acting in capacity of Ringmaster. An incident originating in the Confectionary this past week has caused grievous damage to the canopy and structure of our most splendid big top, namely side panels and awnings, not limited to but including the grand entrance, passage-end flanks and character act banners and the structure of tiered seating, most greatly affecting the important personage sumptuous seating and mechanical structure of folding upper tiers." The Ringmaster paused for thought and turned to slowly pace back and forth in front of the window.

"Further performances are untenable at this time. Engineering report structural progress. Canvas will need to be procured from the merchants at Ganymede. Repairs will run into tens of thousands of Coin. The Confectionary itself sustained significant damage."

Marvel gingerly raised his hand "Actually, Ringmaster, it wasn't quite as bad as it seemed. The oven has come up rather well and we can get by with the odd scorch mark."

"Well then, at least it won't cost *you* quite so much. I assume that your stock is still ruined?"

"Ah, well, yes." Marvel managed a weak smile.

"Please don't talk, Marvel. Continuing, Miss Fitz. Scratch that last."

The Octowriter backspaced fiercely, one tentacle hammering down a single key and another poking a small piece of something white between the paper and type hammer.

There was no expression to read but something about the way it rippled its suckers suggested irritation.

"Discussions with Messrs Marvel and Phyllo Cane have revealed that an experimental recipe was to blame for the fire and that Phyllo Cane himself is yet to exhibit any actual proficiency in the family talent of confectionary. Given the pressures of solvency and credit, it is with great regret that the Circus of Wonder would have to consider withdrawal of residency for any persons unable to contribute to the ongoing success of the troupe."

The Cane family's jaws flapped in unison.

"However, in recognition of the family's long history with the Circus of Wonder, I deem this inappropriate, but other and equal steps must be taken. I invoke the rite of The Circuit, so that Phyllo Cane may pursue his destiny and will provide a Seeker's Passport so that any who will accept him into their troupe will enjoy an accord with the Circus of Wonder."

The Octowriter tapped to a halt a couple of seconds after the Ringmaster had finished speaking.

"That is all," he said and then to Phyllo, "Take that to the Book Keeper for entry. I will expect your response by tomorrow evening.

One tentacle snatched the paper off its roller and then waved it about impatiently. Phyllo gingerly plucked it from the tentacled grip and leant closer, trying to see the Octopus's body around the back. He got a smart smack on the forehead from one of the livelier tentacles for his trouble.

"Good evening, Marvel. Roly. Phyllo." The Ringmaster sat down at his desk and started to examine a document. All aspects of him were turned away, no longer wishing to engage.

"Ah, good evening then, yes," Marvel stuttered, "Boys?" He turned them around and pushed them out.

"Well that *was* unexpected," he said once they were back on the horseshoe and had closed the door.

A horrible sensation of being out of control was rising in Phyllo's chest. "The circuit? What's he on about, Dad? What does he mean? What's the circuit?" Phyllo still didn't understand what was going on. Roly shrugged and shook his head, clearly no better off.

"Well, it's an old-fashioned sort of thing, really. Haven't heard of anyone actually doing it in years." Marvel fiddled with the buttons on his jacket.

This was no help to Phyllo. "And…"

Marvel looked this way and that, as if looking for the answer. "Occasionally talents might skip a generation or just not manifest. It happens. Sometimes. In most situations there are enough relations to ice over the cracks or perhaps find another aspect to excel in. I find you enormously helpful in the ring, Phyllo. We wouldn't sell half as much if you weren't there. It would seem, however, that that is no longer enough."

The Book Keeper's cabin was the last by the gate. Marvel steered them slowly toward it.

"The circuit is a chance to try other talents. Traditionally, a series of two-month adoptions, going on for a year, to be trained as if you were part of other families. One after another. To see if you might be better suited to something else. When the year is up you have to decide." He cringed as he said the final words.

"But I don't want to be something else."

"I know, son." Marvel hesitated briefly, but then squeezed Phyllo's shoulder, "I don't want that either, but if the Ringmaster is serious, and unfortunately he does appear to be, then I don't think that we have any choice."

"No way. I'm not doing it. He can't make me." Phyllo was

the Confectioner's son. He wanted to train to be a confectioner. *That* was his right, not this crazy circuit business.

"It's a flaming insult, that's what it is," said Roly. "He's picking on us because he thinks we won't stand up for ourselves. It's always been the same. Just because we don't throw ourselves around the big top, cavorting like flipping trained monkeys, they look down on us. Well they've got no idea what it takes."

Marvel flapped his arms at Roly, looking back to the Ringmaster's door. "Yes, yes. Quite so," he said in a hushed voice, "and they will probably never understand. Let's not make too much fuss, eh?"

"Dad! I can't believe you're being so calm about it!" Phyllo exclaimed, "Mum would never have stood for this in a million years. Taking away someone's talent, it's outrageous."

"Far worse to be ejected from the troupe. Don't you see? If we got thrown out it would put an indelible slur on our names, across our future. Your future."

"Mum would have stood up to him."

"Your mother," Marvel cut across him, "would have wanted to keep you safe. That's the most important thing. Especially in these darker days." Marvel knocked on the door they had now reached and then pushed it open six inches. "Albertus? Are you free?"

Albertus came to the door dressed for mid-winter, despite it being August. Layers of jumpers filled out his slight frame, a paisley cravat snuggled up to his wobbly chin and two beanie hats, one over the other, topped off his head of fine white hair. He looked at them through large thick glasses.

"Marvel. Nice to see you. Oh, and the boys too. Come in, come in."

A low fire crackled in the grate casting an amber glow

about the interior. It was almost entirely filled with books. Shelf upon shelf clung to the walls. One side of the cabin, which adjoined the Ringmaster's, was double height just like his, but the ceiling sloped dramatically down to the height of the low ticket booth at the gate on the other. A staircase spiralled up to a small mezzanine. It felt like a discovered space, like a cupboard under the stairs, being put to good use.

"The Ringmaster said I should give you this," Phyllo said, unable to keep the anger out of his voice. Albertus took the piece of paper and looked quizzically to Marvel.

"But this is all stupid. It was an accident. An accident! He doesn't have to make me out to be some kind of idiot!" raged Phyllo.

Albertus blinked at him, quite taken aback by Phyllo's fury. "Well, I've not been in on the proceedings, so give me a minute to catch up." His enormously magnified eyes skated over the document. "I'm not sure yet what the Ringmaster might expect me to do. I am, after all, a man of many hats, many hats, yes." He fell silent, reading.

"Hats?"

Albertus gave a series of small nods. "Mmm. Yes. Metaphorically speaking." He paused in his reading. "One for the Book Keeper, you know. Perhaps you might like to think of it as a smart bowler, wearing which I keep an astute eye on the Circus of Wonder's finances." He tapped a thin finger to one lens of his glasses then pointed the same at Phyllo.

"Another is that of the Ticket Seller, which is probably a jauntier affair. Much jauntier." He cast about for inspiration. "Perhaps a pink trilby with a feather in its ribbon. I like wearing that one. Reminds me there's life in the old dog yet. Making the children coming in giggle and getting them excited about the show. You might not imagine it, but I do like pulling silly faces." He stretched his mouth out in a wide grin to demonstrate and pointed to a small door on the low wall. "The booth at the gate is actually part of my cabin, but I keep the door closed out of hours. It's draughty and I wear two pairs of socks as it is."

Roly laughed and Phyllo even thawed a little.

"In other moments I am the Post Master. Letters and newspapers and such come in through the Book Keeper's network for me to distribute. Like I haven't got enough to do." He snorked out a little laugh. "Perhaps a nice flat cap with a peaked brim for that one, hmm? By far my most common attire, however, is that of Librarian, which I wear at this very moment." He wafted a hand at himself, drawing attention to his woolly outfit. "I look after the books of the cast and they're no ordinary books, oh no. Every man, woman and child in the troupe has their own volume which adds up to quite a number, quite a number, I can tell you." He rolled his hand, "and then there's the history, law, geography. All that good stuff." He looked to Phyllo and met his eyes. "That'll be the hat we need I expect, the woolly one."

Albertus went to sit down at his desk, sweeping mounds of curling paper out to its edges so that the note from the Ringmaster could lie flat. He pulled a large desk-mounted magnifying glass across to rest over it and took a few moments to take it in. "Oh well, he's quite clear, isn't he?" He looked back to Phyllo, eyebrows tipped to a slant in sympathy.

"He can't do it, can he? He can't make me? It's not fair." Phyllo couldn't believe this was happening.

"Ah well, it is unusual these days, but it's also an old circus rite."

"I've not heard of it in years," said Phyllo's father, "Didn't think it still went on."

Albertus pressed his fingers to his lips, maroon fingerless gloves on his hands. He got up from the desk and went up onto the mezzanine. He only seemed to take the smallest shuffling steps, but got up there in no time. They could see him pulling books from shelves, quickly replacing them and moving along, searching. "A-ha, a-ha." He tucked a fat volume under his arm and shuffled back down the stairs.

"Historical Precedents and Circus Law," he said by way of explanation, opening the book and running his finger over the pages, muttering. Occasionally, he'd lick the tip of his finger before turning the page. "Yes, yes, here's one. Prunella Devlin, late of Bridle Bay. Don't be alarmed, it's an old book. Let's see now. I think I still have the Devlins." He pushed the book to one side and made off up the spiral staircase again, pulling himself up by the banister this time with a bit more effort. He stopped beside an old carved cupboard, pulled a bulging keyring from his cardigan pocket and sorted through it, holding each key up to the light to examine it through his enormously thick glasses. He had to study a few before he found the one that he wanted and having done so, unlocked the cupboard and disappeared inside. There was some shuffling and banging and then he was back. Albertus was surprisingly quick on his feet considering his apparent old age.

"Devlin," he said, waggling the book about triumphantly, "Now then." He thumbed through the pages and then began to read aloud. "Prunella Devlin, daughter of Jeremiah and Eliza Devlin. Seventh generation juggling act from Bridle Bay."

Over the open book Phyllo thought he could see a mist forming. Albertus adjusted the angle of the magnifying glass and ran one finger along under the words. The mist was pushed into a slightly different shape. "Aged fifteen years, Prunella was issued with a Seekers Passport by Samuel

Barker, our current Ringmaster's grandfather." Albertus picked up an intricately filigreed gold pen from his desk and drew a symbol in the air over the book. The mist shrank and concentrated itself into the form of two figures. One bore the unmistakable outline of a Ringmaster's top hat on its head; the other was much smaller. A girl. The Ringmaster-shaped mist gave her a kind of baton, possibly a rolled-up piece of paper.

"Prunella went to Farthington's Flying Circus initially, training with the tumblers, Andreas Ginnasta took her under his wing." The mist above the book reformed into a wobbling shape throwing smoky balls into the air and dropping them and then attempting a rather clumsy forward roll. "She also tried the knife throwing act, but her nerves couldn't stand it and eventually moved on to Meduso's Circus of Zoological Marvels to try her hand at animal training." Albertus turned the page and the mist wafted away. He read on silently, subconsciously allowing the odd phrase to escape. "Whip... Norwegian mountain lion... despite best efforts... Bridle Bay Cemetery."

"What's that?" Roly exclaimed, pointing to the thin mist forming over the book again. Phyllo couldn't see anything distinct, but Roly had gone quite pale. "Is that what I think it is? Is that lion...?"

Albertus wafted urgently at it. "Nothing to see. Nothing to see. Perhaps we could try another." Albertus snapped the Devlins' journal shut and returned to the circus history book. He licked the tip of his finger to turn the pages more efficiently. He was almost at the back before he found another entry of interest. "Ah yes, here we are. Valentine Dunn. A-ha, a-ha." He looked up to Marvel with a little twinkle of triumph. "Do you remember him, Marvel?"

60

"Valentine Dunn? Now that does have a ring to it..." Marvel crumpled his brow, trying to think.

"Quite famous, quite famous actually. Back in the 1800s." Albertus got up from the desk and made off up the stairs, as best he could.

"Just how old do you think I am?" said Marvel.

Albertus wafted his hand at him, "From the history books." He sorted through the keys on his oversized keyring. "Ah yes now I think that this is the Mechanical Misfits." He's singled out a large brass key with a steel band around the shaft. It was a different key from the one he'd used last time, but it still unlocked the cupboard door. When he opened it a cloud of fumes wafted out. Albertus went inside, crashed about and remerged looking a bit flustered. He cricked his neck and descended the stairs, back to his desk.

Albertus put the book down in front of them. It smelt of petrol.

"Valentine Dunn started off as a confectioner just like you, Phyllo. Now let me see, yes. He started off at Bonko's and didn't make much of a mark for himself. Their Ringmaster was famously a short-tempered old goat. Don't tell him I said so." Albertus wrinkled up his podgy face and snorty laughed, making funny little elbow nudges towards Phyllo.

"Yes, Yes. Oh, never mind. Anyway, Bonko struck an accord with Captain Velocity's Mechanical Misfits. Valentine took to them right away. Created the most famous act of their time." Albertus flourished his fountain pen over the book and the mists swirled into what was unmistakably a tiny smoke man climbing into a large upturned tube. It was Phyllo's turn to point. "Is he getting into a cannon?" He was both fascinated by the misty representation and horrified.

"Oh yes. Such a crowd puller it was that the Mechanical

Misfits went from strength to strength, yes strength to strength. Made them what they are today."

The little smoke man popped out of the cannon and flew over the pages of the book. He plopped to the surface of the desk and dissipated in rippling fading rings.

"So, what we're saying here is that everything'll be alright if I can just get myself shot out of a cannon." Phyllo scrubbed at his hair. "I can't believe this."

"Either that or get eaten by a lion," Roly chipped in.

"Now, now, boys. Look, Phyllo," Albertus said, "This isn't your destiny we're looking at here, its history. This is a marvellous opportunity, isn't it, Marvel? Marvellous."

Marvel cranked his face into a smile. "Of course, yes, absolutely."

"And just because Prunella got herself into a spot of bother—"

"Bother!"

"It doesn't mean that you have to. This could be the start of something great for you, Phyllo." Albertus attempted a light punch on the upper arm for camaraderie's sake, but never actually made contact.

"You might not even have to leave the Circus of Wonder," he continued.

"How's that, Albertus? The Seekers Passport?" Marvel said, hope springing in his eyes.

"Yes, yes, it's an accord with other troupes and he might well need it, but the Ringmaster says he wants him to find a talent. He hasn't specified where."

CHAPTER SEVEN

Moving On

Despite all the drama and mayhem he'd caused, the Confectionary still felt safe. The arched ceiling of the kitchen with all its dangling pots and the shelves, stuffed not quite as full as usual, created a cushioned space that soothed Phyllo's nerves. The rest of the Canes made a beeline for their living quarters and that squishy, if miniscule sofa to kick off their shoes and collapse. Phyllo looked for solace in his old box of ingredients.

The cardboard had been blackened, but flames hadn't caught his carefully curated stash. Still in their small packages, they snuggled neatly together. He pulled out the jar of precious honey and sighed at its greatly depleted contents – just a spoonful left. It didn't matter now, anyhow. He'd never make it work.

"You know you don't have to do it, eh?" Marvel stood in the doorway, "If you wanted to stick with it, stick with us, I'd leave this place for you in a heartbeat. We all would." Marvel came around the counter to look him in the eye.

"You don't have to leave, Dad. It's just me."

"We stick together like raspberry gum, no matter what. If you couldn't handle it, if it was too much, we'd all leave. Start again."

"And go where?"

"Travelling fairs always need a good Candy Man. It might be strange at first, but we'd find our feet."

Phyllo didn't need to ask if he meant it. One thing that was never in doubt was that Marvel Cane would do anything for his family.

"Thanks, Dad, but isn't it kind of dangerous?" He knew that it was.

"All for one." Marvel punched into the air, somewhat half-heartedly. "Just don't mention it to your little sister until you've made up your mind, eh?"

"Course. Thanks, Dad."

Marvel patted him amiably on the shoulder and went back to re-join the others. "Don't be too long out here. It's been a long day. We all need some rest."

Phyllo closed up his box, slid it beneath the counter and rubbed at his eyes. He was tired and his eyes were playing tricks on him: he thought he'd just seen someone in a hooded cloak pass by the front door. He shook it off as a trick of the light and drifted out into the shop for a last look around. The Confectionary was the only home he'd ever known. He knew every inch of it. He walked along the counter and then back along the shelves, letting his fingers run over the smooth polished wood. His memories lodged in the grain. Could he exist anywhere else?

Running footsteps, two pairs. A swish of fabric passed the narrow door.

It was late and very dark. With no show to prepare for the next day most of the troupe were probably asleep. Even the engineers had stopped hammering and packed it in for the night. Phyllo opened the door the tiniest crack and peered to the right, around the horseshoe. He couldn't see anything. He stuck his head out and looked to the left. In the darkness something was moving away. Odd. He stepped out of the door and quietly followed, thinking about Emmett and his strange behaviour before. Was it him?

Urgent whispers hissed on the night air out of sight. Phyllo leant forward, trying to see around the curve. The door to the Quartermaster's store was ajar. Phyllo crept to it. He held his breath and spied through the gap. Flashlights. Their haphazard light revealed the forms of men: six or seven. They swept the contents out of cupboards and climbed racks to take what was hidden on top. Long coats threw monstrous shadows. Faces concealed by ragged makeshift masks. Thieves of the In-between.

Phyllo had to raise the alarm. He stepped back, but a strong arm wound across his chest and a blade pressed into the soft flesh of his throat. "No place for a child," said a rough voice.

Phyllo froze.

His captor kicked the door fully open. "We are discovered," he said and the men inside jolted from their task, stuffing final booty into their sacks and bolting for the door. Out of the shadows blundered a large man with a filthy rag tied around his face for a mask. He tugged on a rope that pulled another from the darkness. His hands were bound in front of him and the rope was attached like a lead. Arif. Their eyes met in recognition and he dipped his head in shame. "I'm sorry, my friend," he murmured as he drew near, "We were captured. I had no choice but to show them the way. It is our ticket on."

The big oaf yanked him along. "No time to chat, ladies," he drawled and Phyllo's own captor tugged him back from the door, clearing the way for the others to escape. When the last had gone, he released his grip and dropped the knife. Phyllo

65

spun to face him. The man was tall and broad, dressed entirely in black and masked – a full face mask with a shape of its own, hard to decipher in the low light but that and the cloak which billowed around him reminded Phyllo of a crow. "Try not to get killed," the crow man said and then ran after the others.

Phyllo gulped for breath and then, after a few moments, gathered his wits. "Help!" he gasped, "Thieves!" His voice came stronger then, "In-between in the horseshoe! Thieves! Thieves! Help!" This day just got worse and worse.

Marvel was first out, Roly at his heels, Dodo lingering at the Confectionary door. Marvel ran to Phyllo's side. "Phyllo. What's happened? Are you alright?"

"That way," Phyllo said, pointing into the darkness.

The Ringmaster thundered around the path, Skinner and Bain a few footsteps behind. They'd been in the big top. The Ringmaster stopped at Phyllo's side, but waved the other two on in pursuit. "Now what?" he barked, glaring down at Phyllo.

Phyllo gulped. "I heard a noise, out here, so I looked out and saw that the door was open." He waved an arm to the Quartermaster's door, "There were men, six or seven, filling sacks. One put a knife to my throat." He touched his neck and felt the fear properly for the first time.

The Ringmaster pushed past him, into the store. "Hector! Hector, are you in here?" Phyllo followed him inside. Hector, the Quartermaster, was slumped on the floor. The Ringmaster snatched a rag up from the ground beside him, sniffed it gingerly then tossed it aside. "Drugged. Help me sit him up."

They leant Hector against the wall and he began to come around.

"We're not safe here," the Ringmaster said, "Time to go."

He stood and strode out into the horseshoe, calling for Skinner who came jogging out of the shadows. "Any sign?" he asked.

"A trail of open doors leading into the bunk room and a jemmied window. That'll be the way out for them, and the way in, no doubt. No-one to catch though. Long gone."

"Can we stack the tiers? Will she travel?"

"The tarp'll make it hairy but she'll go."

"Then let's go. Call it."

"Ringmaster." Skinner gave an obedient nod then turned, put his hand to his mouth and yelled "Jal!" at the top of his voice. He took off at a trot, other voices also taking up the call, "Jal!" "Jal!" It echoed around the cabins and the big top.

"Come on, Phyllo, let's get ready," Marvel said and hurried him back to the Confectionary. Dodo was waiting at the door, her eyes wide with fear.

"It's OK, Dodo. Everything's OK." Phyllo broke away from Marvel to scoop her up. She threw her arms and legs around him, holding on. "They've gone now and we're going too." Dodo was so young, so small. The thought of her outside the big top's protection was terrible. He couldn't allow it. "Come on, I'll help you pack your bunk." He put her down in their living quarters and together they cleared her bed, rolling up the bedclothes and lodging them in the small cupboard at the end. They did the same for his father's things and then his. Roly and Marvel had already cleared the floor. Marvel dowsed the log burner to be sure it was out and moved on to the kitchen, helping Roly to put small items away in cupboards under the counter and ensuring their remaining ingredients were safely tucked away behind the bars of the shelves. Glumberry opened one yellow eye from the top shelf then the other. "Jal, is it?" he said with a yawn.

"Yes, we're off," Marvel said, "Thieves in the stores. Time to go."

Phyllo climbed up to get him, then passed him to Dodo. She embraced Glumberry securely and he flopped a wing over her shoulder to help with his awkward weight. "Too many caramel peanuts," he said and nuzzled into her ear.

"Everyone ready?" Marvel said. He looked all around, making final checks. "Let's go."

Once out on the horseshoe, the noise of activity caught up with them. Engineers had hoisted the canvas right up to the roof and the Machine was stirring. The whump of its pistons sent deep vibrations through the ground, a steady heartbeat that pumped through the Circus of Wonder, the adrenalin excitement of a new destination to come. This time Phyllo knew even greater changes lay ahead.

Engineers engaged gears to wind the tiers of the stand in on themselves. One under the other, each chair folding and sliding beneath the next. The stands closed like a flamenco fan, emptying the space, making room. Metal clanged against metal and the engineers called out to each other, locking off brakes and releasing pulleys.

The troupe were gradually assembling in the horseshoe and the Ringmaster made his way around the heads of each cabin, making departure checks.

"Floors clear for mechanism? All flames extinguished? Loose items stowed?" he asked Marvel, who nodded. "Carry on."

Marvel pulled a fat brass key out of his inner jacket pocket and slid it into the hole beside the Confectionary's smallest door. A twist of the key opened up a small flap under which was a lever. Marvel pulled it smartly down, closed the flap and withdrew the key. The Confectionary's outer skin juddered and then the side door, wall and roof on the left side all started to rise in clicks. After going up about a foot, the width of the cabin started to shrink. The two outer walls moved slowly and decisively in, toward one another. Inside the counters swivelled and aligned. At the back the living space folded in on itself and empty floor slid away, beneath the bunks. The Confectionary condensed itself into a solid mass of furniture and counter and shelving, not a scrap of space anywhere.

Around the horseshoe other cabins did the same. Frú Hafiz, Albertus Crinkle and the others all stood before their shrunken cabins, clutching keys.

"Pack her up!" the Ringmaster called and all together the people of the Circus of Wonder got behind their cabins and pushed them into the now empty big top. Engineers buzzed around them like bees, locking off mechanisms and checking connections to the big top frame. They threw ropes and pumped jacks, bolting the cabins into place, securing them to each other under the big top roof.

The Ringmaster's cabin was the final segment. They rolled it into place, throwing open the tall brass doors to reveal the interface to the Machine. One of the king poles supporting the roof fitted exactly into the shape now created in the fascia. It clunked home and the Machine sighed, reunited.

Phyllo and the others filed into the big top, down the narrow alleyways that led between cabins. They gathered in the ring. It was the only empty floor space and was surrounded by the huddled shrunken cabins of every act. Emmett stood chatting amiably to another clown, now out of make-up and looking considerably better. Marvel went over to greet him, Dodo too. Emmett patted her affectionately on the head.

Phyllo and Roly stood side by side a small distance away,

looking up at the engineers swinging about in the rigging. They were unfurling the canvas again on the sides and securing the outer perimeter.

"Quite a day," Roly said.

"You're not kidding. Quite a week."

"No denying it."

Hands in pockets, they rocked on their heels.

"Look at Bain." Roly nodded up to the burly engineer leaping around the roofs of the cabins. "I think his family talent might have come from mountain goats."

"At least he's got one," Phyllo grumbled.

"Yeah. About that."

Phyllo looked around to his father. He was speaking animatedly to Signor Volante, Emmett nodding along, engaged, brow furrowed. "I'd rather not leave our circus, obviously. Rather not have to leave the Confectionary and you lot. Rather not have set light to the big top, come to that."

"What an idiot."

Phyllo raised an eyebrow at him. "But if I don't agree to do it, it'll mean trouble."

"More trouble."

Phyllo nodded and squeezed his mouth into a thin line.

The Ringmaster swept into the ring and then through the small opening left into his cabin, Skinner on his heels. He held in his hand a wooden stake, two feet long and topped with iron. It was the master stake, the destination marker, and it was out of the ground. Skinner would take the link through the Ringmaster's quarters, on to the next location, Shady Hollow, and drive it into the ground there.

The rhythm of the Machine stepped up a gear. Blue light of electricity ebbed stronger and weaker, stronger and weaker, growing with each phase. Through the core of the metal framework, the Machine started to hum, reaching fingers of power through the skeleton of the big top, through the cabins. Blue light escaped out of the minuscule gaps around rivets, the web of metal that supported the roof vibrated in pulses. The temporary tarpaulin behind the Confectionary fought against its ties, bucking and cracking, whilst the original canvas held firm.

Phyllo considered the people of Tabberstock. They hadn't seen the Circus of Wonder arrive. They'd noticed them there first thing in the morning, pulling up rigging and hammering tent pegs. They'd probably assumed an early start and seen work in progress. Nothing unusual there.

They wouldn't see them leave either.

Beyond the Ringmaster's link, Skinner would be stepping out of the treeline in Shady Hollow to march fifty paces into the centre of the clearing, head bobbing on his thick neck, counting. He'd scan the horizon, turning a slow circle, squinting into the night and then, when he was satisfied no-one was there, he'd push the stake tip into the ground, whirl his heavy lump hammer up, high over his head and bring it down hard. Once, twice, three times. That was how it went.

In Tabberstock, the Circus of Wonder vanished.

When Phyllo emerged from the big top the first thing that struck him was how very dark it was. Yes, it was the middle of the night. Yes, it had been the middle of the night in Tabberstock too, but here the darkness was thick as molasses. He could barely see Roly by his side and the air was so still, it felt like they'd been lost down a well.

"Howling humbugs," Roly said, "Where are we?"

The engineers emerged too, small beams shining from

torches strapped to their heads. They fanned out into a line, twenty men abreast and jogged off around the circumference of the tent, like the great sweeping hand of a clock. They kicked away rocks and hefted debris that got picked up in their dim puddles of light, clearing the space for the horseshoe and cabins.

The Ringmaster and Skinner strode out with a flashlight and set to examining what was left of the tarpaulin. The rope had cut clean through the eyelets of the upper section, leaving it hanging limp.

"Well, it got us here," Skinner said.

The Ringmaster grimaced. "And the sooner we're gone the better. Let's go for a half set, it's too damn dark to do anything else."

The sweep of engineers rounded back to their starting point and then swarmed all over the cabins, which were pushed out and expanded, but fine work would have to wait for better conditions. The Ringmaster sent the rest of the troupe off to bed, where most could sleep until first light.

The Canes settled back into their cabin and retired to their beds. They'd fled Tabberstock and the In-between could not have followed them here, but they'd been infiltrated, pillaged. Phyllo hadn't come to any harm, but it had been dangerously close. The circus only being half set added to their discomfort, an uneasiness not helped by the guard which would prowl the perimeter until dawn. And Phyllo was going to have to leave, leave his family or put them at risk.

He couldn't sleep. His brain whirled with worries and questions. Roly, in the bunk above, seemingly couldn't either. Phyllo could hear him flapping his covers, tossing and turning. He looked across the room to his father where Marvel too lay wide awake. Phyllo could see him silently staring at the window. Was he dreading the new day too? The day when a choice would have to be made, with no good options to be had?

Only Dodo slept, wrapped up and snug with Glumberry softly snoring in the cupboard at her feet. At least Phyllo was grateful for that.

The oppressive darkness lifted gradually and when an apricot haze crept up over the sky, he, Roly and their father all slunk out to the kitchen to share tea and toasted cinnamon bread in silent solidarity. The front door swung open and a cool breeze blew the last of the night and their old life away.

"One more in the pot?" Lazarus Barker said, sidling in through the narrow doorway and into their kitchen. He was pale, dark shadows drawn under his eyes, but he stood tall, shoulders back.

"Ringmaster. Of course." Marvel hurried to provide him with a steaming cup which he took with a nod of gratitude and leaned back against the counter.

"Once we get this jal done with I'm heading off to the merchants, taking Bain with me and Hector, if he's up to it. I think you should come too, Marvel. You've a corn popper to replace and you know your ingredients best."

"Yes, that's a good idea, Ringmaster, thank you," Marvel said.

"We'll have to wait for the canvas to be sized, but I want this whole business dealt with as quickly as possible so I'll not be driving back and forth. There's a chance we'll need to overnight so be prepared. Ganymede has an inn."

Marvel nodded, obediently. "Right you are, Ringmaster. Actually, I had hoped to use our downtime to make a start on replenishing the stock, with what ingredients remain that is."

"This will be a chance for Roly to show us what he's made

73

of, will it not?" The Ringmaster looked meaningfully to Roly, who looked away, suddenly fascinated with the pattern of bubbles on the surface of his tea.

"And while we are at, there are other matters to finalise, a decision to be made."

"Ah, yes, quite right, Ringmaster, once again, you are quite right."

"Phyllo, clearly you'll be no use here. Get some leaflets from Albertus and take them into town. Let's see if we can't squeeze a few Coin out of this miserable place before we get on our way. I'll ask him to date the leaflets for a show the day after tomorrow. Even if we have to rope off some of the stand, we should be able to host something by then. I'll see if there's anyone to help you."

As if giving out leaflets was beyond his capability, thought Phyllo bitterly, but he nodded and gave the Ringmaster a weak smile. This was what he was reduced to.

"Excellent tea, Marvel. Restorative." The Ringmaster took a deep breath and pushed on. "At the gate in ten minutes?"

Marvel's face was briefly brightened by the compliment and then back to all seriousness. "No time like the present, eh?" he said. The Ringmaster touched the brim of his hat and left.

"Right then." Marvel gathered himself up and went off to pack some things. "Stick to your strengths, Roly," he called from the other room, "Toffees are always popular so make up a batch of those lovely peanut ones you made the other day. Best leave the candyfloss until tomorrow though. The floss may flop." He poked his head around the doorway, "Fancy giving the peppermint truffles another try? I think we should be able to cover that with what's here. Wake up Glumberry for it, eh?"

"I'll do my best, Dad."

"Good lad." Marvel gave him a smile and, obviously holding on to it, turned to Phyllo. "The Ringmaster will ask me, son. Have you decided?"

Phyllo didn't want to say it, but had no choice. "I'll do it."

"You're sure?"

"Dodo."

"Yes. Dodo." His father came over and embraced him. "It might not be as bad as you think. I've made some enquiries, just to see if I could find you something here and turns out there is something." He pushed Phyllo to arm's length. "The Fabulous Volante. Aldo's agreed."

"The Flyers? Barnum's britches, Dad, are you trying to kill me?"

Marvel looked uncomfortable. "It is a bit in-at-the-deep-end, isn't it?"

"Off the high wire, you mean, Dad," Roly squeaked, "Galloping gobstoppers!"

"I know, I know, but everything feels a bit like that. To me anyway. At least it's here. At least you'll still be with us. Sort of. And what if it *is* your talent? What if you were *meant* to fly? Wouldn't it be something?"

"Yes, it would." Phyllo shook his head. "It really would be something."

Roly laughed, a short hiccupping burst that he hadn't expected. Phyllo couldn't help it, he started to laugh too. Marvel beckoned Roly over to join him and looped an arm around each of his sons' shoulders. "Canvas protect us," he said.

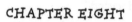

CHAPTER EIGHT

Shady Hollow

By eleven o'clock a small contingent of carnies were making their way across the grass to the village of Shady Hollow. Birdie Volante, Phyllo and two teenage tumblers from the Agile Arethusa: Harric and Garric, each clutched a handful of leaflets.

The sky was clear and the sun shone, but they trudged through inescapably long shadows. Cold pinched at Phyllo's ears and fingertips. Shady Hollow was set at the base of a tall stony ridge and the big top had pitched on the apron of land that lay out before it. Tree-covered hills climbed in a curve in every other direction. The landscape gobbled light and warmth.

They tramped forward in a straggly line, Birdie paying more attention to her little dog, Buffo, than anything else. She held tiny morsels of food between fingertips, encouraging it to walk upright on hind legs. Harric and Garric pushed each other around, squabbling. No-one was happy about being sent out.

When grass gave way to compacted earth, the first houses of Shady Hollow came properly into focus. Clay tiled roofs and clapboard walls, silvered with age. The houses squatted in a loose formation around a cobbled main square with a decrepit stone well in the centre. A woman wearing a knotted headscarf and a severe expression bustled across the far side and disappeared into a dim alleyway. A sign dangled limply over the door of a public house directly ahead. Unhappily it read: *The Well of Tears*.

The group paused to take it in.

"Well this is nice, thanks, Phyllo, for a lovely diversion," said Birdie.

"What a dump." Garric scuffed the sole of his shoe over the cobbles.

"There might be a better bit. Let's have a look down there," said Phyllo, following after the woman. The alleyway squeezed between a grimy bakery, with its blinds pulled down, and a liquor store, open for business but empty of customers. Then it expelled them onto a packed earth road. To the right it wound up the rocky face of the ridge and to the left led to more rundown cottages. "This way," said Phyllo, turning left. They took it in turns to approach doors and post their leaflets.

"This is hopeless," said Harric, "Where is everyone?"

"There." Birdie pointed to a drab net curtain at the window of a house they'd just leafletted, as it flopped back into place.

"Friendly," mumbled Garric.

"Perhaps they're not used to visitors," suggested Phyllo.

"This is the closest village to Ganymede. They must get *some* people passing through," said Birdie.

"Well, maybe once. Would *you* come back?" Garric said. It wasn't appealing.

After that they picked up the pace.

The road curved around to the left to reveal more cottages with peeling paint. One had collapsed. The roof was sunken at one end and balanced precariously on a cracked wall at the other. They gave it a wide berth and continued on around the curve until they were regurgitated into the dismal square.

"Let's try the pub," said Phyllo and they grumbled in after him.

Inside the air was thick with stale beer and tobacco smoke. Shafts of sunlight filtered in through dirty windows to illuminate four or five groups of customers, distributed about the saloon at solid tables. Some looked up at their arrival, but most were more interested in the contents of their glasses. It was the most life they'd seen.

"Yes, love, what can I get you?" A woman with dirty blonde curls and a world-weary face leaned against the bar with both hands. She examined them head to toe.

"Oh, nothing. Thank you," said Phyllo, scanning around the room, trying to judge how welcome they were. So far, she seemed friendly enough. Phyllo put on his circus head and made an extravagant sweeping bow. "I bring you greetings from the Circus of Wonder."

"Do you now? Not here for a sample of the local tipple then?" She pulled a bottle up from under the bar and lined up five shot glasses.

"Oh, no, no. Sorry." He put up a hand to stop her, but she poured one out anyway.

"Mermaid's Tears. You'll never taste finer." She tossed it back and closed her eyes for a moment, savouring it.

"Drinking the profits again, Amethyst?" A man at the bar raised his glass to her. "You'll never get out of here with expensive taste like that."

"Who says I want to? Seems like things are looking up, anyhow. Circus of Wonder, now that's a name I haven't heard in a good long while." She looked wistfully at them and beckoned them closer. "Nice to see some bright shiny faces." She leant over the bar to run a sticky finger under Phyllo's chin. Up close her skin was pallid and pocked, her breath sour.

"Well, we're back in town and putting on a show for one night only!" Phyllo managed, stepping back a little and executing another less elaborate bow. Birdie spun a pirouette, her little dog yipping, and Harric and Garric performed a synchronised backward walkover.

"Well isn't that lovely," said Amethyst, "I'm sure we'd all appreciate the entertainment. A measure of happiness wouldn't go amiss in this joyless place. Here, put a little pile of your pamphlets on the bar and pin one to the door, if you like. It gets busier later."

Phyllo found that the inside of the door already had a poster for the Circus of Wonder tacked to it. It was dirty and torn, the colours muted by time. The main image was a jester in the ruff and robes of yesteryear. A three-horned hat curled from the top of his head. Phyllo took it down and replaced it with the new one.

"How old do you think this is?" he said to Birdie as they headed back across the grass.

"How should I know? Could have been there for decades judging by the state of the place. Who knows when they last bothered to clean?" She gave a little shudder and marched on ahead.

By the time they got back the horseshoe was fully set. Cabins were locked together and the ticket entrance archway was constructed with its lamplit sign in place, *Welcome to the Circus of Wonder*.

Phyllo passed beneath the sign and wondered how much

longer it would apply to him and where Arif and Shadi were now. He willed them both to be OK.

Their group dissipated. Birdie and her little dog skipping off into the big top and Harric and Garric racing back to their quarters, tripping each other up as they went. Phyllo sauntered around to the Confectionary and let himself in.

Roly was in the kitchen, sleeves rolled up with the ingredients for peppermint truffles on the worktop in front of him. A newly boiled kettle belched steam and Glumberry sat perched on the arched spout of the tap, yellow eyes wide.

"Dodo, wind the snow globe," Roly instructed imperiously.

Phyllo hadn't noticed Dodo, but now saw her peeping over the counter. She poked out the tip of her tongue as she wound the globe and carefully set it down to tinkle out its tune.

Roly found the beat of the notes, just like their father had shown them, and pulsed his arms up and down in time. "OK, Glumberry, let's do it," he said.

Glumberry's head bobbed along too, somewhere inside the feathery fluff.

"Ingredients then. Cream cheese, powdered sugar and peppermint essence. All whipped up in a bowl," he squawked and they were off.

Dodo tipped in the cream cheese and Roly launched a scoop of icing sugar into the air. It dropped, rather ungracefully, onto the counter with a *whump*. He wrinkled his nose and tried again, tossing it this time with so much force it pelted the shelves.

He wasn't quite getting it right. "Dodo? Have you got any more of these snow globe things?" he asked.

"Oh yes," said Dodo and disappeared through the doorway to return with a box.

"I've been collecting," she said, plucked out two more

globes and wound them to life. The different melodies layered and merged. Roly screwed up his face in concentration and tapped out the common beat with his fingertips.

Dodo added another globe and another. Roly swept up a scoop of icing sugar and launched it determinedly into the air. This time it fell in a great sweeping arc around him, wide to start with, but getting tighter, finally settling into the bowl.

"Yes!" He cried.

Glumberry wobbled on the tap and flapped his stubby wings for balance. "Peppermint now," he called.

Dodo lined up even more snow globes. Seven, eight. They chimed out their tunes: 'Edelweiss'; a carousel waltz; 'Swan Lake'.

Roly twirled, tapping out droplets of peppermint essence. They swept along a curve to the bowl. Dodo pirouetted on the spot, copying the ballerina in one of the spheres. Then she spun around the counter, particles of icing sugar rising from the places they'd spilt to float above her in the air.

Roly took up the spoon, but it whipped out of his hand and into the mixture, whirling around on its own.

Dodo giggled delightedly and the icing sugar above her turned to snow.

She swept an arm to one side and a flurry whooshed into the shop.

She swept the other arm in a circle and a shower of snowflakes fell from the ceiling.

The spoon in the bowl then started to flick truffle-sized balls of mixture out, across the kitchen. Roly grabbed up a tray and danced about in their path, trying to catch them. Some he fielded, but others rocketed past to splat into the shelves.

A jar of peppercorns smashed. A tin of hazelnuts tipped to spill its contents to the floor like rain. Then a particularly large truffle smacked Glumberry straight between the eyes. He squawked and flapped and fell to the floor.

The spoon clattered into the bowl and icing sugar sank in a sugary fog.

Roly was still clutching the tray like a shield with his eyes squeezed shut, so it took him a moment to realise what'd happened.

"Galloping gobstoppers," he breathed as his eyes popped wide, "Did you see that, Phyllo? Glumberry – oh no."

All three children bent over Glumberry, Dodo stroking the soft plumes on the top of his head and gently calling his name.

He snapped his beak.

"Glumberry!" Dodo scooped him up and squeezed him. "You had me really worried."

"Is there truffle on my face?" he clucked.

She picked out a blob.

"Just my dignity dented." He ruffled his feathers and, when Dodo lifted him back to his perch, he eyed the kitchen mournfully. "It's a bit of a shambles."

"Let's carry on," Dodo said, "We're almost there." She went along the row of globes and wound new life into each.

"Er, hang on—" Roly wasn't quite so relaxed about the kitchen bombsite – things had gotten a bit out of hand.

"Can't stop now." Dodo stared pointedly at him and tapped a single finger rhythmically in the air.

Phyllo laughed.

"Right, well you can hold this then." Roly shoved the tray at her, sloshed hot water into a pan and clonked a bowl on top. He tried to stir the mixture but it had thickened so much that the spoon wouldn't budge at all.

"Don't forget the beat," said Dodo and started to spin.

Roly pushed the spoon in little rhythmic pulses, the movement seeming to get easier and easier. Then it was off, stirring again on its own.

"Peppermint dust!" Glumberry ducked his beak down to the heavy stone bowl at his end of the counter and Phyllo was sorely tempted to snatch it up, but Roly got hold of it and Phyllo contented himself with spinning around and around with Dodo. When she snatched up the tray to start catching truffles, he carried on on his own.

Roly smashed up the humbugs and tipped them out on the counter, then flung handfuls of chocolate into the basin.

More and more truffles fired from the bowl, far more than seemed possible, Dodo stacking them on tray after tray. Roly snatched up a couple of skewers to spear two at a time, plunging them into the melted chocolate and flicking them onto the counter, where they rolled through the dust and ground to a halt, sparkling and white.

Another pair, speared and dunked.

The balls on the trays rocked and rolled, forming themselves into lines that rose into the air; bobbing along to the beat, they floated to the bowl, swirled themselves around and then bowled across the counter. Dodo built them into shining pyramids, like an arsenal of snowballs prepared for battle. More and more. The piles grew.

The children laughed and whooped. They twirled and clapped. Every surface heaved with confectionary. Snow fell from the ceiling. Glumberry flapped and squawked.

The last handful of truffles piled into the bowl in a last-ditch scrum, fighting for the final remnants of chocolate. The bowl rocked and Roly grabbed for it, but it fell from the top of the pan and he just caught it in time, as it rolled off the edge.

The last tinkling snow globe ground to a halt with a ping.

The Cane children looked around at each other, panting.

83

They were spattered with chocolate and sparkling with sugar. Dodo had snowflakes stuck to her eyelashes and fat drifts of snow heaped in the shop corners. The air glittered with a sugary fog.

Roly looked somewhat terrified. Globules of white hung in his eyebrows.

Phyllo pointed and snorted. Roly's jaw flapped then they were all falling about, gazing around the Confectionary, rapt. Snow and truffles: everywhere.

~

It took them the rest of the afternoon to package their handiwork and to clear up the mess.

Roly popped the mint-green striped boxes into shape, Phyllo filled them and Dodo finished them off with sparkling red ribbon.

They'd made so many that the mobile rack in the shop was almost half filled by the time they had finished. They were extraordinarily pleased with themselves.

Phyllo managed to sweep the majority of the snow out of the Confectionary before it melted, and that which did helped wash away any remaining stickiness. It felt as if that was what the recipe had intended – the magic of the Confectionary working with them. A lucky break at last.

Night was falling when they wiped over the last surface.

"I'm starving," said Dodo, "Do you think we'll have to wait much longer for Dad?"

"I think they'd have been back by now, if they were coming," said Roly, leaning his mop in the corner and looking out of their small door. He and Phyllo considered the dimming twilight side by side. "Can't see the Ringmaster wanting to risk meeting up with any In-between. If they aren't here by the time it's properly dark, I reckon they'll be staying at the inn in Ganymede. I could make us some sandwiches?" said Roly.

"What about Emmett? Shall I see if he wants to join us?" Phyllo asked, "He seemed a bit brighter on the jal. Perhaps he'll feel up to it."

"Good idea."

Phyllo felt a gnawing ache in his gut beyond hunger when it came to Emmett. He didn't expect a clown to smile all of the time, but Emmett's bouts of gloom were increasing and his moods swung wildly. One day he'd be colourful and happy, the best fun friend Phyllo could hope for, and the next he was grey and moody, not even willing to give him the time of day. He just never knew where he was with him these days.

The door to the Clown Quarter was ajar so he poked his head around as he knocked.

It opened into the communal dressing room where tables with big, lamp-lit mirrors squeezed in amongst the clowning paraphernalia. Frothy wigs, bulbous shoes and buckets that poured ribbons instead of water hung from pegs on the walls and a riot of make-up pots and sponges fought for space on table tops.

"Hey, Emmett," he called.

Emmett was sitting at his dressing table smoothing out what was left of his natural hair with a paddle brush. He wore crumpled blue linen trousers and a shirt, untucked and open at the neck. In his wrinkled civvies he looked unnatural, like he might be on holiday, sporting an outfit pulled hastily from a suitcase.

"Phyllo." Emmett pulled a full eye-crinkling smile, meeting Phyllo's gaze. His dressing table overflowed with un-replaced lids, stiff brushes and dirty crockery and he seemed to notice this for the first time as Phyllo approached. He hurriedly stacked plate on plate, balancing a handful of cloudy glasses on top.

"Haven't seen you in a while. We've been wondering how you are," said Phyllo.

"Fine. I'm fine," Emmett boomed, "Never better." He rubbed at his stomach, an action Phyllo had seen him make hundreds of times in the ring when he was wearing the Bingo Bongo persona. He stepped in a little closer, bringing Emmett into touching distance. "We've just finished working and Roly's going to make sandwiches, as Dad's not here. I think we've got some cherry buns too, and we just thought, if you hadn't eaten…"

Emmett shook his head emphatically. "That's very kind of you, Phyllo. Very thoughtful." He slid his chair back and moved the pile of plates and cups onto the floor. There were already some others down there. He stood up. "Thing is, I'm just on my way out." He smiled then, but it was rather weak, as if he were making a conscious effort to crank up the corners.

"Where are you going?"

"Oh, just into town, you know, meet the locals."

"That shouldn't take long. I went in earlier with a couple of the others. It's a dump."

"Is it?" Emmett nodded, as if resigning himself to it.

"I really wouldn't bother. Come and have supper with us."

Emmett clasped his hands together, constantly moving them, feeling his nails and squeezing at his thumbs. He squinted at Phyllo and said, "No. I need to. I'll just make it a quickie, I expect. Perhaps I'll catch up with you later?"

"Right. Sure. Well you know where we are."

Emmett turned toward the cubicles which lined the back wall. Four clowns shared this cabin and each had their own curtained space, comprising a high sleeper bed and room beneath for a small desk and a cupboard.

Emmett went over to his cubicle and retrieved a jacket from the top of a heap of jumbled garments on the floor. Phyllo could see more dirty crockery and junk. Emmett followed his eyes and snapped the curtain closed. "Never been much of a housekeeper," he said, "Drove my old mum mad. Come on, I'll walk you back."

"Where are the others? Nubbins and Gus? Are they going too?"

"I expect so. Probably. I didn't really pin them down. Just popping in, you know." Emmett threw a fatherly arm around Phyllo's shoulders. "And how about you? Big changes ahead, I hear."

"You could say that."

"Marvel was very persuasive with Aldo. Given you quite the introduction."

"Has he? No pressure, then."

"Couldn't say enough about your enthusiasm. Aldo liked that particularly."

"No half measures, eh?"

"You sound just like him. No half measures, indeed." Emmett licked his lips. There was a slight tremor in his arm and he removed it. Phyllo hoped he wasn't worried for him. He was worried enough for everyone. They were nearing the Confectionary.

"I'll leave you here," Emmett said and waved through the window to Dodo. She skipped toward them, but Emmett wasn't in the business of hanging about. He was halfway to the gate before she'd even got to the door.

CHAPTER NINE

The Fabulous Volante

Marvel's return the next day was bittersweet. Roly and Dodo couldn't wait to show him what they'd achieved. Even the taste test went well, which in itself could be utterly nerve-wracking. Marvel had stood with his hands on his hips, gawping at the rack for a full minute before even asking to try one. "They taste like terrifyingly good fun," he'd said, which seemed like a fair summary of the previous afternoon.

At the Ganymede market his father had managed to procure a new popcorn machine. It wasn't quite as big as the one Phyllo had blown up, but the corn hopper was still a fair size. "At least it won't take up as much room," Marvel had said and, as space was at a significant premium, that the extra time required for maintaining the flow of kernels would be worthwhile. He'd manage to replenish a good deal of their stores too and even picked up a couple of cases of sherbet saucers to fill the gaps in their shelving, whilst they got back up to speed. All in all, Marvel judged it 'a successful trip', even if it had, unfortunately, soaked up the last of their family time together.

"Lazarus was quite emphatic that you should start with the

Fabulous Volante without delay, I'm afraid. No time like the present though, eh?"

"No, don't suppose there is," Phyllo had replied, but he didn't mean it. He'd have liked nothing better than to stay at the Confectionary forever.

It was a very slow packing of his bag and a rather protracted saunter out of the Confectionary that came next. Dodo threw her arms around his legs at the last moment, slowing him down even more. There were tears brimming in her eyes and it turned out that that was just the motivation Phyllo needed to stiffen his upper lip. "I'm only going twenty yards around the path, Dodo. It's not like I'm actually leaving. You never know, if I'm a success, I might be able to teach *you* how to fly."

"Fly?" Her long eyelashes fluttered rapidly at the thought.

"Oh yes." Phyllo pulled a hanky from his pocket and gave it to her, "I hear that's the secret to all their trapeze tricks." Actually, Phyllo had absolutely no idea how they achieved their high-flying manoeuvres. If he was honest, he'd been trying not to think about it. "Now, I'll be popping back when I can, so see if you can teach Roly how to make some decent toffees while I'm gone."

"Oi," Roly protested, but gave Phyllo a pat on the shoulder. "Try not to break your stupid neck," he said.

Phyllo grimaced. "I'll try."

Now that the Ringmaster and his party had returned from Ganymede, activity levels around the circus had picked up considerably. The faint holiday atmosphere induced by the cat being away had evaporated the very moment Lazarus Barker had crossed the threshold. Not to say that the mice of the Circus of Wonder weren't keen to get on with things. Where the engineers had pretty much ground to a halt, now they swung in the rigging, making ready to install the greatly anticipated new canvas. Down on the ground, a chain of carnies led from the gate right around to the Quartermaster, feeding in boxes and sacks of supplies in a great hungry snake. They replenished what was lost and added more besides. Bottles clinked in their cases and strong men huffed. Phyllo sidestepped around them all and slunk into the big top.

The Fabulous Volante were also hard at work, practising. Signor Volante stood down in the ring, mercifully with his back toward Phyllo, watching the flyers up on the bars. He yelled out instructions and made single loud claps, marking the timing of something Phyllo didn't understand. Two trapeze bars swung back and forth, members of the Volante family alternately dangling and hurling themselves from them. He'd seen the act a thousand times before and knew, of course, that it was performed above the crowd, but now that he came to look at it, it really did seem terribly high. He slid into the bottom tier of seating and tried to keep a low profile.

Columba and Ezio were up on one trapeze together and Salvo was alone on the other. They were working on a trick that involved Ezio hanging upside down, Columba jumping from the bar, turning a somersault and being caught by her ankles, then the pair of them swinging to a sufficient height for Columba to be tossed to Salvo on the other bar. It made Phyllo feel quite sick to watch them.

"I see you, Phyllo Cane." Birdie. She stepped lightly along the row in front toward him, in her ballerina fashion, wiry and thin. Her knees and elbows like bulbous knots beneath the silky flyer's costume. Her dark hair was pulled back into a ballerina's bun, revealing the handful of pink spots that peppered her forehead. She held a sleeping Buffo in her arms and an expression of smug satisfaction on her face.

Phyllo floundered at being discovered. "Er, yes, here I am." He stood up and put out his hand for a shake. Birdie eyed it disdainfully. "Don't be stupid."

She looked him up and down, slowly shaking her head from side to side, tsking. She poked his gut with a bony forefinger. "You're going to have to do something about that. There's no room for gnocchi on the bar." She snorted out a couple of laughs, but then got a hold of herself. Whatever she'd meant; it had gone right over Phyllo's head.

"Ha ha ha," he managed, nervously, hoping that Birdie wouldn't see through him.

"Hmm. You'd better come down." She turned her back on him and walked away with the same prancing steps and Phyllo followed, dragging the lead that seemed to be in his shoes. They descended into the ring where Signor Volante finally noticed him.

"So, it is time. Marvin tells me you have great enthusiasm. This is key for the Fabulous Volante. For me."

Phyllo looked nervously from Signor Volante to Birdie and back again. "Marvin? Marvel, surely. You mean my dad?"

"Marvin. That's what I said. I hope you realise how lucky you are?" He punctuated his words with decisive gestures. "The Volante are a proud family. Very proud. To be admitted like this, well it's never happened before, never and we have been part of the Circus of Wonder for more than a century. Never has a Volante needed a pass from the Ringmaster neither. Is a nonsense, if you ask me, but if Lazarus wills it then maybe you learn some spirit, huh? I don't suppose you'll make a worse flyer than you are a confectioner." Signor

Volante slapped Phyllo roughly on the back and jostled at his hair. His first experience of the sugar-coated spiky strands left him surprised and pulling his hand away with a frown. He rubbed at his palm with the other hand testing for stickiness but found none. "Huh." Signor Volante looked Phyllo up and down and walked around him, inspecting. "Well, you are the skinny one in the family, at least that will help."

"He's squidgy in the middle," Birdie chipped in, reaching over to poke him again, but Phyllo arched away from her and blocked her hand with his own.

"Thank you."

She settled back onto one hip and gave him an acidic grin.

Signor Volante took Phyllo's small bag of personal belongings from his hand, tossed it to the ground and then flexed his arm for him, feeling for muscles. "Shake my hand," he said and as Phyllo took it said, "Grip. Grip it," and nodded to himself. "Ezio! Arnaldo! Here." He waved one beckoning hand over his head at the flyers up on the bars. Ezio and Columba made one more full swing, at the peak of which Ezio released Columba to turn a double somersault and land in the safety net. Ezio pulled himself up onto the bar and then, at the next peak, rolled off backward himself, flipping over on his way down to land on his feet in the net which stretched to accommodate him.

Arnaldo had been on the side platform so descended the rope ladder. It didn't involve any tricks, but the bottom section of the ladder bucked about worryingly with nothing holding it at the bottom. Not that this seemed to bother him. All three came obediently to Signor Volante's side and the difference in Volante and Cane family genes was instantly apparent.

They were older – Phyllo comforted himself with that fact. They were taller – a basic consequence of their difference in years. Sure, you could argue that. They wore snug costumes to allow free movement up on those bars and there was no getting away from the well-defined muscle that covered their chests, arms and thighs. Well, their whole bodies really. Phyllo's eyes skated over them and he'd never been more conscious of his own weedy frame. Arnaldo was the eldest in his mid-twenties and the star solo performer of the troupe. He had dark wavy hair that flopped handsomely on his forehead, a square jaw and laughing eyes. He looked at Phyllo with what could only be described as pity.

Ezio shared his cousin's olive complexion and fantastic hair, which also flopped decadently in waves. Phyllo felt more and more like a puny porcupine with every passing moment. Ezio was shorter and younger, turning twenty next year and better matched to his female flying partner and cousin, Columba, who was petit and blonde. They all looked at him with fixed smiles, but Phyllo knew they were wondering what on earth they were going to do with him.

"Right then, let's see what you can do." Signor Volante wafted an arm and the boys came around to take Phyllo by the elbow, one either side.

"What? Wait," Phyllo managed, scuttling along on tiptoes.

"Is OK. We'll see how you like it."

"Do what I do," said Ezio, "It's all about the confidence. Be sure in your movements. Use your weight, like this." He planted one foot on a low rung of the flimsy ladder and pulled it taut, then placed a hand higher up and started to climb. "Now you." Arnaldo jostled Phyllo in closer from behind, "Take off your shoes, they won't help you."

Phyllo let out an involuntary kind of squeak. "Isn't this a bit fast? I mean you haven't shown me anything yet. I don't know—"

"Is just for fun. See what you make of it."

Phyllo squeezed his hands into nervous fists and leant away from the ladder.

"Right foot here." Arnaldo placed his foot on a low rung and pushed it down. Phyllo absolutely did not want to, but knew he was going to have to screw up the courage. He put his right foot onto the same rung.

"Hold high. Transfer your weight. Up you go." Arnaldo seemed to be getting on behind him and his sheer wilfulness propelled Phyllo onto the stringy ladder. A couple of rungs up and the whole bottom half of his body was swinging around wildly.

"Straighten your body. Push your feet to the floor."

Phyllo flailed about like a hooked fish, desperately trying to gain some control. Arnaldo got onto the ladder beneath him and that stabilised things. "Up, up, momentum is everything."

"I thought confidence was everything," Phyllo squealed.

"That too."

Phyllo scrabbled up the ladder, higher and higher. Simultaneously climbing and staying stable was a big problem. His kneecaps had turned to liquid and his biceps to mallow. Much higher than it had seemed from the ground, the ladder reached a narrow platform. Ezio was already there, waiting. He leant over to extend a hand for Phyllo to take and as much as he did *not* want to let go of the ladder, Phyllo took a deep breath and shot his hand out anyway. Ezio effortlessly pulled him around onto the wooden board, depositing him next to the supporting wires which Phyllo grabbed on to instantly.

As glad as he was to have made it to the top of the ladder, he was now in the unfortunate position of being thirty feet above the ground with not a lot more than air to count on for support.

Ezio caught the trapeze bar with a long pole and pulled it in as Arnaldo joined them on the board, smiling and, Phyllo suspected, trying not to laugh. He had to calm down. Through the cloud of panic Phyllo forced himself to look at the situation rationally. If he thought about it *logically*, Arnaldo's relaxed attitude to this terrifying experience was quite encouraging. It *could* mean there was a chance that *actually* he wasn't in any danger and that he was completely overreacting, that all this knee-trembling fear was just the gut reaction of someone not used to heights.

On the other hand, it *did* seem that they had absolutely no concerns for his safety whatsoever. Was it possible that the Volante gene had other magical properties beyond brilliant hair and dark good looks? Undoubtedly. Was it also possible, then, they assumed he was going to be able to do something naturally that, in reality, it was not possible for him to do? Was he, Phyllo Cane, about to plunge to his death?

"OK?" Arnaldo asked.

Phyllo whimpered.

"So, Ezio will show you a simple swing. That's all we'll do, just so that you can get a feel for it. OK?"

Phyllo nodded mutely.

"Ready," said Arnaldo. Ezio grasped the bar with both hands and bent at the knee. "Hup."

He jumped smartly up and then swung down and away on the trapeze, flicking to propel himself higher. A couple of swings later, he released, turned a somersault and landed in the net.

"*Ready* is the command to bend your knees and prepare to leave the board. *Hup* is the command to go. With the trapeze timing is everything," Arnaldo explained.

"I thought confidence was everything, oh and

momentum."

"You're listening, good!" Arnaldo patted Phyllo enthusiastically on the back, making him wobble about. Arnaldo reeled in the bar and held it steady with the pole. It seemed incredibly far away still. "Now you'll have to lean out to get it, but don't worry. Stand here, toes over the edge. Come on."

He was going to have to let go of the support wires. Phyllo gingerly released them and tested his jelly legs for strength. After a couple of seconds standing free, they still held so he edged over to the lip of the board. "Barnum's britches, it's a long way down," he breathed, peering unavoidably over the edge.

"Eyes on the bar." Arnaldo gripped Phyllo's waistband at the back. "Take hold."

Phyllo whimpered again. "It's too far away, can't you get it a bit nearer?"

"It doesn't come any nearer. You can do it."

"Crackers. This is crackers." He stretched out one arm, turning his body to get more reach. Fingertips brushed the metal. He leant a tiny bit, experimentally. Arnaldo held him firm. He leant just a little bit more and was able to grasp it.

"*Buono*. Now the other hand."

Phyllo's heart beat revved up to a roar and his palms popped with sweat. The ground beneath him swam in and out of focus. He had to turn square on and stuck his bottom out like an alarmed duck trying to find a centre of gravity that didn't send him tumbling over the edge. Arnaldo pulled the bar around to help him with the pole and he grasped it.

"Ready. Hup."

Phyllo hadn't expected the command so quickly, but in all honesty the combination of forces once Arnaldo let go of his waistband put it out of his hands. He didn't so much jump, as get sucked from the platform, whisking away on the bar and swinging to a peak, his legs flailing about once the bar had stopped moving and then he was rocketing backwards. Someone was screaming.

One moment he was hanging from the bar and the next it had slithered from his grip and he was tumbling to the net. He landed on his back, wide eyed and panting, and was surprised to find that it hadn't hurt.

"Off you get," Signor Volante called and Phyllo scrabbled to the edge on his hands and knees and half climbed, half fell off into the sawdust of the ring. Birdie stood next to Signor Volante with her arms folded, pouty-faced.

"S-Sorry. I-I er couldn't quite hold on," Phyllo croaked.

Signor Volante regarded him for a moment and then said, "You're not exactly a natural, but there is an ocean between saying and doing. You got up there and swinging. You followed instructions." He slapped Phyllo on the back and roughly squeezed his shoulder. Phyllo swayed about, his limbs buzzing with adrenalin.

"I'm not sure it's really me, I mean I couldn't even hold on. And it's so high. Barnum's britches, it's so high." Phyllo flopped over at the waist, leaning on his thighs for support. "I'm not sure this whole circuit thing is going to work out."

"U-huh. Will you tell your little sister she has to leave, or will I? Don't be selfish." Signor Volante gave Phyllo a dismissive cuff about the top of his head and he straightened up, frowning. "I tell you what, why don't you go train up as a Ringmaster and then you won't have to do what he says, huh? What about that?"

Phyllo scowled at him. "Yeah, right."

"Right. So, stop the complaining and start with the work. Show me your press-ups. Those arms are too weak."

CHAPTER TEN

The Bird Cage

While the Confectionary expanded widthways during set up the Volante cabin, or *the Birdcage*, as they affectionately called it, grew taller.

On the inside, their cabin, which fitted inside the big top with room to spare like every other, reached as high at the flyers' platforms. The next thing that Phyllo noticed was the presence of a now familiar stringy style of ladder that climbed the rear wall. At the top a fixed trapeze swung from the ceiling. Calling it the Birdcage seemed even more appropriate to Phyllo then, as nothing could have been more at home up there than a giant budgerigar.

Phyllo was sorry to note that stringy ladders were a bit of a theme. Another dangled down the centre of a wall of what appeared to be empty arched windows, rather like a dovecote. He spied glimpses of bedding inside the lower ones.

Once set up, from the outside the Birdcage added an additional turret beyond the big top and sported a flagpole accordingly. It was a flag to which Signor Volante was referring as the troupe bundled inside, after their day of rehearsals.

"This year, that flag will become gold or we will die trying. I will not have anyone say that the Fabulous Volante are not worthy of the Gilded Pennant. We are as good as the Mechanical Misfits even in our warm-ups. Better!" He slapped a loose fist into the palm of his other hand, "Hard work from everybody, huh, and the Gilded Pennant is as good as ours."

The Volantes buzzed about in the small floor space like bees over honeycomb, kicking off shoes and pulling on sweaters. Replies of 'Yes, Papa,' and '*Si*, Aldo,' rumbled around the group.

"I know we can do it," said Arnaldo giving his Uncle Aldo a back-slapping hug. Ezio and Salvo high-fived. Out of the loop, Phyllo shuffled awkwardly from foot to foot, sticking to the wall by the door. He'd never spent any time in the Birdcage before and didn't quite know what to do with himself now that he was there. Even if he was now part of their troupe, he wasn't a Volante. He was a cuckoo in their nest.

Nonna Sophia appeared from the kitchen in a cloud of steam to clonk an enormous dish of spaghetti down in the middle of their large table, which sat at the centre of everything. She was Signor Volante's mother and family matriarch. At eighty-one, she'd long ago declared herself much too old for the trapeze and was dedicated instead to cramming as much food as possible into all of the others.

"Eat, everybody. Eat," she cried without introduction and the family swarmed to the benches on either side of the table. Phyllo wasn't used to this kind of scrum dining, and dawdled behind. Nonna spied him over the ducking heads of those already tucking in.

"You need to eat most of all," she called and waddled over to roughly pinch at his cheek, "Barely any meat on you at all. Ezio, move up, make space for our guest." She peeled the bag from Phyllo's shoulder and manoeuvred him into the small space Ezio had conceded. She leaned through another nonexistent gap to fill a bowl and then placed it in front of him.

Three fat meatballs nestled in a coil of tomatoey pasta. It smelt wonderful and Phyllo's stomach growled with approval. "Eat. Eat," Nonna said again, attempting to ruffle Phyllo's hair and finding it stiff. "What is this?"

"His hair is as stiff as his body," Birdie chirped from the opposite side of the table.

Phyllo shrugged, his mouth completely full of the delicious food. When he'd managed to swallow, he added, "I think it's the sugar in the air. I'm not sure really. Seems to affect my hair more than anyone else's."

Nonna Sophia sat herself down in a chair at the foot of the table, to Phyllo's right, and tucked into her own bowl of food. She was as round as a meatball herself and red in the cheeks from the cooking, but her face was kind and her dark eyes crinkled around the edges with the air of a naughty mouse. She wrinkled her nose with a smile and laid one hand on Phyllo's arm. "No worry. You'll loosen up. Nonna will look after you."

"Thank you," he replied quietly, "Can you go up on the trapeze for me too?"

She roared with laughter, slapped the table heartily and got Phyllo in a surprisingly rough embrace that involved a lot of pinching and slapping. When it stopped, it left him rather shocked and breathless. She wagged a finger at him, "I like you, so funny!"

Signor Volante grunted from the other end of the table, noisily closed the newspaper he'd been reading and flopped it down.

"Huh," he grumbled again.

"Papa?" asked Ezio.

"Captain Velocity in *The Ballyhoo*." He wafted a derisory hand over the newspaper. "The Mechanical Misfits have already worked Star City and have the Gilded Pennant. Again." He puffed out his cheeks. "We can no let them get ahead of us again on the route." He punctuated every syllable with his hand, "Coin is scarce. It's our turn." He plunged a fork into his spaghetti and spun it around.

"They're pretty good," said Salvo who sat to Signor Volante's left on a bench.

"Good. Yes," Signor Volante grumbled, "But they've had their pick of the pitches too many times. *Basta*! We need to get ahead of them for once."

"So, they have a flag, so what? The audiences know that we're good too," Ezio soothed.

"No! Is not enough. The crowd is smaller every year, like the magic is failing. And Lazarus, do you think that he notices, huh? You can bet the net that he does. He wants the Coin just like everyone else and right now, his pockets are emptier than ever before. Magical canvas does no come cheap."

Multiple pairs of eyes at the table drifted to Phyllo who felt the heat of the spotlight. "It was an accident, you know? I didn't mean to."

"Try not to have any accidents here," said Birdie sourly.

"I can't promise anything," Phyllo mumbled, but looked over to Birdie and smiled. After that he thought it might be better to just keep quiet.

When dinner was over, the weight of the day's strangeness hung heavily upon him. He wished more than anything that he could crawl into his own familiar bunk in the Confectionary. He had a sneaking suspicion that he wasn't going to like the bed that awaited him here.

"That's you," said Birdie, pointing to the empty arch up by the ceiling.

"Right." Phyllo rubbed at his eyes. "Would be, wouldn't it."

"Nothing personal. Youngest at the top, oldest at the bottom. You wouldn't expect Nonna to get up there, would you?"

"No. Course not."

Birdie gave him another of her acidic smiles. Signor Volante came over and patted him on the back. "A good night's sleep, that's what you need. You have everything?"

Phyllo nodded.

"Either one, up top. You choose."

He went over to the ladder and tested it for wobble. This one, at least, was tethered to the ground. He looked back over his shoulder. The entire Volante family seemed to be watching him. Looking into their eyes, one by one, gave Phyllo a peculiar sensation of lightness. Where he'd expected to feel self-conscious, he found instead he just wanted the day to be over. He was so tired he didn't have the energy to be afraid. He grabbed on to the ladder and alternated arm and leg movements, almost automatically, until he was high enough to choose the closest empty bunk. He looked down. Every eye looked attentively back up at him. It was oddly comforting. As if, if he fell, they were all ready to catch him. He stepped over to the ledge outside the nearest archway with more confidence than he felt and into the cubby hole beyond. The family down on the ground began talking again and milling about.

When Phyllo awoke, he realised that he must have fallen immediately asleep as he was still wearing the previous day's clothes. Now he saw his bunk properly for the first time. It was entirely enclosed with a ceiling just high enough for him to sit up without bashing his head, but low enough to feel cossetted, like sleeping in a tongue and groove burrow. Only the archway was open to the rest of the cabin, which was big enough for access, but too small to accidentally roll out of in the night. The bag of belongings at his feet held a few changes of clothes, one of Dodo's snow globes, a few personal toiletry items and a framed photo of the Cane family, complete with his mother, taken just after Dodo had been born. He unpacked into a small cupboard at the foot of his bed and placed the photo and globe in a cubbyhole by his head.

A set of Flyers Blues lay neatly folded on the ledge outside, along with a pair of soft shoes. He leaned out of his cot to take in a bird's eye view of the communal space. The large table was scattered with the ruin of breakfast: half empty toast racks and froth-lined coffee cups, and only Nonna Sophia beetled about down below, clearing up.

Phyllo realised with a jolt that everyone had already gone. He must have overslept. He quickly changed into his new clothes and stuck his head out again to map the route down. Funny how looking out to see what was happening hadn't bothered him at all, but looking again with the prospect of climbing down was quite a different matter. It made his head swim.

The platform outside his bunk was about a foot wide, more of a shelf really, and provided his link to the stringy ladder.

"Crackers," Phyllo said in a low whisper, "Even getting out of bed is crackers."

He eased out to stand with his back to the wall and edged along like a petrified crab. Even at the very end, the ladder seemed impossibly far. Panic crept up his legs in jelly waves. "Nope."

He shuffled back along the ledge to reverse into the cot before his shaking sent him plummeting. A different approach then. He took some steadying breaths and came back out, on his hands and knees this time. The ledge was wide enough for his knees, but not quite wide enough for his hips to sit squarely without bouncing his centre of gravity over the edge every time he moved. He hugged the wall as much as possible and scuffled along to the ladder to reach it head first.

This was when he realised that this approach had issues too: his head was closest to the ladder and his feet, miles away. He stopped stock still and racked his brain, but just couldn't come up with any other way and the ground was starting to swim around again. He needed to get down from here before he fell down so, heart pounding in his ears, he reached out a hand and grasped the ladder. First one hand, then the other. He gripped manically at the rope, shuffled his knees forward and then swung a wildly waving foot around to find a rung.

Nonna Sophia finally noticed him then, clattering about as he was by the ceiling and clinging on for dear life. "Down you come, little rabbit," said her calm voice from below and Phyllo felt immediately relieved to no longer be alone in his struggle.

"One hand over the other. Take it slow. No rush. You like some porridge? Maybe some toast? I make some fresh toast?"

Phyllo couldn't think about food whilst in such a precarious position and only noticed that Nonna Sophia had moved to the bottom of the ladder when she launched into one of her enthusiastic roughing up sessions.

Phyllo flinched under her affectionate pummelling.

"You sleep like the *ghiro*, huh? Cozy in the nest," she said with a gentle smile and a rough pinch at his cheeks. Phyllo blinked bemusedly, which she took for confirmation and then steered him over to the table to sit down. "Porridge. I have some left." She ladled a bowl from the stove and slid it in front of him. It was creamy and heaped with caramelised apples in the centre. The smell of cinnamon and honey levitated in its steam.

Life in the Confectionary was all about flavours, subtle scents and textures. His father had trained them to notice these details for as long as he could remember. His enthusiasm lay in the creation of sweets, however. Day-to-day meals hadn't been much of a focus, more a necessity. To be served something so sumptuous for his breakfast was a marvellous treat. He looked happily up to Nonna who regarded him with wide expectant eyes. "Eat. Eat," she said at last, tired of the suspense. Phyllo didn't need telling a third time.

Phyllo found the Volante family practising in the big top. He looked up to the bars as he approached and saw Arnaldo land back on the platform next to Ezio, who caught the trapeze with a hook. Signor Volante called up to them. "The strength is good, but it needs style. More flow. Move with the wind."

Ezio pulled in the bar, Arnaldo took it then peeled backward off the board, rolling his body around the bar before the peak and then spinning like a screw above it as it returned. The rigging thunked and juddered at his landing.

"Better," Signor Volante called out, "But too late, the pirouette needs to start on the turn." He clapped his hands for emphasis and then noticed Phyllo. "Oh, you decided to join us, huh?" he said, raising his eyebrows.

"Sorry."

"Seven in the ring, every morning. Every morning. Everybody." He looked Phyllo over. "This is wrong." He grabbed hold of Phyllo's belt and pulled the knot undone. "Like this." He wound it around Phyllo's waist like a cummerbund, fastening it at the back. Now Phyllo realised that Nonna Sophia had embroidered a small sweet in a purple and yellow twisted wrapper on the panel in the centre. She'd used the colours from his confectioner's jacket. It was his own personal sash.

"There. How's that feel?"

The sash hugged at his middle and made him stand tall. "Good. It feels good."

Signor Volante nodded, approvingly, gave Phyllo's upper arms a squeeze, spun him around and then back. "How would you say is your fitness?"

"Good. Pretty good." Probably anyway. The most energetic thing Phyllo did usually was stirring.

Signor Volante squinted at him. "Physical strength is the core of a good trapeze artist. The body must be strong so the mind can follow. I see the fear in your eye, Phyllo Cane, and is normal. Only a fool would stand up there with no knowledge of how to get down without care. Little by little. That is the way. See my *tesoro*, my Birdie. She has grace. Natural flow. She will dance in the air like her mother."

Birdie pranced along the raised edge of the ring, wafting her arms up and down like a balletic stork. Phyllo thought she was too gangly and sour to be elegant, but kept that to himself. Signor Volante waved to her. "Come, Birdie."

She looked up obediently, but fell into a scowl when she noticed Phyllo standing there too.

"Birdie, I'd like you and Phyllo to train together today."

"But, Papa, I wanted to teach Buffo—"

"Start with ten laps of the horseshoe first and see how he fares, then come back to me."

"Running? But, Papa, I want—"

"Birdie." Signor Volante's tone ended the discussion. Birdie rolled her eyes to Phyllo then jogged away. Phyllo looked from her to Signor Volante. He wafted his fingers to follow.

"Right. Right then." Phyllo stumbled after her. She'd made it out of the big top by the time he'd caught up.

Birdie's running style was much like her prancing about the ring. She bounced in an arc with every step. Phyllo thought that she was so light, it must take no effort at all. He jogged along at her side. "Is this what you usually do? Jogging, I mean. Do the others run too?"

She poked her nose a little higher into the air.

"Birdie, come on. I don't see why you can't talk to me. You never seemed to hate me this much before."

"I never got saddled with you as a partner before," she sniffed.

"Well this wasn't exactly my idea either, you know? I'm trying to stay positive here, but you lot are crazy. Who'd willingly throw themselves off that crackers-high platform? And why can't you sleep down on ground level, like normal people? I mean, no-one needs more than a bunk bed."

"Who wants to be *normal people!*" Birdie stomped to a halt and waved a twiggy finger in his face. "And if it wasn't for you, we wouldn't be in this horrible place. We should be on the Brampton Levels by now, bartering with the boatmen and enjoying the sun, but, oh no, Phyllo *cretino* can't flaming cook and sets light to the place. You really are useless."

Phyllo's jaw flapped about looking for a retort, but nothing came. His face screwed up and he clamped his mouth into a grimace. Birdie's accusatory finger wavered and then dropped. Her shoulders drooped a little and Phyllo turned to huff away around the horseshoe in the other direction, swallowing the lump in his throat.

She didn't follow.

Out of show times the barriers by the Confectionary and next to the ticket gate weren't employed, and without them the horseshoe became a circular path that ran the entire circumference of the big top. Now instead of running past the anonymous cabins of the Book Keeper and the Ringmaster and on toward the Confectionary, Phyllo stomped counter-clockwise, heading for backstage. There was no reason why he had to run with Birdie anyway. He sped himself up into a jog, past the Birdcage and on, pounding toward the Clown Quarter.

He rounded the curve and found engineers blocking the path, repairing the tiers, but caught sight of Emmett ahead as he stumbled out of his cabin. He looked hunched and crumpled but walked determinedly away, seemingly talking to himself and rubbing at his neck.

Phyllo dodged around the engineers, trying to catch up with Emmett, but he dropped out of sight and then Phyllo ran slap bang back into Birdie.

He sighed and pre-empted her bile. "I'm not interested, alright? You don't like me? Fine. I don't have any choice in this so that means neither do you. Just get over it, OK?"

She had her hands pressed together and didn't look anywhere near as aggressive as she had just a few moments ago. "I know," she said in a smaller voice, "I think perhaps…"

"Perhaps what?" Phyllo pressed her.

"Papa always says it's my biggest hurdle. The thing I'll have to learn if we're all to really fly."

"Sorry, I'm not with you."

"Look, I'm just saying I'm sorry. I'll try not to be so, well, me."

Phyllo was rather surprised by this. "Really?" They eyed each other sceptically and then Birdie put out her hand. Phyllo considered it for a second. The temptation to say *don't be stupid* was enormous but he took it and they shook rather uncertainly instead.

After a moment's odd silence Phyllo asked, "Did you see where Emmett went?"

"Emmett? San Giuseppe, what are you associating with him for? Did you see the state of him?" She looked rather shocked at herself and then said, "I mean, yes. He looked a bit... tired. He went in to the Ringmaster, I think."

Phyllo started walking again toward the Ringmaster's cabin, ignoring Birdie who tagged along at his side. "He's a friend. I know he's looking a bit... shabby at the moment, but I'm worried about him."

They stopped on the path outside the enormous brass doors and Phyllo pressed his ear against them, listening.

Birdie looked horrified. "*Sei pazzo?*" she hissed, snapping her eyes up and down the path. Then, with the lightest touch, she silently opened the door and slipped inside. Phyllo goggled at her. She stared at him mutely until he stepped into the darkness too.

CHAPTER ELEVEN

Loyalty

"Better out of sight than to be seen listening at keyholes," Birdie whispered, "What's so important?"

"I don't know," Phyllo mouthed, "But it just doesn't feel right."

The Machine wall shielded them from view while Birdie scoured the mesh of pipes and cogs, searching. Phyllo held his breath and waited, a pulsating crackle of electricity lighting both their faces blue. Then, finding what she'd been looking for, Birdie silently beckoned him over. Between the curve of a pipe and a gap in the teeth of a stationary gear, Phyllo could just make out the Ringmaster standing on the telescope platform by the window, and a rear view of Emmett, who shuffled from side to side ten feet in front. The Ringmaster turned away from the window, to face him. "I must confess, I'm astonished to see you back here so soon."

Emmett looked down to the floor, pulling at his jacket. "I know. I'd hoped—. It's just here, especially."

The Ringmaster descended the platform steps and went to sit at his desk, where he examined a stack of papers. "Yes, this place isn't doing anything for me either." The Ringmaster took a deep breath. "Emmett. It can't go on at this rate, I'm not made of money."

"It can't go on," Emmett echoed, "I know." He looked up to meet the Ringmaster's eye. "I went in myself. Thought I'd save you the trouble."

The Ringmaster's expression hardened. An eyebrow arched.

"But it's so expensive. I couldn't. Just the smallest—" Emmett tailed off, shaking his head and returned his gaze to the floor.

"You surprise me. Fact is, Emmett, you need me. Oh, sit down for Grimaldi's sake." He gestured to the chair in front of his desk and Emmett took it gratefully. He rubbed at the back of his head with a shaking hand.

The Ringmaster's tone softened. "We are a family here, are we not? We all look after each other. I do something for you, you do something for me. Round it goes. It's always been the way of the carnies. Of course, there's a balance to be had, you know that. The books have to balance. Peace of mind comes at a price, for us all." He leaned back in his chair, considering. "I'm not sure you're really in credit anymore."

"Lazarus, please. Ringmaster, don't. You know I'm loyal to the end."

"Are you? But to what end?" The Ringmaster regarded Emmett through stern eyes.

"No. Loyal to you, and the Circus of Wonder. Just as I have been all these years." Emmett leaned forward in his seat, grabbing on to the edge of the desk.

The Ringmaster leaned away a little further and retrieved something from a drawer which he placed on the table with a clonk. "We'll be away from here tonight and no-one will be gladder than I to be back on the route. Just remember who your friends are."

Emmett grasped the item in front of him, but his body

blocked Phyllo's sight of it. "Thank you, Lazarus, Ringmaster." His voice sounded close to tears. Birdie pulled on Phyllo's sleeve. "Come on," she mouthed as the scrape of a chair vibrated across the floor, "He's leaving." Birdie opened the door a crack and they slipped out, Birdie pulling Phyllo away, across the path.

"Hang on." Phyllo paused by the canvas wall opposite and glanced as nonchalantly as he could over his shoulder as Emmett came out. He clutched a turquoise package close to his chest and hurried away down the path.

CHAPTER TWELVE

Life Without a Safety Net

B irdie jogged away. "Come *on*, we've only done one lap. Papa will be wondering where we are." Phyllo caught her up. "What do you think that was all about?" he asked. Birdie shrugged and then said with a sniff, "If I were you, I'd be concentrating on my own problems. You're just lucky that I'm learning too. I know I'm younger, but obviously, in talent terms, I'm miles ahead."

She fussed at her hair. Phyllo could see that Birdie being 'less me' was still a work in progress.

"Well *obviously*," Phyllo puffed. "Although I wouldn't get too excited about that. Being better than me isn't difficult."

She pulled the first genuine smile he'd seen in a while. "We'd better go back."

They jogged in through the next opening and over to the ring. Signor Volante greeted Phyllo, looking impressed.

"*Buono, buono*. Not even broken a sweat. Things are looking better for you."

Phyllo realised, belatedly, that perhaps he should have faked a bit of puffing and panting.

"Strength and balance then. Birdie, show Phyllo the bars."

She rolled her eyes, but bade Phyllo follow her to the rear of the ring and a pair of asymmetric training bars. Birdie grabbed the lowest with both hands, pulled herself into a chin-up and flicked her legs over the top. She came to rest above the bar, balanced on her hips. She grinned at Phyllo and then rolled back down to the mat. "Now you."

Phyllo got to the chin-up position easily enough, but after that it was all a bit ineffectual and graceless. He could see that Birdie wasn't going to volunteer any helpful information. In fact, she seemed quite determined to make it as difficult as possible. He shrugged it off. While he was down on the ground struggling with the bars, he wasn't dangling from a trapeze, and that suited him fine. He spent the next few hours watching Birdie show off and then trying, ineffectively, to copy. Time flew by and before he knew it, it was time to prepare for the show.

Nonna Sophia pulled Phyllo to one side the moment he stepped through the Birdcage door. "I finish this afternoon," she enthused, "Now you are one of us." She held out a performance leotard and pressed it to Phyllo's shoulders. It draped against him in a waterfall of sequins. This was not the low profile he'd been hoping for. He took it gingerly. "Thanks, Nonna Sophia." She gave him a rough squeeze. "Try, try." She wafted a hand up to Phyllo's cot. Getting up to his bed; another trial. He sighed.

The others seemed to be clambering about with ease, scaling the tricky ladder with light steps and flitting in and out of their cots like birds in a tree. Ezio sat on the ledge outside his, pulling on the sleeves of his own leotard. It was almost as high as Phyllo's yet he seemed quite unconcerned. The costume clung to his muscular torso and an image of how Phyllo suspected he would look in *his* plopped into his mind. It wasn't going to be a flattering comparison.

Ezio made two easy sideways shuffles in his sitting posi-

114

tion to reach the ladder, stepped on effortlessly and scampered down. Phyllo made a mental note – that was how they did it. He moved over to the bottom of the ladder and stood looking up for a tad longer than someone happy about climbing it might have. Arnaldo appeared at his side. "Going up?"

Phyllo managed a weak smile.

"I know it's strange for you, Phyllo. I'm here. I'll help you. We all will. You'll never be anywhere safer than the Birdcage. We all look after each other. Trust us."

Just having Arnaldo standing next to him *did* make Phyllo feel more confident.

"This is our home space, our safe space. Do you feel your sash? It knows we are home. Try to feel it." Arnaldo grasped the air and then held it in a tight fist. "Come on, I want to see you in this costume. Remember, momentum is everything. Don't stop." He waved a hand up and Phyllo just got on and climbed, despite himself. Arnaldo seemed to exude a magical propulsion that was impossible to resist. The sash about his waist had become stiff and light and urged him upward. Once he'd got going it wasn't so bad and stepping over to his cot was OK too, so long as he didn't look down. Momentum *did* seem to help. Arnaldo had *somehow* helped.

Keeping up the momentum when it came to getting changed, however, was a bit more of a challenge. The leotard was miniscule. The struggle to squeeze inside it sent him flailing about his cot like a fish on a river bank. The silky fabric clung at the tips of his toes and stuck to his elbows and just when he thought he might never manage it, his shoulders slid into position with a pop.

"Thank Barnum the zip's at the front," he puffed and peered down from his cot to find Arnaldo looking back. He nodded to Phyllo and made a fist. "Feel it," he mouthed.

What Phyllo felt was extraordinarily self-conscious and a bit hot, but he sat himself down on the ledge and prepared to come down. He wasn't sure if it was the silkily snug effect of the leotard or his sudden awareness of the life in his sash, but something about the air in the Birdcage that evening did seem different. He probed his senses trying to get a handle on it. The best he could come up with was that the air felt soft, felt like it was filled with steam from cooking, with the burble of family, with the excitement of the show to come. He sat and absorbed it for a minute, thinking.

The Volantes were getting changed one by one and gathering informally at the table where Nonna Sophia heaped slices of toasted panini and cubes of cake – something to keep them all going until after the show. He got the impression that dinner was always late in the Birdcage, always the whole family crowded around, always noisy and amiable. Together. Being together was an important part of it all.

Arnaldo waved him down and in that moment, Phyllo felt like he could do it, bumped along the ledge on his bottom and swung onto the ladder. Then he was on the ground without really having thought about it. Arnaldo gave him a backslapping hug. "*Buono*. Get something to eat."

He felt inexplicably relaxed and smiled his way over to the food. Until he laid eyes on Birdie and her merciless smirk, that was.

"Gnocchi," she murmured under her breath as he approached, but Phyllo managed to block the probing finger aimed at his stomach. Nonna Sophia looked him over. "How do you like it? How is the fit?"

"It's, er, very nice," Phyllo managed, not quite sure how to critique the outfit which made him feel like one of the stick men he'd made back at the Confectionary. Stick men which had limbs of plaited strawberry laces and bodies and heads of marshmallow. Nonna smiled. "*Buono*. You look the part. Now you can be an extra. You fit right in." She got him in a bear hug and pinched at his cheeks.

"Like one of the family," Birdie murmured.

"Everybody," Signor Volante called out, "All out for the intro and then back here for warm up. Phyllo, just follow Birdie's lead, huh?" They filed amiably out of the door, chatting and laughing.

Ordinarily, this would have been Phyllo's most favourite time out on the horseshoe. Mingling with the customers and showing off toys or ostentatiously scoffing sweets. It was great fun. Usually. That evening however, the excitement was overshadowed by his own uncertainty. What would following Birdie's lead entail, he wondered? He racked his brain, but couldn't remember ever seeing her do anything dangerous. That was something. And what were the Fabulous Volante supposed to do in the crowd? He hadn't learned anything yet.

And it wasn't until he stepped outside that he remembered: the Birdcage wasn't even *on* the Horseshoe Path during show time. The gate by the ticket office and the open shelved door of the Confectionary effectively sealed this part off, making it officially backstage. Their route would take them directly into the big top with no mingling in the crowd at all.

Phyllo felt cheated.

He scuffed his way around the edge of the heavy red curtain that marked the threshold of the ring, but was cheered, at least, to see that the engineers had finally finished their repairs. The far section of canvas hung smooth and smart behind the refurbished upper tier seating. Polished wood now sported a swathe of new cushions that dressed the seats like plump jewels. The big top looked as good as new, better even and Phyllo felt the weight of it lift from him. It was a theatre to be proud of once again.

Unfortunately, there wasn't much of a crowd to appreciate it.

The troupe split up and drifted out to disperse amongst the thin audience, outnumbering its members two to one. Birdie pranced along the aisle so Phyllo attempted a sort of confident stride, hoping that he might look the part even if he didn't feel it. Far from blending in, as they usually did in the bustling masses, the carnies stood out garishly in their flamboyant costumes. Emmett was actually sitting down on a bench near the front, not even bothering with the pretence.

A violin started to play the welcome melody and it rang out around the space, clear and true. He scanned the tiers and softly hummed along. A handful of people occupied the prime seats at the front of the central tier, facing the ring head on. Phyllo recognised Amethyst from The Well of Tears. She was by far, the most enthusiastic of the line-up: her face shone pink against the sallow complexions of her fellows. She alone clutched a small cone of popcorn.

Then he spotted his father and Roly serving a family group further around to the right, and casually wove his way toward them, humming all the while. The volume of the melody grew as more and more of the troupe joined in. Without the buffer of the crowd it felt harder, more conspicuous than usual. The small crowd could see easily where the sound was coming from. Then from the back the singer began and the lighting dimmed.

> *"Come hear our song,*
> *See the Circus of Wonder!*
> *Come join the throng,*

The Circus draws near.
Run! Come along,
It's a Circus of Wonders!
Take your seat, plant your feet.
You're in for a treat.
The Circus of Wonder is here!"

Just like always, the rest of the troupe sang the song again together. Exposed as they were, the audience looked from one to the other expectantly and when the lights shifted to the Ringmaster, their eyes were already upon him.

Signor Volante flourished a hand above his head and the Volante skipped toward him in the long-legged bouncy fashion of gymnasts. Phyllo hadn't even made it to his own family to say hello. He looked to them longingly and raised a hand. They gave him a brief wave back but he had to tear himself away.

Back in the Birdcage the Volante fell into an automatic programme of stretching. Columba and Ezio climbed up to the trapeze in the ceiling to go over timings and polish transitions. Birdie played with Buffo. Phyllo paced.

"No much of an audience out there, huh?" Signor Volante said to Phyllo as he passed.

"Not much of a town," Phyllo replied.

"That's true. Birdie—" he called to get her attention, "You and Phyllo should go out and sit at the front. Fill a couple of seats, make some noise. Put on jackets to cover over your costume. What do you say, Phyllo?"

Phyllo couldn't agree quickly enough. He had nothing to practise or stretch and he might be able to catch one of his family. They chose seats on the front benches and Roly slid in next to them almost immediately.

"Well if it isn't my brother, the trapeze artist," said Roly, elbowing Phyllo and grinning.

"That's me."

"Are we to expect your high-flying debut later in the show?"

"Not likely. It was enough of a trial getting the costume on." Phyllo opened his jacket to reveal the spangly leotard.

"Noticed that earlier. Very nice." Phyllo could see Roly was fighting a grin.

"Oh, shut up."

"I didn't say anything." But he did laugh a bit. "No, it's very you."

Phyllo rolled his eyes.

"Also, nice to see that Mr and Mrs Wood and all the little Woods have come to see your first show." He was referring to all the empty wooden seats that surrounded them.

"I know, right? At least we'll be out of here tomorrow."

Harric and Garric of the Agile Arethusa tumbled across the ring in an extraordinarily long chain of somersaults and flips that signalled the end of their act. Roly, Phyllo and Birdie all whooped and cheered enthusiastically, pulling a little more zest from the sparse crowd.

The Ringmaster appeared in a spotlight, gesturing to the tumblers now taking a bow. "The Agile Arethusa!"

Phyllo, Birdie and Roly stamped their feet and cheered some more.

The lights dimmed around the ring whilst the spotlight remained on the Ringmaster. In the darkness equipment was moved. The silent cogs of the Machine rotated hoists and repositioned platforms.

"For your delight and delectation," he called out, "we bring you artists from around the globe. From the ancient world and our own fair nation, tremendous treasures more precious than gold.

"Our tumblers rolled. They leaped. They spun. Their tale: where this evening's show began. To swell the heart and feed the soul, their talent: our virtue to extol." He clutched proudly at his chest.

"This, dear friends, is the block on which we ask you now to build your faith. Your hope, your will, that those with daring do achieve the dizzying heights we ask them to.

"And we *will* ask them to."

The Ringmaster held his open hand out to the tiers and flitted his gaze from face to face. He nodded knowingly, golden light twinkling on his buttons. Phyllo felt the people of the crowd draw in to him.

"Tonight, you will witness feats beyond the bounds of men. Skills unmatched in heaven's realm. Angels weep to see our fine flyers soar," he fixed his gaze on Amethyst and her friends, "And you might wonder if they, from heaven, fell.

"But I won't tell."

Birdie gasped and Phyllo let out a long 'ooooh'. The Ringmaster nodded at them.

"But first, relax a while. Prepare yourself, tickle your taste buds with a tub of our terrific toffees or perhaps sup on a scrumptious soda, but save some for later." He wagged a finger at them, "You'll crave libation to sooth your throat once all the cheering's done."

At that a gaggle of clowns pushed an oversized pram through the gap where the plush red curtains met at the back of the ring. It had a crudely painted sign attached advertising candy floss and lemonade.

"I'll see you later," Roly said in a low voice, sliding off the end of the bench and heading up to their father and the official

Confectioner's cart. This was their cue to pick up more business.

Four clowns had accompanied the pram out into the ring; Nubbins, Sprockets, Greedy Gus and Bingo Bongo (Emmett's ring persona). Nubbins, a dwarf at a little over three foot six, wore a smart pink and white candy-striped jacket with a matching extra tall stove-pipe hat. He was undoubtedly *The Confectioner* in this tableau. Sprockets skipped along beside him, gangly and appealingly rubber limbed. Quite the opposite, he was tall and skinny in a long tan shopkeeper's coat covered with pockets made from clashing fabrics: sky-blue polka dots on one, swirls of vermillion on another. He pulled a fist from one pocket and tossed a handful of sweets and dancing confetti high over the children on the benches. Greedy Gus encouraged the scrum that followed, but had an enormous lollypop of his own, which he gave great exaggerated licks. Emmett slouched at the rear. His eyes were on the ground. Phyllo was sure that he was supposed to look a bit more enthusiastic.

Nubbins rocked the pram to a stop and mutely beckoned the other three to his side. Sprockets and Greedy Gus came immediately to lean in and coo-chi-coo, but Bingo Bongo drifted. He took his time to gaze droopily over Nubbins' shoulder. He pulled an exaggerated expression of delight, then pushed away, leaning too heavily on Nubbins. This sent him, and the pram, crashing forward into the edge of the ring. The children beyond squealed.

Nubbins yanked the pram back and gave Bingo Bongo a kick in the shins for his trouble. Laughter rippled. An exaggerated nod later, he took the 'baby' out of the pram and launched into their 'don't drop the baby routine' which Phyllo had giggled at from the stands a hundred times before. They passed the bundle between them, letting it pop out of their grip like a slippery bar of soap and just catching it, sliding whistles from the band and surprising honks of horns punctuating their actions. The sharp kick Emmett had just received took the shine off it for Phyllo though. 'Bingo Bongo' wandered over to the ringside and flopped down to sit on the edge.

"What's he doing?" Phyllo hissed to Birdie.

"I don't know. Isn't it part of the act?"

"Not usually." Phyllo was sure that he ought to be playing pass the baby.

Sprockets whistled Bingo Bongo over, sniffing at the 'baby's' bottom and feigning a smelly nappy by wafting one hand under his nose. He appeared to take the hint and got up, but instead of going over, he shambled out through the gap in the curtains. Birdie and Phyllo looked at each other, confused. Then he was back, clutching a baby bath that slopped water over its edges with every uncertain step.

Phyllo knew that a slopping water malarkey was a clowning staple, but he also knew that this wasn't supposed to be happening until later. Nubbins and Sprockets exchanged bemused looks. Bingo Bongo bringing out the baby bath now had just fast forwarded their routine to its mid-point when they'd only just begun. "What are you doing? This is too early," Sprockets growled at Emmett through the corner of his mouth. Emmett either didn't hear or didn't care to answer. One end of the bath slipped from his grip and banged down onto the floor, closely followed by the other. Water, abandoned momentarily in the air, sloshed back into it and then rolled over the edges, soaking them both.

The kids on the benches roared.

Nubbins bristled. Greedy Gus gamely carried on with the

'slippery baby' gag they were working and Sprockets picked Bingo Bongo up by one elbow and marched him out of the curtain. He waved his arms about dramatically, miming that he was throwing him out. Phyllo wondered what he was really saying.

A couple of minutes later, he staggered back in through the curtain, a full bucket in each hand. He made a beeline for the baby bath which had sat ignored since his earlier exit. It felt wrong. The very directness of it told Phyllo that something was off. Water gags involved a lot of wobbling about and teetering around the edge of the ring, kidding the punters that they were about to get soaked. Bingo Bongo wasn't making a play of it at all. He plonked the buckets down and then went back for one with both hands, tipping it bluntly into the bath. The water rebounded out, soaking Nubbins from behind. Nubbins froze mid game and then stomped a wide circle to come face to face with Emmett. Phyllo could have believed it was part of the act, but he knew that it wasn't and flicked his eyes around the group, gauging their reactions. Nubbins might have been small but he was fierce if you poked him. He kicked Emmett in the shin again. This time Emmett crumpled to rub at it. Up this close, Phyllo could see the hint of a snarl under Nubbins' make-up. Sprockets intervened, turning Emmett around, hand on shoulder to march him back out of the ring.

Emmett was barely gone five seconds before he came back around the edge of the curtain, this time clutching a basket of apples. Phyllo knew that the apple bobbing skit came right at the very end. The audience chuckled at the sight of him, but then Emmett tripped over himself and fell headlong. Clutching the basket and unable to save himself, he crashed to the ground. He was still for a moment but then levered himself up, unsteady and uncoordinated, pitching about. Blood dripped from his nose. The basket of apples tipped and rolled in the sawdust. The band's jaunty music faltered.

"You're rubbish," a gaunt child along the benches called out. Someone threw the remains of a toffee apple, which rolled to a stop by Emmett's side. Sprockets dashed over as fast as his unfeasibly long shoes could take him and hoisted Emmett up, onto his feet, but Emmett wrenched himself free in a flopping turn. He staggered to the side, wagging a finger and then dropped to his knees to gather up the apples. With a few in the basket he lurched over to the baby bath and tipped them in. Emmett took an uncertain step backward and flourished his hand as if the crowd should applaud this great achievement.

They stared silently back.

Phyllo suspected that none of the others fancied bobbing for apples Emmett had been bleeding on Nubbins apparently least of all. He launched himself at Emmett and knocked him back to the ground, raining down wildly angry punches. Emmett pushed at him ineffectually. This was most definitely *not* part of the show.

Greedy Gus intervened and then the band was playing noisily frantic music, trying to blend the fight in with the act. Gus held Nubbins out at arm's length while he fought to lash out and Sprockets pulled Emmett to his feet and marched him off again.

Phyllo took in the scene wide-eyed and then spotted the Ringmaster in the wings, watching the proceedings with a thin mouth and flared nostrils. He spoke urgently into the shadows and then Harric and Garric reappeared, tumbling into the centre of the ring to perform an unscheduled fill. The clowns had finished too early so the engineers hadn't had time to reset for the Dirigible Dislocationists, the act that came on next. The band floundered into a piece more suited to the tumblers now centre stage. Harric and Garric looked flustered, but threw themselves into a repeat of their finale and once the band recognised what they were doing, adjusted accordingly.

Phyllo and Birdie looked at each other, stunned. "You really have got the strangest friends," Birdie said.

"Something's wrong. I need to go and see him," Phyllo said, making to get up, but Birdie grabbed at his arm. "No, you'll get us into trouble. We're supposed to stay here and gee up the crowd."

Phyllo deflated.

"See him after," Birdie hissed.

Phyllo had never wished for a show to go faster. The combination of concern for his friend and his looming first appearance with the Fabulous Volante left him squirming. When Birdie finally tugged on his sleeve and said, "Let's go. We're on next," Phyllo's stomach filled with an acidic combination of relief and horror.

The rest of the Volante were already in line behind the curtain. Birdie took her place calmly, but Phyllo shifted foot to foot, trying to see around the engineers who worked at the backstage Machine controls. Beyond them Nubbins was gesticulating wildly at Sprockets who seemed to be trying to calm him down. He couldn't hear what they were saying, but Nubbins' small face was scrunched into angry lines and he hopped up and down with belligerent stamps. Emmett was nowhere in sight.

Next thing he knew, arms around him were flourishing in the air, the troupe was up on its toes and Arnaldo was leading everyone out into the ring, himself reticently included.

Phyllo had seen the Fabulous Volante perform many times and knew that their act was indeed fabulous. In the past, he'd always watched as an enraptured audience member, but that evening he saw it all quite differently. With something that verged on terrified awe.

His one taste of the platform had been terrible. His knees had melted away from under him and his vision reduced to swirling spots. The prospect of going up there again quite frankly filled him with dread. He was utterly relieved that, for now at least, he'd be safe on the ground, playing only the part of an extra.

The ring had reset to resemble a great sailing ship. Images projected down from the lighting rig that summoned the sea and the wooden boards of a deck. The immense king poles that ran up to the roof on either side of the ring now masqueraded as masts that held the flyers' platforms. Webbed nets, furled sails and ropes cascaded from the star-spangled ceiling: ships rigging that would double up as the flyers' stage. Their act wasn't just about circus skills, their act told a story.

All the flyers skipped around the ring, trailing swathes of turquoise organza, dipping and rising to resemble the sea. All but Ezio and Columba, that was. The opening sequence was theirs alone.

Ezio, the Ragged Deckhand, initially came on pretending to sweep the deck, but then unhitched two long swathes of white silk from the rigging. A jet of air from the lungs of the Machine caught them and they unfurled like sails to lift him from the ground. With balletic grace he seemed to run in the air, gears of the Machine lifting him faster and higher to glide out over the audience. Strong and athletic, he climbed and tumbled through the silk until he reached the ground again and Columba made her entrance.

Secretly watched by the Ragged Deckhand, she boarded the ship as a wealthy Lady. The Machine blew azure silks to envelop her like wind and she took to the air, twirling and graceful over the audience, much like Ezio had.

Phyllo snapped out of his trance as her feet returned to the ground. He'd always found this part so beautiful and glanced around the ring at his comrades, also enacting the sea, to nod his appreciation. All their eyes were on her. They all swayed with a dancer's fluid motion and Phyllo realised that he too had been swept along. But it wasn't just the spectacle. He'd felt briefly connected to the action at his core. The sash had buzzed around his middle and, somehow he knew that the energy had been coming from him, not it. It was an odd realisation.

The Ragged Deckhand and the Lady met. Shy at first, soon they were soaring on the silks together in an aerial dance that spoke of love. Even as an awkward twelve-year-old, Phyllo could not help but appreciate it. They were so graceful. He'd seen it all before, but now he was thinking about how difficult it was and it felt a world away. Phyllo's proudest achievements to date had involved the wielding of a wooden spoon. He'd barely managed that and certainly didn't have this kind of talent. Suddenly his mouth was dry and the fear of the enormous task ahead washed over him. He was ridiculously out of his depth.

Arnaldo and Salvo strode into the ring as the Ship's Captain and Second-in-Command. This was where the trapeze elements of the routine began. The troupe abandoned the organza 'sea' and moved to new positions. Some climbed to the platforms whilst others anchored ladders. They all moved around with that bouncy gymnastic grace which Phyllo did his best to emulate, shadowing Birdie.

She spied him out of the corner of her eye, smirking. "You're so stiff, Phyllo. You look like a clockwork soldier."

Phyllo cringed. At least there weren't many in the audience to see how bad he was, even at that.

Arnaldo and Salvo's routine on the two trapeze bars was the part in the story where the Captain also wooed the Lady with his daring feats of strength and skill. Arnaldo and Salvo criss-crossed in the air, switching trapeze bars and spinning around each other. The shapes they formed were in perfect symmetry, timed to the split second and, as the routine progressed, the moves became more and more complex. More and more impossible, to Phyllo's thinking. After every perfectly executed launch came a choreography of moves and solid landings.

Sometimes they moved in perfect symmetry and others Arnaldo would launch from his own trapeze, turning incredible twists at a head-spinning height, for Salvo's sure hands to catch him. Phyllo watched open-mouthed, the hairs standing up on the back of his neck. The biggest tricks, the fastest spins and the highest leaps came with a kind of shockwave that moved up from the ground. He could feel a collective pulse that rolled through the air around him, through him. The troupe together made Arnaldo fly higher, faster. The troupe together joined forces somehow.

The sash around his middle stiffened and tightened, as if it were desperate to join in. He examined the sashes of Arnaldo and Salvo, up on the bars. They twinkled in the spotlight. Phyllo would ordinarily have assumed it was light reflecting on the sequinned embroidery, but now he wondered if that light was coming from the sash itself. He wondered if he was seeing the magic.

There was an unfathomable edge to what they were achieving, an impossibility that bent the laws of physics. The people on the ground somehow donated the gravity they weren't defying and held Arnaldo up just that little bit more. It was electrifying even with this small crowd. Phyllo could only imagine what Arnaldo could achieve with a full house willing him on.

Columba joined him in the air as the Lady, her light form dancing like a feather in a summer breeze. The music from the band changed and the lighting effects darkened. This was the cue for the entrance of Marco, the youngest members of the troupe after Birdie, who played the part of the Pirate Captain. Marco was only a couple of years older than Phyllo and quite similar in height, but still had him at a disadvantage in the muscle department.

Marco, the Pirate Captain, climbed the rigging and hung there to spy jealously on the Ship's Captain and the Lady. The visual effects changed again and projected images of night following day to night again, led the story on twenty-four hours to when the Pirate Captain returned with his men to attack.

Every member of the Fabulous Volante was on stage then, either crew or pirate, tumbling through the rigging or flying from bar to bar. Each member had their own part to play, even Phyllo and Birdie, who, although their characters were earth-bound, were allowed to don an extra layer of pirate costume to menace from the ground. A role that Birdie took to rather too well.

The Lady swung on the high trapeze, trying to avoid the Pirate Captain's clutches as he scaled the rigging to reach her. If Marco could take on an important part like this at his age then perhaps there was hope for Phyllo yet, he mused to himself. He'd never heard that any of them had come to any serious harm, beyond a sprained wrist or a bit of rope burn. They must look after the younger and inexperienced ones, to keep them safe, Phyllo decided. He was nodding to himself with this positive realisation when he suddenly noticed the complete absence of the safety net. He grabbed at Birdie.

"The net! There's no net!"

She shook him off. "Well of course not, Gnocchi, it's show time."

"But what if he falls?" Hadn't anyone thought of that?

Birdie bit her lip in mock panic and then said, "Well, duh. Where's the excitement with a net?"

"But it's dangerous, he's not much older than me!" Phyllo imagined himself up at that height.

She shrugged and looked up to Marco who had now reached the platform. "He knows what he's doing."

An accomplice pulled in the bar and he launched into a swing, reaching out for Columba and missing. A game of cat and mouse. With every swing he got a little closer.

Phyllo's mouth dried. He knew what was coming. He knew that Marco would leap from one trapeze to the other. He knew that Marco was the least experienced, the youngest of the practising troupe. This was his big moment, his trick. There was no net. How had he never noticed that there was no net before? What if he missed? What if he fell? Phyllo couldn't bear to look, but neither could he tear his eyes away.

The music from the band swelled. It rose with the pirates who were winning. Then Marco leapt – spanning the impossible distance from one trapeze to the other. He stepped onto the bar either side of Columba and enveloped her in his pirate cloak. Phyllo thought he might faint with relief.

The Pirate Captain dragged his prisoner down to the deck, where the Captain and his crew stood ferocious guard over their cargo, but made no attempt to rescue the Lady. A spotlight found Ezio, the love-struck deckhand, who leapt to a silk and tumbled through it to the ground to save her.

The music from the band changed and the engineers brought on the effects of a storm. The troupe members on the ground lunged from one side of the ring to the other in unison, as if being tossed about. Phyllo trailed from side to side, after Birdie, who swooned dramatically at every turn. He stumbled about, with reasonable conviction he thought, but was relieved when they were finally 'thrown overboard' by a sweep of light and able to slink off into the wings. From there he watched Ezio and Columba fly away on the silks, higher and higher, until they disappeared from view.

As soon as the show had finished Phyllo sprinted around to the Clown Quarter, but raised voices coming from inside stopped him dead at the door.

"You broke the code. You never break the code." It wasn't Emmett's voice, but one of the others, angry and forceful.

"I know. I'm sorry. I'm trying." That was him, whimpering almost.

"You're sorry? You're not sorry."

"Sprockets, I am. You know I am. I'll make it up to you."

"Sprockets? Great Grimaldi, am I wearing a costume? Do I still have make-up on? No. Be a professional, Emmett. Am I calling you Bingo Bongo?

"I wouldn't mind."

"Well what does that say? It's like you've forgotten everything. Jack. My name is Jack."

"Jackie," Emmett pleaded.

"You're making us look like fools. And don't look at me

like that. The wrong kind, Emmett. Unprofessional. You'll get us thrown out. Very least get yourself thrown out. That what you want?"

There was a long silence and Phyllo pressed his ear hard to the door, trying to pick something up.

"I said don't look at me like that." Jack's voice was much louder now. Phyllo heard a whack and a scuffle. Something glass hit the ground and broke. "This is trouble, trouble for us all. And don't just sit around neither. Hang up your costume." Now Jack was yelling, "Take off your make-up. You're giving clowning a bad name. Have some respect, respect for the rest of us, if you've run out for yourself."

The door snatched open and Phyllo stumbled back. Jack filled the doorway, tall and wiry, all traces of Sprockets the clown removed. He glowered at Phyllo with residual anger still burning in his eyes. He rubbed at his fist. "More trouble," he grumbled and pushed past.

Phyllo watched him go. He'd never seen one of the clowns in such a temper before.

In the cabin Emmett slouched at his dressing table. He stared dejectedly into the glass he was clutching, the last dregs of a pale blue liquid at the bottom. Phyllo sidled uncertainly into the room and when Emmett looked up his face rolled through a series of expressions, as if his brain didn't know which to choose. The forlorn starting point morphed into guilt then panic and then finally settled on tired resignation.

"What in Barnum's name is going on, Emmett?" Phyllo said breathlessly.

"Nothing, nothing, I'm not doing anything." He sank the last of his drink and momentarily closed his eyes.

Phyllo frowned at him. "In the ring, Emmett. Are you hurt?"

"Oh that." Emmett got up from the dressing table, wobbled uncertainly to his small cubicle and swished back the curtain with uncalculated force. It flapped around his legs and he fought it off. "I'm just a bit under the weather." He dug about in the junk on his desk, looking for something, but not finding it. He grumbled under his breath.

Phyllo moved in closer to try to see what he was looking for, unheard by Emmett who started at his proximity when he finally turned back.

Emmett's sparse make-up was uneven and jagged. What was left smeared, splodged and red, into his cheeks. Had Jack done that? Phyllo had heard the whack from outside. White greasepaint above his eyes fell heavily into the creases in his skin. It flaked in dry scales, contrasting fiercely with his eyes, which shone like wet glass.

"I've had the most terrible stomach upset," he mumbled, leaning away and walking around Phyllo, back to his seat at the dressing table, "and a headache." He rubbed at his face, smearing the make-up even more.

Phyllo sat down at the neighbouring table and passed over a cloth, but the pot of remover was smashed on the floor. Emmett bent to scoop up a blob which he smeared over his face.

An unnoticed splinter of glass drew a scratch across his skin, a droplet of blood rolled down his cheek and he paused, staring coldly at himself in the mirror.

"For a moment there, I thought I saw the man I used to be," he said.

Phyllo stared at him.

"He wants me to fail and it's all I deserve. I hear him sometimes. Telling me that I can't do it. Laughing at me for trying. I'm a fool." Emmett lifted his eyes to Phyllo's in the mirror's reflection and there was something different there. He saw it just for an instant: an angular slant to his eyebrows, a sneer at his lip. It was an expression he hadn't seen on him before. It had an edge of nastiness about it that made Phyllo recoil. There was a jarring familiarity too, but Phyllo couldn't place it. Somewhere nearby a tin bell jingled.

"They all hate me. Wish I'd just leave."

"No, Emmett, I'm sure that's not true."

Emmett rubbed at his jaw. "It feels true."

CHAPTER THIRTEEN

Brampton Levels

The troupe had been waiting for it. Willing it. It bounced from engineer to engineer around the Horseshoe Path, sing-song and jovial.

"Jal!"

The mood shifted. They were finally escaping. Shady Hollow could keep its oppressive gloom. Phyllo had hoped that if they could get back on schedule, the rest of the troupe might start to forget it had been he who'd knocked them from it in the first place. And almost destroyed their livelihoods.

The troupe *bustled*, delighted with their improving fortunes, but Phyllo just couldn't summon up the relief. Emmett's troubles weighed him down.

"Cheer up, you miserable git," Roly said, bumping into him on purpose in the ring, "Anyone'd think you liked it here."

The troupe was gathering under the big top, rolling their cabins into place. Roly had just helped push the condensed Confectionary into position and the engineers were still locking it off.

"*I'll* be glad to be shot of this place, I can tell you that. Give me the Brampton Levels any day of the week," Roly continued. Phyllo gave him a weak smile and Roly lapsed briefly into silence, stuffed his hands into his pockets and then produced a toffee, which he passed over. Phyllo unwrapped and ate it immediately.

"Better?"

Phyllo nodded and managed a slightly more convincing smile.

"Shouldn't you be helping your new family pack?"

"Yeah, well I do actually like them better," Phyllo smirked, and Roly shook his head. "Once I'd put all my stuff in my cupboard that was it, though. There are so many of them in there and they know what they're doing. Thought it was better if I just got out of the way."

"Yeah. Probably for the best."

The two of them stood side by side, rocking on their heels. Frú Hafiz's cabin rolled into place and she came into the ring too, escorted by their father. They stood beside it talking solemnly. Roly unwrapped a toffee for himself and popped it into his mouth. "So, Emmett's being weird," he mumbled, through the sweet.

"Very. I went to see him. He's in a bit of a state. Drinking."

"We should do something. Make him something, maybe. Cheer him up a bit."

"Don't think I'll be allowed." Phyllo scuffed at the floor with his toe.

"No." Roly went distant, thinking. "Got any ideas? Would be nice if we could surprise him with something really special."

"Something happy."

"Yeah. Something happy."

Phyllo thought for a moment and then said, "Nothing seems to be making him happy at the moment."

"Something from before, then. Can you remember him

saying he liked anything in particular? I haven't heard him talk about anything in a while. Have you?"

"He talks about his mum, sometimes. Maybe we could do something there?" Phyllo suggested.

"A childhood favourite, yeah." Roly thought for a minute. "Do you think Albertus would let us look in Emmett's book? Have a look at his past?"

The books of the cast were a new area for both of them. "We could ask. I don't see why not and I probably won't be missed for a while yet. Maybe while we pitch?"

"Got to be worth an ask."

More cabins rolled into the big top, the cast gathered in the ring and the buzz of conversation rose. The Birdcage, however, was conspicuous by its continued absence. Only it and the Ringmaster's cabin were missing and the Ringmaster's was always last.

"So how is it then, being a flyer?" Roly asked.

"Terrifying." They both snorted. "The first thing they did was make me climb up to that crackers high platform and swing out on a trapeze. Can you believe it?"

"What was it like?"

"Insane. My legs went to jelly. It's like your whole body knows it's a bad idea and tries to stop you by turning to goo. Well, I fell off, didn't I."

"Fell off?" Roly looked aghast.

"There was a net, not like in the performances. Which is also crackers."

Roly nodded, open mouthed.

"Weird thing is, they kind of make you feel like you can do it, if you're brave enough. I don't know what it is or how they do it, but it's kind of like team spirit. It's like they're all tuned into each other. I think getting me up on the platform was a test, to see if I'd try, even though I didn't know how."

"And you fell off? Are they nuts?" Roly's voice cracked.

A screech of machine gears came from outside and an urgent clang of metal on metal drummed louder and louder. Shouts of panic escalated with the din and then the mechanism went quiet. The shouting, however, continued and Phyllo could pick Signor Volante's voice out in the cacophony, "Ezio, *rapido!*"

Phyllo wanted to see what was happening and pulled Roly out with him onto the last scrap of path, in front of the Birdcage.

Signor Volante had their cabin locking flap open and was wrestling with the lever. The Birdcage itself listed alarmingly to one side about half way up, the upper section swinging under its own great weight. Where the Confectionary sucked in its walls to condense, the tower of the Birdcage collapsed in an accordion fold. Signor Volante had explained to Phyllo how the storage reformatted into a single solid layer and the turret of cots folded like a deck of cards to sit on top. Only they hadn't. Fifteen feet from the ground the tower went crooked, leaning sideways and pivoting dangerously where the mechanism had missed several creases in one corner.

There was a lot of arm waving going on and shouting in a language Phyllo didn't understand. It was probably just as well. Birdie tugged at her father's sleeve, pleading for attention. "Papa, Papa, I bet I know what it is. There's something not put away, it's stopping the fold."

"Aren't you the fox?" Signor Volante snapped back, "Go and play with your little dog, Birdie, leave this to the men." He shooed her away and Birdie turned, her little face scrunched up and hurt. She noticed Phyllo and quickly turned away from him too, dashing with Buffo away from the Birdcage and into the dark field that surrounded them. Signor Volante returned his attention to Arnaldo. "You were supposed to make checks. How has this happened?"

"I did, damn it, I did," Arnaldo snarled back.

"San Giuseppe, you no take that tone with me." Aldo let go of the lever and turned to square up to Arnaldo. "You do your job and no complain about it. *Idiota!*"

Ezio pitched in with something in Italian then and they were erupting into a scuffle of pushing and shoving.

"Team spirit, you say," Roly murmured under his breath.

Phyllo had never seen them behave this way. It was like everything he thought he knew about them was a mistake.

The Ringmaster swept out from the big top and strode past Phyllo and Roly, straight into the centre of the melee, cane aloft.

"Desist immediately," he boomed.

Signor Volante released Ezio's collar and Ezio stepped back. The whole group shrank down from their inflated, aggravated selves, as if a bubble had been burst.

"Aldo, furnish me with your key," the Ringmaster demanded and when it was produced, passed it to Bain. "Locate the release at the back, let's see if we can't elevate it."

Skinner appeared and a dozen other men from the engineers trailed behind.

"Scale the side and brace the riser, it'll get worse before it gets better. Step back now." He spread his arms wide and Signor Volante leant away from the Ringmaster's hand, too close to his face. He grumbled, but Phyllo could see from his expression that he knew this was no time for objections.

The engineers formed a human pyramid to the side of the Birdcage, leaning in and supporting it as the gears ground and thumped inside. The Ringmaster unscrewed the lever and replaced it with his cane, which seem to act as a master key. It took a couple of false starts and worrying lurches, but they got the tower back up so that Ezio and Arnaldo could hurry inside to fix whatever it was that had come out of place.

They reappeared a few minutes later, Arnaldo leading the way. "OK, it's done," he said. The Ringmaster shook his head, agitated. "Your explanation?"

"One of the upper cots. The locker was open, some things on the bed. I expect he forgot. When the storage condensed it would have got jammed."

"He?" The eyes of the Ringmaster flicked to find Phyllo's and that now familiar sick feeling returned to his stomach. He'd put everything away; he was sure that he had. "He who?" Heat rose at Phyllo's neck.

"A mistake, I'm sure. He just isn't familiar yet—"

The Ringmaster pointed forcefully at Phyllo then turned his palm skyward to beckon him over with a curling finger. "Phyllo Cane. A word," he hissed.

Roly gave a little whimper and nudged him in the back.

Phyllo dragged himself over, legs heavy as lead.

"Are you determined to destroy my circus?" the Ringmaster demanded.

"No. No, I definitely put my things away," Phyllo managed before the Ringmaster raised a palm to silence him.

"And yet it would seem that the evidence is to the contrary. You know how the cabins work, do you not? You know the importance of clear space?"

"No, really, I definitely—"

"If I were you, I'd be doing my damndest not to put a toe out of line." The Ringmaster spoke slowly, deliberately, "If I were you, I'd consider myself fortuitous to still be here."

141

"I don't know what happened—"

"What progress has he made, Aldo? Is there any point to this endless torture?" The Ringmaster turned to Signor Volante.

"It's only been a day," Phyllo blurted.

"Enough!" Lazarus Barker's face rippled with restrained emotion, "You will speak when you are spoken to. Aldo, what do you say?"

"So far, is OK. He's trying, I think." Both men's eyes fell upon Phyllo and he'd never wanted to turn and run more. He didn't want to be a flyer. He didn't want to have to try. Only the thought of Dodo at the mercy of the In-between kept him there.

"Then we will see."

Bain came to the Ringmaster's side. "Is she clear inside?"

"Check it. We don't want any more stupid mistakes." Bain disappeared and a minute later was engaging the mechanism. It groaned and complained, but then something thunked back into place and the tower descended in a smooth fold. The Volante family sprang into action, encircling the cabin and, along with the engineers, manoeuvred it under the big top. Phyllo hung back, empty to the pit of his stomach.

"Crikey, Phyllo, you'd better watch it," said Roly, joining him, "Looks like Barker's really got it in for you."

It was starting to feel that way.

The engineers rolled in the Ringmaster's cabin next and then set about unfurling the canvas walls, the final part of the process before sealing up the tent. Signor Volante came to the last remaining gap in the canvas by the Birdcage and called out for Birdie who dutifully returned, looking sullen. They disappeared inside and Phyllo clenched his teeth together. No call for him. He supposed it would be a bit much to expect.

Signor Volante was angry after what had just happened. Phyllo was the outsider, now more than ever.

Roly tugged him into motion as the Ringmaster came out of the shadows, making a last inspection of the perimeter and they scuttled under the flap, just ahead of Skinner who clutched the marker stake.

The ring was crowded, rumbling with low speculation about what had just happened, and Phyllo was glad to turn his back on them, looking instead out the last open flap into the night of Shady Hollow. The white shape of Buffo was visible running about in the field and Phyllo thought he heard his collar bell. Lazarus Barker came in through the gap, turned to survey the field beyond one final time, then came inside. "Seal her up," he said, "Let's get the hell out of here."

When the blue glow of electricity had faded from the big top skeleton, they'd arrived at the Brampton Levels. Skinner's men hoisted the canvas and the troupe poured out at the first opportunity. The sky stretched pale blue to a far horizon. Sunrise was an hour away at least, but the brightening sky reflecting across flat sheets of water doubled the ambient light to a glow.

Phyllo breathed deeply. Warm clean air filled his lungs and cleared his head. The big top had materialised on the Standing Bend of the river, the moored boats of the market a stone's throw away. Distant silhouettes of trees stood sentry on the horizon that reached around them in every direction. The landscape was open, lighter and brighter already than the gloomy dell they'd been stuck in for the last few days. This was better, much better. Phyllo's life was never going back to normal, but at least now, here, for the rest of the troupe, there was a chance to reset.

The Ringmaster strode out ahead of the troupe into the river landscape that had drawn every eye, and turned to face them. "Full set, everyone. We have the light, let's not waste any more time." Rather predictably the Ringmaster's gaze fell to Phyllo.

The Volante family were certainly buoyed by their new surroundings. They came together in a back-slapping huddle. "I'm sorry, Papa," Ezio was saying, "I don't know what came over me."

"We are all hungry, huh?" said Signor Volante, "Let's get set so Nonna can open the kitchen." The group laughed in agreement and he pulled Ezio into his chest for a rough hug. Arnaldo patted Signor Volante on the back and he acknowledged him with a nod. The group moved as one, back toward the big top and, as they went revealed Marco, who stood still, slightly away from the rest and facing Phyllo. A slant on his eyebrow. A curl at his lip. Unsettling and off-beat. Phyllo blinked and then it was just normal-looking Marco, staring out at the view. He turned and then sauntered away, after the others.

Phyllo shuddered. "Did you see that?"

"Huh?" Roly had been looking out at the river market.

"Marco's face. That look he gave me. It was *weird*." He'd seen that expression before on Emmett's face in the mirror.

"They're all as intimidating as each other as far as I'm concerned. I mean, do they all have to be quite so good-looking?"

"It wasn't that." Phyllo thought he'd been starting to get to know them, to understand how it worked. "They were all so supportive—"

"Before, you mean?"

Phyllo stared at him.

"Before you broke their home."

Despite the warmth of their new location, Albertus opened the door to greet them in multiple layers of cardigan and woolly hat.

"Boys, boys. Two visits in as many days. I *am* honoured. The youngsters usually find me dictionary dull." He pushed the thick glasses up his nose to survey them better and snorked out a laugh. "All in a bit of a pickle still, but come in, come in." He shuffled over to the fireplace and bent to arrange kindling in the grate. "I'll just get this going and we can have some tea." The sticks of wood smoked and caught. He added a couple of logs and then shuffled over to the small kitchenette, which was tucked neatly beneath the mezzanine. "Darjeeling? Oolong? Japanese Gyokuro? White Peony? I've probably got some Pouchong in here somewhere—" He rooted about.

"Whatever you're having," said Phyllo, who really didn't know one tea from the next, "surprise us."

"Very well, very well." Albertus flourished a tea spoon and clattered about a bit more, retrieving one thing from a cupboard, another from a drawer and setting the kettle to boil.

The fire took hold, cracking and popping as the thin bark caught and peeled away in twisting ribbons. It threw a comfortable glow into the cabin and not just from the grate, Phyllo noticed, but also by seeping between books that huddled on the shelf above the mantelpiece. Old books, bound in rough leather that was more often than not coming away at the seams.

Both boys drew in closer and Roly's curious finger picked at an edge which, to both their surprise, opened like a door on tiny hinges. On the other side, where there should have been bindings, was a miniature living room complete with old armchair and its own roaring fire. An inch-high man wearing a dressing gown and a cross expression rushed over to grab at an inner handle.

"Do you mind!" he squeaked and slammed the door shut. He had been perfect in every way save for the fact that he was a drawing. A very fine and detailed drawing, but a drawing nonetheless.

Albertus set his tea tray down on the corner of the desk. "Ink Imps. Intensely private. Normally the solitude of my existence suits them perfectly." He popped a couple of fold-out chairs from the wall and set them between his desk and the fire. "They like to live in the books and they don't like to be disturbed. Taking on characters and stories and so forth." Roly undid his jacket and flapped at his face.

"Warm and dry: that's their perfect conditions," said Albertus, noticing Roly's pink cheeks, "Suits my arthritis and poor circulation. Better without milk this one, really, if that's alright?" He poured from the teapot into three mismatched cups. His eyes, magnified to at least twice their actual size, flitted from one brother to the other. Phyllo picked up his cup and tried it. The tea was pale and sweet. "Delicious, thanks."

"The better the book, the richer the colour. They tend to flit from volume to volume as a rule, but this is a bit of a settlement." He waved a gnarled hand at the shelf. "I put them all together here, makes looking after them easier, yes much easier."

"Fascinating." Roly picked at another flap and was

rewarded with a shrill scream. He slammed it shut and came to sit by Phyllo, looking chastised.

"Actually, Albertus, we wanted to ask if we could look in Emmett's book. He does have a book, does he?" said Phyllo.

"Emmett? He does, yes. But books are private, Phyllo. They contain personal information and are not to be shared willy-nilly. We are not a lending library."

"Oh." Roly's face fell with disappointment.

Albertus picked up a biscuit. "And besides, I know I don't look like much of a dare-devil, but dealing with these books is a dangerous business. Barnaby Twitch over on the Funicular Fair got sucked right in. Couldn't get out. Got much too involved and fell into the story. It happens, oh yes, it happens. Didn't get him back until six years later when the unfortunate subject got squashed by a runaway carriage. Lucky for him, Barnaby that is. End of the story, you see? The only way out: the end of the story."

Phyllo hadn't realised people could get trapped in the books.

"Not to mention that these books only respond to their maker, Phyllo, and I wouldn't be allowed to give it to you, even if you *could* read it. Archivist's Oath. We are sworn to protect them. Whatever would you want with it, anyway?"

"It's just that he's been rather down," said Roly glumly.

"And we wanted to cheer him up," cut in Phyllo.

"And sometimes, in our recipes, er my recipes," Roly corrected himself, "You can add in a memory and a flavour from the past and it makes it *more*. A bit of a boost, you know."

"I see, I see." Albertus eyed them ponderously.

"Not just that, it can really transport you. I thought, we thought, if we could just latch on to something, you know, something really happy from Emmett's past, we could send

147

him back there for a moment, help him to feel happy again."
Phyllo smiled hopefully.

"Something like those marshmallows you were making
when you set the big top on fire?"

Roly winced. "We wouldn't do anything like that. I mean,
we absolutely wouldn't burn anything down, honest. There
might be something really simple. If only we could look."

Albertus sipped his tea and considered them.

"I shall look on your behalf. It seems like an innocent
enough request. Innocent and good-hearted. Who am I to
deprive your records of marks of kindness?" His enormous
eyes blinked purposefully and he stood to cross the small
room and climb the spiral stairs, sorting through his bulging
keyring as he went. Phyllo and Roly followed.

When he shuffled to a stop in front of the carved cupboard,
he'd picked out a copper key whose teeth resembled the letter
'W'. Small iron rivets punctured the stem. He unlocked the
door and stepped inside. Phyllo peered in after him.
Outwardly the cupboard had the dimensions of a large
wardrobe, perhaps six feet tall and then about three feet to the
side and back. Looking in through the door, however, he saw a
much longer, narrow room which stretched away twenty feet
or more, with shelves to the ceiling on either side, every shelf
packed with neatly ordered books.

Phyllo leant around the edge of the cupboard to check the
outside dimensions again then glanced over to Roly, who
looked equally as baffled as Phyllo felt. The inside and outside
were different shapes.

Albertus ran a finger along the edge of a shelf, muttering
references as he went, then plucked a book from mid-height.
The cover was a harlequin check of dusky pink and yellow. A
small rubber chicken dangled on a ribbon over the top of the

spine. "Classic Clowning iconography," said Albertus appreciatively and clutched the book to his chest. "Excuse me, boys. Coming through, coming through." They moved aside and Albertus made off down the stairs to lay the book on his desk. Roly followed, but Phyllo lingered, drifting into the impossible cupboard.

He'd almost been afraid to step on the floor, but it was solid enough and the way it was built felt comfortingly familiar. It had the same kind of structure as the Confectionary. The ceiling arched in a polished wooden bow, much like the ceiling over their kitchen, and the shelves were solid and wooden too, with a brass protective rail a couple of inches up that would prevent anything from falling off. The books were pristine initially, but he could see, as he continued to travel along the shelves, that they became older and more dishevelled the further into the room he went.

Down at his desk, Albertus was speaking. "Now let me see. Something happy from the past? Let's have a look. Emmett has been with the Circus of Wonder for a good long time. We should have an accurate record. I hear their Archivist is excellent." Albertus's snorky laugh travelled up to the mezzanine and made Phyllo smile.

On the very top shelf he spotted a whole section of books with spines wrapped in a uniform baby blue satin and, as he strained to look, noticed ladder rungs on the leading edges of the shelves. He checked the door over his shoulder and then climbed a couple of rungs to peer at them. As he'd suspected, it was the Volante family. Birdie first, although her name, as it turned out, was actually Bernice. Her volume was thin, only half an inch. There were others for Ezio and Arnaldo; the whole family was there, Nonna Sophia's thickest and furthest from the door.

Phyllo looked over to the opposite side. Other books were also stored in co-ordinated groups. Dark leather with rivets; mauve silk with long emerald tassels hanging at their spines; scarlet velvet that sparkled with rhinestones. Phyllo assumed that every member of the troupe must have had a book there.

"Come around to this side, Roly, and perhaps you might glimpse something too, through the magnifying glass." Albertus's voice drifted in and Phyllo climbed down from the shelves and came out onto the mezzanine.

"I'll ask the book for something sensory. I assume that's the ticket. A smell? A flavour? At a happy moment, yes?"

Roly nodded and Albertus drew symbols in the air over the book with his filigreed pen. Pages flipped in a rushed fan then settled. Phyllo hurried down the stairs to join them and stood on the other side of the desk to also see the book. Wisps of smoke gathered into the form of a person walking, skipping almost. "It's a garden," Roly exclaimed, getting closer to the magnifying glass. Phyllo could only see a layer of fog surrounding the indistinct human form.

"Happy enough, do you think?" asked Albertus.

The smoky figure reached up to pull something down to its face. "Is he eating something from a tree?" asked Phyllo, unable to make out what was happening.

"Honeysuckle. He's smelling honeysuckle," said Albertus.

"And he's eating a lolly. What do you think that is, Albertus? Looks a bit like a lemon-pop."

Phyllo, really couldn't see that and tried to come around behind them to also look through the glass, but their heads blocked the view.

"Yes, I'd say so," replied Albertus, "They really were all the rage at one time. All the rage."

"Brilliant. That's a great combination." Roly turned around

to Phyllo who was forced to step back as they were now almost nose to nose. "Probably not a toffee, which is a shame because that's the only thing I've really got the hang of. What about a boiled sweet?"

"Or a jelly?" Phyllo suggested.

"Yes! A jelly. Perfect."

Albertus closed the book. "Will that do you then, boys?"

"Yes. Thank you, Albertus. That's brilliant." Roly's face was alive with enthusiasm, "Come on, Phyllo, let's check the stores."

The Horseshoe Path was already taking shape, with more than half the cabins out in position, the Confectionary amongst them. Up ahead, Frú Hafiz tugged at the swags of mauve silk that draped in a canopy over her door. In this half-light her pale face reminded Phyllo of the moon. He was always a little in awe of her, but right then she looked more mystical than ever. She greeted them in her clipped manner, "Are you well, Masters Phyllo and Roly?"

"Brilliant," said Roly, still overflowing with energy for their discovery. She looked faintly amused by his exuberance. "And you, Master Phyllo? You do not seem to share your brother's joy."

"Oh no, I do, it's just, you know."

"One cannot have sweet without a dash of salt." She folded her arms and tucked her hands into the opposing cuffs of her jacket.

"You've been talking to my dad," Phyllo replied with a smile.

"It is better to deal with problems before they arise. The

pen is mightier, isn't that what they say? Did my Page of Swords give you what you need?"

Phyllo's brow furrowed.

"Albertus."

"Er, yes. I think so." Phyllo hesitated. "Roly seems to have been inspired anyway."

"But not you. Of course, he sees it so much more clearly. I find it's best to focus on the ambiguities."

The boys looked at each other. It was going to be one of *those* conversations.

"Right."

Frú Hafiz tweaked a pleat in the silky fabric to smooth it flat and stepped back to take in the whole. "At least one gloom is lifting," she said with a sigh and looked past them to the brightening morning sky. Phyllo hadn't slept at all. Suddenly his eyes were arid with fatigue.

"Destiny reveals at its own pace. The true nature of a thing is rarely presented by the mask it wears."

Phyllo blinked at her.

"Roly! There you are." Their father was hurrying across the path to meet them. "And Phyllo too. How *are* you? Aldo treating you well? You look tired. Exhausted. Are they working you too hard? Shall I have a word, eh?" Marvel gestured over his shoulder.

"Dad. Really, I'm fine." He brushed it off, but felt the relief of having an actual parent there, looking out for him. He suddenly realised just how much he'd missed it.

"That business with the mechanism, everything OK?" His father's face crinkled with concern.

"It seemed OK in the end, but I don't know if it's gone up. I should check." Phyllo worried at his lip.

"Yes. Yes, you should. Apologise. Ice it over, eh?"

"But I didn't do anything to apologise for. I'm sure I put my things away."

"It doesn't really seem like you, I must admit, but you ought to assure him of your best intentions, eh? At the very least."

The last time Signor Volante had engaged with Phyllo he'd been livid with rage. He wasn't sure how a statement of *best intentions* would go down.

Phyllo screwed one foot into the ground. "Dad, do you think you could come with me?" His father's unexpected presence now seemed like a necessity.

Marvel smoothed down the breast of his coat. "I mean, it's only Aldo. He's mostly bluster, isn't he?" Marvel pasted on a smile and stretched out a hand. "Oh, come on then. No time like the present, eh?" But they hadn't even taken a step before the Ringmaster came over to break them up. He'd come from the river.

"By count of moorings the market's expanded appreciably since last season and there'll be just as many day boats." His heavily shadowed eyes shone with determination. "The Coin is here if we can seize it. Finish the set and we can run a matinee. I assume your shelves need filling, Marvel? No time for standing about."

"Right you are, Ringmaster." Marvel's hand dropped and he looked regretfully to Phyllo.

"Get about it then. See if your apprentice can't earn his crust." He patted Roly on the shoulder and turned him around, toward the Confectionary. For once, he ignored Phyllo completely.

∼

Phyllo cut his way back to the Birdcage through the big top. Engineers buzzed around the rafters reinstalling systems, and a handful of the Volante family checked rigging and the solidity of platforms. They were too busy to take any notice of him, but their spirits seemed up and he took this as a good sign.

The Birdcage itself looked completely normal. Outwardly, the tower was up and straight, the striped canvas that covered it taut and correct, as far as he could tell. From inside, he could pick up the rumble of conversation. Signor Volante and some of the others. His feet didn't want to take him over the threshold, but he knew that he'd have to face them all sooner or later. He dragged himself in and found ten or so family members sitting around the table, eating breakfast. Eyes lifted to register his arrival. Conversation faded. Aldo Volante, who sat in his usual chair, carefully put down his cup.

Phyllo's mouth dried. "Er, m-morning, everyone," he managed.

Nobody said anything. Now their eyes were on Signor Volante. Jaw clenched, he beckoned Phyllo to him with large shovel-like hands. Phyllo shuffled over, his insides squirming. The silence was unbearable.

"Last night, Phyllo, we had a problem. A *big* problem." He stared ferociously into Phyllo's eyes. "Our mechanism is specific, unique." He pinched his fingers together and squinted. "Just like the Fabulous Volante, huh?"

Phyllo nodded mutely.

He slapped the back of one hand down into the palm of the other. "You *must* clear your bunk. Everything *must* go into the locker. *Everything*. The door *must* be shut. *Tight*. Our bunks: they fold into each other. When we move, they don't exist."

"I know. Really, Signor Volante, I put my things away. Really I—"

Signor Volante held up a hand to stop Phyllo speaking.

"I have heard. I will no make you swallow the toad. You thought you did your best, but you should know, your best was not good enough. You must be better."

Phyllo blinked down to his toes.

"Now this is enough." Signor Volante picked up his coffee and the rest of the family took it as a sign to go on about their business. Nonna Sophia rounded the table, took hold of Phyllo by the shoulders and steered him into a seat. She poured a little thick coffee into a large cup, topped it up with steaming milk and gave it to him. "Pastries or something hot? Frittata? How do you feel?" She pinched at Phyllo's cheeks with both hands. "You are so pale!" She rubbed his arms up and down violently then pinched at his cheeks some more. Phyllo wasn't sure he'd ever get used to her rough-housing, but he'd seen her give Ezio similar treatment and come to the conclusion that it was nothing personal.

"Just tired, I think." He took an experimental sip of the milky coffee and grimaced at its bitterness. Nonna Sophia heaped three spoonsful of sugar into it and pushed it back to him. A frittata was very appealing, but Phyllo's eyes were drooping so badly, he didn't think he could stay awake long enough for her to cook it. He picked up an almond croissant from the pile in the centre of the table. "This'll be fine, thanks," he said and proceeded to wolf it down.

"Up to bed," Nonna Sophia instructed, "The first show is still half the day away and you'll be no good to anyone without sleep." Phyllo mutely obeyed. The others were drifting off to their cots too, a dozy hush falling over the place. He climbed up to his bed on autopilot. His bed was clear so he had to go into the cupboard to pull out his blanket. The photograph of his family tumbled out with it – the frame was cracked.

∾

When Phyllo awoke he discovered that, once again, he was the last out of bed. The table was clear and not a single other person was in sight, not even Nonna Sophia.

He threw on his blues and, desperately hoping that he wasn't in yet more trouble, dashed to the ring. Eight or nine of the Volantes, including Arnaldo and Signor Volante stood there, looking up. Marco swung on one trapeze, the costume of the Pirate Captain flapping about him, and Columba sat on the other, swaying gently.

"The cape wraps around him too much. Is too clumsy," Signor Volante muttered to Arnaldo, "We need a better design. It's slowing him down."

"We need it for story-telling on the landing. It envelopes Columba. It's how the audience knows she's been captured," Arnaldo replied.

"I no like it."

"It's a modern interpretation. More choreographed. We have to move with the times. Our audiences expect theatre."

Signor Volante sighed. "Shorter at the very least, huh?"

"Alright, Uncle Aldo."

"OK. Marco! Columba! Starting positions. Show me." He clapped his hands and both flyers swung back to their platforms.

"Ready. Hup."

Both swung out, acting out their part in the show where the Lady is trying to escape the Pirate Captain's clutches. Marco stood on the bar, reaching out for Columba every time their trapezes got closer together, but from where Phyllo was standing it was clear: the bars were always much too far apart. Watching Marco lean into thin air made Phyllo's palms sweat. Stepping from one trapeze to the other looked utterly impossible from where he was standing, but he knew that was exactly what Marco would do.

"Really kick it for the next two, Marco," Signor Volante called from the ground and Marco did as he was told, pushing down on the bar at the peaks, driving it on, higher and faster. "Launch high and swoop down on her – a bat capturing its prey. Next peak." He waited for Marco to reach the crest and clapped his hands together at the exact moment Marco should release to fly to Columba. The team on the ground stood with their feet apart and legs bent. The sash at Phyllo's waist felt suddenly heavy and he flexed against it, the rest of the team flexing too. Phyllo's hair stood on end, sucked upward with the energy. Marco seemed to hang impossibly in the air as Columba swung inevitably toward him. The pirate cape billowed menacingly around him and he dropped onto the cowering Lady's bar, wrapping her in the sleek black fabric as he landed. Her bar swung back to the other platform and they stepped off backward, fluid and wrong. Marco's performance was pure evil.

Signor Volante folded his arms and nodded appreciatively. He raised his eyebrows to Arnaldo. "OK, the cape can stay."

The team whooped and cheered as Marco bowed theatrically from the platform, finally stepping off to land in the net. He jogged over to stand by Phyllo.

"I think it is your turn, no?" He raised one eyebrow at Phyllo, but it wasn't the snarky, odd expression he'd seen earlier that morning, the expression that had reminded him of

Emmett's reflection. It was the expression of a gently teasing fifteen-year-old boy.

"Oh, no, I'm fine, really," Phyllo mumbled, taking a step back. Arnaldo noticed their conversation and came over to join in. "He's right. Come on, Phyllo, you shouldn't wait too long."

"No. No. It's too soon."

"It's the perfect time," said Marco.

"Si, si," Arnaldo agreed. And then they were either side of him, guiding him over to the ladder. Phyllo had a distinct feeling of déjà vu as Marco raced up the ladder in front and Arnaldo put one foot on the first rung. He was just considering how he might escape when Arnaldo threw his arms wide, encompassing Phyllo and the ladder within their reach. His left hand rolled over to show the way up. "Confidence is everything," he said.

"And momentum," Phyllo replied drearily. Arnaldo smiled and Phyllo got on.

The ladder didn't buck about in the crazy manner it had done before. For one thing Arnaldo was weighing it down, but for another, Phyllo had learnt a little from his travels up and down inside the Birdcage to his bed. He'd found his centre of gravity and that little bit of knowledge did wonders for him now. He climbed.

"Look up," Marco called from above and Phyllo tore his eyes away from the receding ring. "It's better to know where you are going than where you have been."

"Easy for you to say," Phyllo grumbled, but he made it to the platform and side-stepped over to the left where he could cling on to the rigging. The ground swam about alarmingly and his stomach rolled.

"OK?" Marco asked, dipping a little to look Phyllo directly in the eye. He smiled a gap-toothed smile. His teeth were straight, but there were pronounced spaces in between, like he still need a couple more to fill his jaw. It was a bit of a relief that Marco didn't have quite as much good-looking panache as his older brothers. His hair, although thick and black, didn't fall in the sultry waves of Arnaldo, rather grew directly outward in a hairstyle that just got bigger over time, rather than longer. It reminded Phyllo a little of his own.

"I'll be your board monkey. Come on, it's fun." Marco hooked the trapeze, brought it in closer and tied it off. "Just make a few swings, get a feel for it. Everybody's here to help."

Phyllo looked down over the edge and indeed the selection of the troupe in the ring were all looking back, smiling encouragingly. "But I can't hold on. My grip's not strong enough. Last time, I just slid off."

"With practice you'll get better, but you have to practise, no?" Marco's eyes were bright "Here." He threw a fat pink pouch at Phyllo from a copper bucket attached to the rigging. It hit him square in the chest with a soft 'poof', emitted a cloud of white dust and plopped to the floor.

"You were supposed to catch it, *stupido*." Marco laughed, the whole top half of his body flopping about with mirth. He was too close to the edge. Phyllo wished he'd stand still.

"Pick it up then. It won't help your grip from there." Marco waved his arms about exuberantly and Phyllo released one hand to scoop it up. Chalk. Marco mimed passing it from one hand to the other, nodding, and Phyllo released his other hand to do just that.

"*Buono*. Now come and take the bar."

Phyllo peered over the edge again and didn't move.

"What's wrong? Are you worried you might fall?"

"Well, you know, it's only natural."

Marco folded his arms and nodded sincerely. His heels

159

were right at the very edge of the platform. "What would happen if you fell?"

"Well, you know, it's a long way down."

Marco stood upright but gradually, almost imperceptibly, was leaning back. Further and further. Then he was beyond his centre of gravity and then leaning much too far and then falling. "Aaaaarrrggghhhhh!" he yelled and Phyllo scrambled forwards to see him land flat on his back in the net, a big dopey grin on his face.

Phyllo coughed and spluttered, residual chalk from the pouch hitting the back of his already dry throat. Marco rolled off the net and sprinted back up to the platform.

"Not funny," Phyllo grumbled.

"Ah, come on. Have a go. It's OK. You're safe, I promise. I'll go first. Look. Do what I do." Marco took hold of the bar and bent at the knees. "Ready. Hup," he said, jumped up and swung away. "Point your toes," he yelled, "Aim for the roof and then push through with your chest." He swung backwards, toward him. "Then try to get behind the bar again on the return, push the bar down to get your body up." He swung up a little higher than seemed possible. "And again." He swung away once more. "Then let go after the peak. Sitting position. Arms out to the side." He dropped to the net. He made it look so easy, which of course it was. For him. Marco sprinted back up to the platform, this time having the decency to be a bit out of breath when he got there. "Now you."

Phyllo clambered to his feet while Marco caught the bar and pulled it in.

"Are you sure it doesn't come any nearer than that?"

Marco grinned, got behind Phyllo and gripped the back of his sash. "Bend. Lean. Grip it, really grip it for all you are worth. You can reach it. Do it! Do it! Do it!" Marco's style of encouragement was somewhat less refined than his older brother's.

"Don't let go until I say!" Phyllo snapped, managing to get hold of one end of the bar.

"OK, OK."

He caught hold of the other end and poked his bottom backward, standing like that terrified duck again.

"Ready—"

"No, no, no. Not ready."

Marco sighed, but continued to grip Phyllo's sash, neither talking nor moving. Phyllo glared at the bar and tried not to notice the ground swimming about. He took a deep breath. "Ready."

"Hup." Marco let go and Phyllo jumped.

Just do what he said, Phyllo screamed inside his own head. He squeezed the bar with all his strength and pointed his toes ahead. The peak came and went without him managing to thrust his chest anywhere and, as he swung back, he thought he might have more of a chance of getting behind the bar, like Marco had suggested. He pushed the bar down and rose much higher than he'd expected.

"Again," Marco yelled behind him and Phyllo rushed away through the air, wind pushing into his eyeballs. This time he felt like he at least managed to straighten up at the peak before tearing backwards again.

"Push! Push!" Marco yelled and Phyllo got up even higher behind the bar that time. He flew away once more, toes pointing, although not really at the ceiling, and then he knew he was travelling backwards again.

He heard a clap and Marco's voice yell, "drop," and he let go of the bar, plummeted for a terrible terrifying eternity and then sank into the net. All motion gently stalled. He was amazed, wide-eyed and panting.

The Volante family around the ring broke out in applause. Signor Volante beckoned him to the edge. "*Buono, buono, Phyllo, here.*"

Once he was off, Marco dropped down into the net too and scrabbled to join him. He grabbed Phyllo in a hug and squeezed him. "How do you feel?" Marco demanded.

It took a moment for Phyllo to organise his thoughts. "Wonderful. It was wonderful," he eventually said. Then his legs gave way.

CHAPTER FOURTEEN

Market Forces

There wasn't any more time for practising after that. The Ringmaster had demanded a matinee show and the engineers pulled out every stop to make sure that happened. At midday the big top was primed and, with show time fast approaching, the Agile Arethusa went out into the market to flick-flack through the crowds. They returned thirty minutes later trailing an excitable snake of people who filled the house.

It bode extraordinarily well.

Buoyed by his small, but significant, progress, Phyllo threw himself into his performance, not that this seemed to please Birdie in the least. She frowned and scowled throughout, barely even meeting his eye. It wasn't until after, when the junior cast members were sent into the market to hand out flyers, that he got any sense of what the problem was.

"I can't find Buffo," she said, "I've been looking for him all day. He hasn't even had any breakfast." Birdie wrapped thin arms about her own waist. "I don't know where he could be." Her shrew-like face was even more pinched than usual.

Then Phyllo remembered. He'd seen Buffo out in the field in Shady Hollow, just before they'd left. He'd not rushed out to grab him as the Ringmaster had been right there, he'd presumed, seeing the same thing. And then it was too late and they'd left. Birdie scowled down at the ground. Phyllo was already in massive trouble with the Ringmaster. Telling tales on him didn't seem smart.

"I haven't seen him today either," he said, a compromise which he told himself was true.

"Try and put a smile on it," Roly growled, through gritted teeth, "We're supposed to be selling tickets here." All three of them cranked their smiles up a notch and handed out the leaflets as quickly as possible.

The river market positively hummed with activity. Moored vendors stretched along the near and far banks as far as the eye could see, day boats squeezed into gaps and stacked away into the slow flowing water in a vibrant carpet of packed pontoons and bobbing coracles.

Shoppers gathered on the banks, where they shouted requests to eagle-eyed merchants. Baskets of produce and cork jars for payment passed between the vendors in a constant and instinctive stream. Exotic fruits, spices and vegetables ferried over the water and into shoppers' baskets. Voices battled to be heard and punters elbowed their way to the front.

This side of the river was jam-packed with *ordinaries*. They never ventured to the other bank, put off, they thought, by the rickety bridge that creaked ominously under foot. Phyllo wondered if any of them ever suspected the spell cast over it which meant that only the *charmed* could cross.

Phyllo, Roly and Birdie squeezed through the melee, dropping their leaflets into baskets and pressing them into hands. Further along, coracles gave way to narrowboats, moored side on with gangplanks extended.

The hectic crowd mercifully thinned and gave them space enough to breathe. Vendors became artisans: artists, potters and tailors. A rainbow of fabrics leant against the side of one long boat, copper pots of every shape and size on another, that squatted low in the water. Roly took a fancy to that one. "Let's look inside," he said.

It was like walking into a treasure vault. Gleaming copper shone all around, twinkling in the flickering light of oil lamps, which were also for sale. Candlesticks and lamp bases; saucepans in varying capacities, from a teacup's worth to ten gallons; ornate shisha pipes; coffee pots and toast racks. The variety was as huge as the interior was small. The boat creaked beneath their feet and bobbed gently on ripples that slapped and gurgled between boat and bank. The three of them wandered through the maze of untidily heaped baskets, picking up items here and there to inspect them.

Roly paused at a display of jelly moulds. "I wonder," he said, and pulled out a tray covered with lemon shaped impressions.

"Perfect," said Phyllo, guessing that Roly was considering it for Emmett's surprise.

The brazier himself now sat at a workbench beside the only door. He tapped away with a small chisel and hammer, etching a pattern on a large copper platter. Thick denim overalls covered him from shoulder to ankle. He also wore a grey Hungarian felt hat which folded back on itself like a shirt cuff at his brow, and a full beard of a similar salt and pepper grey. Roly waved the mould above his head to attract attention. "How much for this one?" he called.

The man plucked a small pair of wire spectacles from his breast pocket and peered at Roly through the lenses, without putting them on. "Re-tinned that myself. Best quality. Leema and two pumpkins."

Not Coin. Phyllo had forgotten that the river merchants

had their own lingo when it came to dealing with money and the *charmed*. He was sure it was only to confuse you into paying more.

Roly nodded and said to Phyllo in a whisper, "So a leema, that's seven and a pumpkin, I think that's three quarters, isn't it? So, eight and a half. Eight and a half Coin! For this?"

The man shrugged and went back to tapping away with his little hammer.

"It's not worth more than three, surely," he said to Phyllo quietly, "What's that in the lingo?"

"I think that's a squid."

"Yeah, that's it," Roly nodded. "I'll give you a squid," he said more loudly.

The shopkeeper blew out a breath. "A leema or you can get off my boat."

Roly looked back to Phyllo who was racking his brain for more monetary terms. "Tell him you'll give him five pumpkins and a parrot."

"How much is that?"

"Four and three quarters. They like it when you make the maths hard."

Roly made his offer and it did raise a smile.

"Alright then. My final offer. Three sprouts and a duck pudding," said the brazier.

"A duck pudding? You're making that up!" Roly scoffed incredulously, but leant into Phyllo and said out of the corner of his mouth, "That's not a thing, is it?"

The boat sloshed on a wave. Long-handled saucepans swung above their heads and pots tinked as they slid together on a shelf. The water line portholes revealed a scarlet gondola hull with extravagant golden scrolls gliding past.

"Oh, I think the parade has started," said Birdie, straining to see, "Hurry up, you two. Let's get outside."

They made their way to the door and Roly put down five Coin with a hopeful expression. The brazier scooped it up. "Have a pleasant evening," he said, gave Roly the glimmer of a smile and went back to his work.

The scarlet gondola was the first of many outlandishly decorated boats that travelled in procession from beyond the bend in the river. They were a noisy bunch, all bringing their own little party, honking horns and whirling clackers. Music came from some of the larger ones, where entire bands perched precariously on little stools on deck. The decorations and costumes varied from colourful flag-waving to enormous representations of river animals. A giant rat's head peered up river between bobbing hulls before finally gliding up beside them. Huge, furry and brown, it was the figurehead to a gondola also covered in fur. The people on board danced about, laughing. Phyllo caught the delicious scent of caramelising chestnuts on the air. Roly and Birdie caught it too and they all scanned about for the source.

"There," said Phyllo. He pointed over to the other bank where a gaggle of food stalls crowded around a busy jetty, belching smoke and wonderful aromas. The arching wooden bridge that only permitted the *charmed* to cross provided the means to reach it. They were drawn across the river by their stomachs and tucking into a cone of chestnuts each a couple of minutes later. They wandered along the bank eating and commenting on the parade.

"Ha, look at that one," said Roly to Birdie, "That reminds me of you." A gondola with a great papier-mâché swan's head at its prow passed them next. Enthusiastic revellers in white feathers flapped wings on either side. Birdie sniffed.

167

An altogether darker boat came along next. Black on every surface, its passengers wore the rippling tissue-paper costumes of black birds. Hoods veiled their heads and long black cones covered their faces. They beat a single drum, slowly and evenly. The costume wearers stood with feet splayed and legs bent, waving their fists at the crowd. The crowd on their side of the river booed back with pantomime fervour. A clearly inebriated fellow a short distance away mooned at them to the great hilarity of his friends.

"Who are *they* meant to be?" said Phyllo.

"The Crows, of course. Don't you know the Crows when you see 'em? I'll give you they ain't the best costumes I seen, but still."

They turned to face the source of the voice.

A girl, no taller than Birdie, stood with her hands on her hips, considering them beadily. "'S'pect you ain't had no dealings. Nice law-abiding folks you are, no doubt. I s'pose they've more interest in the oath breakers." She examined Roly's striped jacket. "Candy man?" she said, eyes lighting up with recognition, "You're with the Circus of Wonder. Got any to share?"

"That's right and no." Roly tried on a smile, but it faded.

The girl was filthy. Her face not so much smeared with dirt, as infused. She wore a purple velvet jacket, cut for a boy and too short in the arm. It pulled at her waist on the last remaining button. Her grubby cotton dress drooped at the hem and her ankle boots, although very similar, weren't quite the same colour or style.

"Circus folk don't have dealings with the Crows. They're just for us poor souls who have to pick a living from the road. And the river sometimes."

"Poor souls?" said Birdie. "If you're a criminal then that's your problem. The Crows are here to protect us. If there's no law and order—"

"Blacker than black. Shows what you know if you think they're do-gooders." She looked along the path, as if she were expecting someone. The creases in her expression smoothed out and her eyes shifted into a sad, puppyish droop. "Won't you help a poor stray? Save me from a life of crime? I've nothing in the world, save the few things I'm selling so as I can buy a crust for supper."

Phyllo looked to Roly and Birdie, rolling his eyes at the terrible acting. "What do you mean?" he asked suspiciously.

She snatched up a hanky from the collapsible table she'd been standing in front of and held it out. It was bloodstained. "Only a sprout. I'm sure you could spare it. That little mark'd scrub right out."

Phyllo leant away from it. "Er, no thanks."

"Like the finer things? What about this?" She held up a grimy wallet.

"Come on, you two." Birdie tugged at Phyllo's sleeve to pull him on, "She's a Tosher. Don't buy that. It's probably stolen."

"How dare you?" said the ragged girl, "This here belonged to my old mum."

"That's no recommendation."

"Bedridden she is."

"That'll be the gin."

The ingratiating smile dropped from her face. "You want to be careful, nice young folks like you on this side of the river after dark."

It *had* got rather dark suddenly.

Birdie and the girl looked coldly at each other.

"Look, a Green Finger – I wonder if he's got any honey-suckle," Roly said and broke away.

"You really need to work on your interpersonal skills, Birdie," said Phyllo and they hurried on to keep up with him.

"There's no point being nice. She'd only take advantage."

Phyllo looked back over his shoulder and the girl called out, "I'll fend off the Lord Protector Corvus on me own then, shall I? In it for the Coin, they are, not the justice. They keep what they take, even if that means your life, but don't you worry about me." She put on a pout and folded her arms crossly, but Phyllo could see the act fading.

He turned back and they pushed on through the crowd, heading for the Green Finger's trolley. Birdie, however, pulled Phyllo up short at a stall selling curios made of mirror, while Roly barrelled on. She'd spotted a music box with a tiny balle-rina pirouetting inside.

Phyllo feigned interest, but his eyes skipped from reflection to reflection in the mirrors on the stall, watching the parade float past. The next gondola was a riot of harlequin pattern and cavorting jesters. They waved and capered about, occa-sionally throwing a sweet out to the crowd and waving balloons on ribbon-wrapped sticks. Their striped baggy costumes rippled with the late summer breeze. Then one stepped forward from the middle of the pack. He was much taller and leaner, his costume old fashioned. Battered tin bells jingled on ribbons from the tips of his tri-horned hat, the ruffle at his neck was a murky garnet red that matched his studded tunic. He stepped off his own boat and onto the Crows', leaning forward purposefully, his face set in a sneer. Then there were shrieks and splashes and the reflections were lost in a surge of people.

Phyllo turned around to try to see what was happening.

Some of the crowd were laughing, but others seemed to be stumbling backwards, away from the edge. Phyllo stood on tiptoe straining to see. A bedraggled crow splashed about in the river, their cardboard 'beak' pushed up over one eye. Then there were more screams and the splashes of others falling in.

Phyllo craned his neck to search the crowd for Roly, who'd gone on ahead. Raking the faces he found, not his brother, but a black full-face mask with a long, curving beak, its wearer staring directly back – the Tabberstock thief who'd held the knife to his throat. Icy fear ran down the back of Phyllo's neck. Then the crowd surged into the space between them, blocking him from view.

"Roly!" Phyllo yelled. He fought his way forward, through the dense and undulating waves of people. "Roly?" The In-between were here in the market, of course they were. He'd been a fool not to suspect it. He lunged out into a gap by the Green Finger's cart and found Roly, mid purchase with a smile on his face. "Sounds like someone's fallen in," he laughed, "Honeysuckle." Roly waggled the pot in his hand which held a small leafy plant, bound to a stick.

"In-between," Phyllo gasped.

A large man who'd been one of the mooner's friends, rolled backwards out of the crowd, slopping his mug of beer over the next man to his right. "Oi, watch what you're doin', ya great clumsy oaf!" the wet man shouted. The first man lurched to his feet and angrily gave him a shove. The other shoved back. More people stumbled backwards, tripping over each other, cursing and pushing. The combination of shock and fear on their faces swiftly becoming annoyance and indignation. After that fists started to fly.

Roly's smile sagged. Birdie flopped out of the melee into the space by Phyllo's side.

"Let's get out of here," Phyllo said urgently and they cut around the rear of the stalls to beat a path through the long grass. Back to the bridge whose thin boards flexed and popped as they thundered across.

They shoved through the huddle of *ordinary* shoppers and sprinted across the flat grass, running for the Circus of Wonder.

Phyllo didn't slow down until he'd crossed the threshold of the horseshoe, where he galumphed to a halt and flopped over, gasping. Roly collapsed to his hands and knees. Birdie was hardly out of breath. She rolled her eyes.

They all looked back the way they'd come and a clump of people on the far side of the river could still be seen pushing each other around. But before long, all the hot tempers seemed to have been doused, some by a dip in the river.

The rhythm of movement returned. The tussle between the Jesters and Crows now just a memory from a day at the market.

"It was him," panted Phyllo, at last able to speak, "The one with the knife, back in Tabberstock. The one who took Arif and Shadi. I saw him in the crowd."

"Took Arif and Shadi?" Roly puffed, "The Ringmaster threw them out, didn't he?"

"And then the In-between picked them up. They had him tied up in the stores, I saw him."

Roly's eyes were wide with shock. "Why didn't you say?"

"Everything's been a bit crazy, I don't know. Maybe it was because of Dodo? She's scared enough and the Ringmaster was looking for someone to pin it all on. It's not their fault, it didn't seem fair."

They stared across the field at the market together, their breathing easing. No-one seemed to be following them.

"And it wasn't just him. Did you see that Jester, the one that stepped off their boat?" asked Phyllo.

"What about him?" said Birdie.

"This is going to sound crackers. I knew there was something about him right away, something wrong, but I've only just placed it. It'll be better if I show you. It's in the Birdcage." Phyllo jogged away and the other two trailed behind. He dashed up to his cot and came back to where they waited on the path as quickly as he could and thrust a yellowing piece of paper into Roly's hand.

"It's the old poster from the pub," said Birdie, recognising it.

"Look at the Jester. Look at what he's wearing. The tri-horn hat with little bells? The dark red ruff? That fitted tunic? Any of that look familiar?"

"I didn't see him, mate," said Roly.

"I did," said Birdie, "Just for a moment. I saw his reflection in one of the mirrors." She took the poster in her own hands. "Even that make-up looks familiar, and those pointy eyebrows."

"It's him. I'm sure of it."

"It does look like him, but it can't be Phyllo, this poster's from years ago," Birdie admonished. She thrust it back into his hands. "Look, it'll be show time soon and I want to look for Buffo. Keep an eye out for him?" The boys nodded and watched as she hurried away.

"And that's another thing," Phyllo said in a low voice to Roly. "I don't think she's going to find that dog any time soon."

"No?" Roly asked.

"I think he got left behind in Shady Hollow. I'm sure the

Ringmaster saw him out in the field just as well as I did, but he ordered the seal and left him behind."

"You're kidding."

Phyllo shook his head.

"But why would Barker do that?"

"I don't know, but it's just one more person behaving strangely, don't you think? Since we got diverted to Shady Hollow, I can't help but think something's changed, that people are behaving oddly. There's Emmett, the Volantes fighting last night and Marco's face this morning. What just happened at the market, even. People behaving badly one moment and then back to normal the next. It's weird."

The evening show came quickly around and, despite his delight in performing earlier in the day, Phyllo just couldn't summon up the same level of enthusiasm for a second time around. He had the unshakeable feeling that something was wrong, but couldn't pin down quite what.

When Arnaldo asked if he was OK during show prep, Phyllo snapped, he knew unfairly, and eventually found he was unable to stay in the Birdcage any longer. He needed to pace, to prowl, to think. He made his excuses and slipped out to backstage.

The Brampton Levels crowd was a big one and the evening house promised to be packed. Undoubtedly, this was good news for the troupe, but Phyllo gnawed at his fingernails thinking about who might slip in unnoticed in the mixed crowd. He'd already seen the Crow Man, surely there would be others?

The big top was still closed, that night's revellers being gradually corralled in the horseshoe to spend their money before the show. For now, it offered Phyllo relative peace. Engineers marched purposefully about, making final adjustments and calling out to each other, but they weren't interested in him. He could wander freely beneath the stands at the perimeter, listening to the gathering crowd on the other side of the canvas. Listening for peculiarities, listening for quarrels or screams.

He prised open a closed flap and frowned out at the horseshoe. Only a small section was visible to him: the stretch outside the Ringmaster and Albertus's cabins. At show time it was the start of the path. He could see Skinner and Bain leaning by the gate, their engineer black and tan uniform topped off by red and white striped bowler hats. It was their nod to a costume, but to Phyllo's eye they were plainly security. He didn't have much time for them usually: they were the Ringmaster's lackeys, bull-headed and ruthless, but tonight, he was pleased they were on the same side.

Show-goers were starting to gather. Lamp-lit and jewel bright, the horseshoe presented its temptations. Ilmar, the balloon sculptor, squeaked long balloons of lime and pearly white into frogs and unicorns for small children, who tugged pleadingly on parental jacket hems.

Closer to his vantage point, Taya was delighting a young man with some close-up magic. By rights, she was the magician's assistant, but had stepped in many years ago to help Marvel when he'd found himself alone. Now she worked the entrance confectionary stand before performances and enjoyed it. Not yet allowed to perform her own tricks in the show, she liked to practise sleight of hand with sweets for customers as they arrived. She plucked a strawberry ring from behind the

175

young man's ear. "You'd better buy that one," she laughed and, thoroughly charmed, he did.

The mood out there seems light enough, Phyllo thought. The cast he could see were plying their trade and weaving their magic just like always. More people came and the crowd thickened. Phyllo knew the Ringmaster would keep the grand entrance closed until the last moment to extract maximum possible Coin from their visitors. Frú Hafiz and the Odditorium, toys, confections and mementoes: it was all an opportunity to prise a little more from their purse. Revellers from the banks of the market joined the scrum, many of them a few drinks down and wearing carnival masks. The sight of them made Phyllo's stomach quiver.

Out of sight the automaton orchestra of the steam organ burst into life, the theme of the circus piping out into the atmosphere. It fought against the babble of the crowd and geed them on to be louder still. The base drum pounded inside its box, thumping the beat into Phyllo's chest and the xylophone tinkled out its melody, but the usually sweet notes rang sour and off key: flat notes just shy: uncomfortable and jarring. Phyllo strained to hear it better. A voice called out over the din, peddling cutlasses and ribboned stars on sticks, Taya called out too, sing-song and sweet, "Toffees and candyfloss! Sherbet hearts and chocolate pigs!" Phyllo strained to pick out the organ, but it was lost in the cacophony. Revellers squeezed through ever decreasing gaps to make their way along the path, gossiping and laughing. One woman wore a sequinned cat mask with long feathery whiskers; a man held a black and white harlequin mask on a wand.

Phyllo's heart beat faster and he tried to swallow away the dry knot gathering in his throat. "Everything's OK," he told himself, "Just another night on the path."

Behind him an engineer shouted out to his mate, "Open her up, Carlisle. Final check clear," and Phyllo felt the quality of the air around him change. The big top was open. The audience were coming in.

He jogged around to the wings, keeping under the stands and out of sight. "Just calm down, Phyllo," he told himself, "You're being a baby."

Backstage on the path, he could hear excited chatter drifting out from all quarters; the prospect of a full house was lifting the troupe in a thrill of anticipation.

Marco slapped Phyllo heartily on the back when he stepped back into the Birdcage.

"Tonight, I will show you the best Pirate Captain you have ever seen." He grinned his gap-toothed smile.

"Excellent," said Phyllo, doing his very best to be positive.

"One day, you will do it too."

Phyllo laughed and shook his head.

"No, really." Marco looked sincerely at him. "I will make sure of it." He pulled Phyllo in for a back-slapping hug.

"Er, OK." Phyllo didn't want to rain on his parade, but he couldn't see that happening, ever.

Marco released him and Nonna Sophia was right behind to take over. She pinched at his cheeks and rubbed his arms fiercely. "Where have you been? No food is no energy and then you'll be in a nice pie, huh? You must no leave my table without food!" She spun Phyllo around by his shoulders and spanked him. Phyllo was so surprised he didn't know how to react.

Marco snorted out a laugh.

"You no laugh! I'll get you too."

She grabbed him by the shoulders and Marco shrieked theatrically, trying to get away. They spun in a shrieking, swiping tussle with Nonna swinging at Marco's backside cackling good-naturedly and Marco arching away from her squealing. Phyllo laughed in return at Marco's expression of great indignation.

"Nonna! Nonna!" Marco wailed, "You cannot spank the Pirate Captain!"

Nonna changed tack and switched to cheek pinching. "*Piccolo bambino,*" she cooed.

"Run, Phyllo! Save yourself," Marco mumbled through his squished-up face, and Nonna Sophia released him.

"No. No. Eat please." Quite seriously she pulled Phyllo over to the table and into a seat. Marco flopped down beside him, red-faced and ruffled. Phyllo imagined Marco'd already eaten, but he swiped a wedge of cheesy panini from the plate and stared at Phyllo until he did the same. They ate in companionable silence.

The Introduction went swimmingly well, many of the audience gasping when the Ringmaster was revealed by the spotlight and Phyllo had to smooth goose-bumps from his arms as they skipped out of the tiers for the show to begin.

But still he couldn't settle, and squinted out at the crowd every few minutes, scanning compulsively for trouble. When the Clowns came on, he peered out to assess Emmett, but Emmett failed to make an appearance, Nubbins, Sprockets and Greedy Gus carrying on without him. The act followed similar lines to its usual story line, but leaned into a rather more spiteful humour with far more slapping and foot stamping than usual. The crowd laughed in all the right places, but Phyllo found it rather grim.

Then finally, the call for the Fabulous Volante came. They could get out into the ring at last. Once their act was over, he could try to find Emmett, find out why he'd not come out with the others. Far from the enthusiasm he'd felt earlier, now he just wanted to get on with it.

From the moment they stepped forward through the luscious velvet curtain however, Phyllo felt altogether different. It was clear that the Circus of Wonder had been working its magic upon the audience. The air was thick with anticipation and the audience was packed with row upon row of wide-eyed faces. They whistled and applauded, welcoming them into the ring and Phyllo, who was last to skip in, felt the troupe *expand* on the glut of positivity. The lights dimmed and Phyllo took up the fabric to play his part as a wave, watching the others around the ring for synchronisation. The music began and, as they swayed and rolled together, he became aware of an understanding settling in his mind, a jigsaw piece slotting into place: *together* they were stronger. They were a solid ring of protection. Ezio could not fall. Phyllo gazed up to watch him climb the silks, to walk on air, to fly out above the audience. Phyllo had to want to keep him safe too because now he was part of the force that held him there.

Phyllo let his eyes crawl over the audience just as Ezio's routine reached the part where he tumbled, frighteningly fast, toward the ground. Expressions changed from wonder to alarm, some raising their hands in front of their faces, gasping, others unable to tear their eyes away. The tension thickened the air with enthralment that helped Ezio climb in an impossible sweeping curve, away from the ground, cheating gravity.

Phyllo now understood that the energy of the flyers was amplified by the intensity of the audience. Ezio and Columba danced in the heights of the big top with more grace and athleticism than Phyllo had ever seen. He watched the entire act with fresh eyes. The energy lifted the hairs on his arms, the final applause a thrill through his chest. When it was over, Phyllo bowed hand in hand with the rest of the troupe, feeling enormously proud. He may not have learned much yet himself, but he thought he was starting to understand how it was done. The audience whooped and stamped their feet, they yelled for more and waved hats in the air.

Up in a high tier a group of three people got up and sidled out of their seats. Dark cloaks, the dull shine of leather. One beaked mask. Phyllo's eyes snapped to them. They moved into the shadows at the edge of the audience and out of sight.

The troupe skipped from the ring, beaming at each other, hugging and high-fiving once they'd gotten backstage. Phyllo felt drawn along with them, attached by a visceral chord, but what he'd just seen, that mask, it fogged his mind and he dawdled behind.

The joyful Volante bounced away to the Birdcage and Phyllo felt hugely relieved that good things were finally happening for the troupe. There was positive progress, for them and for him, but Emmett, now he was another matter entirely. Phyllo knew Emmett's troubles weren't any of his doing but also knew he was suffering. He wanted to help.

So as the happy Volantes disappeared, hugging and laughing, Phyllo jogged away in the opposite direction, in search of his old friend.

It became apparent quite fast that something was wrong. Shouting from the Clown Quarter: Gus's deep booming voice, "Where is it? Garibaldi damn you! Give it to me, now!"

Phyllo stopped at the open door. No-one inside looked his way.

Emmett was sprawled on the floor. His make-up was old,

probably left from the matinee. He was rumpled and grubby, his natural thin hair wild and unkempt. Gus leaned over him, fists clenched close to his chest.

"You'll give it to me or you'll be sorry!" he yelled and Emmett cowered away.

"I don't have it," he whimpered.

"What did you do with it? Where is it?" Gus was shaking with rage, tiny globules of spit flying as he spoke.

"Ah he ain't got it." Sprockets strolled out into view, hands on his hips. He took his time with his words, eyes flicking between Emmett and Gus. "Needed the Coin, didn't you, Bingo. How much did you get? How many bottles will it buy you?"

"I didn't. I wouldn't." Emmett scuttled on his hands and knees over to his dressing table and attempted to crawl underneath.

"Oh no you don't." Sprockets pounced and pulled Emmett roughly along the floor by his ankle. Now facing the door, Phyllo was shocked to see the expression on Sprockets' face. Eyebrows pointed and lip curling in a sneer. Even the shade of his make-up seemed darker. Greener. Poisonous.

"You'll give it back then," Gus shouted, closing in.

"I can't, I don't have it," Emmett cried out and covered his head with his hands.

"Do it, Gus," Sprockets growled and Gus snatched up a chair by its back and swung it over his shoulder.

"No!" Phyllo screamed from the door and, in a panic, dashed in. All three clowns snapped to face him and Phyllo saw the expression on Gus's face too, transformed from its usual rounded, jolly proportions to something angular and harsh. It was as if laying eyes on Phyllo broke a spell and their faces melted into something more familiar and confused. Gus

181

took a step back and dropped the chair to the floor, looking for all the world like he didn't know why he was holding it. Sprockets rubbed a hand over his forehead.

"Phyllo." Emmett sobbed out his name and then burst into tears.

Phyllo didn't know what to do. He stopped short of them, only a few paces into the room. "Emmett, what's happening? Why are you—? Why are they—?"

"I didn't take it. I wouldn't take it," Emmett pleaded through tears.

"What? Take what?"

Gus flopped down onto the chair and leaned an elbow on one thigh. "The bracelet. The emerald knot. He took it."

"I didn't!" Emmett wailed.

"It's gone."

Phyllo knew what that was: Gus's treasure. The Clowns were not a family group. The four of them had been thrown together by chance and the circus. Each one of them came from a different place and had their own history, their own path to this point, but one thing united them all: there was no going back. They'd left their roots behind to travel on alone. And they all travelled light, every member of the Circus of Wonder did, but Gus had kept one thing from his past, had kept it with him always: the emerald knot bracelet. Phyllo didn't know how much it was worth, but it was set with at least dozen gems, including one bonbon-sized emerald at its centre. A memento of his homeland, to Gus it was priceless and his safety net should things ever go wrong.

Now something had.

"You can't trust him," Sprockets' voice quavered. "He's smashed, Phyllo. Everything he does is about getting more." He snatched up an almost empty bottle from the floor. "Mermaids Tears – of all things. You're such a cliché," he spat and tossed the bottle to the ground. Emmett scrabbled to rescue it.

"I'm done with you. Keep this up and Barker'll be done with you too."

Emmett hugged the bottle to his chest and shook his head, eyes closed.

"Pathetic." Sprockets spun away from Emmett and lurched toward Phyllo and the door. As he drew level, he spoke in a growl so low only Phyllo would hear, "I'll never set him free."

Phyllo stepped back blinking and Sprockets pushed on, out of the door. Phyllo wheeled around to watch him stride away, broad and purposeful, not Sprockets' usual gait at all. Something jingled as he walked. Light from the oil lamps illuminated him in flickers. Disappointed and frowning. *Flicker.* Jaw clenched and muscle bulging at the temple. *Flicker.* Glaring back at Phyllo, sneer at his lip. *Flicker.* Something spinning, glinting around one finger then snatched back into his palm. *Flicker.* He was gone.

CHAPTER FIFTEEN

Confessions

"He had the bracelet, I'm sure of it."

Birdie stared at Phyllo incredulously then shook her head. "So now you think that not only is the Jester from an old poster popping up to push people in the river, but he's possessing Sprockets to stir up trouble for Emmett?"

Phyllo swallowed. "I know, it does sound crackers."

"You think?" She flopped over in a back bend and then walked her legs over to stand on her feet again.

"Well, I'm not going to be able to do that, so you can just forget it."

"Flexibility is everything," said Birdie sweetly.

"Is it now." Another thing for Phyllo to add to the list.

"You can start off like this." Birdie lay down on the floor and pushed her twiggy little body up in a bridge. Phyllo got to the sawdust beside her and gave it a go.

"If I were you, I'd be more concerned about the masked thief you said you saw."

"I *did* see him," Phyllo puffed out.

"At least he might actually be real. Don't you think you should be telling someone about all this?"

"I'm telling you." Phyllo's arms gave way and he

crumpled.

"I mean the Ringmaster, Phyllo."

He pulled himself up into a sitting position. "I have thought about that, but me and the Ringmaster, I don't know. Even I can see it's a bit hard to swallow. And, I'd say Emmett's got enough problems without the Ringmaster on his back." He made to get to his feet. "Maybe I should tell Dad."

Birdie put out her hand to pull Phyllo up. She was surprisingly strong. "It's almost midday, but if we hurry, we've got just enough time."

The Confectionary was vibrating with activity, the narrow side door pinned back to vent heat. The new popcorn machine rattled with exploding corn and Phyllo could see that Dodo had been put on kernel duty to keep it running. She had several crates already piled one on top of the other, with the uppermost one half filled with bulging red and white striped bags, tops secured by twisted corners. She shovelled freshly popped corn into yet more bags, diligently finishing them with sprinkles of cinnamon and vanilla dust.

Roly wielded an oversized whisk in an equally enormous cauldron of batter, preparing the next batch of apple nuggets for the oven. Rack upon rack towered with their cooling predecessors. Marvel was catching jelly snakes from a tank and slipping them into clear pouches which he tied with a ribbon.

The smell was glorious and, when they stepped through the small doorway into the shop, Phyllo was quite overwhelmed by nostalgia.

Dodo was the first to spot them. "Phyllo!" She sprang down from her stool and bounced across the shop to wrap her arms around him. Her face, lost in the strawberry-blonde froth, pressed against his chest.

"See, some people like me," Phyllo said to Birdie with a grin. She tutted.

"Couldn't keep away, eh?" Roly called over his shoulder, dropping the whisk in favour of a large spoon to ladle out the next batch.

"We had a few minutes, so…"

"Missed your old dad, eh?" Marvel came striding over toward them clutching a dozen jelly snake pouches, which he hung by their ribbons from a wire tree on the counter. "Time to make visits, that'd be a luxury, eh, Roly?"

"Fat chance," Roly puffed. "We're rushed off our feet."

"Team Cane." His father punched a fist into the air rather feebly. "Dodo's become our Chief Popper, haven't you, my little sherbet? This new machine's running flat out."

Dodo stepped back from Phyllo and nodded proudly. "A gross an hour. I'm the fastest popper on the river," she said proudly and their father chuckled, pulling her in for a squeeze.

"Don't know where we'd be without you." Marvel gave Phyllo a weak smile. "We miss you, Phyllo. Need you now more than ever, but there we are."

Phyllo missed them all desperately too, but bit his lips together rather than admit it. He pushed his hands into the pockets of his flyer's blues. His father stood opposite, his hands in the pockets of his own slacks, only on him the striped coat of the confectioner was pinned back by his sides. Phyllo missed that too.

"So, what can I do you for?" said Marvel, turning away and bustling back to the tank.

"Birdie wanted to show Dodo the flyers rigging, didn't you, Birdie."

186

No-one was more surprised to hear this than Birdie herself, but she caught on when she saw Phyllo's wide eyes willing her to play along. Phyllo leaned in toward Dodo and said in a loud conspiratorial whisper, "I mentioned that I'd teach you to fly if I could. Might as well get a tour from a pro." Dodo squealed and bounced on the spot. She looked to their father for approval, who looked quizzically to Phyllo. "Very well, but don't be too long. Lots to do, eh?"

Birdie puffed up at the task and it occurred to Phyllo that she was used to being the youngest, the protected one. Looking after Dodo would be a whole new experience. When they were safely on their way to the big top, Marvel pulled the shop door firmly closed.

"What's this all about, Phyllo?" he said and Phyllo explained.

He told him about the Crow Man in the crowd and the rumpus that had exploded around the Jester. He told him about checking up on Emmett after the show, the Mermaid's Tears, the emerald knot bracelet and the peculiar expressions he'd seen on Gus and Sprockets' faces, Marco too.

Marvel leaned heavily on the counter. "Mermaid's Tears. Oh, Emmett," he sighed, "Well, I can't say I hadn't suspected something of that nature."

Phyllo looked to Roly, who appeared equally perplexed.

"It's just a drink though, right? What's the big deal?" Phyllo asked.

Marvel looked away to the floor. "An intoxicant, not liquor exactly, more of a potion. Terribly expensive and not readily available really, I'd say." Phyllo's father rumpled his brow in thought. "You have to wonder..." He tailed off then said, "There was a time, a few years back, that Emmett became terribly depressed. It's the sort of thing people turn to if they're that way inclined.

"When the Barkers died in that awful fire it hit the circus hard. We were all shocked, of course we were, but Emmett suffered from a kind of delayed reaction. Just when most of us were starting to come to terms with it he lost himself, drifted off into this dreamlike state. He'd come out of it and then we'd lose him again. I thought perhaps he'd taken something for his nerves, but Mermaid's Tears, Barnum's britches."

"But what does it do?" Phyllo pressed.

"It gives the taker a false sense of serenity. Makes all their worries disappear. Of course, it's enormously addictive and I've heard all sorts of terrible things about getting off the stuff. I understand that as you try to rid your system of if it, all your old problems and worries come flooding back only magnified and more terrifying than ever. Some people hallucinate, go mad. Dreadful stuff."

"Do you think Emmett's hallucinating?" Phyllo said.

"Possibly."

Phyllo considered that. Surely hallucinations happened in your own head. "But why would I see it?"

"You?"

"The weird expressions on faces. The same expression really, but on different people."

Phyllo's father stared blankly at him for a moment and Phyllo felt as though cogs were turning behind his eyes and then as if pennies were falling into place. "Vincula," he said.

Phyllo and Roly looked between each other, uncomprehending.

Their father opened the door, "Quickly now."

❧

Frú Hafiz perched upon a low stool in the shaded entrance to her cabin. With both legs tucked to one side, as if riding side-saddle, she balanced a plate of grilled sardines on her lap and expertly stripped the flesh from one with her teeth. As they neared, she returned the bare skeleton to her plate and fastidiously wiped her fingers and lips on a neat linen napkin. Her pale skin glowed ethereally in the shadows. The long red tassel of her cap draped over one shoulder and for a fleeting moment, Phyllo saw her as a mermaid perched on a rock in the shade.

Except, of course, that Phyllo had never seen a mermaid wearing round mirrored sunglasses, imaginary or otherwise.

"Frú Hafiz," Marvel gave a little bow, "I'm sorry to have interrupted your lunch, but time is short." He glanced about, as if keen not to be seen, "Perhaps we could talk inside?"

Frú Hafiz obligingly held back the drape of her doorway then followed them into the booth where she usually accepted paying visitors, keen to learn their destiny. An almost circular bench ran around the edge, save for the entrance where they were standing. It was extravagantly padded and littered with cushions of mauve and emerald green velvet. Two lamps burned low on the walls. Almost every surface was swathed in fabric, even the ceiling, which gathered together the drapes from the walls in an elaborate midnight blue ruffle. Layers of woven rugs littered the floor.

She settled behind the circular table at the booth's centre. A ball of smoky glass, as big as Phyllo's head, squatted on dragon's feet before her and reflected the Canes in its pearlescent surface. Frú Hafiz removed her glasses to look at them with her ice blue eyes. "What brings you to me?" she said.

"I'll come straight to it, Dargun. Vincula, I think there might be one among us," said Marvel urgently.

189

It was rare for Phyllo to hear Frú Hafiz called by her first name, Dargun. Her expression sharpened and Phyllo wondered if his father was going to be told off.

"What have you seen?"

"Not me, Phyllo."

Her eyes slid to Phyllo. She nodded. "And the source?"

"I think Emmett," his father continued.

"Yes." This information appeared to make perfect sense to her.

"Do you know about it? Do you know what's happening?" Phyllo questioned, suddenly hopeful that she could explain.

"Some things I see."

"Mermaid's Tears, Dargun. I think Emmett is struggling with it." Marvel clasped his hands in front of his chest and Phyllo continued, "Do you know what to do?"

Frú Hafiz placed her hands on the table. "Mermaid's Tears, yes. Phyllo, have you seen the face of the Vincula?"

Phyllo thought about the unnatural sneer he'd been seeing in other's expressions. "Possibly, I suppose, on different people."

"Yes." Frú Hafiz nodded meaningfully to herself. "Its control must be slipping so it's seeping out into Emmett's reality, looking for a foothold. It is a difficult road, to be rid of Mermaid's Tears. Emmett will have to defeat his personal demons, but the presence of a Vincula will make that very difficult indeed."

"But what is it?"

"A guard, of sorts. Assigned to their task with dark magic. They become the embodiment of the demon to keep their subject imprisoned by it."

Phyllo shook his head. It seemed like such a lot of effort to torture a clown.

"But why Emmett?"

"His fear is important to someone."

Phyllo shook his head, perplexed.

"So, it's real?" asked Roly, "Phyllo's not seeing things?"

"Not totally out driving. I'm sure you wondered?" She gave Phyllo a small smile.

He nodded uncertainly. "So, what should we do?"

"The obligation lies with the unbound. Follow your instincts. Skills unknown are already being discovered," she said crisply.

Phyllo and Roly looked at each other. Phyllo couldn't see how learning the trapeze was going to help anything. "Look, sorry, but do you think you could be a bit clearer?"

"The cards may reveal more." She produced a deck and held them out for Phyllo to take. "Shuffle. Consider your question."

Phyllo took them, a fat pile of well used tarot that barely fitted in his grip. He manhandled them rather clumsily into a different order then gave them back.

Frú Hafiz held them reverentially for a moment then dealt from the top of the pack to lay a careful pattern upon the table. She paused to take in the picture as a whole and then pressed her forefinger against the first card she'd laid.

"Where we begin: the Seven of Cups is the search for truth," she said gently, "Gut wrenching experiences, you've felt powerless, inadequate."

That sounded familiar. It felt strangely reassuring to have pointed it out so succinctly.

"Your motivation?" She moved to the next card, "The Empress. Overloaded, not surprising. Too much emotion and internal contemplation." She raised her eyes to Phyllo. "There is seldom one wave that breaks for you." She touched the next

191

card and smiled. "Your hopes and fears. Everything you are and hope to be. The King of Wands, why wouldn't it be? It's all there inside you."

Phyllo stared at her, uncomprehending.

"Present and passing. Judgment. All has changed, but there's nothing new there. Now, the forces against you. The Five of Cups." She drooped a little, seeming to feel the weight of it. Her voice wavered. "The longing, Phyllo. It drives against you. Your desire for them to return: it's exhausting." Frú Hafiz's brow crumpled, but she didn't look up. Her white eyelashes batted furiously. Instead she rushed on to the next card, her speech becoming faster, more urgent.

"Near future. Knight of Pentacles, inverted. Travel? Always we travel." She waved a dismissive hand. "Love. Everything comes down to love, but the struggle, the struggle goes on. The path you must follow is your own."

She rolled one hand over and over.

"Follow your instincts. Evolution. The Knight of Wands, inverted again." She tutted and then shrugged. Her fingertip passed to the next card. "So much change. Your world will never be the same again. It's difficult, stressful, but I see success there. Yes, there is hope, but the road is hard. Blind is a bookless man, you must learn. But how does the future feel? The Five of Pentacles. Can nothing be easy?"

She slammed the table with her palm causing the cards to jump and the crystal ball to judder on its stand. When she continued speaking it was in a lower voice, consoling.

"Confusion, suffering, loss. The end is not clear. This card is unfocused. It isn't over, but someone is waiting for you. A divine order sustains you. The time draws near. That is all."

She covered her eyes with her hands and drew in a long slow breath.

Phyllo lowered himself onto the bench on the opposite side of the table. He'd never had a reading from Frú Hafiz before and fought to make sense of it.

"Right then." He screwed up his face with the effort. "So, I want to know what's going on, because I'm feeling over-whelmed and I want everything to go back to how it used to be, but that's holding me back?"

"And," chipped in Roly, "You're a nice kid, who might be going places, but it's all a bit of a struggle."

Frú Hafiz lifted her eyes to look at him disdainfully.

"And someone is waiting for me. Who?"

"The cards do not say."

"And I don't see how this helps Emmett."

"The cards help you see the view from the window. The Vincula's aim will be to keep Emmett enslaved. Only you can discern how this falls in with your own destiny. While Emmett becomes more lost in his fear the Vincula gains strength. The only way to stop it is to take its weapons away."

"Mermaid's Tears."

"Yes, but more than that. The fear itself is what truly binds him."

From what he understood, depriving himself of Mermaid's Tears made Emmett feel worse, made him want it all the more. The fact that Emmett's demon was so close to the surface now made Phyllo think that he was already trying.

"Should I go to the Ringmaster?" Phyllo asked.

Frú Hafiz glanced up at his father for a moment, then looked away. Marvel quietly cleared his throat. "The Ring-master doesn't need to be troubled with this, eh? I don't think that drawing attention to Emmett's struggles will be of benefit to him, do you?"

Phyllo had thought the same himself, but if was good to get confirmation. "What about the Crow Man?"

"Our Ringmaster is eternally on guard for the In-between. I'd say he's got it well in hand. Best to stay off his radar, Phyllo."

"Right." Phyllo didn't need attention drawn to *himself* either.

~

That night, Phyllo tossed and turned in his bed. Both shows had gone well, considering. Even Emmett had appeared for performances. Looking shaky, but participating. In the ring you would never have known that the previous evening had gone so awry. Backstage, however, the atmosphere was frosty.

"Don't worry," Emmett had dismissed it, blasé, "They've had their say and now it'll blow over."

"But, Gus, what about his bracelet?" Phyllo had insisted.

"I've told them. There's nothing more I can say."

Phyllo couldn't help but feel Emmett wasn't giving the matter enough weight and didn't know how to broach the subject of Mermaid's Tears.

"Do you think you'll be alright? Can you try to get over it, what happened before I mean?" He meant to say the terrible moment you felt you had to block, the fire, the loss of your friends, but he couldn't find the words.

Emmett broke eye contact, "Bingo Bongo, life's a breeze," he'd said and turned away but placed a hand on Phyllo's shoulder before he went. "I'm used to it, I'll be OK," he said and there was a glimmer there, just for a moment that Emmett admitted the huge pressure he was under.

But Phyllo knew that he was not OK and that he didn't know how to make him better.

The blankets tangled around Phyllo's legs and he struggled against himself. The Birdcage was dark and quiet. Only the faintest crackling ripple of the canvas broke the silence. Night air seeped in to clear the humidity at the top of the tower where Phyllo slept. It wouldn't help Emmett to go to the Ringmaster. He'd seen Emmett's shambolic performance in Shady Hollow. Emmett's card was already marked. Phyllo would not make it worse for him.

The Crow Man was another matter, however. Surely, he was a common enemy. An enemy who'd held a knife to Phyllo's throat and been the catalyst for the Circus of Wonder to flee Tabberstock. The Ringmaster had taken them seriously enough then, why wouldn't he now? The trouble was the Brampton Levels was proving to be a great, profitable location. The crowds were good, the market much bigger than last year. The Ringmaster would not want to move on before it was time. It was Phyllo's fault that they needed to make up the funds, but what if they were in danger? Was he putting them more at risk by saying nothing? He had no doubt: the Ringmaster would *not* like it, but did Phyllo have any choice?

When seven o'clock came the next morning, Phyllo was already pacing the ring in his flyer's blues. Signor Volante was next to arrive and gave Phyllo a surprised salute with his coffee cup. "You had breakfast?"

"Not hungry." Phyllo shook his head. He couldn't eat with his stomach tied in knots.

"Ready to get going then?" He came to a stop in front of

195

Phyllo, the many sundried wrinkles of his face undulating as he chewed on his breakfast pastry. "We teach you something today, huh? You held on the other day. How did you like it?"

The experience had been both terrifying and exhilarating. Phyllo shrugged, "It was OK," but a smile broke out on his face.

"Unfortunately, we have to do more than just hold on." He waved the pastry to and fro in front of Phyllo's face. "Forward and back. Forward and back. It's not such a good show. Nobody's paying for that. We'll teach you a catch, huh?"

The smile fell from Phyllo's face.

"Something easy." He called to Arnaldo and Salvo who'd just sauntered into view, gave them instructions and moments later they were climbing up to the boards.

"This is the straddle knee hang. Is pretty simple and the easiest way to be caught by a partner. Not so much flying involved."

Salvo swung out first. After a couple of momentum raising passes, he lowered himself to hang from the bar by his knees, arms outstretched.

"Ready, hup," called out Signor Volante and Arnaldo launched too. He swung out and, on the return, brought his legs up around the outside of his arms so that by the time he'd reached the reverse peak he was able to let go with his hands and hang only from his knees. He swung back toward Salvo, arms outstretched, and their two trajectories brought them close enough together that they could grasp each other's hands. Arnaldo released his own bar and swung away with Salvo. They swung back again, Salvo released him and he dropped easily to the net.

"Just like that," Signor Volante said, brushing his hands against each other. "You think you could get your legs up?"

196

It wasn't a complicated move but, to Phyllo, it didn't look any more possible than any of other the other tricks they performed.

"Low bars first. I see that face. It's easy, you'll see."

The low bar was set over to the side with a fat red mat beneath it. He climbed up on the box at one end and shuffled his way out into the middle.

"*Buono*. Now, legs up around the outside of your arms and hang by your knees."

Phyllo tried to locate the muscles required to achieve this and struggled to lift one foot as high as his head. This seemed to him to be quite an achievement, but it wasn't very close to the bar.

"Both feet together."

He tried to lift them both simultaneously, his stomach muscles shrieking in protest. If anything, they were farther away.

"Don't lean forward, lean back," Signor Volante ordered.

Phyllo puffed and sweated. He flailed and fell off.

"Again."

Phyllo climbed back up on the box and shuffled out into the middle once more. Signor Volante came to stand beside him, put one arm behind Phyllo's back and scooped the other behind his knees bringing them up to hold him like a baby. Phyllo felt deeply uncomfortable with this but tried to ignore it. "Head back," he commanded and then shifted to push Phyllo in the small of his back until his feet rose high enough to touch the bar. Phyllo's grip slipped and he plopped once again to the mat.

"No enough strength. Strength is everything."

Phyllo looked up at him and laughed.

"Is not a joke." Indeed, Signor Volante looked quite serious.

197

"Core muscles." He thumped at his own chest. "And grip is flabby. Work on these and we try again."

More of the Fabulous Volante gathered in the ring. Some performed eye-watering stretches while others lugged in sets of weights, which they lined up for anyone to use. Arnaldo and Salvo were back up on the trapezes and Signor Volante made to join them, but before he walked away, he said, "Train. Make your muscles strong, especially your core. Run. Be fit. This is how you must begin. We try again tomorrow, and the day after that." He rolled his hand in an indication of the unending expectation Phyllo was to rise to.

Perhaps a run was just what he needed. Even though by this time, he'd already been up for hours, the sleepless night had left him feeling clouded and dull. The flat open plains of the Brampton levels might just give him the space to clear away the fug.

Phyllo jogged out of the gate and turned immediately away from the gathering rainbow of bustling market to throw himself, headlong, into the cool blues and greens of nature. He found a path that wove between stoic trees and lost himself in their dappled shade. He pounded the trail, initially with a bit too much enthusiasm, getting so out of breath he had to stop to lean on a tree for a bit, but eventually adopting a slower, steadier rhythm that was easier to maintain. Mechanically, automatically, his body found its beat and Phyllo no longer had to think. It was a relief, a meditation, but as the challenge of it subsided, his brain found other things to do.

It pondered, for instance, what exactly it was that Frú Hafiz had seen inside him on the cards? And, what exactly were the obligations of the unbound? Did that refer to Emmett's demon? Were *they* the bonds that held Emmett? If so, did that mean because he was free of it, he could help?

The woodland path scooped away in a curve, rounding the back of the field where the Circus of Wonder sprawled: a canvas stronghold in foreign lands. He didn't usually see it from the back and the unfamiliar angle revealed the imposing structure to him anew. The outer walls of the cabins were painted with depictions of the artists within. Scenes that merged fluidly one with the next: jugglers grinning up at spinning clubs; Peaches and Rosemary: the fat ladies of the Odditorium balanced on the tiniest of balls; Frú Hafiz stooped mystically over her crystal ball. Within the horseshoe, the red and gold striped canvas of the big top stretched high, the dual king poles of the Machine lifting its roof into flag-crowned points. The additional towers either side, one of which was the Birdcage stood like sentries, flanking their commander. Phyllo was at once proud to be a part of it and terrified of the perturbing unknown through which they endlessly journeyed. On he ran and the river market came into sight once more. People ebbed and flowed. Single shoppers and family groups. Day trippers and stall holders, rootless wanderers also at its heart.

He skirted the cabins and jogged in through the gateway, past Skinner and Bain playing cards on a barrel. They looked up only briefly, Bain's eyes following Phyllo without greeting. Up ahead the great brass doors of the Ringmaster's quarters swung open and Phyllo braced himself for an unwelcome encounter but, instead of the man himself, Gus stepped out onto the path.

Hunched and sweating, he pulled at the braces holding up the great weight of trouser at his barrel-like waist and mopped his brow. As he moved away from the door he turned, unwittingly, to face Phyllo. Instantly his features transformed with guilt and Phyllo knew at once what he'd done. Gus shook his

head and bit his lips together. Phyllo slowed to stop beside
him, but Gus didn't want to talk, didn't even want to look him
in the eye. He turned and hurried away.

"Phyllo Cane?"

The very voice he'd hoped not to hear.

"A word."

Phyllo edged around the Machine wall to find the Ringmaster
scanning the market through his telescope. He twisted the
focus and slid from boat to boat, stall to stall, face to face.

"The crowd is gathering nicely and it's still quite early. I
might even wander down myself, maybe I'll pick up a nice
dragon fruit for breakfast."

Phyllo shuffled from foot to foot and the Ringmaster took
his time to turn. His right hand clutched the head of his cane
which he tilted away at an angle.

"Were you planning on coming to see me?" he said
blandly.

Phyllo didn't answer.

The Ringmaster continued, "Group dynamics are a tricky
business. One bad apple and it upsets the whole barrel. Or
pie." He looked to Phyllo for acknowledgement, "Apple
nuggets or whatever. But of course, that's not you anymore, is
it." He looked thoughtful. "One slippery rung on the ladder
perhaps? Well anyway, you get the gist, I'm sure." He smiled
and Phyllo got the distinct impression of a grinning crocodile
with rows of glistening teeth. "Important to iron out misun-
derstandings before they take hold. As it happens Emmett is
already on my radar. It doesn't do to protect that which works
against us."

Phyllo shook his head.

"Perhaps there might be more to the situation? Something that might help me to see it in a different light?"

Phyllo considered telling the Ringmaster about the mental breakdown Emmett appeared to be having, but wasn't convinced it would help.

"No?" Lazarus Barker stepped down from the platform and crossed to sit behind his desk. To his left the Octowriter's tentacles undulated gently, as if rippling in the current of a stream. He tossed something to it from his pocket. A single tentacle snatched it from the air then tucked it out of sight.

"Something fresh from the market for Miss Fitz too, I think." He smiled again but Phyllo backed gingerly away.

"There was something else." Phyllo wanted to get the Ringmaster off the subject of Emmett and now seemed like as good a time as any to say the thing that had been on his mind. The Ringmaster raised one expectant eyebrow.

"The other day, in the market, I saw someone. One of the thieves that raided our stores. The one with the knife." Phyllo searched the Ringmaster's face for a reaction.

"I see."

"He has this mask," Phyllo indicated the beaky shape with his hands, "I've never seen another one like it. It was him, I'm sure of it."

The Ringmaster raised his chin. "The In-between are our constant companion, Phyllo. We are vigilant. The windows they came in by are barred. It was luck on their part."

"And I saw him at a show, in the audience. At the back."

"There have been a lot of masks. The parade is always full of them."

"Yes, I know but this one's quite—"

"Phyllo, we cannot allow ourselves to fall into histrionics.

We are quite secure. The big top protects us." The Ringmaster's tone was changing now, sweet persuasion lost to sour impatience.

"They have Arif and Shadi," Phyllo blurted.

The Ringmaster laid his palms on the desk, his eyes narrowed to a squint.

"I, I saw him, Arif, in the stores, when the thieves—"

"You saw him in the stores and you didn't say?" The colour was rising above the thick sculpted beard on the Ringmaster's chin. A small vein popped up at his temple.

"It didn't seem so important then. They had him tied up, clearly a prisoner. I know it wouldn't have been his fault, not his choice, but now they're here—"

"Not important?" The Ringmaster got to his feet.

"You wanted to blame them for the fire and I knew it wasn't them. I didn't want to add—"

"That was not for you to decide," he bellowed.

"I, I—"

"Are you determined to ruin us, Phyllo Cane? Your pernicious zeal against this circus is mind-boggling! Get out."

He stormed around from behind the desk and Phyllo turned tail and ran. He slid around the Machine wall and out of the door. The Ringmaster stomped after him, but leaned out of his door rather than follow. "Skinner," he roared, "Here. Now."

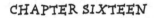

CHAPTER SIXTEEN

Onward and Upward

The river market closed at the end of September and without it the Brampton Levels became a quiet haven of nature once more. Idyllic as that was, it was not the place for a big top with seats to fill. So, with great reluctance, the Circus of Wonder concertinaed, stacked and stowed itself away to travel on. At midnight, Bain hammered the marker post into the centre of a clearing in Upper Loaming and their journey up river began, the big top winking out of existence to re-emerge from the darkness a hundred miles north.

Each successive pitch now would take them a little higher up Pilgrim's Peak until they reached the top and Star City, their final destination and the home of the Circus Guild. There, they would perform one last time for the Master Aficionaster and his panel. It was their chance to showcase the talents they'd spent a full tour perfecting. Each act's chance to win a coveted Gilded Pennant.

If the Circus of Wonder could secure just one, Phyllo knew it would make all the difference for next season. Pennant holders had their pick of the routes, able to plan and hit destinations at optimum moments, ahead of rivals or avoiding

Shindy Fairs of the In-between. In their current financially precarious predicament, it was nothing short of essential.

Upper Loaming was still busy. Although nothing like the numbers attracted by the river market, while the weather held, its residents were happy to venture out into the great outdoors, happy to sample the delights of the circus and soak up the last rays of sun before they faded into autumn. They held shows afternoon and evening to half full houses, which Phyllo thought wasn't bad, considering, but then he was determined to stay positive.

The Ringmaster's determination had a different focus. He made spontaneous inspections, day and night, questioning the inactivity of idle hands, and could be regularly spotted at that great circular window of his cabin, scouring the horizon through the lens of his telescope.

To Phyllo's initial relief, Lazarus Barker seemed to have taken the threat of the Crow Man and his companions very seriously indeed. Now that he knew Arif and Shadi were involved, willingly or not, the In-between's threat had swelled in his estimations. Men from the engineers were posted around the perimeter, burning campfires into the night, declaring to any who might like to chance it that the Circus of Wonder would not be easily breached.

They patrolled the horseshoe too. Now working much longer hours than they were used to, the engineers developed bad-tempers and bullying attitudes. They demanded to know what everyone was doing or where they had been. Once the circus was set up, operation of the Machine during performances had previously been their only responsibility, but now the constant weight of security stretched their patience thin. A cantankerous Skinner declared that the horseshoe gate would be kept locked at all times outside of shows so that his men could rest, Skinner guarding the gate from the inside while Bain prowled around outside.

Inevitably, the mood sank. The pressure of their looming appearance at Star City bore down on high spirits and, more oppressively, the snarling aggression of the engineers made even usually happy-go-lucky cast members twitch and snap.

The Fabulous Volante trained like they'd never trained before. Signor Volante filled every spare moment, his determination to win a Gilded Pennant for the troupe shining in beads of sweat on the brow of every flyer. Phyllo unavoidably trained too and, despite his own misgivings, found that there were muscles beneath his doughy pre-teen flesh after all. Every day he felt a little fitter, a little stronger, but his enthusiasm to climb to the height of the board never increased. A shortcoming Marco found hilarious.

"You can take the boy out of the Confectionary, but you can no take the confectionary out of the boy!" he roared and when Phyllo gazed up at him confusedly said, "Your legs, they are made of jelly, no? Or marshmallow perhaps?" He howled with laughter again as Phyllo wobbled to the edge of the platform, peering down to the ground, which swished about beneath him in nauseating waves.

Learning a trick on the ground had been Marco's idea and Phyllo could not agree to it fast enough. "I'm gonna teach you how to be the Pirate Captain! How about that?"

"On the ground?"

"*Si*. Well closer to it anyway."

Marco arranged to borrow a pair of platform swings from the Agile Arethusa for their morning practice sessions and soon he and Phyllo were swinging about on them like a couple of hooting apes.

Their frame was of a triangular construction, the base of

which rested solidly on the ground. The swing which hung from the apex had a platform large enough to hold three enthusiastic Agile Arethusa, or one nervous ex-confectioner. Phyllo found he was much happier up on his feet than he had been dangling from a bar, and he and Marco were able to get a good rhythm of swinging going without all that worry of being thirty feet or so above death. Before too long Phyllo screwed up the courage to lurch from one to the other as they came together at the top of their swing. Following Marco's effortless lead, he over-egged it and sent them both tumbling off the back.

Phyllo gave the wide-eyed Marcus a sheepish apology, "Sorry. Too keen maybe?"

Marco, who was sprawled out flat on his back, shook his head and laughed. "Never."

When it dawned on Phyllo that he hadn't seen his family in days, he made a point of dropping in. After the matinee, he side-stepped Skinner on the path and slipped in through the Confectionary's narrow door. Roly was there alone.

"How's it going?" he asked, leaning against the counter to pick at a bowl of fizzy hearts.

"Busy." Roly tipped a scoop of violet sugar into the candyfloss spinner and readied the wands. "Seen any more of your pal in the mask?"

"No. Thank Barnum."

"Let Barker worry about the In-between, Phyllo. He's got Skinner and Bain on it now."

"Don't we know it." There was no escaping them.

"I'd say our first priority ought to be Emmett's demon,"

said Roly, sweeping a wand around the candyfloss drum and pulling out an untidy clump. "Although, what I've seen of Emmett over the last few days, I'd say he's pulled himself together a bit."

"Hard to know what that means though, isn't it?" said Phyllo, "Is he beating the Mermaid's Tears or has he given in?" They both nodded wearily. "Any joy with the jellies?"

Roly shook his head. "I thought we were laughing when I got that little plant from the Greenfinger, but there's not a single flower on it. I've been leaving it out in the sun and everything."

Phyllo sagged. They needed the honeysuckle flowers for the recipe. "Frú Hafiz said that stopping too quickly would bring the Vincula to the surface. We want him to stop, but we don't. How are we supposed to know what to do?"

Roly stuffed the ragged ball of floss into a bag and knotted it around the wand. "The whole thing is giving me the creeps."

Over the days that followed Phyllo felt things were settling down. He made numerous visits to Emmett, sneaking past Skinner to pop in, between training and shows. On the whole Emmett was evenly cheerful and when Phyllo had spotted the evidence of a cloudy glass or the twinkle of a badly hidden bottle, he'd reminded himself that slow and steady won the race. He definitely didn't want Emmett to go into any kind of meltdown and bring that horrible Vincula back.

They moved on again to Revel Brook, a destination rising in altitude, but falling in temperature. The air there was clean and sharp, a beauty spot that drew mostly *charmed* visitors, no matter the weather. It provided healthy houses for the increasingly focused troupe and the days passed in a flurry of shows and extra rehearsals with little spare time. When they moved on again it was to Fortune Falls – the final stop before Star City.

Fortune Falls clung to the upper slopes of Pilgrim's Peak in a series of climbing plateaux. Its remote location meant that visitors outside the magical community were very few and far between. But it was popular, with those who had the ability to get there, for its out of season market. Named after the great waterfall which plunged down the sheer rock face to the north, it was also famous for the extraordinary span of glasshouses which clung to a more accessible southern ledge.

Now high enough to rise above the clouds, Fortune Falls was bathed in sunlight almost all year round. Its huge ornamental greenhouses grew crops quite out of season, even tropical. Their produce was in high demand from enthusiastic shoppers.

The crowd was drawn too by the chance to experience shows destined for awards from the Circus Guild. Star City was always packed out, chock-a-block with the circus fraternity and specially invited guests. Tickets to shows there were like gold dust, whereas Fortune Falls buzzed with possibility.

When the Circus of Wonder pushed out its cabins on one of the lower plateaux, Phyllo had felt sick with anticipation. Whether it was down to excitement or the increasing thinness of the air, looking out from the edge of their outcrop, he'd felt breathless and wobbly kneed. Far below, lights twinkled in a clutch of houses and the moon sparkled in reflections on the tumbling river. It felt like drifting above the world. His life had changed so much in the past months it didn't feel real and now so much depended on an achievement out of his hands.

Even if he trained every minute of every day, he could not hope to gain the skills required to earn a Gilded Pennant. That task was down to the rest of the troupe. Even if he'd still been a Confectioner, earning the award for confections was unheard of. Not that he had the skill there either.

He sighed, utterly disappointed with himself. He was bottom of the heap. He'd cost the troupe dearly and had no way of repaying them. He desperately wanted there to be more to him than this, the kid who was trouble, who drifted from one mentor to the next without ever really gaining a talent. Was that who he'd be? He had until the end of the season to grasp being part of the Fabulous Volante and then he'd have to move on to another act and Barnum only knew what that would be. He sighed. It wasn't coming easy.

Perhaps nothing of value ever did.

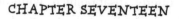

CHAPTER SEVENTEEN

A Moment in the Sun

The next morning, Phyllo drifted easily out of sleep to consciousness. The feathered mattress of his bunk had blended with the quilt to make a perfect cocoon of exactly the most comfortable temperature and softness. He poked his nose out to find that the air at the top of the Birdcage was cool. It drifted across his senses, clear and fresh. In the preceding weeks, he'd awoken most mornings in a slight panic, wondering if he'd overslept and then being gripped with foreboding at what the day might hold and his impending clamber down a flimsy ladder to the ground. He'd awoken most mornings with his body aching to its very core.

Today, he felt stronger, felt his posture was straight and correct. He felt fitter, physically, the best he'd ever felt. As if he were shedding childish puppy fat. Perhaps it was the quality of the air in Fortune Falls. Perhaps it was knowing that the Circus of Wonder *might* be on the brink of redemption. He felt like something was coming and his head was clearing to make space.

The Birdcage was entirely quiet. He poked his head out of his cot and saw that the great scrubbed dining table remained clear from the night before. No cooking smells drifted up from Nonna Sophia's kitchen. He listened hard and picked up the snuffling breathing of Marco in the bunk below. Phyllo, it seemed, was first awake. A feat he'd never managed before, his bed too unfamiliar, the hours they kept too unsociable. Life in the Birdcage was just becoming life.

He shuffled to the ladder and down a couple of rungs to sidle back along to the opening of Marco's cot. Marco lay unapologetically star-shaped, head thrown back and mouth open. Phyllo smiled to himself. Marco's cot, although identical to his own, was in as much of a mess as was possible. Empty crisp and sweet packets littered the small shelves, and what Phyllo assumed to be the majority of Marco's wardrobe was screwed up and wedged into the corner beneath one of his large feet. Snapshots of Marco with his brothers, arms flung about each other's shoulders, were pinned to the ceiling alongside an empty, flattened popcorn cone from the Confectionary and a smoothed-out sweet wrapper. Phyllo looked up at them curiously. The cone was an old style he just about remembered: faded turquoise with purple scrolling writing which declared its contents 'caramel-sweet'. And the wrapper, golden and nameless, was a generic style they still used on lots of different candies, depending on what they were making at the time.

"You're wondering why I've got rubbish pinned to my roof." Marco had awoken and was watching Phyllo through sleepy, still half-closed eyes. Phyllo shrugged and Marco reached up to give the flattened cone an easy tap. "Papa gave me this on the day I first performed in the main show. It was only a small part. Just one perfect catch. It was the day I really joined the troupe and I knew."

"Knew what?"

"Knew I was destined to fly. It was in my blood. I could feel it."

Phyllo nodded. "How old were you?"

"Eight."

Eight. It was five years later for Phyllo and he still hadn't experienced such a moment. "And the wrapper?"

Marco's face fell into an easy smile. "It was the best day, ever. Sitting in the sun, backs to the cabins. Papa thought those bonbons were the most incredible thing he'd ever tasted. *'Like sitting on Nonno's lap in the olive groves'*, that's what he said. When I closed my eyes, I could taste it too. I could feel the dry heat and smell the rosemary growing in the scrub. It made me homesick for a place I've never been. But Papa's been. Somehow, I felt it too. Your mother made them." Marco's eyes fell to Phyllo's and something shifted. "It felt like home."

Phyllo's eyes prickled and he looked back up to the wrapper. But he smiled. "She was good at that, making it feel like home."

Marco laid his hand on Phyllo's shoulder. "*Si*."

"No, *I've* got the list. Nonna gave it to *me*." Birdie pulled the paper from Marco's hand.

"I've got the Coin. I'm the oldest." Marco tried to snatch it back, but Birdie whipped it behind her back and danced from side to side. Marco cursed under his breath.

Phyllo and Roly strolled shoulder to shoulder, hands in pockets. They stole looks at each other and smirked. Dodo skipped along in front, a small basket looped over her arm. Marvel's ingredients list and pouch of Coin, originally given to Roly, already in her possession. "Girls," Roly breathed.

"*Rompipalle*," Marco muttered.

They climbed the first of the hundred steps that linked

plateau to plateau in snaking paths. Boxy dwellings huddled together in the limited space, doors painted scarlet and sapphire and emerald green. Plumes of wood smoke rose from outdoor kitchens with enticing smells of roasting meat and spiced berry wine already heating on their stoves. As they climbed, they rounded the slopes to the south to find the first of the great greenhouses clinging to the sheer rock face. Intricate ironwork framed thousands of panes in a shining cathedral of glass.

The Conlis, residents of Fortune Falls, bustled industriously about. As a race they were short and stocky, with tanned, leathery faces that crinkled deeply at their eyes. Phyllo squinted at them in the bright inescapable light, watching as they transported produce out to tiered racks, baskets on their backs almost as big as they were. They moved with a geisha grace, barely lifting their feet from the ground, but speeding forward with apparently little effort. Phyllo could see why they'd adopted such a style of moving about: most of their party puffed and panted from the effort of the climb. Roly burned puce.

"Howling humbugs, where's all the oxygen," he gasped.

"This way." Birdie bounced ahead, toward the double height entrance.

"How is she *doing* that?" Roly wheezed.

"Virtually nothing of her, is there," Phyllo puffed, "Doesn't need much to keep going."

"Come *on*." She waved them impatiently forward, but flailed ineffectually at the enormous door, only managing it eventually with Marco's assistance. She swept her nose into the air and flounced in, past him. The door swung back and Phyllo, as the last of their group, was propelled inside by its closing weight.

213

Once over the threshold the incredible structure truly revealed itself. Its arching metal rafters seemed to hold up the sky itself. Like great ribs inside the chest of a whale that breathed with the life of the plants it contained. Phyllo's lungs absorbed the oxygen greedily and his senses buzzed with colour and smell. Zingy lemon trees, trimmed into fruit-spotted globes, ran away to their left and to the right: perfumed peaches blushed on thickly leaved branches. The Conlis drifted between them, checking fruit and harvesting prudently. The river, which would eventually plummet from the falls, ran gurgling and clear over rocks and through gullies, feeding a spider's web of tiny pipes which fanned out into the beds.

"Get a basket, Marco. There are things in this part on the list." Birdie pointed to a drooping tower of wicker baskets beside the doorway and Marco grumbled over to pull one out. Phyllo got one too. "You pick for Dad, Roly. I'll carry."

"Brilliant, thanks." Roly flapped at his shirt front and Dodo produced the list from her own little basket, which was only really big enough to hold herbs. "Bergamot, cherimoya and mulberries if we can find them," she chirped, "and he said to look out for horned cucumbers because, apparently, you never know."

The Canes and the Volantes drifted through the greenhouse in an amiable group, buying things from their lists and taking risks on others that weren't, having second thoughts and then eating them as they wandered. The green and yellow ciruela were sweet as honey and the mangosteen, soft and tart. The flavours were intense, Phyllo's mouth watering with delight at each new taste. When they left the first greenhouse, they were already loaded down. And quite sticky.

One set of doors led quickly to the next. The second glass

house was fully circular, its roof sweeping up into a point, like an upturned onion. The ground was carved into row upon radiating, swirling row of alternating herbs. Yellow and green, deep red and purple. The pathway swept above the ground on metal gantries, allowing shoppers to look down to make selections whilst immersed in each plant's wonderful aroma. The Conlis sashayed below, snipping bunches or snatching up full plants upon request.

"Lavender. That's on the list," said Dodo, pointing down to the jolly purple tufts.

"Let's say we couldn't find any," said Roly, wrinkling up his nose. Phyllo snorted.

"There's something on *my* list though," Roly said and when Phyllo looked, he saw that Roly was pointing up, out of the roof. There, above the greenhouse, sprouted a cloud of yellow honeysuckle, growing determinedly out of a crevice.

"How did that get up there?" There seemed to be very little earth for it to be growing in. Phyllo wondered how it had survived.

"What is it?" Marco squinted up too.

"Honeysuckle. We need it. Roly needs it for a recipe. A special one."

"Is there any for sale?"

"Maybe. We should look." Now the shopping trip felt a bit more interesting and when the Conlis vendor came over to help them Phyllo quizzed him about the plant, but he pursed his lips. "I have horehound and hyssop? Saffron, sage and sesame?"

"No, honeysuckle. Honey. Suckle." Phyllo tried to say it as clearly as possible. The vendor shrugged then tucked his hands to rest inside a wide central pocket on the front of his woven tunic. It looked a bit like he was wearing one of Frú Hafiz's carpets.

Roly pointed up to the branch visible through the roof. "Hon-ee-suck-lll." He enunciated as clearly as he could, pulling exaggerated faces with every syllable. The vendor's eyes drifted up to the plant. Then he flopped a hand at them and started to laugh. "Why would you buy if you can pick it for free?"

The boys frowned at him.

"Herbs?" He waved a hand across the plants at his feet, "Lemon verbena, liquorice, lavender?"

Roly sighed. "Fine, we'll take some liquorice, but definitely no lavender. In a pot please." The man seemed to hover across the plants, gliding a handful of rows counter-clockwise to scoop a pot from the ground and then returning to pass it up.

"Thanks," said Roly and, after trying to wedge it into the top of Phyllo's basket gave up and held onto it himself. Marco had armfuls of herbs in pots – basil with enormous fragrant leaves and bushy tubs of marjoram and oregano. It seemed Birdie's need for control stopped short of actually carrying anything.

A revolving door spat them back out onto the mountain-side, where they found themselves rather precariously balanced and weighed down. The Conlis, it transpired, were aware that shoppers might be a bit overwhelmed at this point, struggling to carry their purchases, as this was where they had stationed a herd of pigmy butterphants.

The butterphants were milling about in a broad pen or straining over the small fence which held them back, parping at shoppers as they came out onto their grassy knoll. A considerably smaller and far hairier version of the butterphants kept in the circus's magical menagerie, this sub-species was a furry footstool of a creature. Knee high with shaggy long brown hair, it had a wide back on which the Conlis strapped two large, lidded baskets. Much like an elephant in many respects with its short stocky legs and a stubby trunk, the pigmy butterphant had ears patterned in jewel-bright colours that could be flapped to lift it into the air, heavy load or no. It offered a most convenient way to transport purchases up and down the levels of Fortune Falls.

"Brilliant," said Phyllo, as the Conlis herder removed his back basket and beckoned to the nearest butterphant, which trotted happily over, snuffling its trunk in the grass as it came. He expertly repacked Phyllo's shopping into the butterphant's baskets and then did the same for Marco with a second animal. He gave each of them a twist-cornered paper bag, which turned out to be full of white chocolate mice. Phyllo tossed one into his mouth.

"Not for you. For him." The shepherd nodded to the pigmy butterphant carrying Phyllo's shopping. It had wide, hopeful, deep brown eyes that stared at Phyllo hungrily. He tossed a chocolate mouse in its direction and the butterphant caught it on the end of its stubby little trunk with a sniff, deposited it in its mouth and chewed delightedly for a few seconds before making a production of swallowing it down. It trotted over to Phyllo's side and proceeded to explore him with its trunk, alternately sucking and then blowing little cool puffs of air at him through his shirt. Phyllo giggled.

"Make sure to keep at least one until he's carried it all the way to wherever you're going. He's your best friend now, but when you run out..." The shepherd chopped his hand through the air, indicating the sudden end to the friendship they could expect. Marco's butterphant blew air into his ear and made him jump. Even Birdie cracked a smile.

They ploughed on, into the final glass house, vegetable crops of every imaginable kind within. Nonna Sophia's list had many that Phyllo had never heard of, but Marco and Birdie picked them out with familiar ease. Phyllo gazed about in awe of the tropical world the Conlis had created inside this glass house in particular. Towering palms brushed their leaves against the glass ceiling. Tiny coral, gold and turquoise hummingbirds buzzed around their giant trunks and visited long trumpeted lilies. No doubt the nectar was on sale here somewhere too. It was the most incredible indoor garden Phyllo had ever seen. The butterphants waddled along beside them, occasionally hooting for their next mouse and searching any pockets they could reach on the off-chance. Roly led the way, sighing impatiently every time they caught him up.

"I can't see any for sale in here either, can you? Maybe we *can* pick it out there." Roly craned his neck to search the perimeter of the green house once more. "There's definitely none in here. There won't be time to look for it if we don't hurry up."

Roly hustled everyone outside, but when he announced what he wanted to do, Birdie shook her head petulantly. "I am *not* going foraging for weeds. There's only an hour until the first show and I want some lunch. Nonna's making cannoli."

Lunch. That got Dodo's attention.

"I'm helping," announced Marco. Phyllo had the distinct impression that he was going to do exactly the opposite of whatever it was that Birdie wanted.

"Fine. Anyone else coming? Or are you all staying here, picking weeds?"

Dodo screwed one of her feet into the ground, wearing her most innocent smile. Phyllo thought it would have been the tiniest leap to eyelash fluttering. "Hungry, Dodo?" he asked.

She nodded. "It's OK. Why don't you go with Birdie? She might even be able to get you one of those cannoli." He looked to Birdie who swelled with responsibility.

"Come with me, Dodo." She put out a hand which Dodo eagerly grasped. "We'll leave the silly boys to it." They trundled away, Birdie's long prancing steps being pulled out of rhythm by Dodo's haphazard gambolling. Phyllo could see that Dodo was delighted to have Birdie all to herself *and* be heading back for food. And Birdie, much as she liked to play the high and mighty card, looked thoroughly delighted to play the responsible sibling instead.

The girls took the path down, curving around the outside of the glass houses to return the way they'd come. The boys and the butterphants climbed the path in the opposite direction, looking for a way to double back above the greenhouses.

The path wound steeply up and brought them to the next plateau, a considerable distance from their aim and they had to trek across rough ground to bring themselves to a point above the onion-roofed glass house. Out of breath, yet buoyed by the suggestion of the Conlis vendor that honeysuckle grew wild, Phyllo had rather been hoping that they would find bushes of it happily sprouting. Alas this did not seem to be the case. Indeed, the only glimpse they had caught of it was now fifty feet or so below, poking rather unhelpfully out of an unreachable crevice above the pointed glass roof. Phyllo's butterphant searched around his waist for a pocket. He pushed the tickling trunk away.

Roly stared down at it too. "Convenient," he puffed.

Marco stood on the edge, hands on hips. "It's not so far."

"You *are* joking!" Roly exclaimed.

"No." His face was deadpan.

"You're right, Phyllo. They are mad. Don't heights mean

219

anything to you?" Roly squeaked.

Phyllo had to agree. "We haven't got a safety net, Marco. It's too dangerous to climb it. You fall here and it's glass for a landing."

"That's true."

"If only we had a rope," Roly said, peering over the edge in much the same way Phyllo imagined he did, up on the flyer's board. Marco's butterphant snuffled its trunk down the back of his neck.

"We've got something better than a rope," said Phyllo.

Roly frowned.

Phyllo pulled the bag of white chocolate mice from his pocket and showed it to the butterphant. It flapped its wing-like ears and gave a snorty sneeze. He jogged over to a slope that was faced with a six-foot drop and puffed and panted his way to the top, then held out the bag and jiggled it. "Here, boy. Come and get it."

The butterphant trotted over and stood up on its hind legs. It stretched its trunk out, but still couldn't reach. Phyllo shook the bag some more. "Come and get it." He sniffed the bag himself for effect. "Mmm, lovely mice."

The butterphant paced back and forth, eyes on the bag. It shook out its ears and gave an experimental flap.

"That's it. Up you come." It flapped its ears again, more convincingly this time, and the thin fabric of ear stiffened to beat at the air. "That's it. Come on, boy."

The butterphant's wing-ears swept back and forth, pushing against the air and driving it up, its thick fuzzy legs dangling beneath it. Up. Trunk reaching out for the paper bag. Up. Its wing-ears beat against the air and then its feet were on the same raised ground as Phyllo's. It trotted forward to suck at the bag.

"Good boy." Phyllo gave it a mouse and looked to Roly, a glint of triumph in his eye.

Roly stared back, nonplussed. "Can you teach him to pick flowers too? Because if you can't, I'm not sure how this helps us."

"All you have to do is get in a basket."

"All *I* have to do?"

"It is *your* recipe. *I'm* not the Confectioner, am I?"

Roly grimaced. Phyllo grinned and led the butterphant back down the slope and carefully emptied the baskets out onto the ground.

"This must be quite a sweet you're making." Marco watched them, amused.

Phyllo wasn't sure how to explain the importance of it to Marco. They were just becoming friends. He didn't want to scare him off with tales of Mermaid's Tears and demons or how he thought he'd seen the Vincula on Marco's own face that morning on the Brampton Levels. As much as he wanted to help Emmett, he was worried that Marco would think he was crackers. "Old family recipe," he said.

Roly gave Marco a thin smile of confirmation.

"In you get then."

Roly's smile transformed into thin-lipped determination. He took a deep breath and came over to pat the butterphant on the head. "Nice butterphant," he said uncertainly.

Phyllo held the bag out in front of its trunk and it sucked enthusiastically through the paper, pretty much ignoring Roly. "Get in, quick, while he's distracted."

Roly hauled himself up onto the edge of the basket and rolled clumsily in, head first. Marco roared with laughter. "I think we have the wrong brother learning to fly!" He clapped his hands.

"Funny." Roly's face reappeared over the edge. "Now what?"

"This way, little fella." Phyllo backed away, holding the paper bag out in front of him. He moved toward the edge and, when they'd all got there, took a single mouse from the bag and held it up.

"Phyllo, what are you going to do?" Roly's voice took on a quaver.

"Fetch!" Phyllo tossed the mouse into thin air and the little butterphant hooted and lurched forward, launching itself off the edge in pursuit. Roly screamed. The pair of them plummeted down and Phyllo thought for a moment that he'd made a terrible mistake. They were falling – rushing toward the glass roof. Then the butterphant reached out its trunk, captured the mouse and threw out its winged ears so that it and Roly soared away, skimming the roof in a sweep. It flapped its ears some more to gain enough height to return to the plateau where Phyllo stood and settled once more by his side, chewing happily.

Roly was white and speechless.

Marco hugged Phyllo and slapped his back. "*Buono! Buono!*" He laughed some more and went on to clap Roly on the back too.

"Hilarious," Roly managed with a sour grimace. "Fun as that wasn't, I still don't have any honeysuckle."

Phyllo could see that they had a problem. "We need to steer him."

"Well, it's obvious isn't it. Carrot on a stick," said Marco.

"Right."

They foraged about for a stick of suitable length then pushed its tip through the paper bag so that it swung on the end. Roly took hold of it and the butterphant immediately thrust out its trunk, trying to reach the chocolatey contents and broke out into a canter. It scampered off, up the hill and in the wrong direction, Roly yelling out from his basket, "The other way! The other way!"

"Swing the stick to the side, Roly. To the side!"

Roly and the butterphant hurtled headlong into a patch of scrubby bushes and out of sight. Phyllo and Marco dashed after them to discover a furry bottom sticking out of a much leafier bush and the sounds of Roly spluttering, "He's eating them. He's got the bag!"

The butterphant sneezed and hooted and made unmistakable munching sounds. Phyllo grabbed on to a back leg and pulled. "Out you come. Come on, out."

Marco pulled on the other side, but only when it was good and ready did the beast finally reverse out of the bush, swallowing down its prize and turning a trunk on Marco to sniff about. Phyllo pushed past, into the spot where it had been and came back with scraps of paper. "It's eaten the lot."

Marco brandished his bag. "I've still got some."

Marco's butterphant was aware of this too, and increasingly conscious of the chocolate mouse free-for-all that was happening without it. It parped and sneezed and stamped its flat feet at being left out. Marco threw one to him and he golloped it down. "*Bravo.*" He gave it a pat on the top of its head. "Let's try again." Marco emptied the bag, bar one, into his pocket and thrust the bag onto the end of the stick before offering it to Roly.

"Woah, whoa – I think someone else should have a try. I mean, I'm obviously not a natural. There are two flyers here after all."

The second butterphant made for the bag and Marco had to grab its trunk to stop it.

"Get out then." Phyllo climbed in to take his place and took the stick from Marco. He held it directly up out of reach and the sudden disappearance of the mouse-bag seemed to stall things.

"OK?" Roly said to Phyllo, now looking much happier with his feet on the ground. "Wherever you put the bag in his vision, that's what he's going to head for."

"Got it."

"And it looks like holding it up like you are now so he can't see it, stops him. Well, on the ground it does anyway."

On the ground. Phyllo blanched.

"Ready then? Let's go." Roly was definitely enjoying himself now.

Phyllo gingerly lowered the stick until his steed spotted it and then they were off, weaving and turning in circles until they managed to navigate their way to the edge and then *over* the edge before Phyllo had time to do anything about it.

This time the butterphant flapped immediately, aiming to keep its trajectory and eye on the chocolatey prize. They swept out in a wide arc and back toward the rock face where the honeysuckle sprouted. The butterphant's wing-ears beat steadily, and they neared the branch but, when Phyllo reached for it, the stick slipped from his fingers, dipping the mouse bag and sending his ride into a dive. Abandoned by gravity, his knees left the bottom of the basket and he grabbed for the rim, fighting to stay in.

"Again. Go round again," Roly yelled from the ledge. They swooped up just before the glass roof, climbing again, butterphant wing-ears beating, Phyllo's heart pounding.

The bag tore a little at the stick and started to flap in the wind. They curled around for another pass. This time Phyllo's fingertips brushed the petals, but he just wasn't close enough to get a grip. The bag caught on a twig and tore in two. The chocolate mouse fell free for a moment and was then sucked onto the trunk of the butterphant and eaten mid-air.

"Damn it!"

The butterphant swept back to the plateau where Roly and Marco were waiting.

"Oh, bad luck," said Roly, deadpan.

"Now what are we going to do?" Without a bag it was impossible to dangle anything from the end of the stick. Marco turned out his pockets. "Three left." Marco's butterphant stretched a trunk over his shoulder and sucked one up. "Oi!"

"Make that two," said Phyllo. He kicked off a shoe and pulled off his sock. "Pass one up here." He dropped the mouse into the sock and sniffed it.

Roly wrinkled his nose but the butterphant rolled its little trunk over its head, trying to get at it.

"He doesn't seem to mind. Let's give it a go." Phyllo knotted his sock onto the stick and dangled it ahead. The butterphant took a bit longer to think about it this time, but soon they were teetering over the edge once more.

They swooped away, stick bending with the extra weight of the sock and Phyllo steered them around for a pass. He got them in closer to the rock face earlier this time, taking a head-on course to the honeysuckle. Twiggy strands of creepers thwacked at his arm and face and suddenly the sock caught on a particularly thorny bramble. In a second it had pulled back and snapped.

The butterphant started. Frightened by the noise, it beat its wings the other way to stop, twisting and dropping away. With it went the baskets, but not Phyllo, who found himself out in mid-air with nothing between him and the brittle glass roof of the greenhouse.

A piercing whistle filled his ears. He looked up to see Marco, who whistled again and the creature looked this time too. Marco dropped the final mouse. The butterphant twisted itself level, scooping Phyllo out of the air as it turned, and dove after its quarry. Phyllo's outstretched hand brushed foliage and he grasped it, tearing the stem out at its root. Then the wing-ears were beating and they were climbing. Up. They curled back around Phyllo in the effort of a longer, stronger sweep. Up. They swooped along the ridge, the butterphant turning to return to the plateau. They landed with a wobble and Phyllo fell out. He flopped to the ground, and collapsed onto his back. The honeysuckle was grasped in his hand.

The atmosphere inside the Birdcage was lifted greatly by the arrival of an extravagant array of fresh ingredients. Nonna Sophia, aided by Signora Volante, Marco's mother, cooked up a storm in their small kitchen. Mozzarella stuffed arancini with generous slices of fat tomatoes; rainbow-coloured ragu and home-made gnocchi; knobbly pizza topped by fresh San Marzano tomato sauce and olives. Every meal a delight. Conversation bubbled rowdily around the hearty table and the troupe pushed itself ever harder and higher in the ring. Signor Volante expanded every flyer's part so that they had choreographed moves to perform at every turn. The routine grew daily with complexity and skill.

Phyllo and Marco's friendship had been cemented by their adventure with the butterphants who, once they'd realised mice supplies had run dry, hadn't wanted to hang about. The boys had managed to delay them long enough to empty out Marco's shopping and together they'd made makeshift hammocks from their tunics to stagger home, laughing and hooting.

They continued to spend a small slice of their mornings practising together, launching themselves from the low ground swings to ever braver heights. The troupe had acclimatized to the thinner air over their stay and now found itself with a new buoyancy. All the extra energy they found in their much-improved menu fuelled stronger performance which in turn fuelled team spirit. This, in further turn, fuelled the supportive magic of the Fabulous Volante which Phyllo felt he understood more day by day. In their upward spiral they flew higher and further and more impossibly than Phyllo had ever seen. With every show he was more and more hopeful that a Gilded Pennant could be within their grasp.

On their last morning in Fortune Falls, when the troupe took a well-earned break, Marco found Phyllo waiting patiently in the tiers. "How do we look?"

"Fantastic."

"Fabulous," Marco corrected.

"That too. Actually, really quite incredible." Both boys beamed.

The Volante family settled around the ring to sup on coffees brought in by Nonna and nibble on biscotti or fat Saturn peaches.

"I'm on a break for half an hour. Let's have another go," said Marco, pulling Phyllo up.

"Don't you want to have a break too?" Phyllo asked, but Marco flexed the muscles in his arms in reply and they hurried over to the swings, positioned just out of the way to one side. They jumped onto one apiece and kicked down together to start the swinging pattern they'd been practising.

"Volare!" Marco called out on his next upswing and Phyllo

echoed it, "Volare!" Their inner rascals bubbled to the surface, noisy and joyful.

Marco took to the edge of the swing and leaped. "Hup," he called as he left the board and the eyes of the troupe were upon them. He rose in the Pirate Captain's stance, arms and legs spread wide and angular. Even without the cape he was bat-like, hanging in the air and then landing the leap at the very last moment, as the boards swung apart. He glided past Phyllo and off the back of the board, just like he did in the show on trapezes. Then Marco ran around to remount his board on the next swing. "Now you," he called out.

"Volare!" Phyllo shouted and Marco called it back, "Volare!" They pumped the boards and gained in momentum. The hearts of the troupe were with them. "Hup," shouted Marco, and Phyllo launched from the board. With every cell, he willed his body into the air. He rose beyond what was possible, and threw his arms and legs out, channelling the Pirate Captain. He too was bat-like and sinister, he stretched toward Marco, the impossible distance to his prey closing. And then his foot touched the board. Lightly. Surely. And he stepped forward to throw his imaginary cape around Marco and they both moved together, backward off the board and onto the ground.

The troupe erupted into cheers. Arnaldo was the first to find Phyllo and squeeze him in a rough hug. "*Buono*, Phyllo. I knew you could do it!" Then Ezio was patting him on the back and then Signor Volante himself. "San Giuseppe, the Confectioner's boy can fly!" he said.

It was true. Phyllo had felt the air thicken around him, felt time slow, so that placing his foot in the perfect spot had been natural. Easy. His body had found its mark and now Phyllo's chest felt fit to burst with happiness. He'd done it.

"And what great timing," Signor Volante continued, "There is no better place to make your debut than Star City."

"Star City?" Phyllo choked out the words, "Debut?"

"The first night shall be yours, Phyllo."

"What? No. That's insane. Marco, you need the warm up before the big one, don't you?" Phyllo looked to Marco as his mouth dried.

Marco beamed with the same smile as the rest of the troupe, like a happy band of meerkats, all standing tall, all looking at him, all eager to see him succeed. "I have played this part every day for months. I know the move backwards."

"But Star City, Marco. Surely you don't want to miss it?"

"Miss it? First night is for set up and checks. I'll take my place in the other shows for the Guild, don't you worry about that! Try and stop me. Yes, I think you should do it – to perform in Star City, Phyllo, it will be good for you."

"Good for him? Is extraordinary for him!" Signor Volante exclaimed, clapping Phyllo on the back, "An experience like this, you can no turn down." He wagged an admonishing finger. "The atmosphere? The people?" He clenched a fist, high to his chest, "It will feed your talent like nothing else could. Now that you can perform, you must."

"But it was just once. And I'm down on the ground." A clammy sensation spread over Phyllo's back. He wasn't ready.

"You were in the air, Phyllo. It is the same at five feet or twenty, huh? It is time for the chick to fly the nest."

Phyllo's jaw flapped. His eyes skipped from Signor Volante, to Marco and then Birdie, who he noticed for the first time standing in the ring. Her eyes were wide with eager expectation. His gaze returned to Signor Volante, who laid a hand on Phyllo's shoulder. "Belief in yourself is everything," he said.

CHAPTER EIGHTEEN

Star City

P hyllo pulled at the neck of his tunic, desperate to release some heat. The ring had never felt more crowded, every person pressing in. Too many bodies in a shrinking space. Shoulder to shoulder and babbling mouth to ear. The air was filled with excitable talk and waving hands and Phyllo felt buffeted. Felt sick.

Low whumps of pistons rumbled through the ground beneath his feet – the Machine: preparing to take them on. Vibration hummed through the big top frame. Electrical charge buzzed bolts in their holes. The inescapable process whirred forward, whilst Phyllo did everything he could to retreat. He tried to close his mind, but the Machine pulled at every nerve ending and refused to be ignored.

The Ringmaster swept into the ring, the lumpy and grace-less Bain trundling in his wake.

"Good people," he called over them and the chatter died down. "The time is almost upon us." He held up the master stake. "In mere moments this post will be driven into the earth in Star City and our hopeful troupe will begin its pilgrimage to glory. The Circus Guild awaits."

Excited chatter bubbled up and Phyllo knew he should feel excited too. Perhaps the thin air of Fortune Falls was finally getting to him. His vision rolled uncomfortably and he closed his eyes until it settled. Marco and Ezio high-fived. The family Volante pulled together in a group embrace. Phyllo sidled a little further away.

"Bain, if you would." The Ringmaster passed the master stake to his thick-necked companion who clomped into the cabin to take the link. "Good fortune to us all," the Ringmaster crowed then spun away with a showman's flourish.

The slow heartbeat of the Machine became fuller, stronger and then faster, beating along with Phyllo's own. Blue light rushed through the veins of the big top and then they were cut loose from Fortune Falls. Free, lost and nowhere: reality spun and yawed, but the canvas of the big top stayed rigid and true. When static pulled his hair out in a puff and stuck the silky tunic to his chest, Phyllo knew they had arrived.

At once, the canvas sides were hoisted to the roof and engineers jumped to their task. Sweepers dashed out to form the wave. Phyllo couldn't wait. "I just need some air," he mumbled to Marco and then wobbled out through the nearest gap. But if it was peace that Phyllo wanted, he was right out of luck.

His senses were immediately ambushed by a city that thrummed with life. Huge, noisy crowds rolled through the streets. Coloured lights, banners and bunting looped lamp-post to street sign and away over rooftops. Somewhere high in the city, a trumpet parped out jazzy melodies. Closer, raucous singing drowned out a band. Sound seeped from neighbouring shows. Smells crept from unfamiliar food, exotic and sweet.

Phyllo reeled, overwhelmed by it all. The Circus of Wonder had settled on one of the five triangular plateaux that surrounded the pinnacle of Pilgrim's Peak, forming a star. The plateau's wide base butted up against the rising nest of streets that was the city itself, whilst the furthest point of it reached out, seemingly, into the night sky.

Phyllo turned his back on the city. Chilly air prickled his skin into goose-bumps, but he welcomed it. The cold felt clean and he was desperate to feel free of it all.

The plateau was bordered by a thick stone wall. Strings of lights swayed and tinkled at pretty lampposts spaced along it and led him, surely as a funnel, to the furthest pointed corner.

It was like standing at the prow of a ship, the sky: his ocean. Stars, in their millions, shone from pinpricks in the inky blue fabric of the night. If there was a heaven, Phyllo thought, surely he was closer to it here than he had ever been. Could his mother see him? He'd have given anything to see her.

"What should I do?" he asked the stars, "The trapeze scares me half to death. Is flying the same, no matter how high? Do you think I can do it?" He searched the sky for a sign. "Shouldn't a person keep their feet on the ground?"

He hung his head. He should be better by now. A few months ago, he'd never have believed he'd even be thinking about leaping from a trapeze without a safety net to catch him. A few months ago, the most pressing thing on his mind had been perfecting marshmallows. How times had changed. Would he ever feel like he wasn't taking his life in his hands? Was he going against his true nature or finding it?

He scrubbed at his hair, frustrated. *Believe in yourself, Phyllo. You're a flyer now.* He laughed bitterly at the thought and the sound hitched in his throat. He leaned heavily against the wall and peered down, over the edge. The wall fell away into darkness hundreds of feet below and he closed his eyes against it.

"Not thinking of jumping, I hope."

Phyllo started. The Ringmaster was standing behind him, leaning on his cane, hip dipped and leg crossed. The velvet of his purple tailcoat shone silky and plush in the moonlight. Machine goggles rested on the brim of his black stovepipe hat. He looked faintly amused.

Phyllo bristled. "How long have you been there?" He swiped at his eyes.

The Ringmaster twirled the curl at the end of his long, pointed beard. "Long enough to see you're troubled."

"Just getting some air." Phyllo turned back to face out to the sky and pull himself together.

"Aldo tells me you've made great progress. Not hankering for a return to the Confectionary, surely?"

"I was just wishing that my mother was here to see it." It was only half a lie.

"Your mother. Yes."

Lazarus Barker joined Phyllo at the wall. Considerably taller, he bent at the waist to lean with straight arms against it. Phyllo folded his own across his chest and turned his face away.

He felt the Ringmaster looking him over and flinched at the scrutiny.

"This world is not a fair place, sultan or pauper," the Ringmaster said at last, "There are no special considerations. Our world turns and there is nothing you or I can do about it." His voice turned sour. "Destiny and time conspire against us." The Ringmaster took his eyes from Phyllo and turned them out into the distance. The landscape rolled sharply away beneath them, dark clouds of forest melting into the darkness. "Both our lives could have been very different had we not lost the ones we loved." The words left him in a tone Phyllo wasn't used to hearing. He snatched a glance up and saw the expression in the Ringmaster's eyes. Grief. Phyllo had the urge to console him, to confirm that they shared the same pain in the

233

loss of a parent, a whole family for the Ringmaster, but there just wasn't time. The Ringmaster snapped himself upright before Phyllo could move.

Lazarus Barker cleared his throat. "If your mother had lived it would be a brighter world for everyone." He laid a hand on Phyllo's shoulder and Phyllo was so surprised, he couldn't think of a single thing to say in response. "I'm sorry, Phyllo," the Ringmaster continued, "This is our destiny." He released Phyllo, straightened his collar and lifted his chin. The familiar aloofness returned. "Let's see what you're made of."

A few members of the band had drawn loose chairs into a huddle in the ring by the time Phyllo returned. They blossomed in the energy that poured down from the city, strumming out tunes and drumming on chair backs. The Circus of Wonder musicians belted out old familiars whilst engineers cranked the tiers into place and, out on the horseshoe, cabins were expanded and bolted down. The melodies dragged lyrics from long buried memories to the lips of anyone close enough to hear them. Phyllo found Roly leaning against a king pole and tapping his thigh.

It dragged a smile to Phyllo's lips, despite himself. Even Emmett had been lured by the music of the past.

Doink doink doink doink. He sat amongst the band, twanging at a metal spring. It added a daft comedic edge to proceedings and the musicians beamed amongst themselves. It was a joy to see his old friend the clown in the thick of things. *Doink doink doink doink.* Emmett bobbed up and down with his own bouncy beat and joined in with the singing, taking the lead.

"Masters and mistresses, come fly with our show. Just tuppence for your ticket now, come take a bow."

Roly threw an arm around Phyllo's shoulders and gave him a brotherly squeeze, then dipped in a mock bow to which Phyllo couldn't help but curtsy. Roly hooked Phyllo at the elbow and proceeded to skip around him in a circle, pulling him in a spin. Faster and faster, Phyllo, initially not a willing participant, had to run to keep up. His feet occasionally lifted from the floor as Roly spun him round and round. The surprise of it made Phyllo burst out laughing; a crazy welcome release from the oppressive tension he'd struggled with all day.

"Lion tamer's got it wrong, lost his whip, now his legs are gone." Emmett got up on his feet and jigged about, hopping from one foot to the other. He doinked his spring with great enthusiasm, but appeared to be having trouble when it came to sticking with the rhythm. Out of time and uncoordinated, he bumped against chairs and musicians alike, knocking their instruments out of their hands.

Emmett continued to sing, but they weren't lyrics that Phyllo recognised now. His voice had dried to a rasp.

"Spits out the bones, blood spread like jam. Call for the Jester, 'cause that's what I am."

Emmett staggered around the circle, and the music faltered, only one banjo player gamely trying to continue. Phyllo and Roly slowed their spin, drawn to the spectacle Emmett was creating.

"What are you looking at?" Emmett pushed one of the musicians on the shoulder, "Don't you know a classic when you hear it?" Emmett lurched suddenly to one side, losing balance and tripping over himself. He landed awkwardly on the lap of the banjo player, who yelped as they both rolled over backwards on the tipping chair.

"Emmett! Emmett! For pity's sake." The musician flailed beneath Emmett's awkward weight and the trumpet player jumped up to help. He hauled Emmett off, kicking and cursing.

"Oi, oi! Don't handle the merchandise!" Emmett tried to disentangle his limbs from the legs of the chair and tore his legging on a splinter. He stumbled backward and took them with him, back to the sawdust.

"Gerroff me." Emmett slapped at their hands as the heap of bodies pushed and pulled at each other, trying to escape the jumble. Phyllo dashed over with Roly. They each took one of Emmett's hands and hauled him up.

"Hey-heey!" Emmett attempted a kind of can-can, kicking his legs in a misinterpretation of the situation. He started to sing again, "Just tuppence for your ticket, missy. Hum-te-hum. Aw, how's it go again, Phyllo? What's the next bit?" He screwed up his face while Phyllo and Roly struggled against his buckling legs.

The banjo player also got to his feet: grumbling and sour and brushing himself down. The neck of his instrument was snapped from the body. His face now wearing a sneer. Phyllo didn't like the look of it.

"I think, perhaps a little lie down, Emmett. What do you say?" He quickly cut in before anything could develop.

"I'm alright. We're having a party!"

"Oh, no, everyone's really tired, aren't they Roly."

Roly feigned a yawn and a stretch, blocking the line of sight between Emmett and the infuriated musicians. "Oh yeah, so tired. Come on. We'll walk you back. Take the party with us, eh?"

Roly scooped an arm under Emmett's and Phyllo did the same on the other side. Between them they steered him out of the ring and around to the Clown Quarter. Emmett chuckled between them, the spring now dangling limply from one hand. "Yeah, we'll take the party with us." He bobbed about, trying to dance and bouncing haphazardly, pulling all three of them in a staggering zigzag. It was like trying to hold on to a sack of struggling monkeys.

Phyllo was relieved to see that the Clown Quarter had already been set. Its communal dressing area was clear and empty, freshly reconstructed after the jal, but Emmett's personal quarters were a disaster. Congealing plates of who-knew-what teetered on his desk in a forest of filth. It was clear that when the time had come to pack, Emmett had simply tossed everything he owned into his curtained cell to get it out of the way. Or perhaps Gus had. Or Jack. Either way, when Emmett threw back the drapes the smell and sight of it was quite overpowering. Emmett dropped to his hands and knees to dig through the rubbish and discarded clothing on the floor. "Some here somewhere. Have a drink with me. It's early yet." He scooped armfuls of junk out of the way, shoving it out onto the floor at the boys' feet. Phyllo and Roly looked to each other. Roly's nostrils twitched.

"Tell you what, Emmett, I'll look for it. Let's have a pyjama party, like the old days. You and Roly climb up to the bed and I'll find it," said Phyllo.

After an initial wide-eyed look of terror from Roly, the boys picked their way over to the short ladder up to Emmett's bunk. In a low voice, Phyllo said, "You go up first so you can pull and I'll push."

Roly grimaced, but climbed up anyway. "It's foul up here," he grumbled.

"Come on then, Emmett," Phyllo called in a much louder voice, "Let's get this party started."

"Hey-heey!" Emmett struggled to his feet and stumbled over, falling heavily into Phyllo and almost taking them both down.

"Roly, help me."

"Emmett, up here." Roly leaned down from the bunk, hand outstretched.

"You boys. I can do it." Emmett chuckled and made an unsuccessful grab for a rung. On his second attempt, Roly caught Emmett's wrist and together they lurched and wobbled upward, Emmett's malodorous bottom way too close to Phyllo's face for his liking. Emmett flopped at the waist and onto the bunk, dragging himself further by means of clenched fists of blanket – a method of locomotion both clumsy and apparently practised. Phyllo returned to the mess on the floor and started searching.

"What are you doing?" Roly hissed down over the edge, "You're not seriously looking for that stuff, are you?" Suddenly and impulsively, Roly gagged, "It's disgusting up here."

"We need to find it." Phyllo pulled a bottle with an inch of blue liquid inside from a desk drawer.

"Oh, Roly, Roly lad, I don't feel so good," Emmett moaned.

"Phyllo, quick, a bucket or something." Roly thrust down a hand and Phyllo tipped out the contents of a small paper bin to pass it up just in time. Phyllo could only see Roly's face and hear Emmett's retching, but that was more than enough. Roly scuttled down from the bunk, looking pasty and not quite escaping the sour smell of acid which chased behind him.

"Help me look." Phyllo resumed his digging. "We have to get rid of it. All of it. Now."

When Phyllo awoke, he discovered that the normal order of things had returned. He was, once again, the last out of bed. Marco was still at the breakfast table though, wolfing down porridge.

"Why didn't you wake me?" Phyllo grumbled, sliding onto the bench beside him.

"I would have soon," he said between mouthfuls, "Heard you come in late. Thought you could do with a lie in."

"Mio piccolo ghiro!" Nonna Sophia waddled over to the table, smiling unreservedly, and pinched roughly at Phyllo's cheeks. Marco put his head down to shovel in more porridge. He was definitely smirking.

"For you?" She indicated the bowl Marco was devouring and Phyllo nodded as best he could, under the face-squishing circumstances.

As he followed the ever-grinning Marco out of the Birdcage a few minutes later, the warmth of it glowed in his stomach. The horseshoe teemed with cast, all keen to practise their parts and jostling for the space in which to do it. They picked their way backstage and into the ring.

"Phyllo, *buono*. We no have our schedule yet, but I think try now just in case there is no time later." Signor Volante extended an arm to scoop Phyllo on.

"We can no keep the net and rigging up much longer," he said, then added loudly, "I'm already being pestered."

He shot a look to the front row of benches where the Agile Arethusa were glaring back. At one end Harric and Garric, the youngest of the Arethusa, sat slumped and petulant.

Arnaldo and Salvo were practising their spins and catches high above and, as their set concluded, Signor Volante clapped his hands. "Everybody! Let's switch to the capture sequence and give Phyllo a run through."

Flyers skipped and clambered to new starting positions.

"OK, Phyllo. I think you are already good with the ground work. You know the climb and the gestures. You have shadowed Marco for long enough, I think, *si*?"

Phyllo nodded mutely. Crackers! They were getting straight to it.

"Into the mouth of the wolf then." Signor Volante gestured to the board.

Marco grinned, "That wolf doesn't stand a chance." He bobbed in a small gymnastic bounce and made straight for the ladder, already performing. Phyllo stared after him, but didn't move.

"Phyllo," Marco hissed. He'd have to follow. He managed a half-hearted skip of his own and tried to catch up, but Marco hadn't waited; he'd scampered up the ladder and was already on the platform by the time Phyllo reached the bottom. Arnaldo stood with one foot on the lowest rung to hold it steady. "Captain," he said with a nod.

Phyllo swallowed hard. Arnaldo looked coolly down at him, not with the usual smile of encouragement, but deadpan, acting as if Phyllo truly were the Pirate Captain. It seemed the time for growth was over. There would be no encouragement to *become*. It was time to *be*. Phyllo looked up the ladder and saw Marco's wide eyes waiting. He took a deep breath, straightened his back and climbed, fighting down the fear and looking out around the big top as he ascended. Other acts sat on the benches waiting for their turn in the ring. Small groups were dotted here and there in the lower tiers, eating breakfasts from their laps and arguing over details to be fine-tuned. The higher he got the more eyes were upon him.

By the time he'd reached the platform his mouth was as dry as the sawdust that mocked him from the ground. Squeals and vibrations from engineers' power drivers faded as they too paused in their work to see the new flyer. In the silence, a tinkle of bells. Whispers rippled around the tent, like waves on the Fabulous Volante's imagined sea, snatches drifting up to his ears.

The Confectioner's boy. He's on the platform. Can he fly then? It's a bit of a risk. I wouldn't do it. They shouldn't let him. They shouldn't make him.

"Ready?" Marco was holding the bar in one hand and gripping the rigging with the other. Phyllo knew the pattern of instruction by now: *Ready. Hup.* To delay might break the spell. The breakfast he'd enjoyed so much only a few minutes previously churned ominously in his stomach. He inched a little closer to the edge.

What if he falls? Fat lot of good that will do us. It's all wrong.

Phyllo looked out into the largely empty seating and tried to imagine it filled with people. He tried to feel the thickening of the air. Tried to believe. His eyes skimmed the empty wooden benches. Mr and Mrs Wood and all the little Woods come to watch. He thought of Roly and smiled for a second. Was he here perhaps too?

Marco cleared his throat. Time was short. Phyllo stepped forward and leaned out to grasp the bar with one hand.

"Ready."

Phyllo dipped slightly at the knee and scoured the big top again, looking for that friendly smile. He found the distinctive profile of the Crow Man.

"Hup."

Balance already committed to the moment, Phyllo half fell, half leapt from the platform. He tore through the air on the trapeze and pushed himself forward just like Marco had taught him. Up above him, shadows played upon the canvas roof in the morning sun. The black outline of a tri-horned jester's hat stretched long and distorted. Phyllo reached the peak and swung backward.

From the other platform, Columba launched. She was the prey the Pirate Captain hunted. In the shock of what he'd just seen, he had forgotten all about her.

Phyllo searched the spot in the tiers where he'd seen the Crow Man, but he was gone. Of course, he was. Where? There! Phyllo spotted him running and then disappearing through a side exit that led backstage.

His swing reached its peak and, as he started the return, Columba's trapeze suddenly dropped on one side and she slid, shocked, off her perch. Her pin-sharp reflexes threw out a hand and she snatched the very end of the bar. Phyllo yelled out, "No!"

She looked up at Phyllo and then at her own trapeze. It dropped again, both sides this time and she let go, plummeting down. The net caught her and she rolled quickly, expertly, off. Phyllo gripped his own bar for dear life, still swinging, but losing momentum.

"San Giuseppe! Phyllo!" Signor Volante clapped his hands and Phyllo's stunned eyes snapped to him. "To the net. Now." He clapped again and Phyllo let go. He fell with a sense of relief, of failure, of fear. His emotions spun, none pausing long enough to stick. Columba's trapeze hung wonky and sick, Phyllo's own, bucking and off. Signor Volante had an arm around Columba who looked pale and shocked. Phyllo stumbled over. "Are you alright? What happened? Are you hurt?"

"I'm OK, but my wrist—" She rubbed at her right hand and flexed its fingers, wincing. Signora Volante rushed to her side too. "We must wrap it," she said, "Ice and a pepper bandage right away. Come." She put an arm around Columba and with a nod to Signor Volante, swept her away.

Signor Volante's face had turned a dangerous shade of purple. He returned his glare to the lame trapeze. "Skinner!" he bellowed, "What's wrong with my trapeze? Skinner? Get down here, damn you." He stamped away toward the engineers' box, which lodged high above the furthest tier.

Phyllo's head swam. Had he forgotten to breathe? In the corner of his eye something black flashed past an open backstage doorway. Phyllo scanned around the audience seating again. He'd seen the Crow Man, he was sure of it. Was he out there still? He caught the eyes of cast in the seats, mouths agape, heads turned to whisper, hard stares.

It's not right to meddle. It will bring us all down. He's bad luck. Bad news. A raised eyebrow. A curled lip. Something jingled in the rafters. Those bells again?

Phyllo's gaze flitted from face to face and then he caught sight of the long distinctive shadow of the Jester falling for a moment through a sunlit doorway that led out onto the horseshoe. Then the blur of a black cape and a crow mask running by. Who was out there? Phyllo launched himself in pursuit.

Where's he going? Knows it's not right. Yeah, you better run.

Phyllo dashed along the aisle.

"Phyllo, wait." Behind him Birdie bounded along, trying to reach him, but Phyllo did not slow. He made the doorway and skidded around the corner, slap bang into Skinner.

"What's this holy show? Where are you running to?" Skinner growled.

"In-between," Phyllo gasped.

"Get away with you. The gate's guarded, been guarded since we arrived." Skinner pushed Phyllo away.

"Skinner!" Signor Volante bellowed from within the big top. Skinner strode into the tent. "I'm here already, will you not eat the head off me."

Up ahead in the horseshoe, Roly was unloading his cart at Taya's confectionary stand, oblivious. Birdie clattered to a halt beside him. "Phyllo, you mustn't—"

"Come on." He ran toward Roly and the now unguarded main gate.

Roly noticed them as they hurtled closer. "Phyllo, what are you—? Where are you—?"

"The Crow Man," Phyllo blurted, "and worse, the Jester."

"You can't be serious."

"The shadow, Phyllo," Birdie said, "I saw it too."

"He's getting away. Come on." Phyllo ran on, out of the main gate and onto their triangular pitch. The flat expanse was open and airy with nowhere to hide.

They ran for the city, its walls the only source of cover, and dove into the rising twist of streets.

The road was narrow and flanked either side by old, uneven buildings. Some were shops, selling canvas wax and tacks or bolts of sparkling cloth. Others had shuttered windows; residences and guest houses, but the majority were eateries or drinking holes of some kind. Doors were thrown open and tables and stools spilled out onto the cobblestones. Even at this time of day, they were busy with customers, munching their way through great mounds of bacon or heaps of sticky pancakes, and slurping on tea.

The road wound steadily upward, bending in a clockwise rising spiral. Phyllo sprinted on. He dodged around plodding shoppers and stuck to the inside of the curve, cutting his line of sight to a few short feet. A handcart parked outside a shop blocked the path and he only just managed to hurdle it. Then he was brought up short and apologising as he blasted into a huddle of coffee-drinking ladies outside a smart café.

With failing momentum and stamina, he slowed to a stop in the centre of the street. People milled about him on every side; flamboyant and noisily conversing, shopping, bustling, locals and visitors from faraway lands travelling on links just like him. He turned slowly on the spot and examined their faces, but couldn't find what he was looking for.

Birdie caught up first, Roly, huffing, puffing and puce, a few seconds later. "Are you sure they came this way?" Birdie gasped.

"Where else is there to go?"

Together they continued to climb the street, scouring their surroundings and catching their breath.

"They could be inside any of them," said Roly, squinting to make out the interior of a shop. It was true. Periodically, narrow alleyways of stairs squeezed through gaps between buildings, offering steep shortcuts to the next turn of the spiral.

"Let's try one of these," Phyllo said and led them up the next set of stone steps, worn low in the centre by time and the thousand feet that had gone before. It spat them out opposite a patisserie with a chattering line spilling out of the door.

Another alleyway revealed itself a few doorways along. At the far end a black cape swished off the top step, turned left and moved out of sight.

Phyllo threw a wide-eyed look to Roly and Birdie and then dashed up the steps.

"Be careful, Phyllo," Birdie hissed.

What would he do if he actually caught up? Phyllo didn't know, but something was going on here that he didn't understand. He pressed his back to the corner and slowly rolled himself around it, searching the thickening crowd for the Crow Man.

Bright bunting crisscrossed the street, fluttering alongside silky star-pattern flags, which now adorned the buildings at regular intervals. A busy inn encroached on the path, where customers perched on tall stools at barrels that served for tables.

His black cloak stood out in the riot of colour. Hunched with his back to them, he was greeting another man, sitting on a stool and blocked from view. Phyllo, Roly and Birdie snuck toward them, careful to stay in the shadows. The seated man rose in greeting. Lazarus Barker. Phyllo stopped in his tracks.

The Ringmaster removed his hat and swept in a low bow. "Lord Protector Corvus," he said, "Thank you for finding the time." Then side by side, the two of them set off up the hill. The Ringmaster strode forward, straight-backed, his tall rabbit skin hat adding even more to his already impressive height. He towered over the man in black. It was odd, Phyllo thought, that he'd seemed to be taller.

They gave chase, but quietly now. Birdie danced between shadows while Roly and Phyllo kept to the doorways or dodged behind others heading the same way. Phyllo squinted at them. The beaked mask had gone. The man's shoulders hunched beneath the soft leather cape. His gait was staccato, reminding Phyllo of a bird that paced and pecked for scraps on the ground. The two men took an alleyway of steps leading up and then another, Phyllo and the others having to hold back at the bottom each time or risk discovery.

Eventually, they found themselves at the top of Star City: a flat cobbled meeting place that stretched broadly in a circle. Star pattern flags ran around the edge, fluttering on poles to conclude at an ornate doorway, beside which a gold-lettered sign said 'Le Crevette Rose'.

Phyllo, Birdie and Roly kept to the covered walkway that ran around the edge, whilst the Ringmaster and his associate cut directly across. They managed to get slightly in front – enough to see their faces and hear them speak.

Everything about the man beside the Ringmaster was black, aside from his skin which was sallow to the point of grey. Dark eyes lodged in shadowed hollows, his hair, black as jet, hung in a straight flat curtain that ended at his chin and was held off his face by a stiff pillbox hat. Beneath the cape, his fitted suit of velvet looked fine and expensive and his heeled boots tapped with the chime of steel. His nose hooked like the beak of a bird, but he did not have the Crow Man mask and Phyllo could not see where he might be hiding it.

"The Circus of Wonder thanks you for your vigilance, Lord Protector Corvus," the Ringmaster was saying as they neared Le Crevette Rose.

"Not at all," Corvus replied, "The Master Aficionaster wouldn't have it any other way."

They passed through ornate doors held open by two Conlis, looking uncomfortable in stiff high white collars. But, as Phyllo, Roly and Birdie approached, the Conlis looked them up and down, then closed the doors quite definitively against them.

Apparently, it was an 'invitation only' kind of a place.

Shut out on the doorstep, they bumbled around each other for a moment and then settled on a stroll along the front of the building, just as if they'd never really meant to go inside at all. They feigned interest in only each other, but threw searching looks through the tall multi-octagonal-paned windows, when they thought that no-one was watching.

Opulently decorated, Le Crevette Rose was clearly a restaurant club. Finely dressed patrons perched on soft crimson chairs at elaborate tables. Antiqued smoky mirrors tiled the walls between huge oil paintings in gilded frames. A broad staircase, that Phyllo could just see the bottom of, swept up with delicate ironwork scrolling beneath its rails. The Ringmaster and Corvus ascended to disappear from view.

"I wonder," said Birdie and then jogged away, examining first one stairwell then another before coming to a stop.

"Now this looks better," she said, as Phyllo and Roly drew up next to her.

"What does?"

"The route to the roof."

Phyllo looked up and saw that the buildings' roofs all fitted together, one slotting snuggly beneath the next, as the buildings themselves spiralled down in a curl.

"Le Crevette Rose is the last in the line. If we can get up on one roof it's as good as being on any other," added Birdie. She pointed to an enormous lantern of timber and glass, perched in the middle of Le Crevette Rose's otherwise opaque roof. It was a vantage point with great potential.

"How do we get up?" said Phyllo.

Birdie walked away and Roly was just about to protest when she turned and ran at them, past them. She jumped, placed one foot on the furthest wall of the alleyway, pushed off it, planted the other foot on the other wall, pushed off again and stepped up, onto the top of a bay window. From there it was a matter of easy steps to the first section of roof. Roly goggled at her.

"Up you come," she said.

Roly snorted out a laugh.

"Help me, Birdie, if you can," said Phyllo. She nodded and

he pelted at the wall, got one foot up, but after that crumpled in an unsuccessful heap.

"Again," Birdie hissed from her perch. "Think about coming up this time, not through. And hurry, people are starting to look."

Phyllo scrabbled to his feet, rubbing at a bruised elbow. "I am *trying*."

He wandered pseudo-casually back out into the piazza, past Roly, scanning about for anyone interested in what he was doing.

"Roly, can you give me a hand? I reckon I might manage one bounce, but two…" he shook his head. "A boost on the first one and then maybe I've got a chance."

"Alright," Roly sighed and went to stand by the wall where Phyllo had just crashed to a heap. He bent and meshed his fingers together as a step. "It's your funeral."

Phyllo ran at him and, to give Roly his due, he did not flinch. He took the weight of Phyllo's foot with an 'oof' and strained to boost him upward with as much force as he could muster. Phyllo's other foot connected with the opposite wall and he pushed off again, rising more than he'd expected and lurched onto the bay roof, bowling Birdie over. Roly shook his head and laughed until the shopkeeper, and likely owner of the bay window, snatched open his door and rushed out. Clapping eyes on Roly he instantly started berating him.

"What the devil is going on? What's all this racket?"

Roly's jaw flapped. "There was a bird," he invented randomly, "Really enormous, huge bird."

"A bird?" The shopkeeper made to turn and look up at his roof where Phyllo and Birdie were flapping about with nowhere to hide.

"Over there," said Roly pointing in the opposite direction, "Flew off." The shopkeeper squinted into the sun.

Phyllo and Birdie ducked low and scuttled up onto the next level of tiles.

"Can't see it. Made a hell of a din. Thought it was coming through.

"Oh yeah, it was really big. Fat. I think it had stolen some-one's pie."

"Someone's pie?" The shopkeeper scratched at a buttock.

Roly chanced a glance over his shoulder and locked eyes with Birdie who patted herself down and mouthed, "Fat?" Roly smirked then continued to the shopkeeper, "Reckon he was having trouble holding on to it."

The man gave Roly a derisory snort, dismissed him with a wave of his hand and went back inside.

Phyllo and Birdie looked down at him from the ridge of the roof. Roly would never get up there alone. He shrugged and waved them along and Phyllo grimaced apologetically. They'd have to go on without him.

The rooftops curled to the lantern of Le Crevette Rose, its octagonal form providing, as Birdie had suspected, a bird's-eye view of every table in the upper salon. Peeking inside they found the Ringmaster sitting uncomfortably with Corvus at an otherwise empty table for eight. A small window in the lantern was open a crack so they settled beside it just as Corvus got to his feet. For one horrible moment Phyllo thought they'd been spotted, but then saw that he was striding toward a third man, now coming to join them.

He was quite the roundest person Phyllo had ever seen. His inflated head wobbled on his shoulders, pink-cheeked, bulbous-nosed and topped by a swirl of unnaturally red hair. He wore a creamy, business-like suit with a jolly colourful tie.

In each fat fist he clutched two or three leads at the ends of which scampered brightly dyed poodles. Turquoise, lemon, lime, cerise and lavender candy-floss puffs on lolly stick legs. They turned in yipping circles, the shortness of lead and girth of the man's stomach keeping them from the very real danger of being trampled underfoot.

"Master Aficionaster," said Corvus with a low bow.

The fat man rumbled with a chuckle that jiggled his jowls. "No need for such formalities, Malum. It's breakfast time after all, not some stuffy dinner."

"As you wish, Monsieur Gourmand—"

"Ronnie. Ronnie, please."

The Ringmaster stood as they got closer to the table. "Master Aficionaster."

"We're all friends here, aren't we? Can't breakfast with strangers. Ronnie, I tell you. Ronnie. Now sit, Lazarus. I'm starving."

The Ringmaster obediently sat.

"Blimey," whispered Phyllo to Birdie, "I've never seen him look so nervous." Birdie gawked down at him too.

"Now I see you've already met Malum. Malum Oswald, Lord Protector Corvus. Top Crow in the pecking order, as my minions would have it and here to keep us all safe." He smiled warmly at the cold creature in black.

"Master Aficionaster," said the man they now knew to be called Malum Oswald.

"Now, don't make me tell you again. Ronnie, I say. Malum, this is Lazarus Barker, Ringmaster at the Circus of Wonder. Of course, I knew your father. Verne and I went way back. And your mother too, Seren was a beautiful woman, if you'll forgive me for saying so."

He disentangled the first of the leads. "Up, Margo."

The pink poodle hopped up onto a dining chair and sat down.

"You all came here on Beau's birthday one year, do you remember? You and Beau and Boddington, like the three musketeers you were. A long time ago now, of course. Such a shame."

The Ringmaster's face had turned a stony white.

"Up, Betty." The blue poodle jumped up onto the next seat. "Such a gift, Verne had. Such a shame that things have, well, shall we say, slid a little?"

The Ringmaster looked down into his lap.

Phyllo goggled at him. It was the most peculiar thing. The Ringmaster was the most formidable man he had ever encountered, but in the presence of these two, Ronnie Gourmand and Malum Oswald, he seemed to have been reduced to a little boy. A scolded one at that.

"Hugo. Beryl. Lavender." Gourmand seated his remaining dogs at the table. A snake of Conlis waiters appeared, balancing great silver trays at their shoulders.

"I've taken the liberty," said Gourmand as they encircled the table. He rubbed at his enormous round belly.

"Know what I like, don't you?" he said with a chuckle and then, in a co-ordinated whirl of movement, the waiters deposited plate after plate of delicious looking food on their table. Mountainous heaps of scrambled eggs, sausages, bacon, bagels smothered with cream cheese, hot buttered toast, muffins and pastries. The smell of it wafted out of the crack in the window. Birdie's stomach growled and Phyllo grinned at her.

"What? I didn't have time for breakfast this morning. Some of us got up early." She rubbed at her tiny waist, "and apparently I'm fat."

"I think that was my fault."

"Not the lightest of landings."

Gourmand immediately shovelled wobbling mounds of scrambled egg onto five small plates and pushed them in front of his dogs who yipped with delight and stood on their chairs to tuck in. Five pom-pom tails waggled gleefully.

"Dig in, dig in." Gourmand waved an all-encompassing hand over the table, "The sausages are excellent." He speared two on his fork and took a greedy bite. The Ringmaster served himself a helping and Oswald placed a single piece of toast on his plate whilst looking with great distaste at the gobbling poodle next him.

A few moments slipped by without conversation. Gourmand, napkin tucked under his many chins, loaded up his plate with food and then turned his full attention to emptying it again, into his sizeable stomach.

Oswald pecked at the tiniest morsel. The man was wiry – thin but not frail, although his back arched uncomfortably. He sat at the table like a predator hunched over its prey. His beady eyes flicking around the room. Watching. Black and crow-like as the man was, Phyllo was now certain he'd never met him before.

Gourmand pulled an envelope from his jacket pocket. "Your schedule, Lazarus. Five o'clock slot. I'll attend on the third night for final judging, but my panel will visit unannounced, here and there, to take in all the acts. Give me the skinny." He smiled broadly. "Five big tops here at any one time and we have to get round it all. Anything in particular you want to highlight?"

The Ringmaster smoothed out his jacket front and sat a little straighter. "Our flyers have put together an excellent act this year. It gets better every day," he said in a rush.

"Well let's hope they've peaked by Friday, eh?" Gourmand's gaze slipped from the Ringmaster, over his shoulder and out to a spot beyond view from the lantern. He shot one hand into the air in a wave. "Vizier! Good morning to you, sir!" He pushed against the table and up to his feet. "The Rings of Ra have been here since Monday. I really must say hello. I hear they have a fire-eating act that's quite extraordinary."

He lumbered away, each candyfloss-puff of a dog jumping down from their chair to trail behind him, their leads dragging and hopping along the plush carpet. Oswald pushed his plate away and leaned back to stare pointedly at the Ringmaster.

"You have a contribution for the Crows?" he said the moment Gourmand was out of earshot.

The Ringmaster nodded, carefully put down his cutlery and produced an envelope of his own. It was small and thin.

"Not in need of much protection then?" Oswald said stiffly, eyeing it with derision.

"We have had a time of great expense. A fire. Enchanted canvas doesn't come cheap."

"A fire? Indeed. It would be a great shame if any other accident were to befall you."

"We are careful."

"You'll need to be." Oswald slid the envelope from the table and under his cloak. He too got up from the table and stalked away.

Malum Oswald swooped across the piazza toward the stairwell where Roly waited, patient and oblivious, lost in the examination of the sole of his shoe. Phyllo and Birdie scurried along the crest of the roof.

"We'll never get to him first," Phyllo panted, "Look up, Roly, for the love of toffee, look up."

Roly scratched at his head, bored, and finally looked around. Phyllo could have cheered. Roly, on the other hand, blanched and scarpered down the steps.

Phyllo sank low to the roof, pulling Birdie with him and, when Oswald had passed by, they scrambled around to the shop, with its convenient bay window, to climb down. Birdie, of course, made it look ridiculously easy, her thin-limbed body floating to the ground like a delicate dandelion seed. Phyllo didn't see himself being quite so graceful and considered his route to the ground uncertainly.

"Let's go," Birdie hissed, urgently waving him down.

It wasn't as high as the trapeze, but peering over the edge still gave him pause. "Yes, OK, I'm just…" Perhaps if he lay down on his stomach, he could swing his legs over? He got down onto his knees, scanning about for onlookers. To his horror he saw that the Ringmaster had now also left Le Crevette Rose and was heading straight for them. They were out in the city without permission and Phyllo didn't need any more trouble. He stormed along, scowling at the ground, but if he looked up…

"The Ringmaster!" Phyllo hissed, "Go. I'll see you back there."

Birdie nodded and dashed down the steps.

Phyllo flattened himself to the roof, hardly daring to breathe, and screwed his eyes shut as Lazarus Barker drew closer. The sound of his footsteps, louder and louder, then echoing in the stairwell, gritty and fading.

Time passed without incident until Phyllo felt sure he was gone. Now he just had to climb down. He'd gotten up there. That was harder, surely? He summoned his bravery and forced himself over the edge, dangled momentarily, then dropped to the ground on wobbly knees.

He paused to pant in the shadows at the base of the stairwell. By now Oswald should be long gone and the Ringmaster around the curve of the road at very least.

He checked the street. Shoppers bustled past; people took time over coffee, just like before. Relieved, Phyllo stepped out, but from nowhere, a muscular arm clamped around his chest. A reeking cloth smothered his face and his lungs filled with a chemical sting.

Phyllo struggled and clawed, but his captor was strong, too strong. Gradually, inevitably, his strength faded and the Crow Man dragged him away.

CHAPTER NINETEEN

Darkness Falls

He was cold. Wrists bound behind his back and leaning, slumped into a corner. The air was thick with decay. Phyllo's eyelids fluttered. Darkness. Thin bars of light. Distant voices. He moved his head and his thin grasp on consciousness swam and failed.

Pain. His back protested and he tried to move. Now he found himself slumped forward, over his knees. Hands tied behind his back. He remembered now. Pain. Sharp and biting. He flinched and found he could move a little. Adrenalin surged through his veins and blood pounded at his temples.

Where was he? He couldn't see much in the inky blackness, but knew he was somewhere small and stinking. He strained at the bindings around his wrists and found that they weren't tied well. They gave a little as he pulled. He fought against them. The cord pinched at his flesh, but gave more and more, until he'd loosened them just enough to drag one hand painfully free.

The relief of bringing his arms around to the front of his body was enormous. He clutched at himself and swayed in a wave of nausea. The ghastly smell penetrated his nose and throat, vile, putrid. He felt around. A stone floor, cold and sticky. A wall, rough and wooden. The other side: cold, metal,

257

dented. In front, wood again, planks, rough with tiny spaces between, just big enough to peer through.

On his hands and knees, Phyllo pressed his face up to it. Behind him something scampered.

What was he doing here?

His head throbbed with the effort of thought. He'd been with Roly. Birdie too. Out in the city. Chasing someone. Black. Malum Oswald. A new man. Not *the* man. A strong arm across his chest. The sickly-sweet reeking rag. A voice he'd known. *This isn't really trying.*

Beyond the gap between planks was a yard, small and walled. Dark. Quiet. He felt around, tried to stand up and found that he couldn't – the ceiling was too low. He had to be in some kind of store cupboard. A bin shed by the smell of things. He pushed against what he thought had to be a door, but to no effect. He felt further along. A larger gap – big enough for a finger. Something metal. He got beneath it and pushed up in the hope of it being a latch. It moved and the door in front of him pushed open, scraping noisily over the floor. Phyllo squeezed himself out of the gap and gratefully into the open air of the yard.

He straightened up. Night had fallen. Empty crates teetered in stacks and bulging hessian sacks leaned in an orderly group by a closed door. A tall gate.

Phyllo staggered toward it and found it unlocked. He stumbled through, into an even darker alleyway.

Where was his captor?

At the end, movement and light. He staggered toward it, squinting and shading his eyes as the light became brighter. He thought his head might explode from the pounding within.

He was back out on the spiralling streets of Star City. Wherever he was on it, the Circus of Wonder had to be down, so down he went. Weaving side to side and stumbling at uneven cobbles. Strangers' laughter. People. Lots of people. Bumping and jostling. An eternity of scraping himself back up from the ground and stumbling on. Grass beneath his feet and then the familiar curve of cabins and the bulb-studded sign that arched over the entrance to the Circus of Wonder. He almost cried with relief.

The booking office window was closed, shutters in place from the inside. The gate was open for a show. No Skinner, no guard. Phyllo staggered into the horseshoe.

On the other side of the canvas the show was in progress. He could hear the band, hear the whoops of performers and gasps from the crowd. He staggered on.

The ground beneath his feet was well trampled. Hundreds of imprints of shoes. Sweet wrappers churned into the earth. A good crowd tonight, Phyllo thought to himself automatically.

Up ahead the steam-organ piped out its merry little tune. Odd for it to be running even though the show was on. It tinkled out the melody, but missed a note. The next one: too long and off key. Had there always been those bells in the mix?

Phyllo's blood chilled in his veins. The main entrance to the big top was just around the bend. He stumbled on.

The automaton orchestra sped up, playing the tune unnaturally fast. The bass drum hammered harder, louder. Phyllo clutched at his head.

The Grand Entrance canvas flaps were down, but Phyllo fed himself beneath the flap of heavy fabric and staggered forward to the edge of the tiers. He gripped the guide rail and looked around. Every seat was filled; the big top packed to the rafters with rapt faces, entranced by the act in the ring.

Marco scaled the rigging in the garb of the Pirate Captain. It should have been Phyllo. This was the show he should be performing in. The off-kilter tune of the steam organ drifted to Phyllo's ear through the canvas and merged with the atmospheric music being played by the band. Bells. There were bells. Nausea gripped him and unable to hold it, he puked spectacularly over the man in the first seat of the row. Outraged, the man leapt to his feet, shouting. Other people howled in disgust and got up to move away. Performer eyes in the ring found him.

Phyllo sank to his knees. The Pirate Captain swung out on his bar, the first groping attempt to capture the lady. Phyllo watched him swing back. It should be him. His eyes were watery, blurry. He blinked it away. Up on the ceiling, the shadow of the tri-horned jester's hat stretched across the painted stars. Arnaldo and Ezio had noticed Phyllo on the floor out in the audience. Their character expressions, lost to arched sneers of disgust.

Marco made his approaching swing to launch, the perfectly timed leap that would leave the audience gasping. The bar of his trapeze suddenly dropped.

Not like Columba's had earlier. Not partially nor lopsidedly, but completely. It fell from the air like an axe had severed it at its root. Marco, unable to get the purchase for launch, dropped too. Like a marionette snipped from its strings he sank like a stone and crashed to the ground.

Several members of the audience screamed. Men jumped to their feet in horror. Now the puking child in the aisle was nothing. Nothing beside the crumpled remains of the boy in the ring.

Bedlam.

The crowd didn't know what to do. They'd been held in the palm of the performers' hands as they'd teetered on the edge of danger, as they'd taunted death. It was expected, part of the circus experience, but never had they seen someone fall so convincingly, so devastatingly. Should they help him? Should they applaud? Should they run? The masses surged toward the ring, toward the exit. They gawped, slack-jawed. They turned their faces away.

Phyllo, still on his knees, was buffeted by the stream of punters flooding from their seats. By the time the big top had cleared enough to see the ring it was crowded with cast, their backs turned. Marco. That was all they cared about now.

Phyllo got to his feet and pushed his way to the edge of the ring. The Volante family were a solid barrier around their fallen flyer. Even through the gaps in their legs, Phyllo could only glimpse snatches of costume. "Marco!" he wailed, "Marco!"

He clambered over the low barrier and clutched at arms, trying to pull them back so he could get to his friend. Signor Volante pushed him hard in the chest. "No! Get away. You. You are the Devil!"

Phyllo gawped back at him, shocked. "I, I—"

"Wherever you are, there is trouble!" He thumped at his own chest, "My son!"

"I didn't do it. I wasn't even here. I just got here."

"Oh, I know that! How could I not know? That should have been you. Where have you been?" Signor Volante's face twisted with fury.

"I, I don't know." Phyllo's voice cracked, his throat closing. Signor Volante threw his hands into the air.

"Out of my way!" Marco's mother stormed though, Arnaldo and Salvo behind her hauling a stretcher. The family pulled back and, between them, Marco was revealed. Crumpled. Twisted.

She carefully, gently, rearranged his limbs into a more

261

natural position and the three of them manoeuvred him onto their stretcher.

Both legs had sharp bends where there should have been none. Moving him like this should have drawn screams of agony, but Marco remained utterly silent.

Phyllo lurched to a different gap to see his face. Eyes closed; expression gone.

"No!" The word escaped Phyllo's lips as he gawked in horror.

"Gently now," Marco's mother instructed Arnaldo and Salvo. "We must get him to the Guild Infirmary as quickly as we can." The Volante family moved as one, Marco at their heart. They swept out of the big top, the stragglers of the crowd standing away, a shroud of horror holding them back. Birdie trailed at the rear. She looked at Phyllo mournfully.

"Birdie. I'm so sorry."

She shook her head and turned away.

The ring emptied and Phyllo found himself alone. The shock of Marco's fall had flooded his body with so much adrenaline that the woozy nausea he'd been drowning in had washed away. It left him only with the terrible headache that grated the inside of skull. He rubbed at his face and looked back up to the ceiling. He *had* seen the shadow of the Jester, he was sure of it.

Up in the rigging engineers swarmed around the trapeze fixings, shouting recriminations at each other and the equipment. One caught Phyllo's eye. One eyebrow arched, lip curling.

Phyllo snapped away. He wanted to get away from them. He got to his feet and made for the exit out on onto the horseshoe. Even before he got there, he could see it was crowded with people, looking for someone to blame, wondering what had gone wrong. Where had the Confectioner's boy been? Why hadn't he shown?

Phyllo ducked under the tiers and went as far as he could into the void. He squeezed himself into the smallest corner. Out of sight. Just for a while.

"Skinner! Skinner? Where the devil are you, man?" The Ringmaster. Phyllo cringed at the sound of him. He had a scolding in the bank.

Phyllo peered through the footwell gap to see Lazarus Barker, crimson with rage, at the edge of the ring. Skinner ran out from the wings.

"Tell me you fixed this morning's problem properly. Tell me we didn't send our star act up on shoddy equipment." Spit showered from the Ringmaster's mouth as he raged.

"I swear it." Skinner held his hands up, "I went up myself. Put new couplings on to be sure. It was a good job."

"Then why is there a trapeze in my sawdust? What in the Devil's name is going on?" The Ringmaster's voice raised in pitch and ferocity.

"It should have been sound. I came in to watch it. Wanted to make sure there was no twitch in it. No-one was more surprised—"

"No-one?" Barker brayed, "No-one? What about Marco Volante? I think he was exceptionally surprised. And Aldo. Barnum help you when he gets a hold of you. And did you just say that you came in to watch?"

Skinner backed away a step. He wrung his hands. "I just wanted to see it with my own eyes—"

"And who was on the gate? Your job was to safeguard the gate."

"The show was almost over. It was just for—"

The Ringmaster lunged at Skinner and grabbed him by his jacket front, pulling him up onto his toes.

"Do you know what you've done?" he yelled into his face. "You've cost us everything. We *need* that Gilded Pennant. Are you going to earn one for us, Skinner? With your dazzling protection skills?" He spat out the final words and then pushed Skinner away from him. He stumbled backward. "No, Ringmaster. I'm sorry, Ringmaster."

Barker strode over to the trapeze, lying ruined on the floor, and bent to snatch up the rope. There was no coupling, it ended in a blunt cut. He snatched up the other and found it the same.

"Not the Machine, Ringmaster. It couldn't have severed it like that."

"Sabotage," he breathed.

"Who? How?"

"It would help if you stayed at your confounded post, wouldn't it, man?"

Skinner hung his head. The Ringmaster pulled in a deep breath and rubbed at his face. "Double the guard. Day and night. No-one leaves, no-one comes in outside of show time. Keep the horseshoe clear. Everyone in their cabins unless they're in the ring. Keep the troupe locked down so we can spot whoever's left on a clear field."

"Yes, Ringmaster."

"Get the guard started now and then fix this. And make sure you do it properly, for the love of Barnum."

Skinner lumbered from the ring. The Ringmaster kicked at the sawdust, then turned out to look around the big top, hands on his hips and chest still heaving. He walked slowly, examining the rig from edge to edge. His eyes ran over the engineering ladders and around the top-most rows of seating. His expression, intense and thoughtful. He scanned the aisles and examined the sides of the tiers. His eyes ran along the rows and, as if drawn by a magnet, found Phyllo, horror-struck and peering out of the footwell in the lowest section.

His hand shot out to point. "I see you," he yelled and ran toward him, jumping over the ringside benches, manically chasing him down. Instinctively, Phyllo bolted. He squeezed out of his hidey hole and ran for the gap between canvas and the tier structure. Lazarus Barker ran too and skidded to a halt, tailcoat flapping in the space that Phyllo need to get through to escape. He was no match for the Ringmaster's speed in his current condition and skidded to a halt in Barker's shadow.

"You."

Phyllo closed his eyes and deflated.

"Is this where you've been hiding? Thought you'd give it a miss today, did you?" The Ringmaster dodged to one side to look around him. "Anyone else you're hiding under here?"

Phyllo looked up, shocked. "Anyone else? No. Like who?"

The Ringmaster glared at him, venom burning in his eyes. "Who cut the ropes, Phyllo?"

"I, I don't know," he stammered, "I thought I saw…" He trailed off, unsure what to tell him.

The Ringmaster grabbed Phyllo roughly by his upper arms and shook him. "What? What did you see?"

"The Jester," Phyllo blurted, "The old-fashioned kind. The one from the poster. I saw him at the Brampton Levels. When I saw the In-between thief. The one in the mask. And I saw him here too. Both of them." Phyllo rubbed at his head. His eyes prickled madly. "There was a shadow, on the ceiling."

"A shadow?" The Ringmaster spat out the word. Derisory. Scornful. He released Phyllo and pushed him away. "Get back to your quarters and don't come out for anything but the ring.

I don't want to see you anywhere else. If I do, so help me, you'll be out of this circus before you've a chance to throw a damn shadow. Get out of my sight."

Phyllo scrambled away. The cast still lingered on the horseshoe and their eyes followed him as he ran. Phyllo tried not to look, tried not to see their cold expressions, the mask of the Jester that he was seeing everywhere now.

The Birdcage was silent as the grave. Every member of the Fabulous Volante had come together as one to spirit Marco away and were currently somewhere between the horseshoe and the infirmary, trying to save him.

Usually the hub of life and family, Phyllo felt its emptiness keenly. He dropped to sit at the table, laid his head on his arms and the last of his energy drained out of the soles of his feet.

It seemed like madness to consider it, but had Emmett's Vincula possessed an engineer to sabotage Marco's trapeze, *his* trapeze?

The shadow.

Those bells.

That expression, everywhere.

The Jester was getting stronger, out of hand.

Phyllo clenched his fists, trying to think. Destroying the last of the Mermaid's Tears might have been too rash a move. By making Emmett go cold turkey he'd not only upset it, but put himself up as a target.

And what about the Crow Man? Was it possible that he was in league with the Jester? He'd escaped his impromptu prison, but that brief encounter in itself didn't really make sense. He couldn't help but feel that it had to be connected, that it wasn't over, that this was just the start of something he didn't yet understand.

Pieces of the puzzle were missing. His head whirled, confused and exhausted. He closed his eyes.

It was the sound of the family returning that woke him. They poured into the room, some slumping at the table, others climbing silently up to their cots. Signor Volante was the last to cross the threshold and closed the door.

No Marco. No Signore Volante.

Phyllo rubbed at his eyes and looked from one face to the next, searching for the terrible truth. Signor Volante lowered himself into his usual seat at the head of the table. His movements were measured and slow. Phyllo's heart beat heavily in his chest. He stared at Marco's father and didn't dare to ask.

"He lives," Signor Volante said evenly.

The relief of it poured down Phyllo's back and he threw back his head in an involuntary laugh. "Thank Barnum."

Signor Volante's jaw clenched. "Both his legs are broken. His back is damaged. Twisted. We don't know how bad it is yet. It could mean the end of his flying days. His mother is by his side." Signor Volante's voice became rough, almost unrecognisable.

Phyllo gulped down a choke. "Oh. Oh no."

"What were you doing out in the audience, Phyllo?" Signor Volante brought his gaze up from the table and fixed it upon him. His eyes were bloodshot and dark, and dissolved what remained of Phyllo's composure.

"You broke the spell. We could have saved him if it hadn't been for your sideshow. Never mind that you should have been playing the Pirate Captain yourself. That was your trapeze too."

Phyllo knew it to be true. "I think perhaps it was meant for me," he said quietly.

Signor Volante's eyes widened a little and he nodded slowly. "Bad luck follows you around, Phyllo Cane. Give me a reason to keep you as one of us."

His mind was blank. He couldn't think of a single thing he added to their act, in fact he was putting them all in danger. As far as he could see, he added nothing to anyone or anything.

"I can't," he said wretchedly, "All I can tell you is that I *am* trying. I never meant for anything bad to happen. I meant to play the Pirate Captain tonight."

"You were afraid. This morning you didn't have the stomach for it. Even before—" He tailed off. "If you meant to do it, where were you?"

"In the city." He caught Birdie's eye and she glared daggers at him, as if daring him to dob her in for being out of the circus without permission. He flicked his eyes away.

"This morning I thought I saw In-between, the thieves from Tabberstock. The one in the mask. I recognised him in the big top and then the thing with Columba's trapeze happened and I chased after him."

Signor Volante clenched his lips together. He was listening, even if he didn't know what to make of it.

"And I think he got the better of me. Put something over my face and it knocked me out. When I woke up, I was locked in some kind of shed and it was dark. I got back here as quickly as I could, but it was too late."

Signor Volante rubbed roughly at his face, squeezed his eyes shut and sighed. "San Giuseppe. This kind of thing, it has to stop. You invite the trouble in. No more crazy risks. No more chasing after thieves. We have security, leave it to them. Let them do their job. Do yours. Everybody has a role to play,

268

especially in the Fabulous Volante. We all fit together. It has to work." He slapped the back of one hand into the other, "It has to work for the Guild. There is no fall-back plan, Phyllo. My son," Signor Volante cleared the rumble from his throat, "Marco cannot come to your rescue anymore. He will no perform in Star City now. The routine is too complicated to swap anyone out. Are you going to let us down, Phyllo Cane? Is this another disaster waiting to happen?"

"I can try."

"No." Anger rose in him and he pounded the table, "Try? What good is 'try'? Do! You are here as a favour to your father, the memory of your poor sweet mother. You let me down, you let them down."

"I won't, I promise."

Signor Volante nodded. "Then we will see."

∼

Their time in the ring the following morning was short. Tumblers, balancing acts and the magical menagerie were all vying for a slot.

The Ringmaster had sent around word that tomorrow's show was going to be the one that really mattered, the one where the Gilded Pennant would be won or lost. This was the last opportunity to hone their acts before the big one the following day. Phyllo, of course, had already known that Ronnie Gourmand would be attending then for the final judging.

Just like he knew that the Crows wouldn't be trying too hard to protect them.

One more day to keep his nose clean and get it right.

The Fabulous Volante skipped about the ring with their

usual gymnastic finesse, but the showmen's whoops and finishing poses were tight and forced. Their gazes tracked Phyllo wherever he went, as if they were scared of what he might do.

Birdie partnered him for stretches and some warm-up moves on the low swings, but she had returned to the pinched expressions of the past.

This was the equipment he and Marco had made their own. Every dip and push from the ground made Phyllo think of him. It made his throat constrict. He couldn't concentrate and Birdie wasn't heavy enough to make it work properly. Their timing was mismatched and off, Birdie shouting at him to concentrate and Phyllo bumbling, apologising when really, he had no idea how to do it any differently.

Signor Volante soon tired of it. "Up on the trapeze, Phyllo. Our time is running short. Let's at least get one sequence under our belts."

Phyllo climbed the ladder up to the board, blocking out the height in his mind. It hadn't helped last time to look out into the audience, so he kept his eyes front and centre. Arnaldo waited on the platform, holding the bar for him with one hand. Phyllo's mind's eye saw Marco standing much too close to the edge and grinning like a fool; saw him pretend to fall only to be caught laughing by the net; saw him drop from mid-air to land crumpled and broken.

He shook the image from his head. Arnaldo waited, holding the bar, expression neutral, and Phyllo took a step toward him. The depth of his view to the ground revealed itself. Phyllo swallowed down the fear and thought about what he needed to do.

A strong swing out, legs up and over, then up onto the bar. He'd done as much before, on the low bars and in the air. Then he just had to pretend that he was on the ground swings. He could do it. He had to do it.

He grasped the bar with one hand and gave Arnaldo a nod. The ground refused to remain unseen and zoomed into focus. Phyllo gritted his teeth.

"Ready. Hup."

And he was away, swinging out. *You can do this.* At the peak he swung his legs up and over and the return swing began, the motion almost helping him pull up onto the bar. He needed to get up onto his feet by the second peak but, as the momentum slowed, his foot slipped and he juddered down, sending the swing off sideways.

His palms sprang with sweat. Columba had already launched on her trapeze for the sake of timing.

A rumble passed around the troupe.

Down on the ground Signor Volante clapped his hands once. "No matter. Reset."

Columba swung easily back to her platform. Phyllo had lost all momentum and his trapeze drifted haphazardly. He turned and saw Arnaldo holding out his hand, frowning. Phyllo's memory served up Marco, jumping up and down and egging him on. He slid off the bar and dropped to the net.

"No. No." Signor Volante waved one hand at him. "You could have swung back to the board. This is a waste of time."

"S-Sorry." Phyllo shuffled to the edge of the net as quickly as he could, "I didn't think—"

Signor Volante's brow furrowed. Phyllo dashed to the ladder and clambered up, the base of it kicking about as he struggled to maintain some kind of control. The platform couldn't come quickly enough and he stepped out onto it, sweating and dragging his hands down the front of his costume. He fumbled for the pouch of chalk in its bucket.

Arnaldo hooked the bar in and held it stiffly, waiting, while Phyllo passed the powdery pouch from hand to hand, taking deep breaths. When he couldn't put it off any longer, he stepped up to take the bar.

"Ready. Hup."

He was away again, heart hammering. He pushed the bar high with his chest and curled his legs up and around and hoisted himself to standing. Columba launched from the other side. Salvo stood on the platform, eyes boring into Phyllo.

He tried not to see it, tried not to see the Jester's mask merge with Salvo's own features.

Phyllo and Columba's trajectories came close enough together for the Pirate Captain to make a wild grab for her – the grab destined to miss. He played his part clumsily.

A second rumble rolled around the ground. He knew they were comparing him and he was coming up short. On the next approach he resolved to be more convincing and leaned out further, grasping with vigour. Too far. The bar kicked back-ward before its allotted moment and swung off centre, losing timing.

The sound of a clap rocketed up to Phyllo's ears from the ground. "Again." Signor Volante scowled up from the ring. This time Phyllo kicked the bar into motion and swung back to the platform. Arnaldo took his hand to guide him back but the grip was loose, Arnaldo's expression drifting from neutral to annoyed.

Again, Phyllo tried and again. His grip slipped. His timing was wrong. His stance was too forward, too straight, too low. Around him the energy of the group became oppressive. He hardly dared look them in the eye for fear of what he might see. In the end Signor Volante called them all down to the ground.

"You're driving me crazy with this, Phyllo. What's the matter with you?"

The troupe stood away from him, arms folded across their chests, mouths hard.

Phyllo's muscles screamed from the effort of it all. His eyes burned. "I don't know."

"You're hopeless," Birdie yelled at him "You've done it on the swings, we've all seen you. It's like you're not even trying. You're going to ruin the act. Don't you even care about what you've done?"

"Of course I do—"

"You're selfish. The most selfish person I've ever known. I bet your own family couldn't wait to get rid of you and lumber us. You ruined their lives, now you're ruining ours." Birdie burst into tears.

Signor Volante put an arm around his daughter's shoulders. His voice remained steady. "The Ringmaster watches us all, Phyllo. The Circus of Wonder needs a Gilded Pennant to survive another term. If the Fabulous Volante cannot win one, what's to stop the Ringmaster replacing us with an act who can?" He raised a cold questioning eyebrow.

Phyllo stared at him, dumbly.

"Arnaldo. Ezio. Time's up. Back to the Birdcage. We must try to rearrange the troupe to cover Marco's loss. This one is of no use to us." He turned his back on Phyllo.

One by one the rest of the Fabulous Volante did the same. They left the ring and the Agile Arethusa dashed in to take their place, lowering the net and casting it aside.

It took a moment for Phyllo to take it in.

He turned and ran from the big top.

The open doors of the Confectionary drew him home.

The candy cart was parked in the middle of the small shop

where Roly tossed packets into its shelves. An enormous weight lifted from Phyllo to see him there.

"Roly." He came in to lean heavily on the counter, chest still tight with pent-up emotion.

Roly lifted his eyes, but didn't get up. "Oh, it's you."

They'd not seen each other since parting company at the top of Star City the previous day. He'd expected Roly to be full of questions and concern, but he didn't seem to be bothered in the least.

Seconds ticked by. A muscle spasmed under Phyllo's eye. "Don't you want to know what happened to me?"

Roly's hand flopped to his side. "To you?" He raised a sarcastic eyebrow.

"Well, I thought you might be vaguely interested to know why your brother went missing."

"Went missing? That's a bit strong. Just got cold feet, didn't you? Decided to let someone else carry the can." Roly jammed bags of raspberry sherbet into the trolley, "For a change."

Phyllo glared at him. "Are you serious?"

"Not like you've ever done anything like that before, is it? Oh, wait, hang on. I seem to be doing all your work." Roly scowled at him.

"Right." Phyllo squeezed his eyes closed. So, that was it: everyone was against him now. He mashed his lips together and fought away the choke in his throat.

It was a pity he'd thrown all the Mermaid's Tears away; in that moment he would have gladly drunk it himself. How marvellous it would be to make all his worries disappear with a swig of potion.

Understanding clicked into place.

It would never have occurred to Phyllo to do something as stupid as take Mermaid's Tears, not ordinarily. Something else was at work on him. He was being manipulated. Being manipulated into needing it, needing the crutch. This was the Jester's modus operandi. The dawning realisation spread through Phyllo and soothed the clench in his chest. His words came out in a whisper, "This is what it does. This is how it got a hold of Emmett."

Roly glared at him, confused.

"The Jester, Emmett's Vincula. It keeps him at bay by magnifying his worries, by keeping him anxious. Now it's redirected to me because it knows I'm trying to get Emmett clean. It's taking away all the friendship and support, trying to make me weak too."

Phyllo looked blindly around the shop, thinking out loud. "I knew something was off, but I couldn't pin it down. The magic of the flyers is in the support that they give each other."

"If you say so." Roly was still looking at him like he was nuts.

"It is. From the moment I arrived, they made me feel like I could do it, now suddenly all that's gone. It's like poison's been dripping on us. Acid, eroding the magic, until it can't function anymore. When did you last see Emmett?"

"That waste of space." Roly stuffed another bag into the trolley.

"Roly, listen to yourself. What are you saying? Why would you say that?"

"Because he didn't even bother to come out for the show. The others had to cover for him, again. Probably off his face somewhere." Roly screwed up his nose, disappointed. Disgusted.

"You know that can't be true, Roly. Think about it. We took it all away."

Roly stared back at him and, as Phyllo watched, the

scathing conviction fell. "You're, you're right. Why did I think that?"

"It's what it wants. This isn't just about Emmett anymore, it's affecting all of us. The Jester, Emmett's Vincula, it's getting desperate."

"Do you think Marco...?" Roly said in a low voice.

Phyllo nodded. "But I think that was meant for me."

Roly stared at him, horrified.

"Now we really do have to find a way to help Emmett, before it affects anyone else."

Hope blossomed in Phyllo. There was an explanation behind what was happening to him.

"The jellies. Yesterday I had another go." Roly dashed to the cool box and pulled out the tray of lemon-shaped moulds. Yellow liquid sloshed about.

"Consistency has been a bit of an issue," he admitted, "To start with they were really sticky. Couldn't get them out of the mould. This lot are looking a bit runny." He tipped the tray from side to side. Gooey liquid dripped to the floor. "The last lot stuck my teeth together."

Phyllo puffed out a small laugh. "If you can get them right, they might buy us some time."

Roly dumped the tray into the sink. "I'll make another batch. What else can we do?"

Phyllo bit at his lip. "We need Emmett's book. Do you think we could persuade Albertus?"

CHAPTER TWENTY

The Currency of Magic

The following day Phyllo found his activities to be considerably curtailed. The Ringmaster's new security regime had every cast member restricted either to the ring or their cabins and as Phyllo's services were no longer required in the ring, this left him with nowhere to officially be but the Birdcage.

Morning practice lightened the load of filthy looks and bad energy as it left him with only Nonna Sophia. She was less inclined to ply him with her rough affection, but still couldn't help feeding him and, for a change, his breakfast was not peppered with pinched cheeks or slapped bottoms. It didn't taste as good.

Mid-morning the family noisily returned, giving Phyllo enough notice to scramble up to his cot and out of the way. They spilled in with an arm-waving argument in full flow.

It transpired that covering for Marco was no simple task. They argued back and forth about who could abandon their own role to take on the Pirate Captain and everyone had an objection. All of them short-tempered and snappy, they worried over Marco, bickered about remembering last-minute changes and agonized that they might not come up to the Master Aficionaster's extravagant expectations.

The hours stretched on, the Volante squabbled and Phyllo grew ever more restless. Trapped in his cot, he had worries of his own. He twitched with frustration, willing an opportunity for escape to present itself and, when the family finally filed out for the intro, Phyllo seized his chance.

The backstage Horseshoe hummed with cast, all concentrating on their impending performances and, he hoped, too involved in themselves to take notice of him. Heart in his mouth, he ducked out onto the path, weaving quickly between them and into the wings. Just in time, he picked out the black and tan of engineers who paced side by side, making security rounds. Phyllo sucked in a breath, flattened himself to slip through a flap in the canvas and then was out, into the auditorium as their eyes swept the spot he'd stood moments before.

The big top rumbled with movement and chatter. The air was thick with expectation. Multicoloured spotlights danced over the crowd and Phyllo spotted cast members already integrated in the throng, the low hum of the welcome theme just about discernible.

Phyllo hurried up the aisle to blend himself in, then slowed his pace to move with the flow of people finding their seats. He scanned about and found Roly up ahead, handing out cones of popcorn. Their eyes met and Phyllo motioned for Roly to meet him over by the side door, then slipped away to get under the tiers at his first opportunity and out of sight.

Roly found him a minute or two later. "I've told Dad I'm refilling the popper," he said and the pair of them stole out onto the horseshoe, creeping against the tide of visitors.

Early evening sun lit the scene in a golden glow that stopped just short of Frú Hafiz in the shadow of her doorway. Statuesque and ethereal, her silver dagger glinted from the long chain at her waist. She watched the steady stream of visitors heading for the grand entrance through dark glasses and picked out Phyllo and Roly as they dodged and wove against it.

"A good evening to you both." She bowed very slightly as they approached.

Just the person they needed, thought Phyllo, after all it had been she who'd explained the Vincula's presence in the first place. He looked about nervously for engineers or even the Ringmaster. "Actually, could we just step inside for a minute, I'm not really supposed to be out on the horseshoe?" She bowed them into her booth.

"The Vincula," said Phyllo, in a rush, "It's getting out of hand."

Frú Hafiz removed her glasses to look at him more closely with those ice-blue eyes. Phyllo's neck prickled.

"You believe that Marco's accident was no such thing?"

"That's right."

She nodded. "And Emmett? What progress has he made?"

"He can't drink Mermaid's Tears now, even if he wants to," said Phyllo, breaking eye contact, "I, er, threw the last of it away." Now he was unsure of how wise that had been.

Frú Hafiz didn't look surprised. "Well, it floats as long as it doesn't sink. Tell me of your encounters with the Vincula – has it laid hands on you?"

Phyllo was rather perturbed to learn that this was a possibility. That gave his mugger in the shadows the leeway of an alternate identity after all. He thought about the stature and the voice and in that moment became more certain than ever that it had been the man from Tabberstock, the same man who'd held a knife to his throat. The Crow Man. He shook his head. "I've seen shadows and reflections and I see its face everywhere, on all kinds of people and I'm sure it influenced someone to cut the trapeze ropes. It's like it's haunting me."

Frú Hafiz seemed relieved, which Phyllo didn't appreciate at all.

"The day it finds solid form there will be nowhere to go but onward to the red dead. Your intentions?"

Roly gawped at her, but Phyllo answered, "I feel like there's something we're missing. I thought perhaps if we looked in Emmett's book again, if Albertus will let us that is."

She nodded sagely. "And if he does not, understand it is the pen that holds the key, rather than the man. Be careful what you say to persuade him. These times are still best kept in confidence. Danger lies in the revelations. Does our Ringmaster know of your suspicions?"

"I've tried to tell him, but he's not very receptive. I'm not exactly his favourite person. Maybe an adult would do a better job of convincing him." Phyllo thought that Frú Hafiz was perfectly placed to be taken seriously. She didn't seem to agree.

"No. This is not his time. Even those of sweet disposition should not be disillusioned now. *Conscience* and *conscious* are two different things. Now, on with the butter." She shooed them back out into the horseshoe, "The show is beginning. Good luck."

The awning flapped closed behind them.

Phyllo and Roly looked at each other.

"OK," said Roly with a slow nod, "Excellent. So glad we dropped by."

Phyllo smirked, "You can always rely on Frú Hafiz."

"To put the wind up you," Roly muttered.

Phyllo laughed and looked around them. The horseshoe had emptied out considerably, just a handful of stragglers now, squeezing through the entrance as it closed. The clock was ticking. They jogged around to the Book Keeper's door, knocked and slipped immediately inside, snapping the door shut behind them.

Albertus Crinkle looked up from his desk.

"Sorry to just burst in," said Phyllo, "It's just—"

"Come in, come in. Refreshing to see young 'uns taking the Ringmaster's security so seriously."

Phyllo didn't know if Albertus knew quite how seriously he was required to take the Ringmaster, but he seemed quite happy to get them off the horseshoe so that worked well enough for now.

Albertus got up from his desk, pushing up the woolly sleeves of his cardigan. "Your timing is excellent. I was just about to make a cup of tea. Tempt you?"

"Lovely. Thanks. Any kind you like," said Phyllo, spotting the unspoken question.

"Right you are. Right you are." Albertus twirled two fingers in the air in a kind of saluting wave and shuffled to his little kitchenette beneath the mezzanine.

Phyllo and Roly drifted into his cabin. A small fire crackled low in the grate and Albertus's desk was littered with books in haphazard piles, curls of paper and a selection of pens, ornately filigreed and resting in individual wells. A fat tome with row after row of figures in columns lay beneath the giant magnifying glass. Despite the mess somehow the small cabin felt more spacious than usual.

"You look busy," said Roly, "Sorry, have we come at a bad time?"

"Not at all, not at all. A Book Keeper's work is never done, isn't that what they say? Something like that." He snorked out a little laugh. "High time I made sure the financial records were up to date, given our current situation. A forecast for the Ringmaster is in order, Gilded Pennant or no."

He clattered some mismatched cups and a teapot onto a tray and jingled across the room with it to set it on the corner of his desk. Light from the fire caught on a patch of worn gold leaf on the teapot lid.

"I seem to remember you enjoyed the Pouchong. Pop out a couple of chairs, there's a good lad," he said to Roly, indicating the outlines on the wall.

They settled to sip at the tea, Albertus's thick glasses steaming over as he drank. Wisps of grey hair poked randomly out from under his knitted hat.

"Looks complicated," said Roly, breaking the companionable silence and aware that they had to move things along.

Albertus swept a hand over the book currently open on the desk.

"Not to toot my own horn, but it is quite complex, yes. Not just Coin to consider, is there? Records of favours and kindnesses and of contracts of obligation, both spoken and written. All currency of the trade. Exchanged favours – amicably arranged. They're like money in the bank, money in the bank, yes." He ran a finger down one column and then the next. "Kindness given freely is stored against your name too." He tapped at the page. "That's a sweet one, a background wealth that cannot be eroded nor stolen."

The boys leaned in to look.

"You won't see anything from over there. Come around, come around. It takes a gifted Archivist to bring a book to life," he gave them a cheeky wink, "And one of these, of course." He patted affectionately at the enormous magnifying glass, suspended over the book by its heavy brass stand.

Phyllo and Roly got up from their seats and came to stand

behind Albertus, each looking over a shoulder. Albertus drew a symbol in the air above the book with one of his pens and the surface of the page seemed to twist. It was as if Phyllo had moved his head a fraction to one side and discovered that the perfectly aligned lines of the page were nothing but an optical illusion. That, in fact, the page was a three-dimensional scene, which had been perfectly lined up to form a flat page only from that one perspective. Which he wasn't looking from anymore. Phyllo blinked and shook his head. It was the oddest thing he'd ever seen.

Roly, on the other hand, settled down to the view immediately. "Cool," he breathed.

A ball-round woman, who Phyllo recognised as Rosemary from the Odditorium, was clearly visible in the page. Not an exact representation, but a paper model, words wrapping around her body to give her form.

She waddled across her paper room to fetch a plate of something Phyllo couldn't quite discern then returned to another figure, who'd also popped up out of the page. She could only have been Peaches, her fellow *Fat Lady*. Peaches took the plate gratefully and Rosemary went to stand behind her now seated friend. Wispy curls of paper like wood shavings sprang from the miniature Peaches' head, and Rosemary worked to curl them around tiny rollers.

"These two are the sweetest," said Albertus with a little shrug, "They'd give each other their last pennies. Back and forth it goes. They're really like a little ecosystem on their own. Tiny kindnesses in the bank, constantly given and repaid."

"Are all the books like this?" asked Phyllo

"Ink Imps take care of day-to-day events so I don't always get to see it, but all the books have an internal world of a sort.

If you're careful, you can peek through the window without falling in."

"Falling in. I'd forgotten about that," said Roly.

"It's not dangerous if you're careful. Besides, if I kept books the *ordinary* way people would ask me, what was that payment for, Albertus? And I'd have no idea!" The skin at the top of the old man's nose wrinkled with mirth. "And this one? What about that? There'd be no recollection. I'm no good at remembering, that's why I write things down. Lists and lists." He wafted a hand in the general indication of his desk. It was littered with long curling slips of paper. Phyllo craned his neck to decipher one. Apparently washing his socks and ordering more ink was still outstanding.

"Intertwining transactions with memories is just so much more sensible. Sometimes the big ones link together. Ambitious projects. There's a lot about repairs to the big top canvas in this one." He tapped at the large leather-bound book on his left and looked at Phyllo over the top of his spectacles.

Phyllo's face went hot.

"The books track the threads of existence and weave them together, just like life. Do you see?"

"They're amazing," breathed Roly, "How do you do it?"

"Years of practice. Years and years. It's a family talent, of course, and being in the Archive is important." He waved his hand, indicating the cabin at large. "Then there are the absorption and peace charms cast about the old place that go back generations. Generations, yes. And the Ink Imps help with focus, certainly. Outside of this room it would be extraordinarily difficult to see anything in the books, but facts and figures." He patted affectionately at the small pile of volumes on his desk. "Each is utterly individual and special to us. Not at all like the kind of thing you'd find in an *ordinary* library. No definitely not."

Both boys deflated a little at that. Phyllo returned to the other side of the desk. "Actually, Albertus, we were hoping that we might be able to borrow Emmett's."

"Borrow? Certainly not. Weren't you listening to what I just said? There'd be no point taking away his book, not that I could allow it. Especially not at the moment."

"Not at the moment?" The boys looked at each other.

"The books are in lockdown, just like everything else. The Ringmaster insisted upon it."

Roly groaned with disappointment.

"Even Emmett's? Please, Albertus, what harm could it do? Emmett's just a clown and a really unhappy one at that. We don't want to look at anything official. None of the important circus finances or anything."

Albertus frowned at them. "We've already looked at his book. I gave you the information that you requested. Why do you need to see it again?"

How to explain without revealing too much? Frú Hafiz had been quite clear that they shouldn't be telling anyone else what was going on. It was the only thing she'd said he'd really understood. Phyllo thought quickly.

"Well, the idea for the sweets was really great and Roly's doing his best, but they haven't exactly been a big success so far."

"One of them nearly pulled out my filing." Roly rubbed at his cheek for effect and Albertus gave him a look of mild concern.

"And I had no idea that there was so much to see, either. I mean, I think Roly got a much better look before. It's actually amazing." Phyllo fired a pleading look at Roly for assistance and he stumbled into the conversation.

"Yeah, it's only fair for Phyllo to see it properly. And, to be honest, he's much better at coming up with ideas than me and if he could just see that bit of Emmett's story, I reckon we could come up with something really cracking."

Albertus sighed.

"And it's the judging tomorrow. We just thought that if we could get the clowning team up to full strength it can only be to the good. Emmett's so off colour he's not even making it to the shows." Phyllo looked hopefully at Albertus this time and added, "I'm sure the Ringmaster would be really pleased."

Albertus pursed his lips and rolled his eyes in deliberation, his dark mole-like eyes magnified hugely through the thick glasses.

"The Ringmaster, yes, I suppose. It would be a shame not to have all pens to the page. Perhaps one more look wouldn't hurt."

Albertus must have triggered something unseen because at that moment a whirring began at the mezzanine level followed by a series of clunks and the sound of gears engaging. They looked up and Phyllo suddenly realised why the small cabin had felt so spacious initially: the spiral staircase had been missing. Now, however, it uncurled itself from the mezzanine ceiling, step after step unclicking from an inner mechanism and dropping into place. Around and around it spun, inching closer to the floor with every turn. Phyllo marvelled at it. The Machine really was exceedingly clever.

"Lockdown," Albertus said by way of explanation, "Closing off the mezzanine protects the link. Now then—" He pulled the enormous keyring from his belt and after a second or two sorting, singled out the small brass W-shaped key that was the Circus of Wonder's. "You two stay here."

He trotted up to open the cupboard and returned quite quickly with the pink and yellow harlequin patterned book they recognised as Emmett's. He put it on the desk.

"Let's go for the full immersive experience, shall we? In for a penny, might as well go for the full doubloon." He snorked out one of his laughs.

Phyllo and Roly fell in behind and peered over his shoulders. Albertus took up a golden pen with slivers of topaz twinkling in its filigree and drew a symbol in the air. Pages began to flip in a fan, then settled to lie open and flat.

The viewpoint shifted. Flat paper became disjointed, edges formed and perspective dropped away. An open village square formed in the letters. Quaint houses came into focus at its edges, ink stretching and blurring to form clapboard walls and tiled roofs. Cobbles popped into being like wrinkles in tissue. A stone well unfolded itself in the square's centre.

"I know this place. I've seen it before." Phyllo raked his memories, searching.

Flowers curled into being in window boxes and glass glinted in the sunshine. Albertus drew another symbol on the page but the ink, if indeed there were any, did not leave a line. Instead colour bloomed from the nib, painting the scene in the watercolour wash of summer.

Wisps of people solidified into shapes. They strolled across the square in the heat of the day, arm in arm or sat at pub benches, supping on drinks. The sign over the pub door scrolled into existence. *The Well of Tears*.

"This is Shady Hollow," said Phyllo excitedly, recognising it at last, "Looks a lot nicer here than it does now. How long ago was this?"

287

"Oh, a good long while ago, I'd say a decade? Half that again even, I shouldn't wonder." Albertus touched the page with his pen in the corner. Their perspective shifted and they sank further into the page, new houses and people revealing themselves in gentle blurs.

Posters were up for the Circus of Wonder on the board outside the pub, declaring it to be in town for three weeks and giving daily evening shows. It was the poster they'd found tacked inside the pub door.

Three weeks would be an interminable stint in Shady Hollow these days. That length of visit was usually reserved for the premium pitches.

"Galloping gobstoppers, it's really gone downhill, hasn't it?" said Roly.

They moved on through the scene, their viewpoint twisting to look through the pub window, no wait, to look at the reflection *in* the pub window. The tri-horned Jester's hat cut its unmistakable outline and perched on top of a familiar face. A much younger and happier face. The face of Emmett.

"Crackers! Look at Emmett, Roly!"

Albertus gave a little sigh. "He used to wear that costume all the time. I expect he was out in the town, fooling around to drum up customers."

Emmett turned away from the window and capered toward a group of children who were kicking a ball about. He joined in and larked about, shaking a Jester's cane that bore bells at its tip. One of the children skipped over and gave him a lemon pop, sent from their mother.

It was like watching a silent movie that had been coloured in by an artist on his holidays. Fascinating and frustratingly quiet, it sucked them further inside. The children swarmed away from Emmett and around the parent for their own ice

288

pops and Emmett strolled on, climbing a path that led eventually into a garden. He took off his hat.

"This is the bit I saw before, Phyllo," said Roly.

Flowers erupted from the page borders. Fuchsias in pink and white, their dancing ladies bobbing on the breeze. Honeysuckle sprouted and twirled from a tree – ink grew and stretched in a never-ending ellipse, its buttery yellow blooms swirling into being. Emmett paused to sniff at them. Up ahead, a cottage. Yellow stone walls piled up to a curving slate roof. The summer sun bathed it in magical light.

The view spun.

Coming up the path was another figure, as yet no more than a dark blur.

Suddenly Phyllo was back in the Book Keeper's cabin, learning over Albertus. Roly turned to look at him, confused. "What happened?"

"Oh, sorry about that," said Albertus, "Must be a smudge somewhere." Albertus turned the page and tapped with his pen. The paper fell into three dimensions again. The text had changed: now it was darker and closer together. It smoothed into a surface which found circular edges. A table. The borders shifted themselves into walls. A cup formed and morphed into a goblet, no, a glass. Slender and ornate. Albertus's nib touched the page and it filled with turquoise liquid. The wisp of a person began to form at the next seat around the table.

And they were back in the cabin.

Albertus tutted. "What the devil's the matter with this book?" He turned a few pages to try one further on.

The font had become jagged and messy. Words rippled in waves that turned to long grass and then revealed the figure of Emmett sitting upon it. Emmett held the Circus of Wonder poster in his hands. The Jester's face laughed out at him. The imaged blurred out of focus and then in again. Suddenly, violently, Emmett tore the poster to shreds. Turquoise seeped across the page and ink melted into a dirty puddle.

They were back in the cabin.

Albertus puffed out a sigh. "Well I never. What a peculiar thing. Troublesome. Troublesome indeed." He closed the book and slid it from the table. "I think, perhaps, the book is trying to tell us something. Best left alone, I'd say. Personal. Highly personal. I should never have shown it to you."

Albertus's mole-like face pinched with concern and he stood to spirit the book back up to the cupboard to be locked away. The staircase disappeared in much the same way as it had formed, step after step sucked into the ceiling, the spiral shrinking a piece at a time until nothing was left. Phyllo didn't see how he'd triggered it that time either.

"I think perhaps you boys ought to go."

Their visit was over. "Yes, of course," said Phyllo, but he felt disheartened.

"Dad's waiting for me. I should be going anyway," added Roly, "Thanks, Albertus."

Albertus gave them a distracted wave.

Back out on the horseshoe, Phyllo felt more perplexed than ever.

"I'm going to have to get back. You'd better go too," said Roly. The words of the welcome theme could be heard ringing inside the big top. Soon the introduction would be over and the Volantes would return to the Birdcage. Roly jogged away to the left and Phyllo peeled off to the right, churning over what they'd just seen.

Up in his cot, there was plenty to think about. He lay with his back pressed into the thin mattress and stared up at the ceiling. So, Emmett was the Jester. It was his former self. What had happened in Shady Hollow all those years ago that had made him give it up? What had happened that had made Emmett turn to Mermaid's Tears and how could they find out if Emmett's book wouldn't co-operate?

They were well beyond a nice surprise of happy sweets. It was looking increasing like their only option was to lose the subterfuge and ask Emmett directly.

If, when the Fabulous Volante had filed out for their slot in the programme, the mood had been tense, it was as nothing compared to the brawl that was their return. Signor Volante was the first to crash in through the door.

"This is no possible," he yelled, "How can all my work, a whole season's hard work, amount to this?"

Phyllo cringed over the edge of his cot to spy on them from above. Signor Volante stood in the centre of their small living space, squaring up to Arnaldo. "You make the catch. You return for the twist. It's simple!"

Arnaldo stamped and threw frustrated hands away to his sides, "It's impossible, I have to be back on the board by then."

"No. No. No! Ezio is on the board then." Signor Volante gestured emphatically at Ezio.

"No, Uncle, he has to be on the rigging then."

"No! I know. I know where you all should be!"

"Then maybe you'd better get up in the rig because no-one else has a clue what's going on!" Arnaldo spun away to stomp indignantly out to the kitchen.

It seemed to Phyllo that at times of crisis the Volante answer was always food. Nonna Sophia was already putting the finishing touches to dinner, the smell of which had been drifting up to his spot near the ceiling for almost an hour, making his stomach growl.

Arnaldo tore a hunk of bread from the board and ripped into it with his teeth. Signor Volante turned his attention to Columba. "You missed your mark. Where were you?"

"You know where I was, Uncle. There isn't enough time to turn the move around if I'm going to be on the ground covering for Ezio in the section before." She flicked her blonde ponytail over her shoulder, but she looked more likely to cry than rage.

"Ugh!" Signor Volante threw his hands into the air and then scrubbed wildly at his hair again. "I thought you were professionals! What's happened to you all?"

Nonna Sophia beetled over to the table and put a steaming bowl with dumplings bobbing on the surface down at its head.

"Aldo," she called in a soft, coaxing voice, "Come eat. Eat and think."

"I can no eat," he snapped.

"Sit. Sit." Nonna Sophia came behind him and put her hands up on his shoulders to guide him to the table. Phyllo suspected that she was the only person in the room who could get away with not doing exactly what Signor Volante told them. Being the matriarch definitely had its advantages. She put a spoon in his hand. "Everything is better with a full stomach. Food for the brain too, hmm?"

He begrudgingly sat down and spooned a small amount into his mouth to placate her. She gave him a pat on the shoulder and then, with the aid of Arnaldo, brought the rest of the family's supper to the table: a great steaming cauldron of stew with dumplings and fat hunks of warm crusty bread.

The family gathered around the table. Slowly the shouting and arguing and bad feeling died away as they tucked into the food, Nonna Sophia topping up bowls, fetching olives and butter. She soothed them with it. She fed them *home*.

Down on ground level it might not have been so obvious, but from Phyllo's high perch he saw it clearly. Saw how being back in the Birdcage affected them all. How it changed them. Phyllo's stomach growled.

Bowl empty, Signor Volante leaned back in his chair. "Where is Phyllo?" he asked and Nonna looked up to Phyllo's cot, catching him peering out over the edge. Signor Volante followed her gaze. "Come down," he said plainly.

Phyllo's empty stomach hollowed even more. They had already told him he was useless, but there he still was, the cuckoo in the nest. What more was there to say? Reticently, he descended the ladder, feeling the burn of their eyes on his back.

Signor Volante beckoned him to the table and looked him in the eye. "You made the Pirate Captain's leap once, did you not?"

This was an unexpected question. Phyllo had been expecting something more along the lines of 'Pack your things'. "Yes," he mumbled.

"How did you do it?"

Phyllo frowned at him. "I, I, kind of jumped from one swing to the other."

Signor Volante nodded, but then said, "That is not the Pirate Captain's leap. That is stepping from one piece of equipment to another. How did you do it?"

Phyllo looked from his face to Arnaldo's, to Birdie's. "I did it with Marco. We did it together." The mention of his name closed Phyllo's throat.

Signor Volante rolled his hand and looked at Phyllo a little harder.

"It, it was fun. We, we gave it everything, I suppose." He looked at the other faces at the table and tried to find the meaning Signor Volante was waiting for. "Everyone was watching, willing us on. It, it made the difference. It made a difference to me."

"What difference did it make, Phyllo?"

Phyllo looked him in the eye. "Everyone was with me. I was one of the troupe. I completely believed I could do it. So, I did."

Signor Volante nodded, "So you did. *Si*." He stood to lean on the table and looked around at his family. "I don't know what's happening to us out in the ring, but I know that we believe in each other. That's how it's always been. That is how we fly, that's how Arnaldo has become the greatest flyer the Circus of Wonder has ever seen. That's what makes the family Volante *fabulous*!"

The troupe shuffled uncomfortably in their seats, faces puzzled. Ezio nodded "I've felt it, Papa. Like something is dragging us down. Like something is wrong."

Phyllo knew that he was right. Something *was* wrong. The Jester was gaining in strength every day that Emmett suffered. They would never be able to perform at their best while its negative force was acting against them.

"We've lost sight of what's important. We've lost sight of love and support. We've lost sight of family and believing in each other, but now, at last, I can see it again." Signor Volante actually smiled at Phyllo. He gawked back at him.

"If we can just remember who we are, Phyllo can fly."

"What?" Phyllo wasn't sure he liked where this was heading.

"It's what Marco would want. You can do it, Phyllo. Do it for Marco."

Phyllo's mouth fell open. "I, er…" This was a bit of turn-around. In the space of two minutes he'd gone from being of no use to them to doing it for Marco. "I'm, I don't…" Phyllo looked back to the table. A low rumble of whispers had broken out amongst the family. Some looked at him with hope in their eyes, others, including Birdie, still wore hard masks of scepticism.

Nobody liked being a failure, but Phyllo had been rather glad not to have to climb the dizzying rig to take his life in his hands anymore. It had given him time to focus on his other problem and that problem still hadn't been resolved. It was all very well Signor Volante magnanimously declaring that the family would believe in him, but once they were out in the ring, once they were out in the Jester's domain, what then? "I, I don't know, Signor Volante."

"You don't know?"

Phyllo shook his head.

"It seems to me that without you, we cannot do it. The routine is so complex now, to make changes, to switch roles. We are all over the place. We must do the original routine or die trying."

"Die trying?" Phyllo squeaked.

Signor Volante hurriedly waved his hands as if trying to rub that last remark out. "We will protect you, Phyllo. Remember how the Volante magic works. I can see you are unsure and if I'm honest, I don't blame you. I don't know what's come over us lately. But I can see it now, I can see where we've been going wrong."

Nonna Sophie beetled over then with another bowl and spoon to set on the table for Phyllo. The others shoved up to make space.

"Eat. Eat. I'm sorry, Phyllo." She patted his cheek gently.

"I'm sorry too," said Ezio. An echo of it rumbled around the table. Phyllo followed it around with his eyes but stopped on Birdie. She still glared at him, stony-faced.

"Sleep on it, huh?" said Signor Volante in conclusion, "In the morning we'll show you we are good as our word."

CHAPTER TWENTY-ONE

The Truth Will Set You Free

The sudden friendliness was almost more unsettling than the Jester. At least he knew where he was with the snarls and the doubt. How could he let himself relax? What if this was just another cruel twist of the knife? What if, duped and trusting, he found himself up on the rig surrounded by flyers with sneering expressions who would let him fall to his death?

OK, they *seemed* genuine enough. Signor Volante had had tears in his eyes, for Barnum's sake: his beloved act crumbling around him; his son in the infirmary, possibly never to fly again. Phyllo knew that Signor Volante wanted that Gilded Pennant more, possibly, than even the Ringmaster. The Circus of Wonder *needed* that Gilded Pennant. Phyllo had put them in debt with his mistakes and now he'd put them in danger too. This was all his fault.

He tossed and turned in his cot. Did he really have any choice?

To not trust them would almost certainly spell disaster. They couldn't run the act without him. They couldn't win a Gilded Pennant without him.

What was he going to do? Aside from his crippling fear of heights and unfortunate lack of talent, he had a Vincula out to ruin him. A Vincula that wasn't worried about hurting people. If he wanted to survive a stint on the rigging tomorrow then time was running out. He knew he had to get rid of it. Tonight. He had to do something. Now.

Adrenalin rushed into his veins. He'd need help and Roly was his best bet. In the darkness Phyllo got hurriedly dressed in his blues and then, quietly as he could, felt his way down the ladder, crept for the door and stole out, onto the horseshoe.

To his left golden light jumped and flickered through the dark and voices rumbled.

Engineers.

Phyllo guessed that a couple were keeping watch near the entrance. He went the opposite way, sneaking around the path, heart up in his throat and hoping desperately that no others were out on patrol. Half way around, Phyllo re-emerged into the light, flames illuminating more and more of the path until he was forced to stop in the last sliver of shadow.

The Confectionary door was twenty yards away and danced in the flickers of the fire. He leaned out as far as he dared to spy Skinner and one other, playing cards by a brazier. They'd posted themselves outside the Ringmaster's cabin.

Phyllo watched until they seemed their most distracted then pelted across to the Confectionary's thin door to slip inside. It too was in darkness, but Phyllo knew this place better than anywhere and easily found his way.

He discovered Dodo asleep in his old bunk, all frothy curls and soft breath, and it reminded him of their squabble for the sofa. Prime positions in the Confectionary were hard to come by and she'd clearly decided his bunk was superior. Like chocolate bowls with remnants to be licked, both were hers now.

Roly slept in the bunk above. Phyllo poked him.

"Mm, no thanks," Roly mumbled from the depths of a dream.

"Roly, wake up," Phyllo hissed.

One of Roly's eyelids peeled up and then rolled back down again. "It wasn't me."

Phyllo poked him a bit harder. "Roly, get up and be quiet. Come on."

Roly's eyes opened again and he stared blearily out. Phyllo beckoned him on.

Knotting his dressing gown in the shop and looking groggy, Roly listened while Phyllo explained how he was now expected to perform in the show, and how he'd quite like to survive the experience.

"We have to confront Emmett. It's the only way," said Phyllo.

Roly nodded then retrieved a small yellow box from the counter which he opened for them both to see inside.

"They worked. Ninth time lucky."

A pile of lemon-shaped jellies nestled in tissue paper, sparkling with sugar.

"Brilliant, Roly. Well done."

He shrugged. "For what they're worth."

"Let's go."

They peered out onto the shadows that led around to the left and the Clown Quarter. To their right, Skinner and the other engineer no longer sat at their post. Odds on they were making rounds. To move in either direction now was a risk. Equally, there may never have been a better moment.

"Crackers, where are they?" breathed Phyllo.

"No time like the present," said Roly. He was an echo of their father and under different circumstances, Phyllo might have laughed. Instead he took a deep breath and nodded. They ran, lunged for Emmett's door and dived inside.

The occupants of the Clown Quarter were definitely asleep, the curtains that closed off each cell all but rippling with their great gusting snores. Every cell but Emmett's, that was. His curtain sagged open half way, a dim light glowing inside. They stole toward it, rounding the bank of dressing tables and listening for activity.

But Emmett was not up in bed. Instead, he sat at his dressing table, shaking. The shape of him was revealed only as they came around to the other side of the mirrors. He clutched a wad of paper in his hand.

"Emmett," said Phyllo, taken aback, "What are you doing?"

Emmett stared into space. His eyes drooped dejectedly. His face shone with shed tears and as they watched, another rolled silently over the brink, to trickle unheeded down his face. A flicker of a crinkle formed and then faded between his eyebrows. He was the picture of utter misery.

"Emmett," Phyllo said again and reached out to touch him on the arm. Emmett started, as if only just noticing them. A hint of light ignited in his eyes, the wish of a smile pulled at the corner of his mouth and his eyes filled so comprehensively with tears that they flooded his face and ran to his chest. He heaved against the weight of them, a gasp which turned to sobs. Emmett wept and Phyllo thought his heart would break to watch him.

"Whatever's the matter, Emmett? What's this all about?" Both boys fell to their knees to look up at him.

"I never meant to," he moaned through the tears, "It was

always for them. I did it for them."

Phyllo and Roly looked at each other, perplexed. "For who? What was?"

Emmett moaned and his head rolled on his neck. "No job, no money. What kind of husband is that? What kind of father?" He looked pleadingly into Phyllo's eyes.

"I don't know, Emmett. I don't know what you mean."

"There wasn't any choice. No choice at all." He wrung his already red-raw hands, crumpling the papers. "Just to get us on our feet. But the circus moves, doesn't it? Of course, it does. On and on, further and further. It's like floating along on a dream."

An odd sort of smile spread across his face. "Peanuts for elephants. A smile for a song." Emmett's voice cracked. "The magic of the circus. Especially this one." He waved one hand. "Especially then. I didn't want to leave, to go back to that struggle. I loved them but I loved the circus more. Loved myself more." He spat out the last words, disgusted with himself. "I left them to it."

"Who? Who are you talking about, Emmett?"

"Rosie. My Rosie," he thrust the paper in his hands at Phyllo, "And our little Bumble." Phyllo took the letters and Emmett dissolved into more wet sobs.

The letter was dated one week previously. Phyllo shuffled quickly through the wad. One was from a few months ago, another, a few years. Letter after letter, all in the same neat handwriting. He went back to the one on top that Emmet had been reading.

Dearest Emmett,

Sometimes I wonder if I dreamt you. If it wasn't for Bumble, I could believe it. She's grown into a beautiful young lady. And she

301

*bakes so well, better than me now. You should see her. I wish that
she'd gotten to know her Daddy. I've always hoped that one day she
still could, but the longer this goes on, well, now I just don't know.*

*I'd promised myself I wouldn't write again. After all these years
I ought to just let you go, accept that you're never coming back, but
I chanced on some cherry buns at the market and it reminded me of
you. Silly, isn't it. Do you remember when I used to make them for
you? The bakery we always said we'd run? It made me smile to
remember it all and then it made me sad.*

*I've missed you so much. Are you OK, Emmett? Please, just let
me know.*

Love always, Rosie & Bumble x

Phyllo looked up to Emmett's tortured face. "You have a
family?"

"Had. Had a family. I'm nothing to them now." His brow
furrowed again and his eyes searched the table top. He swept
an angry arm across it and knocked the clutter to the floor.

The loudest snorer of the three cells faltered, but then
continued at a lower volume.

Phyllo knew that in that moment, if Emmett had had it, he
would have taken a good long slug of Mermaid's Tears. This
was what his mind returned to without it. He looked desperately to Roly and remembered the jellies.

"We brought you a present," he said and nodded to Roly
who proffered the box.

Emmett's eyes drifted down to it. "A present? For me?" He
looked from Phyllo to Roly to the box and his eyes swam with
tears again.

"Just some jellies," said Roly, "Happy ones. I made them
especially for you."

"For me?" he said again, like he wasn't worthy of such a

magnificent gift, "You're good boys," he said as he ran the back of his hand under his nose, "I don't deserve it."

Roly opened the box and Emmett took one. "They look excellent, Roly," he said, attempting to gather his wits, attempting to play the part of the doting uncle he'd always been. He popped it into his mouth. "Delicious," he said automatically and sucked upon it, wiping at his eyes with his sleeve.

Slowly his expression changed. The furrows in his brow smoothed out, the pinch in his eyes relaxed. He sat back in the chair and took a great deep breath. Phyllo could almost see the memories that swam before his eyes.

"When I think about it now, it does seem like it was all the *more* magical back then. Years ago, I mean. I suppose time changes everything, doesn't it? Changes people."

"Time sure has changed Shady Hollow," said Phyllo.

Emmett's eyes widened. "Shady Hollow, yes, that's just where I was thinking of."

Phyllo and Roly stole a glance at each other.

"We used to love stopping off there. You'd never believe it now." He looked out into space, picturing it in his mind's eye. "Used to be teeming with visitors all summer long. So busy I'd walk away, out of the village, just to get a bit of peace at lunchtimes. Along the lane." Emmett's hand snaked in the air in front of him, remembering the path.

"There was this one particular cottage that had the most beautiful garden. Honeysuckle like you've never seen. Overgrown, but just lovely. I shouldn't have really, but I used to sneak in there to lay in the shade and hide out, just absorbing the smells and the warmth and the peace. It became a bit of a habit." Emmett laughed to himself and Phyllo could see that Roly had really hit the spot with his jellies.

Emmett continued. "But I wasn't the only one that visited that cottage. Another man came every day too. Carrying a bag or a box and he never saw me. He didn't live there. Just stayed a while and left again. I noticed him because he looked like he didn't want anyone to, if you know what I mean. Always wearing black and a cloak." Emmett's face started to take on a different expression.

"He never noticed me until one day I surprised him and jumped out. I don't know what made me do it." He looked down into his lap. "I am a fool. I've always been a fool." The brief moment of happiness was dropping away.

"He was nice enough to start with. Took me to the pub and we got talking and before long he knew me better than I knew myself. We've all got things we don't want other people to know about, things people wouldn't understand. That's what he said.

"And he was right about me, wasn't he? I didn't want people in the circus to know I'd abandoned my family. And he, well, he had his own secrets. He said neither of us would tell and he knew a way to make me feel better about it all. More like, he knew the way to seal the deal so I couldn't go against it." Emmett's face crumpled and his eyes flicked up to the mirror. He flinched.

"Who was it?" Phyllo pressed.

Emmett almost laughed, but it came out in a choke, "I can't tell you that! That's the point isn't it?" He sat up a little straighter in his chair.

There was a sound like a metal nail scraping across glass. Long and jagged, it pierced the night. Emmett's face convulsed into the snarling expression Phyllo had come to recognise then disappeared again. Phyllo and Roly both got to their feet.

"I'm not allowed to talk about it." Emmett's expression had

become frightened now, "Bad for the circus is bad for the clown. A secret for a secret, sealed with the tears of a mermaid. That's what makes it go away." He nodded to the boys as if he were a teacher giving a lesson.

A cracking sound issued from Emmett's mirror and they all jerked around to look at it. The Jester stared out at them. The darkly golden tri-horned hat perched upon the head of a younger Emmett, but now the face was so twisted with years of pain it snarled back at the world. Its skin was deathly pale, a dirty blue diamond painted over one eye. This was the eyebrow that arched and pulled the face into a sneer. "Naughty, naughty. Not supposed to tell." Its voice was rasping, harsh.

"My demon," Emmett breathed, staring at it as if mesmerised.

"What does it want, Emmett?" Phyllo asked, looking between them.

The Jester curled its lip, "No real friends. No love for Emmett. No joy. Worthless, pitiful, pathetic dropout!"

Emmett whimpered.

"No! It's not true. Don't listen to it, Emmett."

"Left the wifey and the ickle baby. Disgusting excuse for a human being. Selfish pig! Selfish swine!" the Jester roared.

Emmett started to cry again. Phyllo pulled him up to his feet, turned him away from the mirror. "What does it want, Emmett?"

"Tears and more tears. One kind or the other. The deal's been struck. My fate is sealed. To break it is to break the promise. The deal is better for the circus and better for the circus is better for the clown." He wailed the words, as if by rote, and covered his face with his hands.

The sound of a crack splitting across glass came from the

mirror. "Blabbermouth!" the Jester squealed, "Stupid Emmett. Can't break the promise. Can't tell the secret!" It hammered its fists on the other side of the glass. Phyllo tried to turn Emmett away from the mirror but somehow it always dragged him back.

"What does it want, Emmett? How can we make it stop?"

"My demon! It knows I'm not worthy. It knows that I'm scum."

"No. Emmett, that isn't true."

The Jester roared and hammered so hard on the mirror that it broke. Shards of glass sprang from its frame and showered the floor. One hand reached through to Emmett's dressing table, its palm slamming down on the surface.

"No other way," the Jester drawled. The hand reached across the table and grabbed at the edge. "There is nothing left for you. Drink the tears, Emmett, or shed your own."

Phyllo stared wide-eyed down at the Jester's arm as it flexed and he realised that it was pulling itself out, through the mirror.

"I can't!" Emmett screamed, backing away.

Another arm slammed down, its hand gripping the table's edge. Blood oozed from a gash at its wrist. The Jester heaved itself forward, the dirty-gold horns of the hat thrusting though the frame, the ragged red ruff at its shoulders. Then it was crouching on its haunches on top of the table, breathing hard.

Phyllo stepped between Emmett and the Jester. "It's gone. I threw it away," he yelled.

The Jester's head turned while its body remained still. Eyes as dark as night bored into Phyllo's. They were the eyes he'd seen stare out from Jack's face back in the Brampton Levels. The Jester's nostrils flared. "Well if it isn't the rehabilitator," it drawled, enunciating every syllable, "Don't you know a lost cause when you see one?"

Phyllo lifted his chin a little higher and the Jester launched at him. The table bucked at the sudden force. It tipped and clattered sideways, the Jester with it.

Phyllo and Roly jolted backward. Emmett cowered behind his own hands and dropped to the floor. The Jester squealed. A terrible sound. Ten thousand nights of anguish, bottled, stored and now finally released in a torrent of frustration.

"He belongs to me!" The Jester sprang and Phyllo bolted for the door, Roly hot on his heels.

"What are we going to do?" Roly squeaked.

"Run!"

Phyllo tore along the horseshoe, leading the way. The Jester tumbled out of the Clown Quarter door after them. Skinner. Skinner was here with another guard. They pelted around the path, leaning into the curve. Into the dark of the far side, away from the gate.

"He belongs to me!" the Jester shrieked out behind them. Phyllo didn't dare look back to see how close it was. Where was Skinner when you needed him? Phyllo could feel Roly falling back, struggling to keep up.

Light from the fire flickered ahead. They were almost around to the other side, almost completed a full circuit. No Skinner.

"This way." Phyllo dived through the flap of the Grand Entrance and into the big top. Maybe Skinner was checking inside. Phyllo and Roly pelted down the aisle and drew up at the edge of the ring. "Skinner?" Phyllo yelled out.

Metal of the stands ticked. Phyllo squinted out into the darkness, spinning on the spot. "Skinner? Are you in here?"

Something moved under the stand but there was no reply.

Roly came to Phyllo's side. "Can't move for the man usually," he puffed.

Something flashed in Phyllo's peripheral vision and he spun to his left to try to see what it was. Darkness. The edge of the ring, sharply drawn against the sawdust. Footsteps, moving quickly.

Phyllo and Roly twitched in unison, twisting this way and that, squinting into the shadows.

A rustle of fabric. Phyllo stepped into the ring, drawn by his instincts. He crept forward, eyes peering into the wings. There was a scuffle ahead. The canvas flapped open and the unmistakable profile of the Crow Man flashed for a moment against the pale flickering light of the brazier. The flap closed.

Phyllo's heart, already pounding, doubled its pace.

Beneath the tiers something was moving, tapping against the metal frame as it went. Phyllo and Roly's heads snapped this way and that, trying to see, trying to pick something out in the gloom.

"Skinner?" Roly shouted out this time.

"Skinner?" The mocking voice of the Jester came from under the stand.

Phyllo scoured the tiers, searching. He suspected that the Jester was moving under the seating to his right, heading for the wings, but something crashed to the ground backstage to the left. Both boys spun to look, stepping slowly backward, edging away.

"Mine," breathed a voice in Phyllo's ear.

They whirled around. The Jester had crept up behind them, loathing and bitter amusement dripping from his very fingertips. Phyllo and Roly screamed and bolted, but in different directions.

Roly pelted into the darkness and away up the aisle.

Phyllo ran across the ring, spotted movement backstage then abruptly changed direction. The Jester made a grab for him, catching hold of his shoulder and reeling Phyllo around. He skidded in the sawdust. The fabric of his tunic tore. Both of them dropped to one knee but Phyllo was up first, sprinting for the rig and onto the ladder.

The ladder bucked and twitched and he fought to control it, climbing away as fast as he could. He got into a rhythm, starting to feel in control, but then realised that this was only because the Jester was on the ladder too, weighing it down.

He scrabbled onto the board, clutching at the guide ropes. What the hell was he thinking, coming up here?

The Jester's face appeared at board level. It climbed evenly, apparently un-perplexed by the height. He stepped out onto the platform and gave Phyllo a wicked grin. "Well isn't this nice?" he said, waving a carefree hand.

Phyllo backed away. There really wasn't far to go.

"I thought I'd have to wait until tomorrow, for the big show." He pulsed 'jazz hands' either side of his hideous smile, "But this works for me. I'm not fussed."

Bloody hell, it was going to push him off. He looked around wildly, looking for something to help him. The trapeze was tied back to the rigging with an anchor rope. Phyllo grabbed at it and grappled with the knot. The Jester brought its hands up to its face again and pulled an expression of mock shock. His voice oozed with fake concern.

"I don't know what could have gotten into him. We thought he was doing so well, but the pressure, oh the pressure must have been too much." It took a step forward. "Crumpled. Crumpled in a little interfering heap. So sad."

Phyllo stole a glimpse up at it.

"And so dead." The Jester lunged. Phyllo yanked the

anchor rope in and leapt for the trapeze, grabbing it with both hands. He swung away, gripping that damn pole for all he was worth. His palms sprang instantly with sweat. He flexed his chest at the apex of the swing and then began his return journey. Going back to the Jester. Crackers!

Phyllo panicked and tried to look over his own shoulder. The Jester hung on the rigging, reaching out. He was level with the board, no, rising above it. He pushed the bar down and straightened himself out. The Jester snatched and flailed, but couldn't reach him.

"Ha!" Phyllo sailed away again. His hands slid around the trapeze, slick against the metal. He rolled himself up to sit on the bar and moved his shaking hands to the supporting ropes. This felt safer, less likely to fall. He didn't propel the swing and it lost momentum, not reaching anywhere near the same height before beginning its return journey.

Phyllo turned to see the Jester as he swung back toward it, but not near enough, nowhere near enough to be in danger. That familiar sneer had returned. The Jester clicked its fingers above its head and popped its eyes for Phyllo's benefit then hurried to get back onto the ladder, going further up now, heading for the rigging at the roof.

"Oh no." Phyllo leaned back and forth on the trapeze trying to get it swinging again. He had to get back to the platform. It swayed slightly then a little more. This wasn't enough. The Jester would be up at the anchor points before he could get off. He wiped his hands on the blues and lowered himself back down to hang by his hands. The ground beneath him lurched up into his vision and his stomach turned. *No time for that now. Get off this trapeze or you're going to die!*

He swung his legs and pushed with his chest with every joule of his energy. Higher. Further. Laughter came from above his head. Phyllo looked up and saw the Jester, walking as if on a tightrope, arms outstretched and pretending to wobble as it made its way along the gantry. Nearer and a little nearer, Phyllo fought against gravity and pushed his body on. Not quite, with the next swing it would be enough.

"Tears or tears," the Jester called out from above and one side of the trapeze jolted.

Phyllo was on the return journey. He lurched forward, releasing the trapeze just as the tension failed. He stepped onto the board and grabbed for the rigging, hauling himself in. The trapeze went slack, and one side dropped. Adrenaline roared through Phyllo's veins. He dived for the ladder and scrambled down.

The Jester was still up at the ceiling, giggling and tearing at the other support rope when Phyllo's feet hit the ground, legs wobbly as jelly. He lurched for backstage and out onto the horseshoe. Roly? Emmett? He staggered for the Clown Quarter, stumbling and gasping. He burst through the door.

Gus, Nubbins and Jack were all awake now too. The three of them plus Roly stood in an arm-waving circle, arguing.

"Let him go, if he wants to." Nubbins was pulling at Roly's dressing gown, attempting to drag him backward.

Roly swatted his hands away, "No. Emmett, please don't go, not now. We need you." His round face shone with disappointment.

"He's not leaving. I won't have it, not while my emerald knot is still missing." Gus dropped to the floor and, as Phyllo rounded the dressing table, he saw him pulling clothes from a suitcase on the floor as fast as Emmett was stuffing them in.

"I've already told you," Emmett wailed, "I don't have it. I've never had it."

"You don't know what you're doing half the time." Gus

311

ploughed on through Emmett's things, shaking them out and searching through pockets.

"Roly," Phyllo gasped, "What's going on?"

Emmett jumped up and hurried to his desk, tossing unwanted items roughly aside to snatch up a couple of photographs in frames. "Now I've gone and done it. Blown it. Blown it. The cat's out of the bag. Can't stay here, not now." He tossed the frames into his case.

"Emmett, the Jester. It's trying to kill me!" Phyllo shouted, "You can't leave now, we don't know what to do. What should we do, Emmett?"

Emmett paused in his scuffle with Gus to reclaim his clothes and looked Phyllo in the eye. His expression told how he realised that his trouble shared was just that. "I'm so sorry, Phyllo. You didn't ask for any of this, but now that you're in, I can't see a way out."

"What?" gasped Roly.

"It'll never give up. Never. But now I've got a chance to escape. It's out of my head, Phyllo."

"I know!" said Phyllo, "It tried to push me off the rigging!"

Emmett wrung his hands. "It's no good. The other one, he'll never let me forget. I can't stay here anymore. I'm sorry. I'm so sorry." He snatched the lid of his case up and snapped it closed. Then he was barging past Nubbins and Jack and heading for the door. Gus dove straight into Emmett's cell, digging furiously through what remained.

Phyllo chased him to the door. "Emmett, please. Tell us what to do. Tell us how to get rid of it."

Emmett struggled past them and out onto the horseshoe, walking as fast as he could under the weight of the case. He shook his head. "I've tried for years and never managed it.

There have been better days, but this is it, the best it's ever been. This is my moment to escape. It's out and I have to go."

"Emmett, please."

"Can't you understand me?" Emmett roared, then took a hold of himself. They were almost at the gate now. He put down the case and grabbed Phyllo by his upper arms. "Listen to me. Go to see Albertus. Ask him for my book. Look up Shady Hollow. That's where this all began. Find the secret." He threw his hands into the air and looked up to the sky. "There, it's as good as told. Now I've really done it."

"Emmett, we've already—" Phyllo began but Emmett had snatched up his case again. He fumbled with the bolts and then swung open the gate.

"Look after yourself, Phyllo. You too, Roly." Phyllo looked over his shoulder to see that Roly was just behind him. Emmett kissed his fingertips and blew it at them. "That one's for Dodo." He gave them a desperate smile and struggled out of the gate.

Phyllo goggled at the receding figure. He was really leaving. It took him a moment to react, but then his legs seemed to wake up and he ran after him. Ran to the gate and out of it. The sounds of a scuffle broke out. Up ahead, in the darkness, three figures converged. One, unmistakably Emmett. The other two, much taller. Phyllo thought that it might be Skinner and Bain finally putting in an appearance, but when he saw the figure of Emmett drop to the ground, a second revealed itself to be the Crow Man. Phyllo faltered, not knowing if he should run forward or back, but the men out in the darkness didn't hesitate. They scooped Emmett up and hauled him away.

CHAPTER TWENTY-TWO

Present and Passing

P hyllo sat on the floor, his back to the wall. Something solid behind him felt reassuring. Something solid beneath him too. He clasped his knees to his chest. Roly, beside him, sat in exactly the same way. They both stared out into the blank gloom of the Confectionary. Both were squeezed into the small galley kitchen. Both hidden beneath the countertops.

"So that's it then," said Roly quietly, "Emmett's gone."

"Yep."

"I can't believe he's left us to it."

"Although to be fair I'd say he was more abducted there, at the end."

"Yes. Worrying, that."

"Mmm." Phyllo nodded his head and mulled over the shocking experiences of the past hour. When he'd come to his senses enough to run out onto the pitch after Emmett, there'd been no sign of him. Nor the other two.

Frú Hafiz had been waiting for him when he returned.

"Emmett, he's gone," Phyllo had gasped and she'd nodded. "The cards are rarely wrong," she'd said, "Will they be wrong about you?"

Phyllo hadn't known what that meant. "No?" he'd hazarded. Frú Hafiz was so frustratingly obscure.

"I'd get off the horseshoe, if I were you," she'd said and disappeared herself, behind her awning. The closest thing to advice he'd received.

Holing up in the Confectionary felt like the safest bet. Roly was heading back there and Phyllo wasn't going to let them be separated now, not when he needed someone at his side that he could trust.

Where was the Jester? Now that it had broken free, was it tied to Emmett at all or were its sights purely set on Phyllo?

Despite their efforts, his prospects had not improved. They'd lost Emmett, but not the Jester, and if he was going to get up on that trapeze tomorrow, it *had* to be out of the equation. Just the thought of performing in the show flipped Phyllo's stomach, never mind with a demon after him too.

He let out an enormous sigh. "It's impossible," he moaned.

Roly groaned in agreement and flopped his forehead to his knees.

They sat in desperate silence. Phyllo stared into space, then let his eyes drop to slide along the floor level shelf and fall upon his old box of precious ingredients.

Its corners were rounded and scuffed by time. The cardboard blackened by smoke. He pulled it onto his lap, loosened the carefully tied ribbon and removed the lid. The ingredients inside were simple enough: flaked almonds, gelatine, sugar and the precious jar of honey. He held the jar up to catch a glimmer of light. The tiniest amount of golden liquid remained.

Why had producing the marshmallow been so hard?

Phyllo stood up at the bench and laid the ingredients out in a line. At the bottom of the box were pages of tried and unsuccessful recipes with extra notes scribbled at the bottom. *Too sticky. Too solid. Too sad.* Why hadn't he been able to make it work?

He examined the packages, each fastidiously tied with yet more ribbon, half empty now and ruined. He imagined himself getting out a bowl and a whisk. Imagined himself tapping at the side of the step with his foot for luck before he began and that was when it occurred to him: he wasn't standing on the step.

It seemed he had grown in his time away, tall enough now to stand easily at the work surface unaided. He looked around the tiny kitchen with fresh eyes. Perhaps it was all the time he'd spent in the voluminous Birdcage, but now the old place felt smaller.

A new kind of clarity crept into Phyllo's brain. In the past he'd so desperately clung to the good old days that perhaps he'd forgotten how to exist in the present. Perhaps that was why his marshmallow recipe had never worked. He'd never seen the memories in their purest form, always with a tinge of regret, with a shadow of sadness and longing.

In that moment he realised, he had to lay the past to rest to move forward. He tossed the old ingredients back into the carton and pushed it away. His mother was *not* in that box.

"On your feet, Roly," he said, "I've got an idea."

Birdie was not happy to see him. "Get off my ledge," she hissed.

"Birdie, please. You have to listen to me."

She turned over in bed and put her back to him. Phyllo clambered into her cot.

"What in Giuseppe's name do you think you are doing?" she fumed, "Get out!"

"Shhhhh!"

"Don't you shush me!"

"Birdie, please," Phyllo begged, holding up his hands, as if she were about to wallop him, "I wouldn't be here if it wasn't absolutely essential."

She narrowed her eyes.

"I need your help, Birdie. The Jester, it's loose and rampaging around the circus."

"Of course it is," said Birdie sarcastically and pulled the covers up over her head. Phyllo immediately pulled them back down. She glared at him, open-mouthed with outrage.

"It is, Birdie, I swear," Phyllo insisted in an urgent whisper, "We have to get rid of it or it's going to kill me."

"So dramatic. Does anything happen in this circus that isn't about you?"

"I'll prove it to you. Come on, come with me. Please. I can't talk to you here. We'll wake everyone up. Come on, Birdie, please."

She sighed hugely and then waved him away so she could follow him down in her pyjamas.

Roly waited by the door, shuffling awkwardly and staring up at the multitude of cots.

"Which one's yours?" he whispered as Phyllo came close. Phyllo pointed up to his bunk near the ceiling.

"Gobstoppers!"

"Tell me about it," Phyllo confirmed.

The three of them slipped outside and straight across the path into the big top. Immediately Phyllo drew them into a huddle, their backs to the canvas.

"We aren't exactly sure where it is at the moment-," said Phyllo, looking nervously at Birdie and then scanning about.

"How convenient," she snapped.

"But the last time I saw it, it was up on the rigging hacking through the support ropes for the trapeze."

Phyllo pointed through the gap in the curtain. The prone trapeze could just be made out, lying in the sawdust. Birdie gawked at it and the three of them moved to the curtain to peer through.

The Jester's stick, complete with its silver bells, also lay in the sawdust. "It's trying to kill me."

Birdie looked horrified. "But why?"

"It's Emmett's demon," said Phyllo, "Roly and I found it in Emmett's book. It's got some kind of power over him to do with Mermaid's Tears. We've been trying to get him to stop drinking it. Well, it didn't look like he was managing too well on his own so we—"

Roly cleared his throat.

"Sorry, so *I* threw it away and Emmett went into some kind of withdrawal depression, but when that happens the Jester starts acting up, trying to get him to drink it again. That's when all the trouble starts, when Emmett's trying to get rid of it."

Birdie looked to Roly for confirmation and he nodded gravely.

"And then we tried to cheer him up with those special jellies that Roly's been making and it did cheer him up for a bit, but then the memories became overwhelming and Emmett kind of crumbled. It set the Jester free."

Birdie's eyes were getting wider and wider.

"It chased us in here, Birdie. Chased me up the rigging. I was on that trapeze while it was cutting the ropes!"

"Marco," Birdie breathed.

"It was supposed to be me, Birdie. All this time it's been the Jester sabotaging us, spreading suspicion and distrust. It's been doing it to Emmett for years, whenever he tried to escape. But it had to start pursuing me when it realised that I was being strong on Emmett's behalf. It wants me to fail. It wants the Fabulous Volante to fail and if that happens the Circus of Wonder won't survive. Help us, Birdie. We can't tell anyone else."

Birdie's delicate features took on a steely resolve. "What do you want me to do?"

Skinner was back at his brazier outside the Ringmaster's cabin. He and the other engineer Phyllo now recognised as Cace were both sitting on barrels by the fire looking dishevelled. Cace moaned and clutched at his head. Skinner thrust a water bottle at him. "Take a drink. Clear your head and don't be making a racket about it."

Cace took a swig and groaned.

"The Ringmaster'll have us down as eejits if he thinks we let the In-between get the better of us again. Be on your guard now. We can't let anything else past us."

"What've they done, Skinner?"

"We'll find out soon enough."

Phyllo carefully allowed the canvas flap to close and turned to whisper to Roly and Birdie. "They're back, but they look in a state. Something's happened to them to put them out of action for a bit, I'd say and they couldn't be sat in a worse spot. We'll never get into the Archive with them sat there."

"Let's give them something to do," said Roly.

Birdie nodded back to the ring and the trapeze, "We just need to get them to notice."

Phyllo squinted up into the darkness. The engineering box lodged high in the tiers. "Can't be that hard to switch on the lights," he said.

They scaled the steep steps, jumping at shadows. The door to the box opened easily and, to everyone's enormous relief, did not reveal the Jester hiding inside. Machine control panels glowed, illuminated labels helpfully identifying the bank of switches they needed.

"Everyone ready?" Phyllo asked, "When I flip the switch we need to get down from here pronto. Getting caught at the scene is the last thing we need."

"Agreed."

Phyllo flipped the switch.

He'd expected the ring spotlights to come on, but instead, the full house lights flickered into life.

"Crackers," Phyllo gasped. He dithered over the switches, but not knowing which one was correct and just said, "Let's go!"

They shot out of the box and pelted down the stairs. If Skinner hadn't seen the light seeping around the canvas immediately, then he definitely heard them thundering down the steps. The metal clanged and echoed as they charged toward the ring and then away to the left, through the silent sawdust and out of a side flap. They drew up, panting in the shadows, then edged their way around the inner curve, breathing hard. Sure enough, once again the brazier flamed alone.

"Who's acting the maggot in here?" growled Skinner from inside the big top.

"Over here." It sounded like Cace had spotted the trapeze.

"They're in there," said Phyllo, "Quick."

They dashed to the Book Keeper's cabin and slipped inside.

Albertus had said that his cabin had peace charms cast over it and Phyllo felt the change in atmosphere the moment the door had closed behind them.

A soothing glow came from dying embers that rippled scarlet and gold in the fireplace. Tranquil and warm, Phyllo could imagine that even the books were peacefully asleep.

They crept carefully forward.

Albertus's desk was tidy, all the books put away. All the pens standing in their wells.

The mezzanine was dark and inaccessible, its spiral staircase sucked away into the mechanism.

"First things first," whispered Phyllo, "We need the key."

Albertus's bedroom took the form of an extraordinarily tall four-poster which, with its extra wide top, created a small curtained chamber whilst also supporting the mezzanine above. The curtains were closed. They tiptoed toward it, hardly daring to breathe. Phyllo pinched the fabric back just enough to poke a slice of his face through the gap, and peered inside.

Phyllo was amused to see that Albertus wore just as many clothes in bed as he did during the day. Burgundy woolly arms pinned the blankets down to his sides and a matching burgundy bed cap covered his head. His mouth slightly open, puffing out gentle breaths of dream, he gave the impression of an enormous sleeping paperclip.

Birdie poked her head around the curtain too, then slid inside. Together they searched for the keys. Phyllo pointed out clothes hanging on a peg which Birdie squeezed top to bottom, without success. Then he felt about in the fluff under the bed and Birdie reached around to the hidden side of the small wardrobe. She pulled back with a big smile and the bulging keyring in her hand. She'd found it. Phyllo gave her an enthusiastic thumbs up and they snuck away, back to the desk.

There were hundreds of keys. Short and stubby, long and curling, wooden, brass; copper, steel. Some had intricate teeth all the way along, others just one square nodule at the very end. They examined each one, methodically working their way through the ring, until they came to a copper key whose teeth resembled the letter 'W'.

"That's it," Roly breathed and Phyllo recognised it too.

"OK, Birdie," Phyllo whispered, easing it off the ring to give to her, "The cupboards up there. When you get inside, all the books are organised by families. Emmett's book is distinctive, it's pink and yellow and there's a rubber chicken dangling on the spine."

She nodded, like this was the most normal thing in the world.

Phyllo didn't know how she'd get up to the mezzanine, but thought that if anyone could, it was her. "Any ideas?"

Birdie tucked the key into her pyjama pocket and paced about, looking up, then came to a stop beneath a long light which hung from two cables over the kitchenette. She beckoned the boys over and mimed for them both to mesh their hands together so she could step in and stretch for it. They swayed precariously left and right, but still weren't tall enough.

"Put me down. This is hopeless," she hissed and clipped them both around the backs of their heads.

Roly rubbed at his ear and grumbled.

Birdie paced some more, sizing up the boys and the height of the ceiling, then brought them together in an 'A' frame this time, Phyllo and Roly's hands on each other's shoulders.

"Ready?" she whispered.

"Hup," said Phyllo.

She rolled her eyes, to Phyllo's amusement, but he stopped smirking when she used the back of his knee for her first foothold. He flinched at the digs from her bony clambering toes, until she stood with one foot on each of their shoulders.

"OK, I've got it," she whispered and lifted her feet to test if the light would take her weight.

"Good job there's not much of her," said Roly. He gawped at Birdie, who hung from the light like a knobbly twig.

"Now give me a bit of space," she said and started to swing then tucked herself up to hang by the knee. She stretched for a rail at the edge of the mezzanine, just managed to touch it, but her hands slid away.

Back she swung, driving the momentum on for more height. Cables creaked. She snatched for the rail and grabbed hold.

"Well done!" Phyllo squeaked.

Birdie let the light swing away, dangled for a moment then curled her legs up to push pointed toes between her body and the edge of the mezzanine. She slid her legs through the bars of the balustrade and then paused to dangle by the backs of her calves.

Phyllo followed this progress through splayed fingers, prickling with sweat.

She walked her hands up the bars, pulled herself up to standing, rolled over the top and disappeared. A moment later her grinning face popped out of the dark. She bobbed in a curtsey and waved down at them like a queen, acknowledging her subjects.

Roly turned, nodding to Phyllo, wide eyed.

"See what I have to put up with?" Phyllo grumbled and Roly rattled his lips with a puff of air.

"Yeah, yeah," Phyllo mouthed and waved her on.

Through the darkness they heard the click of the lock then nail-biting silence. Phyllo squeezed his eyes closed to listen harder and wished he could have seen Birdie's shocked expression when she saw the inside of the impossible cupboard.

A few moments later she was back, holding Emmett's distinctive book and looking amazed. She pointed back at the cupboard over her shoulder.

"I know!" Phyllo mouthed with a resigned kind of shrug and then tried to position himself directly beneath her. She dropped the book into his outstretched hands and he hugged it to his chest.

She flipped easily over the railing, swung down from the base rail and dropped noiselessly to the floor.

Trying and failing to keep up with Birdie was par for the course, but for Roly, who was staring shamelessly, it was a new experience.

Birdie beamed.

Phyllo tutted and took the book to Albertus's desk where he opened it reverentially beneath the magnifier. What he found on its pages, however, was a bit of a disappointment. The excitement he'd been feeling evaporated.

He'd been expecting the story of Emmett's life.

He'd been hoping to flick to the chapter entitled 'Demon Jester', or some other useful heading, and find everything they needed, but it wasn't like that at all. Instead, they were presented with entries in columns, numbers and item descriptions. It was an accountant's log of transactions.

Share of the gate was the most regular entry. Costs for food

324

and general supplies were listed regularly too. Phyllo turned pages and scanned for something meaningful. Then he found an entry for Mermaid's Tears and pointed it out to the others. "Look."

"Wow, look how expensive it is!" whispered Roly.

Phyllo continued to turn the pages and as Emmett's time went on Mermaid's Tears appeared more and more regularly, against ever-increasing costs.

Phyllo flipped back to the first entry he'd seen. "It's just sucking up all Emmett's Coin. We should start at the beginning, right?"

The other two nodded.

"But how do we see the story?" said Roly, "Albertus said, only an Archivist could really read the book."

Phyllo had already thought this through. "He said the book had to be in the Archive and under the magnifier," said Phyllo, "But Frú Hafiz said that the pen was more important than the man."

Roly picked up the pen with topaz in the filigree. "Albertus used this one when we visited, and I think I can remember what he did."

"Brilliant." Phyllo had been prepared to give it a go but if Roly could remember, all the better. He ushered Roly into the chair then crowded in behind with Birdie, to look over his shoulders.

"I think the shape he made was like this." Roly waved the pen about and they all looked expectantly down through the magnifier.

Nothing happened.

"Maybe, a bit more like this then." He tried again, moving more fluidly. The surface of the page rippled encouragingly, but that was all.

"I think you nearly had it there," Phyllo urged and Roly made the symbol once more. Bigger this time, and pointier.

The uppermost page rippled. Once, twice, then again. Ripples grew into waves then swirled suddenly into circles. Phyllo blinked rapidly, trying to clear the blur. Patterns grew in hypnotising flurries. Words left the page and rushed up to his eyes. They filled his peripheral vision and swept over his head, spinning his senses until he felt compelled to squeeze his eyes tightly shut.

"Roly, I don't think this is quite right," he trilled.

"Is it meant to be like this?" Birdie squeaked beside him.

"I, I don't know how to make it stop!" said Roly, an edge of panic creeping into his voice.

Waves of changing air pressure crashed around them, buffeting Phyllo's eardrums, squeezing the air from his lungs, and just when Phyllo thought he couldn't bear it any longer, the commotion started to fade.

It was replaced with an overwhelming sensation of being somewhere else.

Distantly, birds tweeted. There were unfamiliar voices, chatting and laughing. The sounds of daytime activity some-where busy. It did not sound like the middle of the night in an archive. Phyllo opened his eyes.

If they were still in Albertus's cabin, it had undergone an incredible transformation. The walls were now papered with a creamy vellum, handwritten words and figures stretched around surfaces to define their shapes. There was a wall with three windows that looked out to a village square and tables were spaced around the representation of a room, at which papery people chatted over drinks.

The air was utterly still. Phyllo's nose twitched at the

dryness of the place and he licked his lips. "I don't think this is quite right," he whispered.

"It's brilliant!" Roly replied.

"Yes, but I think we're actually in the book, Roly. This isn't what Albertus did at all. I think we've fallen in!" Alarm spread through Phyllo's chest.

"Yeah, but this is way better!" Roly moved forward to walk around and Phyllo looked at him for the first time.

"Roly, you're made of paper!" He looked at himself, "I'm made of paper!" He felt at his own body which he now saw was intricately constructed with folds. He had become an origami figure, the like of which he'd only ever seen once before, but he'd been outside the book then, looking in. He tested the joints in his fingers with a flex.

Roly passed a hand down his own smooth printed dressing gown. "This is incredible!"

"This is bad," Phyllo breathed, "Albertus said that if you fall into the book you can't get out."

"We'd better not be stuck like this!" squawked Birdie. She too had become a paper person, knobbly and slight with fragile-looking limbs.

"Yeah, but look how thin you are," Roly quipped and then seeing her scowl said, "No. No. I'm sure it's fine, I mean, I've still got the pen." He waved it at them, "I just have to draw the right thing."

She glowered. "Which is?"

Roly shrugged and had the decency to look a bit sheepish.

There was obviously more to this book-keeping talent than any of them had realised.

"Er. Well, we can experiment, I suppose."

"Experiment?" Birdie's scowl didn't look any less fierce for being two-dimensional, "You'd better have a plan, Phyllo Cane!"

"Of course," said Phyllo with as much conviction as he could muster. He caught Roly's eye for a moment then turned away, taking in their surroundings. "Let's just work out where we are."

Around them the scene continued to form. More tables flapped into existence, words stretched around corners and paper people peeled from the page to inflate with a pop. A long chest-height structure appeared behind them, and behind it, a young woman with dirty blonde curls that sprang from her head. Even in her basic paper form, Phyllo recognised her instantly.

"This is The Well of Tears," he said, "That's Amethyst."

Birdie peered at her. "She looks very young."

"We're in the past, remember."

Paper Amethyst looked up and smiled. "What can I get you?" she said and Birdie jumped.

"Can she see me?"

"No, look out behind," said Phyllo and Birdie spun to see two paper people lolloping toward them, their flimsy limbs flexing oddly in curls. They were little more than ill-defined sketches compared to themselves and the others around them, flat and devoid of detail. Words on a tickertape scroll appeared in the air above the nearest. "A bottle of your finest home brew, Amethyst," it read.

"Right you are, sir, and right away." She dipped out of sight and pulled up a sketchy bottle which she placed on the bar. "Two glasses, is it?"

"And one for yourself," rattled the tickertape.

"Very kind," she said and placed three small glasses beside

328

the bottle, then made to pop out the cork. The tickertape figure placed a flat hand over hers.

"If you don't mind," it said, "from a different bottle."

"Of course, I quite understand," she replied and the flimsy figures picked up their purchase and lolloped over to a table in the corner.

"Why can't we see and hear these two properly, when we can see and hear Amethyst and everyone else so well?" asked Phyllo.

"It's like the book is trying not to show us," said Roly, "I wonder." He leaned in to touch the bottle with the nib of the filigree pen. Colour flooded through the tip to seep into the bottle. Turquoise liquid shimmered and the label completed itself in a scrolling hand: *Mermaid's Tears*.

"Try that on him," said Phyllo, indicating the figure who'd just bought the drinks. Roly touched his arm with the nib and black ink spread in spidery veins across the paper's surface. It settled in crevices and creases, but did not complete the picture in the way that it had on the bottle. The effect was that of an ink spill, soaking into damage. An accident which disfigured the no longer blank form. Phyllo stepped back a little. "I think I liked him better before. What about the other one?"

Roly touched him too. Crimson and gold swept across the figure in swirls, but sank into the paper like a wave into sand. Randomly, a mark remained. A smear here, a line there. A tri-horned hat curled from his head and then receded. It was Emmett.

"A hot day," said the thin sketchy Emmett, words appearing on a tickertape above his head too.

"Thank Barnum for The Well of Tears, eh?" rattled out the tape above the figure of black.

Emmett nodded and looked thirstily down to his empty glass.

"Emmett told me to find a secret," said Phyllo, "These two look like they're trying to hide something, don't you think?"

Roly and Birdie nodded in agreement. The figures were odd and stood out from the whole.

"I think I've found a kindred spirit in you." The ink-smeared man stretched out a thin, curling arm to pat Emmett on the shoulder. "A man with a past, just like me. We are men with a bond."

Sketchy Emmett shuffled in his seat.

"What do you say we seal our newfound friendship with this bottle of Amethyst's home brew? Tried it before?"

"It's a new one on me," rolled Emmett's tape. He shrugged.

"Then you're in for a treat. Would you mind being mother?" the ink-spill man asked and pushed the bottle over. Phyllo noticed that now something extra was around its neck – a heavy metal ring inscribed with symbols. It looked old and magical. It looked like trouble. Phyllo was getting a bad feeling.

He continued to talk. "As it's your first time, I say we do it properly. You should pop your own cork for the full effect."

"Alright, if you like."

Emmett pulled the stopper from the bottle and, instead of the foaming bubbles that Phyllo might have expected, wisps of black mist rose from the bottle mouth. Faint at first, but then thickening and growing. Phyllo took another step back, but the flimsy paper men at the table took no notice at all. They could not see it, just like they could not see Phyllo, Roly or Birdie.

Fluid and oily, the mist coiled around the arm that held the bottle. Snaking upward, it climbed to twist around Emmett's neck.

"San Giuseppe, what's that?" Birdie yelped.

"It must be the demon," said Phyllo, horrible realisation prickling at his neck, "It's coming out of the bottle and that ring. This is where it starts."

"We need to get it back in there," gasped Roly, leaning over to swipe at the mist, trying to send it back to where it came from. His hands slid through the smoke. "It's impossible!" he flapped.

Phyllo gawked at it. He'd never fought a demon before, never been inside a book before either. How was he supposed to know what to do or how to do it? He wracked his brain desperately. It was like being forced up to that trapeze platform all over again, not knowing anything, but being pushed inescapably on.

The image of Arnaldo plopped into his mind's eye. *Confidence is everything*. Phyllo had felt sick with terror that day too, yet he'd summoned up the confidence to climb. Marco and Arnaldo had helped him push through the fear.

"We can do it," he told Roly, "We'll find the way." The sash at his waist glowed with a pulse of warmth. Phyllo'd forgotten he was wearing it. Dressing in the blues had become second nature. The sash, just the thing that stopped his tunic flapping about.

The expression on Roly's face brightened, Phyllo's conviction rubbing off on him. Emmett too seemed to relax in his chair.

"There was something on your mind, back there in the garden. I've an eye for it." The inky figure's tickertape unfurled and melted away as the words were spent. He snatched up his glass to hold it out. "Fill her up. And your own. That's it. To new friends."

331

Their conversation continued, oblivious to the demonic mist.

Emmett poured the drinks, looking more self-assured than he had moments earlier. They clinked glasses and drank, the figure of ink just pressing the glass to his lips; Emmett, the full glass thrown back thirstily. Roly jabbed the pen against Emmett again and colour swirled across him revealing an expression of delight. He closed his eyes and sighed. The figure of black emptied his own glass into the pot on the table.

"Crackers! He drank some!" cried Phyllo, "No, Emmett, please," he begged, but Emmett did not respond.

"He can't hear you," said Birdie and, as they watched, the collar of smoke around Emmett's neck started to grow again, creeping up, over his head. It expanded to also flow down over his chest, his legs, his feet. It engulfed him completely, wrapping around him in a murky shroud.

"Good stuff, isn't it?" said the inky figure, reaching over to give Emmett a refill. "Tell me about her then, the one that got away."

Phyllo, Roly and Birdie all stared at Emmett in horror. The smoke surrounding him became a solid mass, but then began to fade and Phyllo thought, for a wonderful moment, that it was melting away as he began to see Emmett through it – Emmett in his Jester's costume, coming clearly into focus. The rich red ruff at his neck. The matching doublet with stars shining in its embroidery. The golden hat and little bells.

"My Rosie, yes." Emmett sighed, "We'd known each other since forever, grew up on the same corner. She had this crazy curly hair. For years she brushed it into this wild, out of control fuzz ball." He held his hands out, at the side of his head, indicating the size of it and smiled wistfully.

"We used to laugh about it. A couple of scamps running

free. Playing pirates on the river or charging about the fields with Gofer, my dog. We spent every moment together." Emmett seemed lost in the memory.

"Then one day she found out how to tame that crazy fuzz into curls and transformed, almost before my eyes, into the most beautiful girl I'd ever seen. All this time, I'd never seen her that way then *BOOM*. She wasn't smeared with dirt and there weren't leaves stuck in her hair. She was something else even more amazing."

Emmett leant on the table and the other figure leaned in beside him. Their heads formed a conspiratorial huddle. Emmett colourful and fully drawn, the inky figure blank and tainted.

"Ah, the joy of a beautiful woman. Another toast." The figure lifted his empty glass high, above Emmett's eye-level. "What'll it be?"

Emmett thought for a moment. "To love."

"To love." They clinked again and the inky figure pretended to knock back the drink. Emmett followed, throwing back his own then clunking the drained tumbler down onto the table.

A terrible sound filled the air, a tearing, ripping noise that twisted into a growling moan. Low and pained. Sudden and loud. Shocking to Phyllo's ears. Emmett folded in on himself and the cloak of colour and smoke that had encased him pulled backward, piercing through the paper Emmett's chest. It shot out of his back then poured itself into a new form, a mass of oily tendrils which writhed mid-air. Arms and legs grew like tentacles, curling out from the whirling cloud. A torso. A head. A tri-horned hat. Still for a moment, it drank in a great long breath then solidified into three-dimensions. The Jester.

Now there were two: paper Emmett, thin and featureless, slumped in the chair and the Jester, fully formed and as real as any person might be outside of the book. The Jester shook its cane with glee, jingling the little bells, and jigged about on the spot.

"Oh crackers," said Phyllo.

"He's got to stop drinking it!" Birdie shrieked, "For the love of Grimaldi, Emmett, if you won't help yourself, how are we supposed to help you?"

"Still can't hear you," said Roly, and Birdie gave him a scowl.

"Who even is this?" puzzled Roly, touching the other man at the table again with the pen. Gelatinous black rolled across the surface and settled to give the vaguest suggestion of a face. They drew closer and looked into it, searching for something to recognise. But the ink sank away into the paper and told them nothing. "Who'd want to set a demon on Emmett?"

That was a mystery Phyllo still didn't understand.

Tickertape unfurled above the inky man as they stared at him, "So, who broke the spell? Did she catch you in the arms of another? Tell me, what happened?"

"No, nothing like that." Tape rolled above paper Emmett as he leaned dejectedly on the table, "We were happy. Got married. Had a baby. Our little Bumble." His shoulders drooped even further. "She was the sweetest dumpling of a child.

"We had plans for the future, but they just never came to anything. A happy-go-lucky guy like me finds it hard to hold down a job, you know? Rosie wanted to open a bakery. She could bake – oh boy, could she bake. But somehow, we never could save enough to get started." He shrugged and fiddled with the glass.

"The Circus of Wonder was hiring clowns and it had me written all over it. The pay was good, for just goofing around, so I stuck with it and moved on to the next stop, sending the money home. I moved on to the next stop and the next." He sighed and shook his head, the words on the tickertape: smaller. "It draws you in."

"I know exactly how that is," rattled the tape above the ink-spill man. He filled Emmett's glass to the brim, dropping the merest splash in his own. He waved his hands expressively as he talked and Emmett followed them about. "The circus, it's a magical life. To be part of that, to be a cog in the machine and doing your part. You can see how people live just for that. To be all that they can be for the good of the circus. It gives men purpose."

Emmett nodded, seeming to contemplate the words.

"Another toast," said the man of ink, lifting his glass, "To the good of the circus, yes?"

Emmett lifted his glass to clink. "The good of the circus."

The Jester pogoed up and down behind Emmett's chair and giggled maniacally. "A toast! A toast!" he cackled and waved his stick about, jingling and banging about.

Emmett drank the Mermaid's Tears.

"Ha ha! I love a captive audience!" the Jester cried and threw his arms wide to take a bow, theatrically tossing away the cane.

As it dropped, silver chain flew out behind, the silver bells elongating and replicating; the chain forming from them, one link after another. It heaped on the ground, metal chiming on metal. The Jester caught up the chain and whirled a loop of it around Emmett's chest. With a foot in his back, he yanked it tight.

Emmett stiffened, then slumped back, defeated.

The Jester laughed, high and mean. His face wrinkled, make-up drying and sinking into the creases. He danced away to jump up on the bar and skip along it.

Paper Emmett's tape continued. The writing: smaller still. "But I never went home, did I. I've never been back and years have gone by. Twelve years. My Bumble will be a grown girl and my Rosie, well."

The figure patted Emmett on the shoulder. "You did the right thing."

"You think?"

"No, Emmett, no!" Birdie scolded, "For Barnum's sake, the man's got no self-control." She threw her arms into an angry fold across her body. Phyllo joined Roly at Emmett's side and reached out to the chain. It was solid to his touch and held Emmett firm, constricting his chest like a great leaden snake.

"We have to get it off," Phyllo said, straining at the chain. It was heavy and awkward but somehow, he had to get it up and over Emmett's head. His flimsy paper arms struggled against the weight.

"Help me!" Phyllo shouted, getting the chain as high as Emmett's shoulders, "I can only get it so far on my own." Roly grabbed on too and together they heaved. Phyllo was still stronger, even in his papery form, but his brother pushing with him too made all the difference. The chain crashed to the floor.

"Brilliant," cried Phyllo and threw up one hand, hoping to meet Roly's in a high-five, but Roly didn't respond. Face pained, he was staring down at his paper fingers. They were buckled and torn.

Phyllo looked at his own: they were still smooth, still whole.

Tickertape reeled over the inky figure again. "Woman like

336

that, beautiful child like that, they don't need a deadbeat, they need a man, out there providing. Am I right?"

Emmett flinched at the words.

"You're providing, right?"

"Maybe I don't send home quite as much as I did." Emmett shifted uncomfortably.

The inky man paused to nod. "What's done is done. No point clinging to the past. Some things are better forgotten. Some things are best kept between friends. Good friends, like us. Not the sort of story everyone would understand."

Emmett crumpled more in his chair.

"Just like my visits to the cottage on the hill." The words hung a little longer on the tape above the inky figure.

Emmett took a moment to consider him then said, "Secret is it?"

"A man's personal business is just that. No-one needs to know. No-one does, but you." The inky figure reached out, it seemed to Phyllo almost involuntarily, to spin the ring around the neck of the bottle.

"Well I've no reason to tell anyone."

"That's right. Secrets between friends." The figure sloshed a refill into Emmett's glass and held up his own. "To keeping each other's secrets."

Emmet chinked his own glass against it, but said rather less exuberantly, "Keeping secrets." The words on his tickertape were becoming rather untidy, missing the line and varying in intensity.

He drank the Tears.

"No point being sad about it. Good times lie ahead. Just keep going the right way and all your mistakes can be forgotten. Everything can be forgotten. Down the hatch. Another toast. To forgetting our mistakes."

"Forgetting," said Emmett blurrily. They drank, or pretended to.

The Jester, who'd been cavorting about the bar knocking over drinks, returned to scoop up the chain and skip around Emmett, jumping up onto the table to swirl it around him, in two loops this time. He bent to sit on his haunches, knees and elbows bent to sharp angles that made Phyllo think of a venomous spider.

He chucked Emmett under his papery chin. "You're mine now," he said and the sneer Phyllo had seen on so many cast members contorted the Jester's face.

"No way." Phyllo grabbed for the chain and pushed against it "We have to get it off. We have to keep going!" Roly took hold too, trying to avoid the rips in his hands.

Birdie scowled, "Can't you see that it's pointless if Emmett keeps drinking?"

"We have to stop the demon taking hold, Birdie. Today is the day, the one that matters. You're a Volante, you understand the power of a team. We're his team. We're all he's got."

Birdie pursed her lips.

"Getting here was the hardest part, getting started. Now we have to carry on. Momentum is everything, remember?"

That first time climbing up to the bar would never have happened if it hadn't been for Arnaldo, his sheer wilfulness had driven Phyllo on. *Up! Up! Momentum is everything.*

Birdie looked down to Roly's hands and Phyllo could see the concern in her eyes.

"Actually, I said that *flexibility* is everything," she said with a sniff.

"Then be that too. Flexible in your thinking. Give him a chance."

Birdie's features were scrunched in a scowl. She looked

from Phyllo to the Jester, who sneered evilly at Emmett. Birdie examined its face and lifted a hand to her own as if feeling the features she could see on the demon's. Her scowl melted away into horror and she jumped to grab the chain too. "Together," she said and they heaved.

Phyllo felt the sash become something more. Now his limbs felt freer. He was able to manoeuvre into better positions to lever against the chain. His mind felt clearer, the way to proceed: becoming more obvious, more possible. All three of them fought for Emmett and the chains fell away.

They landed with a great clattering that juddered through the papery room and the Jester wobbled on his perch up on the table.

His black eyes found Phyllo's.

His nostrils flared.

"What is this?" he slowly said, the hollow gaze flitting from Phyllo to Roly and then Birdie.

"Gobstoppers," breathed Roly.

Their actions had brought them into focus, somehow.

"We're here to stop you," Phyllo croaked, drawing the Jester's attention back to himself, his heart suddenly racing.

The Jester stood up to tower over them. He rippled with laughter. "You can't stop *me*. I am Vincula made human. I am spirit from spirit, summoned from the underworld. I am dread made real."

"No." Suddenly everything had become clear. "You are self-doubt and insecurity. You're made of weakness and fear," Phyllo said.

Emmett fidgeted in his chair. He and the inky-spill man still seemed oblivious to their presence and even that of the terrible Jester.

Emmett gave a great sigh. "I don't think I've made the right choices," he said, "I've always thought that there was no way home, but suddenly, I can't help thinking that was a mistake. Funny how you can think one way, so completely for so long, but then suddenly see things differently. I've been weak. I've acted this way out of fear."

"Did you hear that, Phyllo?" Roly said, "I think what we're saying is getting through."

The Jester stamped his foot. "I am *his* weakness and *his* fear and he is *mine!*" The Jester leapt down from the table. He snatched up his cane and snapped the chain like a whip. It cracked at Phyllo, Roly and Birdie's feet. It pushed them back, away from Emmett.

"You've had it now," Phyllo yelled, "he's started to think for himself."

"You know nothing," the Jester laughed. He launched the cane at Phyllo like a spear. Birdie dived to push him back so that it sailed past, but it had a life of its own, swinging away to the left and dragging the chain behind it like a comet's tail. It soared past the windows and turned sharply at the corner, then again at the next.

"It's coming back!" Phyllo shouted and ducked away. Birdie was fast to follow, but Roly was slow. He threw his hands up in defence. The cane connected with his fingers and spun him away before turning again to complete its circle and speed on.

Round and round. The chain trailed behind. Row upon row of snaking metal formed into a furious cyclone that separated Phyllo and the other two from Emmett, the Jester and the bottle of Mermaid's Tears.

The Jester roared with laughter again and through the haze of metal, Phyllo could see the sneering lip, the mocking eyebrow.

"Roly!" Birdie rushed to his aid.

Phyllo glared back at the Jester and edged toward the chain cyclone.

"Phyllo, no!" Roly shouted, "You'll be shredded! Look at my hand!"

Phyllo glanced back at him. Roly clutched at his wrist – his hand was torn to ribbons.

The chains whistled in a rising roar, heat beginning to come from the spinning mass. Faster and faster. The smell of scorched paper worried at Phyllo's nostrils. The Jester cackled and danced about. The inky man poured another drink.

"We have to get through to him," Phyllo shouted and turned back to watch the silver chain as it began to glow, getting hotter. The more time that passed, the more solid a wall it became. His instincts told him to reach out and grab it, but the heat pushed him back, the front of his body stiffening as it crisped. It was too dangerous. It was madness.

Timing is everything. Launching on the trapeze at the right time was crucial. Co-ordinating with your partner's moves, essential. Get that wrong and nothing else worked.

The vortex of metal spun and spun, ever more blade-like, solid and scorching. Then Phyllo saw it: the cane within, leading the chain in its deadly path. It was the way in. He locked on to it with his eyes, mapping its trajectory, estimating when it would next come into range.

The sash glowed with warmth at his waist. He felt light, he felt free to move wherever he wanted, he felt clear and fast.

"If not now, when?" he asked himself aloud and when the cane came into sight again, he knew he was ready.

Hup.

The vortex seemed to slow as Phyllo thrust one hand forward toward the mass of metal. Every link in the chain became clear. Every wave that rippled through it, visible in minute detail. The Jester's cane moved sedately into reach and Phyllo plucked it from the air like a feather floating on the breeze.

The cyclone immediately began to unravel. Chain thumped haphazardly to the floor, sending the Jester skittering about. Emmett was revealed and tickertape rolled above his inky companion's head.

"No point being sad about it," it said, "Good times ahead. Just keep going the way you're going and you can forget about it all. All your mistakes forgotten." He'd sloshed out two more shots and held one up to eye level.

"Some things I don't want to forget," said Emmett.

The inky man floundered for something to say. He rubbed at his chin, considering, then said, "You've been gone too long, Emmett. Now's not the time to make rash decisions. We have an accord. We have our new friendship." He lifted his glass, "To new friends."

Emmett shook his head. "There's never going to be a better time than this. If not now, when?"

Phyllo gawked at him. "It's working! Roly, Birdie, it's working!"

"No!" The Jester snatched up the chain and started to haul it in. "No, he's mine. *Mine!*" Metal scraped on metal. It clanged link against link, mounding at the Jester's feet.

Roly and Birdie got themselves up from the floor and scrabbled to either side of Phyllo.

"How did you do that?" Roly gawped at the Jester's cane in Phyllo's hand.

"Timing is everything!" Birdie trilled, "I think you might actually be becoming a Volante."

Phyllo huffed out a laugh, but then saw Roly's hands. Both

were battered, but one was devastatingly torn into strips. "Roly, you're hurt!"

He winced. "Stings a bit. I just hope it will stick back together."

Phyllo flexed his own fingers. His hands had not suffered in the same way. Even before, when they'd been hauling the chains together, his had not got hurt. Was he stronger? Had this experience made him stronger?

The sash felt like a power source at his core. Everything was clearer and easier. A whole lifetime ago he'd been sent out on a run by Signor Volante, the start of his mission to become strong.

The open plains of the Brampton Levels had given him time to think. Running around the back of the cabins had shown him a whole new perspective. All the acts of the Circus of Wonder represented in the elaborate murals that reached around the outer wall. Each merged seamlessly with the next. All were connected. All were part of the whole. They encircled the big top. Suddenly he could see that he was just at the beginning of a circuit of his own.

His apprenticeship with the Fabulous Volante was only the first stop. Was he a flyer? How could that work when his fear of heights still didn't seem to be going away? He realised that it didn't matter. Even if this wasn't his true talent, Phyllo knew that the next apprenticeship would come. He could be literally anything, the possibilities were endless. He would try and that was his strength.

"I'm feeling more and more weedy by the day, next to you," Roly puffed out a sigh.

"No, Roly. You carried on even when it must have hurt. That's real strength, right there," Phyllo said and threw an arm around his brother.

At the table, Emmett pushed the glass away and leant back in his chair. "I don't want it," he said, "This is the coward's road."

The Jester tried to flick the chain up to snare him, but couldn't get it to rise from the ground.

A smile tugged at the corners of Phyllo's mouth. Emmett had the strength now too.

For all the worry of the last few months, at last resolution was forming. All those times he'd doubted his own sanity, seeing the face of the Jester on so many others. It had taken Frú Hafiz's confirmation to allow him to believe his own eyes. Now Phyllo knew not to get bogged down by the mistakes that he'd made: all that terrible marshmallow, all that time wasted wishing for the impossible, wishing his mother alive.

He remembered the ground swings and their cries of 'Volare!' Marco had believed in him. That day in the ring they'd all believed in him, but more crucially, he'd believed in himself.

"Belief in yourself is everything," Phyllo said, willing the meaning to get through to Emmett.

He stepped forward and thrust the Jester's cane down, into the bottle. It sank all the way in, disappearing beyond what was possible, the links of the chain trailing behind and shrinking to fit through too. In it went, dragged back to where it had come from. The chain rattled in, faster and faster, clanking against the sides. It looped and writhed about the table. The Jester danced about in horror, grabbing up the chain and trying to haul it back.

But on it went, sucked into the bottle, ever more like fat silver spaghetti, flopping about and shrinking. The Jester held on, pulling and shrieking until his hands were at the bottle mouth, then pulled *inside* the bottle mouth. His body puffed out like a balloon: air squeezed from one part to inflate the next. His head grew disproportionately as his arms were sucked down into the bottle too, then his chin. A bulbous fore-head bulged then deflated as the Jester screamed, a high-pitched squeal that faded as his legs were sucked in and curly-toed-shoes flailed in the last raspberry blow of air.

He was gone.

Emmett stood up and at last they actually heard his voice. "You know what? I don't think I've really got time for a drink. I've already kept my Rosie waiting too long. I've a bakery to open."

He snatched up the cork from the table and poked it deci-sively back into the bottle. He hammered it once with the heel of his hand. "I've got to get home."

He pushed the chair back and strode for the door. With every step his lolloping gait became smoother. The papery curls of his limbs straightened and filled out. The colours of his costume swirled and filled in.

He snatched open the door and the Emmett that stood in a bright halo of sunlight seemed stronger than Phyllo had ever seen him before. He stepped out into the square and the door slammed closed behind him.

Silence.

Phyllo, Roly and Birdie stood panting and wide-eyed in the suddenly still papery world. Words and figures that had filled the walls faded away. Their absence taking with them any sense of shape and depth. Tables and chairs, people and their drinks all melted into nothing.

Pure creamy vellum, rough and sweet smelling, in every direction, as far as the eye could see. Phyllo stood in no space or time and waited for words to appear. None came.

"He's gone," Roly said.

"And taken everything with him, by the looks of it," Birdie added.

"I think that's it," Phyllo said, "The book, this book, it's just about Emmett's time at the Circus of Wonder. Emmett's gone home. It's the end."

An odd tightness formed in the back of Phyllo's throat. They'd freed Emmett from Mermaid's Tears. All those years he'd spent its prisoner, now he'd never have to suffer it. They'd put a stop to the pain before it had begun.

But the crushing aspect of this reality now dawned. Emmett had gone home, so now Phyllo would never get to know him. He'd saved his friend, but lost him too.

Ripples swept across the vellum. A familiar pressure pushed at Phyllo's ears, at his lungs. His vision blurred and everything became lost in a monotone void. Then his feet pressed suddenly harder into the ground, as if he were whirling and fighting against gravity. He pushed back and found he could support his own weight.

Birdie gasped, Roly let out a short sharp "Ha!" and Phyllo opened his eyes. They were back in Albertus's cabin.

CHAPTER TWENTY-THREE

The Magic of the Circus

Phyllo closed his eyes and breathed in the magic. It was the strongest that he'd ever known it. The air was thick with awe. The aromas of caramel popcorn, of sawdust and canvas, of new costumes and greasepaint, of fear and joy: they swirled all around him and filled his head. They filled his heart. The music rose in waves and he let his hand fall to the sash at his waist.

Nonna Sophia had added to the embroidery and now a rather flattering depiction of Glumberry flew across its front panel, the pre-existing sweet clenched tight in his beak. The fat little bird on the wing was Phyllo's own version of flying: the impossible dream realised.

The Fabulous Volante leapt and twirled around him. This show was the one that really mattered and they were making it count.

It was time.

He strode out into the ring to pursue the Lady. He was the Pirate Captain and she would belong to him. He scaled the rigging while she fled. He chased her out onto the bar.

One swipe to grasp her, another try and then again. She pulled away, but she would not escape.

He drove his own bar on. Higher. Higher still. The battle

raged around them, beneath them, but the Pirate Captain would not be dissuaded. She thought she was far enough away to escape, but no.

The Pirate Captain leapt. High. Slow. Still. He hung in the air and waited for the bar to come to him. The crowd held its breath. They were so high and there was nothing to catch him. Surely this was a step too far? Surely, this time, they would fall.

Phyllo felt the air thicken and time slow. He drew in his legs and shaped the cloak, a malevolent bat, then simply stepped on board to envelop his prey. Together he and Columba swept off the back of the trapeze and onto the board.

He'd done it. His big moment. The feat the Fabulous Volante had needed to make it all work. They continued to fly, continued to tell the story. Phyllo's part now was all based on the ground. He was safe.

The story wound on and Ezio came to Columba's rescue. They whirled on the great silks that billowed like sails. They soared over the audience and Phyllo felt the gasps from the crowd speed them on.

He understood the magic now. He could feel it. The Pirate Captain and the Lady escaped and the show was over.

The big top exploded with applause. Men, women and children were all pulled to their feet by the extraordinary show they'd been privileged to witness. The Ringmaster swept out into the ring, the entire cast jogging behind and then encircling him. They skipped into position to take their bow. The final bow of the season.

Phyllo looked around the troupe. Every one of them had given their all. They absorbed the cheers and joy that rolled down into the ring and every one of them deserved it. Greedy Gus, Nubbins and Sprockets all bowed together, waving happily out to children in the front row. No Emmett, for them there never had been. Phyllo tried not to be sad. Emmett was happy somewhere, with Rosie and Bumble. Maybe he'd meet them all one day, maybe buy a cherry bun from that bakery.

Phyllo understood now that sometimes you lost people. There was nothing you could do to change it.

He would dearly have loved for his mother to have been there too, but that wasn't possible. Their moments together were in the past. They'd been wonderful and magical and full of love. He'd been lucky to have them. Now it was up to him to fill his future with something new.

Then someone stepped out of the tiers and started to make their way down. Quite the roundest man Phyllo had ever seen. In his white suit, with a handful of colourful cotton-candy puffs jumping up and down at his feet, it was unmistakably Ronnie Gourmand. He stepped into the ring and the Ringmaster strode forward to greet him. Ronnie Gourmand shook the Ringmaster's hand delightedly and then with the other, handed him a fold of golden fabric.

The Gilded Pennant.

The cast erupted, jumping up and down and cheering, their eyes wide and their smiles even wider. All around Phyllo carnies roared in triumph. Harric and Garric sprang into impromptu flick-flacks. Arnaldo and Ezio threw arms around each other's shoulders and fist-pumped out into the crowd. Signor Volante burst into tears.

Phyllo and Birdie jumped around and around in circles, whooping with delight. They'd done it. Then his vision was filled with candy-stripes and strawberry blonde curls.

"Well done, son. I couldn't be prouder."

Birdie scooped Dodo up to whirl her around and Marvel

349

squeezed Phyllo tight to his chest then stepped back to put out his hand.

For a moment it was bizarre. Then Phyllo took it, surprised, but feeling, unexpectedly, like this was the moment he'd been working towards.

Suddenly his throat was constricting and he felt like even if he'd had the right words, he wouldn't have been able to say them. His father nodded reassuringly, then released him. There were other hands to shake in the crowd. His father stepped away to reveal Roly, who raised his eyebrows and nodded with an appreciative smile. He came to stand by Phyllo's side.

"How's the hand?" asked Phyllo.

"Just a paper cut," Roly quipped, but then admitted, "Actually, it hurts like mad. Dad took me to the infirmary. Got it bandaged." He lifted his right hand to show Phyllo the fat white wad. "Saw Marco there and his mum. He said to tell you 'Volare', whatever that means."

For a moment they were silent, happily watching the mayhem and rocking on their heels. Then Roly punched Phyllo lightly on the arm with his good hand.

"That was incredible," he said.

Phyllo grinned into the air ahead, "Not bad, if I say so myself."

Roly laughed. "You're a genius."

Thank You
from the Author

So that's the end of this first adventure with Phyllo Cane and the Circus of Wonder.

If you'd like to find out what happens next please sign up for news at www. sharnhutton.com/cowsign-up/ or scan this QR code with your smartphone camera and I'll keep you informed about new stories as they become available.

As an extra little thank you I'll send subscribers three of the character portraits I drew whilst writing this book. I hope they make you smile.

I'm so delighted to have this story in the hands of readers so my thanks, lovely reader, go to you. This book is the product of years of devouring and loving magical stories and the resulting desire to create my own fantastical world. Thank you for coming along for the ride and daring to believe.

If you've enjoyed it, please do **leave a review** - it makes all the difference to an independent author like me.

My gratitude goes also to Anna Bowles, a wonderful editor who shared with me her enormous experience in middle grade fiction and gave invaluable insight into how to make this journey with Phyllo a joy. I hope I've done your advice justice.

Enormous thanks to Andy Catling, whose cover illustration makes me smile every time I look at it and to Julia Gibb, who squeezed me in to polish up my terrible punctuation when I was laughably disorganised, thank you.

My final thank-you goes to the indie community, individuals too numerous to mention, whose support through the process makes anything seem possible – you guys rock.

~

Sharn W. Hutton lives in Hertfordshire, England with her husband, two children and scruffy Tibetan Terrier, Pip.